"Greeley's talent for spinning a good, lusty yarn is undeniable. Fans of his first science fiction novel, GOD GAME, will want this."
—Library Journal

"Greeley is a hell of a good writer. His naturalness and right-on characterization make his fiction very real."
—Science Fiction Review

The Final Planet

Andrew M. Greeley

The Final Planet

TOR

A TOM DOHERTY ASSOCIATES BOOK

THE FINAL PLANET

Copyright © 1987 by Andrew M. Greeley

Published in association with Warner Books

First TOR printing: May 1988

A TOR Book

Published by Tom Doherty Associates, Inc.
49 West 24 Street
New York, N.Y. 10010

Book design: H. Roberts

Cover art by Boris Vallejo

ISBN: 0-812-58338-8
CAN. ED.: 0-812-58339-6

Library of Congress Catalog Card Number: 86-40415

Printed in the United States of America

0 9 8 7 6 5 4 3 2 1

For three friends, both old and new, out of the mists—

Roger, Rita, Marilyn

SONG OF THE WILD GEESE*

My Maire bhan! My Maire bhan,
—I've come to say good-bye, love;
To France I sail away at dawn—
—My fortune for to try, love.
The cause is lost a stoir mo chroi,
—All hope has now departed;
And Ireland's gallant chivalry,
—Is scatter'd broken-hearted.
Ah! pleasant are our Munster vales,
—Encrowned in summer sheen, love,
But now no more the autumn gales
—Unfold our flag of green, love;
And say, could we remain and see
—In ruin and dishonor
Far o'er those valleys waving free
—The foeman's blood-red banner!
No, sweeter in far lands to roam
—From Lee's green banks and thee, love,
Than live a coward-slave at home
—To plighted vows untrue, love,
And better ne'er to grasp thy hand
—Or view those tresses shining,
Than 'mong the cravens of the land
—Crouch down in fetters pining!

Mo bhron! 'tis hard to part from thee,
—My heart's bright pearl, my own love,
And wandering in a far country,
—To leave you sad and lone, love!
But spring's young flowers will crown the glen,
—And wreath the fairy wildwood,
And Druith's feet will pace again
—The mountains of my childhood.
Farewell, farewell, mo mhuirnin bhan
—Time flies, I must away, love;
'Twill soon be dawn, 'twill soon be dawn,
—My steed begins to neigh, love;
Farewell, preserve thine heart as true,
—As changeless as yon river,
And Druith's will be true to you,
—Anear, afar—forever!

*The Irish soldiers of fortune who "flew" from Ireland to escape English tyranny
and continue to fight for Irish freedom. At the time of the *Peregrinatio* of the
Iona, the term had been extended to include all pilgrims who bore weapons.

TECHNICAL SPECIFICATIONS: TIPV/*IONA*

The Taran Intergalactic Pilgrim Vessel *Iona* is an ion-hyperspace exploration vessel suitable for both in-flight and landing configurations. The basic propulsion system is ion-hyperspace drive powered by matter/antimatter conversion generators. Energy is created during the matter/antimatter conversion cycle and is utilized for propulsion, life-support, and defense systems. The mass created on the energy conversion cycle is used by the gravity-pods located on each deck, and the excess goes back into a breeder reactor, which holds it for emergency use in the conversion engines.

The life-support system maintains a total internal environment, and basic protein is produced in the hydroponic farm. The communication system consists of multiple banks of telepathic neuron transmitters that amplify and modulate the total telepathic capacity of the members of the crew. Weaponry consists of CDLs of varying sizes, located at strategic points. These Capacitor/Discharge/Lasers are fed energy from the basic power generators.

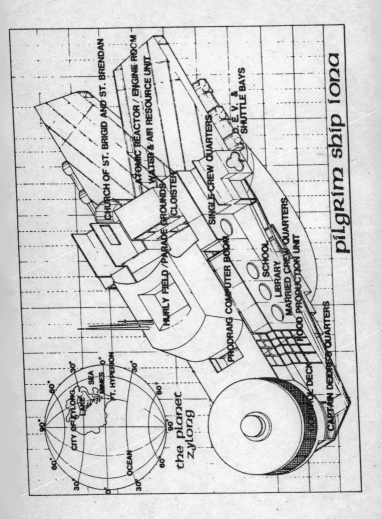

pilgrim ship Iona

CHURCH OF ST. BRIGID AND ST. BRENDAN

ATOMIC REACTOR / ENGINE ROOM

WATER & AIR RESOURCE UNIT

CLOISTER

HURLY FIELD / PARADE GROUNDS

SINGLE-CREW QUARTERS

D.E.V. & SHUTTLE BAYS

PADDRAIG COMPUTER ROOM

SCHOOL

LIBRARY

MARRIED CREW QUARTERS

FOOD PRODUCTION UNIT

NO. DECK

CAPTAIN DESMOND QUARTERS

the planet zylong

CITY OF ZYLONG

SEA

LAKES

MT. HYPERION

OCEAN

90° 60° 30° 0° 30° 60° 90°

60° 30° 0° 30° 60°

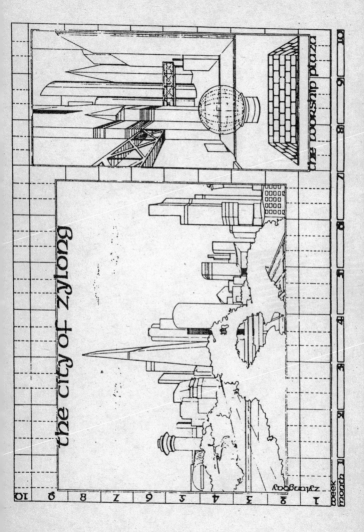

the city of zylong

zylongboy

the worship plaza

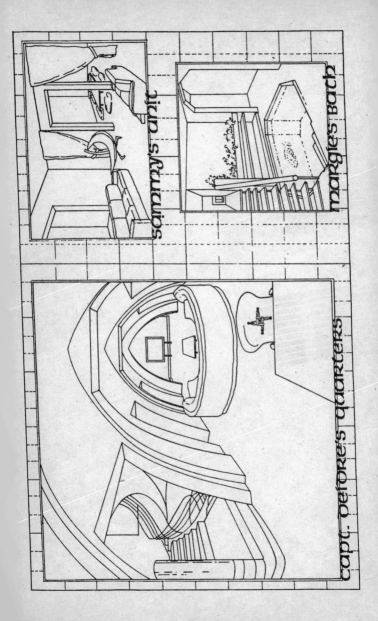

sammy's attic

margie's bath

capt. petore's quarters

PART
ONE

THE CITY

1

Seamus O'Neill moved his finger to the button to fire the last retrorocket, glanced quickly behind at the inky blackness where the TPS *Iona* continued its silent orbit. A twinge of sentimentality, not totally uncharacteristic, jabbed at his soul. The *Iona* wasn't much to look at, you understand—an old battered titanium hulk fixed up to look like a monastery, yet it had been home for the quarter century of his life, the symbol of the Spirit of Exploration for which the Holy Order of Saint Brigid and Saint Brendan stood. Like all the second-generation Wild Geese, he had railed against its confining walls.

Still, he reflected with a sigh of self-pity that came as natural to Tarans as breathing, *at least up there you were with your own kind, not set down alone on a heathen planet.*

Sure they call it loneliness, he told himself ruefully. *Would you believe it, Commandant Seamus O'Neill, lonely, and on the first day too. Ah, 'tis going to be a grand adventure, isn't it? Just grand.*

Irony was as natural among the Tarans as self-pity.

He scanned the countdown readout ... five seconds to fire. He thought of Tessie's blond hair and white limbs. *You win some, you lose some. 'Course, so far you've lost them all.* Seamus was good at the first stages of courtship, something less than sensational at all later stages. He sighed again, a sigh which other earth-descended folk they met on their pilgrimage thought indistinguishable from an acute asthma attack.

He softly pushed the firing button; the shuttle-craft *Eamon De Valera* jumped in faint protest, then slowed its descent toward the jungle clearing. Seamus O'Neill, not a paragon of religious devotion by a long shot, but not exactly an agnostic either, breathed a short prayer.

"If it's all the same to Yourself, I'd like it to be a safe landing; well, one I can walk away from anyway.

"And while I have your attention, I'd certainly not be rejecting any help and protection you be after willing to provide for this little jaunt of mine, begging your pardon for seeming forward."

Seamus assumed that Himself (or Herself, as you pleased) was fully aware of the situation. Still, it didn't hurt to bring matters up occasionally—with proper respect, of course.

The old shuttlecraft settled onto the firm red soil of the clearing with as much dignity as its weary hull could manage. There was little dust, just as Podraig the foulmouthed computer had predicted. "Touchdown," Seamus informed the stars, in case they were listening.

And then he sighed for a third time, this one intended for Himself, the stars, the Lady Deirdre, and anyone else in the cosmos who might be listening—the immemorial protest of the Celt against his unfair destiny.

It was a historic moment about which no one cared, the landing on a new planet. *Even a thousand years after the Second Great Exploration, landing on a new planet should be a major event, shouldn't it?* he asked the Deity.

The latter Worthy did not deign to answer.

Well, admittedly, the dominant species here is supposed to have come about the same time the Proto-Celts came to Tara. We became pilgrims because we wanted to keep alive our culture; they because they wanted to build a perfect society. So my belated arrival here is something of an anticlimax.

But still . . .

But still, what?

Repressing an urge for yet a fourth—and even louder—sigh and removing his crash helmet, Seamus gazed out the shamrock-shaped observation window above the *Dev*'s console. A terrible, unfriendly, lonely heathen planet it was—as well as the final chance for the end of the *Iona*'s pilgrimage. Still, Zylong was indeed the most beautiful planet he had ever seen—perhaps, as Commodore Fitzgerald had said, one of the most beautiful in the galaxy. During the decades of the *Iona*'s erratic and dubious pilgrimage in search of a world that wanted its scholarship and service, O'Neill had set foot on many life-supporting planets. Sometimes he had landed in peace, sometimes armed to the teeth in the company of his fellow soldiers of fortune, the Wild Geese—mind you, only in self-defense, for the Tarans were basically a peace-loving and noncombative people.

Why fight with others when you can fight much more constructively and with no bloodshed among yourselves?

Anyway, the Rule of the Holy Order was strict: their mission was to keep alive the Spirit of Exploration during the long interludes between the Great Explorations and to land and establish a permanent monastery on only the planets that needed and wanted them.

God knows, if herself's analysis is to be believed, they need us. Ah, but do they want us? That's the issue, my boy, isn't it?

The Holy Order no more made converts than did St. Columcile in Switzerland or St. Donatus in Italy or St. Killian in Bavaria long ago during the First Exploration. *Peregrinationes pro Christo.* If the natives were so impressed by the scholarship and service of the monks that they became interested in the Faith, that was another matter.

Would they be interested here in this great, terrible heathen place?

Seamus doubted it. Moreover, he doubted that they would want anything to do with the *Iona* or anything it stood for. Of course, there were ways of interpreting the regulations.

Heathen place it was, but luxuria
wonderful place to bed a "proper woman
supposing that you could find one such
with.

None of the planets he had visited compared
with the pictures of the *Iona*'s home planet, Tara,
to say nothing of that misty island on Earth from
which his remote ancestors had come, but Zylong
in its lushness approximated the beauties of those
homes more closely than anything he had seen.
The painter who had created the scene in his window had laid on all the colors with a wild and
heavy hand. It looked like a slick picture taken
from one of the tattered old books in the monastery library, too rich, too lush to be real. The
greens were too thick, the blues too deep, the reds
and purples too rich.

And best of all, it was not rushing through
hyperspace at a rate several times the speed of
light.

"Ah," Seamus O'Neill murmured to himself,
" 'tis the perfect planet for us to settle, save that
the locals might not exactly want us, worse luck
for them. Give us the slightest hint that we're
welcome, and sure we'll be here, bag and baggage,
to stay. We'll not interfere with them at all, but
give us a few years and they'll be after sighing just
like us."

O'Neill disliked this mission. If he had come
on the *Napper Tandy* with his lead platoon of Wild
Geese, he would not have to wait for the initiative
of the other side. He did not think of himself mainly

as a soldier; it was something he did because on a pilgrimage you had to have soldiers. Mind you, he was not altogether incompetent as an officer. Weren't there those on the *Iona* who, bad luck to them, argued vigorously that he was better at being an officer than he was at his other profession of bard. Spying, however, was not his line of work.

Not at all, at all.

He was prepared for death, if needs be. If it were all the same to Himself, he'd postpone death for a few years. A few decades, even. There were a number of tasks he'd just as soon finish before the account books were closed. Like persuading a proper woman to share his proper bed for the rest of his life.

That thought caused him to sigh again and indulge in a number of harmless if very distracting fantasies about amusements one might enjoy with such a proper woman. *First of all, you kiss her very gently and then ... Well, if it's all right with You*, he interrupted whatever the Deity was about with another request, *I'd like a few years of someone like that next to me at night.*

However, mortality rates on pilgrimages were high among both monks and Wild Geese. If his life were to be as short as his parents' lives had been, well, there was no good purpose served by complaining about it. Spying was different; whatever fancy names the Commodore gave to his mission, he was still a spy. He came along on the tiny *Dev*, armed not with a laser pistol but with a small harp, dressed not in the proud uniform of a commandant but in the dull gray of a wandering minstrel. There would be no electronic communication with the *Iona;* the Zylongi were not to be aware of her existence until a final decision to land was made. Only his own telepathic powers would be in use—weak and skittish as they were.

I'm to charm them with my wit and song—and Himself knows I'm a great bard no matter what those blatherskites on the Iona *say about me. But while I'm awing them with my songs and stories, I'm supposed to be finding out what makes this heathen place tick.*

A hazy sun, turned rose by the thick upper atmosphere, was beginning to decline from its zenith. Its light softened the edges of the surrounding thick green foliage and deep crimson flowers, and the golden stream flowing nearby. *A nice place,* O'Neill thought. *I wouldn't mind raising wee ones here at all, at all.*

It was in the nature of things that the proper woman in your proper bed, properly disrobed and loved, was a requisite for having wee ones to raise. So far, Seamus had not done all that well, despite his brilliant fantasies, in dealing with that requisite. *I'll probably end up a crusty, lonely old bachelor, if I live long enough to become crusty.*

Then, having enjoyed his self-pity almost as much as he enjoyed his imagining about the proper woman, he got reluctantly from the pilot's couch. It was time for work.

He had been briefed to expect a hot humid atmosphere, but the wall of moisture he met leaving the *Dev* startled him. The fragrance of the flowers was as strong as their color, an overwhelming sweet scent, like the monastery greenhouse at Easter. Or a wake. O'Neill's poet's gown began to stick to his body. He unzipped the front of it, thinking again about the proper woman and about the possibilities of zipping and unzipping her garments.

Steady, now, Seamus O'Neill, Commandant in the Wild Geese, you have better things to think about than undressing a woman.

Have I now? Like what, for instance?

Well, like the fact that the Lady Deirdre is monitoring all your thoughts.

Ah, sure she's a woman of taste and discretion. She wouldn't be after monitoring my harmless little fantasies, would she?

You'd better not be taking a chance.

Ah, 'tis yourself, Seamus O'Neill, who has a good point there.

Virtuously, he raised the zipper on his poet's gown.

"Peace to this planet." He repeated the usual Taran greeting and knelt on one knee, making a perfunctory sign of the cross. " 'Tis neither ours nor theirs," he added a prayer of his own, "but Yours. Protect it and us and them from all evil. Grant that I may bring to the good that is here something that is better, and to the bad, healing to make it good."

He paused to consider the elegance of his

prayer, simple, heartfelt, appropriate. *Not all that bad for a spur-of-the-moment effort.*

Pleased with his creativity as a man of prayer—and resolving that he would jot it down as part of the record for future historians just in case the Lady Deirdre missed it—Seamus O'Neill walked around the perimeter of the small landing site. The jungle looked impenetrable. Even so, the briefing officer chose it over the desert, which was supposedly dominated by aborigines; as interesting as those original Zylongi might be, they were not the primary object of his mission.

Podraig, *Iona*'s foul-tongued computer, had refused to advise about the landing. To set down on the plain outside what seemed to be their capital might be seen as a warlike invasion; the *Dev* might be blasted out of the air before it touched ground, and Seamus with it, worse luck for him.

"Do they have the weapons to blast anything out of the air?" Seamus had asked the computer.

"No frigging data," snarled Podraig.

On the other hand, if he landed in the desert or the jungle at some distance from the capital, they might not even notice him. Or if they did, they might not think it worth the effort to rescue him. Maybe they were a race of mystics, like some of the solitary monks on *Iona*, heaven save and protect us all.

So with the computer refusing to make estimates, the decision was to drop him in the jungle. Better to be marooned in the jungle with plenty of water and food—all of which might be poison—

than to be blasted out of the air or die of thirst on the desert.

"Why not put me down on one of the mountains?" Seamus had demanded ironically. "They say freezing to death is a pleasant way to die once you get used to it."

No one had bothered to laugh.

Anyway, here he was in the jungle. Did the locals know he was here? Did they care? Did they have any intention of rescuing him from this fragrant, hellishly hot landing site? He had nothing but a harp to ward off any animals that might lurk there. In the briefing the monk Kiernan—Kiernan Pat, the one with the Ph.D. in biology, as distinct from Kiernan Tim, the subnavigator—had said, "Sorry, we have little information about nonhuman fauna. There are herds of cattle, which the dominant race—vegetarians, you see—keep for their milk and fur. . . ."

"Fur . . . cattle with fur?" Seamus protested.

"Heathenish, isn't it? The subordinate race are omnivorous and consume small animals, so there's probably a predatory food chain. There is no reason, of course, to assume that there is an absence of large predators. I'd be interested," he smiled faintly, "to learn that any of them were hominivorous."

"You mean man-eating?"

"That's right."

"I'll try to let you know, Kiernan, me boy."

"You do that, Seamus."

Seamus sat down in the shadow of the *Dev*

and peeled back the top of his poet's gown. Strumming his harp, he crooned an ancient and mournful Celtic melody, adapted to fit his situation. It went on—interminably, he himself was willing to admit—about a woman mourning for her sweet lover who had gone off to a strange world to spy on the enemy.

If the Zylongi had sound-scanners focused on him, they knew he was a minstrel—that is, if their culture had any sense of such a person. And if they had the good taste to enjoy his music.

Do they even have music here?

All rational life forms have music, the teacher had insisted in the monastery school's class in xenology.

How do we know? Seamus had demanded.

Well, he had not been designed to be a scholar anyway. "You're not stupid at all, at all, Seamus Finnbar O'Neill," the Lady Deirdre had said with some sympathy. "It's just that your talents are not in the scholarly direction."

"Not anywhere near it," he admitted ruefully. "I find it hard to concentrate in a classroom. . . ."

"Especially when there are young women present."

"Well," he admitted with a winning smile, "they do make concentration a little more difficult."

"Sure you'd be thinking about them even if they weren't there."

"It might even be worse," he agreed.

"You'll be the death of me yet," she had sighed. "You're a terrible cross for an old woman to bear."

Seamus had refrained from denying that she was old. His instincts said that her displeasure over his grades was not to be turned away by compliments—even accurate ones.

Seamus had no objection to accurate flattery, but he never considered his creativity to be limited by accuracy—especially when women were the issue.

The Captain Abbess's comment on his intelligence was motivated by a mistake he had made in one of the planning sessions for this mission. She had been giving the standard lecture about the origins of space exploration. In the middle of the twenty-first century, it was said, the abundance of cheap energy, combined with a long period of tranquillity on Earth, had produced the Second Great Exploration, during which many pilgrimages went forth for wealth or adventure or faith or ideology or in search of a better world.

Seamus had been daydreaming about the glorious swelling breasts of his "proper" woman. He felt he ought to say something to indicate that he was listening.

"Columbus and Leif and Brendan and them fellas, and them all being Irish too . . ."

Herself was quite upset. "No, that was the First Exploration, a thousand years and more before the settlement of Tara.

"Our Holy Order exists," she said icily, "to keep alive the Spirit of Exploration that brought our forebears to Tara so long ago."

" 'Tis true," Seamus had said, as though giving

14

the woman good grades on her historical knowledge. The Tarans wanted to keep alive the era of adventure, and the Zylongi, apparently, wanted to forget all about it.

While he sang of the lamentations of his unfortunately imaginary lover, O'Neill considered his chances. Carmody, a Brigadier serving as the *Iona's* Operations Officer, assured him that the best data indicated no serious danger in this reconnaissance. The Zylongi were far below normal on the aggression scale; they would probe, find him harmless, and release him.

"Will they now?" O'Neill strummed a chord on his harp that was supposed to indicate irony. "Would you care to offer an estimate of the probability of such a happy outcome?"

Carmody, shrugging his massive shoulders, a frown crossing his craggy face, muttered, "Between sixty and seventy-five percent."

O'Neill laughed out loud. Fitzgerald, Carmody, even the sainted Podraig were guessing.

A lavender twilight was descending, and with it a powerfully sweet, enticing smell, one which brought back all of his virtuously dismissed fantasies. *It would be a good place to bring the proper woman on a proper honeymoon. Sure wouldn't the smell turn her on too?* His daydreams returned to the issue of her breasts, a subject on which Seamus had a tolerant and open mind, so many different arrangements were there that might prove satisfactory.

You bed the woman here and then you take her

back to Tara, where you've never been yourself, and maybe on the Green Hills impregnate her there, and then you go on to Earth and your child is born in the Old Ground or on the shore of the Great Lake. 'Twould be a fine honeymoon and religious pilgrimage all combined into one. He made the sign of the cross reverently. *Sure there'd be nothing wrong after you're married with mixing lovemaking and praying.*

With the Transit stations developed half a millennium ago, Tara was only two weeks from Earth. If ever the components of such a station, long stored in the hold of the *Iona*, were assembled here on Zylong, it would be only a little more than two months from Zylong to Earth, and the Transit circuits were not crowded in this era between Explorations—save of course for Tarans, who were incorrigible travelers and pilgrims.

The Holy Rule said that no pilgrim could return to Tara or to Earth, unless his monastery had found a planet that would accept it. Then that planet became your home, but you could visit previous homes for reasonable times, "so long as the purpose is educational and religious."

Sure that was all I had in mind. Education and religion.

The pilgrim ships were wisely forbidden contact with the planet they had left behind, save for purposes of canonical obligations (like the Captain Abbess's participation in Roman elections). Zylong was, of course, even more isolated because, except for an occasional wandering space tramp, it had no contact with the world its founders had left behind for a millennium, by their choice at that. They wanted no part, the Abbess said with a twist of distaste in her aristocratic mouth, of the "corruption" of earth.

She was not exactly naive about human nature, but as she added, "Seamus, corruption comes with the genes and not with the place. Isn't that true?"

He had agreed, of course, though he did not know either Earth or Tara. Born on pilgrimage, he had never seen either, save in pictures. To visit the Old Worlds with your proper woman would be almost as much fun as making love with the proper woman.

He was so pleasantly occupied with his daydreams that he almost missed the Zylongi patrol. They crept stealthily through the jungle, like the pack of heathen savages they probably were. O'Neill read their presence before he heard them. His rather dull psychic sense—dull compared to the real experts like herself, anyway—felt five "persons," anxious but not hostile. That foulmouthed computer, Podraig, insisted that they would be humanoid. "Somewhat different from us in their biology after a thousand years and more," Commodore Fitzgerald said at his briefing, "probably not so different as to exclude crossbreeding," adding, with a faint touch of irony, "not that you need feel obliged to make any experiments in that direction."

"Persons" probably meant humanoid. And as for breeding, all thought of anything related to that praiseworthy and perennial process faded from

Seamus O'Neill's frightened head as he waited for them.

I'm not an anthropologist, I'm not an explorer. I'm a soldier and a second-rate bard. What the hell am I doing here?

And you're just as dead if you're killed by "anxious" folk instead of "hostile" folk.

Then the Zylongi slipped out of the jungle. Seamus lost some of his fear. They didn't look all that scary. In fact, they looked almost as frightened of him as he was of them.

"Sure isn't that always the way," he spoke his profound wisdom aloud. "Everyone is scared of everyone else."

The Zylongi stopped in their tracks at the sound of his voice, as though his words had frozen them in place. There were three men and two women. Shorter than Tarans, with darker skin, brown hair, European faces, the Zylongi showed their Earth origins. Four of them carried spears; one of the men had a rather ancient carbine-type weapon that he pointed directly at O'Neill's skull.

The women were lovely—short and full-figured like vest-pocket Venuses. Their dark arms and shoulders invited a caress despite the wicked spears they carried. One was a little older than the other, a dusting of gray in her curly brown hair.

Well, they don't know what to make of my voice. What will they think of my music?

He reached for the harp. The man with his weapon raised it warningly. Seamus struck a chord. The fellow lowered the weapon—a little.

Mostly to offend the Lady Deirdre, whom he was sure was listening, he devoted his long song to highly clinical praise of the women and their attributes, which would have made them proper bed partners indeed.

The Zylongi listened, their faces still blank and wary, but their bodies relaxing as the melody went on.

Sure they know it's sensual music and they can't help but like it. Good thing for me they don't know exactly what I'm suggesting might be done with those wee lasses.

Finally he stopped and waited. The man who seemed to be in charge spoke, softly but as though giving an order. The younger woman walked gingerly toward him, touched his harp, and when she realized that he would not resist, gently took it out of his hand. She strummed its strings with a nervous smile. O'Neill patted her approvingly on her head. *Well, they know about music,* O'Neill thought.

There was nothing about the men's slender, smooth bodies to suggest they would be particularly competent in a brawl. They were handsome in a diminutive sort of way—much like Taran boys in their early teens.

I could lick a dozen of them without working up a sweat. I could disarm this crowd in a couple of seconds. Knock out the men and carry off the girls. They'd probably come willingly enough. They seem fascinated by my six feet four and red beard.

Seamus O'Neill, you're an idjit for even thinking such things.

Well, it's all right to think about them as long as you have no intention of doing them. The Rules say you don't exploit the locals sexually or any other way. And God knows, Seamus O'Neill, you've always been one to keep the Rules.

All of his captors were clad in wraparound, turquoise-colored kilts with markings that suggested they were uniforms. The men's garments were fastened at the waist; the women's under their arms. Despite the heat and humidity, the light fabric showed no sign of wilt or wrinkle.

There ought to be no trouble removing such garments, if it ever came to that.

Hey, Seamus O'Neill, what about the Rules?

I'm only thinking those things because I have no idea how to be a spy. A man is entitled to calm his nerves, isn't he?

The local with the gun approached the captive and began speaking in a soft musical language. O'Neill was reluctant to reach for his universal translator with a spear point just an inch from his bare chest. He kept his hands high and smiled in what he hoped was a winning way. The young girl tentatively touched his red beard. *Don't they have such things here?*

In a sharp tone the armed man spoke directly to her. She blushed, pulled her hand back quickly, lowered her eyes, and murmured what sounded like an apology to Seamus.

" 'Tis no problem at all, at all," Seamus said soothingly. "Sure, even Taran women like red-bearded men."

The girl blushed more deeply. *Isn't it remarkable now, how much you can convey by a tone of voice.*

Seamus began to relax. The police patrol probably had orders to bring him in alive if he didn't seem hostile. (Carmody's prediction had suggested this.) They hesitated. The man with the gun gave an order and the older woman set down her spear. There were a lot of fancy gold stripes at the top of her uniform, which didn't hurt the view of her full breasts at all, at all. Probably the insignia of some kind of senior medical type. She looked efficient and competent, the kind that was used to giving orders and being obeyed.

She took from a pocket in her wrap something that looked suspiciously like a syringe. *The police doctor,* thought O'Neill slowly and carefully, for the benefit of the readers on *Iona, must have been ordered to put me under.*

The woman approached O'Neill slowly, apprehensively, a gauzelike pad in one hand, the needle in the other. The others moved a step closer, their spears poised, ready to strike. Her head came barely to his chest, her deep brown eyes looked up into his blue ones. She seemed to plead with him not to hurt her. O'Neill felt a wrench of desire. His heart went out gently toward her fear. For a moment their eyes locked. She looked away quickly. Then resolutely she looked up at him again. Her brown eyes, deep, dark, and inviting, were even more frightened. O'Neill had always been a sucker for terrified women.

She's probably old enough to be my mother.
There were lines around her eyes, hints of wrinkles
on her pretty face, touches of fleshpads on her
neck and chin. She was, however, very nicely built
and poignantly attractive.

"Don't be afraid of me." O'Neill touched her
cheek. "I'm not going to hurt you, and unless our
biologies are more unlike than they seem, whatever you have in that great terrible needle isn't
going to hurt me much either."

She lowered the needle and waited, as though
submitting, not at all unwillingly, to a heathen
greeting ritual.

"I'm not the heathen." Seamus laughed. "You
are."

She laughed lightly too, probably assuming
that was part of the ritual.

It was a pleasant face to touch, warm and
smooth. Almost without realizing what he was
doing, Seamus caressed it lightly, first with his
fingers and then with his whole hand. The woman
seemed to sag, as though she were yielding to him
completely.

Seamus glanced around. The others did not
seem angry or offended. Rather they watched with
intent fascination.

So, because it couldn't possibly do any harm,
he kissed her forehead. The woman tensed in surprise but did not try to fend him off. Her friends
gasped. *More in astonishment than in outrage,* he
thought.

"Keep your hands off the women, Seamus,"

the Captain Abbess had said, "and yourself with more than enough of the chemicals of the young in you."

Well, she didn't forbid a little ritual kiss at the beginning, did she? Besides, what kind of a Taran bard would it be that didn't brush his lips against hers? His kiss was quick, and her startled lips were firm and warm. Her eyes widened, her jaw dropped, and her head tilted down. Seamus noted with interest that firm nipples were pressing against the fabric of her uniform.

Ah, now, it wasn't that much of a kiss. But then, you've never been kissed by a red-bearded giant before.

The second gasp from the rest of the gang seemed more like envy than anything else.

See, Your Ladyship, I am skilled at this spy business after all. The kissing isn't really to calm my fears. Sure I'm not afraid at all, at all.

Well, not as afraid as this poor thing is.

Hesitantly, the woman lifted the syringe and nodded at it, as if asking his permission.

"No problem at all, at all." Seamus took her hand and guided it toward his arm. She was trembling; he felt her pulse racing through her arm and imagined her heart beating rapidly.

"Nothing to be afraid of." He rolled the gown off his shoulder and pointed at his upper arm muscle. "Is it here you're wanting to stick me?"

She nodded dubiously, still not sure that he wouldn't break her back.

He thought about kissing her again but, instead, drew her hand to its target. He hardly felt the needle when it plunged into his arm.

Well, it was a pleasant enough feeling to go out with.

As his limbs began to weaken, he wondered vaguely whether the programming the geniuses on the *Iona* had built into him would resist probes for lust. *It won't do to have the Zylongi know how you reacted to one of their mature police medical types. They might not approve at all of such exchanges. Still, they didn't object too strongly. Maybe they don't object to a few minor exchanges of affection now and then with weird outworld giants.*

Even if he's the first weird outworld giant they've ever seen.

O'Neill felt very peaceful and very sleepy. He began to slide toward the ground. The medical woman threw her arms around him and shouted. The others raced to help her. Very gently they lowered him to the turf that he had so recently claimed, albeit tentatively and subject to approval by the locals, for the pilgrimage of the *Iona*.

Everything's gone according to plan so far. Isn't that nice.

His second-to-last thought was not of the Zylongi woman or his mission; it was of herself, the Holy Captain Abbess Deirdre Cardinal Fitzgerald. His last thought was that it had suddenly turned very dark.

Ritual kiss or not, the woman doctor tried to kill me.

2

"Commandant O'Neill, reporting for final in-structions, Your Ladyship, ma'am," he said, salut-ing sloppily, his tone containing just enough servile respect to stop a half-step short of insolence. This time the black-haired witch was going to have to tell him the whole truth, not the half-truths that she liked as a matter of political principle even when expediency did not demand that she be evasive.

The Cardinal took her hand off the quartz rock that transmitted psychic impulses to the huge view-ing screen on the oak-paneled wall of her throne room. Zylong faded away; thick red curtains fell back to cover the screen. The matching observa-tion port remained open, revealing the cold stars staring implacably from the darkness of eternal night. O'Neill, who did not like darkness, shivered slightly and turned away from the port.

"Oh, yes, Seamus," she said absently. "Do come in." There was always a faint twinkle in her eyes when he entered. Seamus knew that he was half a son to her, a replacement for her own slaughtered children. It made for an awkward relationship, especially since neither of them would ever dare mention it. On the other hand, it never hurt to know that the Cardinal Abbess had a soft place in her heart for you.

"Having a look at our friends down there?" he asked with elaborate casualness.

Sorting through papers, she began to read a summary: "This report, Seamus, has been compiled basically from four sources: (*a*) reports from the occasional traveler who landed on Zylong, usually by mistake, and lived to tell about it; (*b*) estimations from what we know of communitarian utopian societies of similar perfectionist bent; (*c*) our own physical scanning—which they do not seem to have intercepted, by the way; and finally (*d*) our psychic reading, which, like the physical scanning, is less than completely satisfactory at this distance. Clear?"

" 'Tis," he said curtly.

"I will," she shuffled through the papers, "have some comments of my own after I summarize the data. All right?"

"Sure you don't often sound like a social scientist."

"I use the jargon whenever it seems appropriate," she colored slightly, indicating that in the endless sparring that was essential to Taran culture, he had scored a point, but had hardly won the battle, much less the war.

"It is, in all likelihood, an old utopian culture entering its last phases before disintegration. The communitarian zeal that once animated it is long since spent. The pretense of unanimous shared decision-making will have long since turned into an empty ritual. It will be very civilized, very sophisticated, very gentle and polite as long as no one challenges the basic assumptions or the real power structure—and make no mistake about it, Seamus Finnbar O'Neill, these utopian communities have a very strong if unacknowledged power structure from the very beginning."

" 'Course we don't know what happens to one after a thousand years, now do we?"

"An intelligent observation—" she raised a thin eyebrow "—as welcome as it is rare. In any case, they will be very supportive of one another, but that very support will be a form of social control. There will be little personal freedom as we know it and very little creative vitality."

"Not exactly like us," Seamus said with a grin.

The Abbess did not find it amusing. "There could hardly be greater differences between them and the band of half-mad, individualistic anarchists over which I seem to be destined to be responsible." Her slender fingers drummed thoughtfully on the desk. "We are contentious, troublesome, independent, given to decisions by a handful of votes. . . ."

"Except for reelecting yourself every year."

". . . That does not alter the point," she went on, the drumbeat of her fingers increasing its pace, "that we are neither polite, nor cultivated, nor civilized and that we not only permit individual creativity to the point of eccentricity—as you yourself exemplify—" she smiled, rather like an amused parent with an indulged child, "—we actively encourage it. We are, in fact, rather proud of our oddities and our eccentricities.

"Ah, sure we're at least alive."

"We are that, Seamus Finnbar O'Neill. Our manners and our morals may not have improved much since the days of the proto-Celts on Tara. We drink too much, we argue too much, we talk too much, we fight too much. . . ."

"On occasion, begging Your Ladyship's pardon, we wench too much."

The Cardinal frowned. "That is neither here nor there. Our men are often rather timid in these matters; they talk a much better game than they actually play, or do I cut too close to the bone, Seamus Finnbar O'Neill?"

Seamus had nothing at all to say to that. So the Cardinal, pleased that she had scored a point, continued. "Our relations between the sexes are usually marked by interminable verbal sparring."

" 'Tis not true at all, at all." Seamus grinned genially at her. "Pure calumny."

"We daydream too much and justify it in the name of mysticism. We pray a lot but mostly because we think God is a Gael like we are. We take interminable showers and baths—in the water all the time—and make a fetish out of personal hygiene and at the same time are incorrigibly sloppy in our domestic hygiene. Have you ever seen anything in all the galaxy as sloppy as this vessel? And despite my endless efforts to keep it neat and clean?"

"It works." Seamus raised his hands in excuse.

"Well, perhaps not much longer. Now where was I? Oh yes, we are very good at hating and not very good at loving. We sing when we're unhappy and cry when we're happy. We laugh and drink and make love at wakes and cry and drink and often don't make love at weddings...."

"A terrible lot altogether...."

"Well—" she straightened her alloy-stiff back a little more "—until you consider the alternatives. In any case the culture contact between deteriorating utopian communalism..." She shuffled through her papers. "I believe that is what our scholars call it, yes. Impressive words, aren't they, Seamus Finnbar O'Neill? ... between, as I say, deteriorating communalism, and incorrigible—let me see, yes—anarchic individualism can be fraught with problems."

"Anarchic individualists? Is that what we are? Well, it seems reasonable enough. Sure I like us better."

"Precisely. But our friends down there might be forgiven for reacting as our ancestors did to the arrival of the Vikings. In almost any scenario, there could be serious trouble."

"We're not going to do them any harm." Seamus twisted uneasily in his foam chair. "Sure won't we leave them alone?"

"Not going to do them any harm?" She fingered her ivory pectoral cross nervously. "That's what the early missionaries on Tara said when unwittingly they brought contagious diseases that killed most of the locals off. We can cope with the medical problems well enough now. But our approach to life could be as deadly to them. Could you imagine, to cite a minor point, a Zylongi woman trying to deal with the endless stream of blarney that pours from the mouth of a Taran male?"

"Or a Zylongi male trying to sort out which of the thousand ways a Taran female says 'no' actually mean 'yes'?"

"That is neither here nor there." Her tough jaw set in its usual hard line, an indication that someone had scored a point against her. Turnabout was never fair play with Cardinal Fitzgerald. Sauce for the goose, never sauce for the gander, even though her tone indicated that she did not totally reject the truth of Seamus's observation. "To take a much more serious matter, what might happen in a culture in which political democracy —as we know it, anyway—has not existed for centuries when it faces a culture in which politics is the favorite form of daytime entertainment?—"

"And often nighttime too."

She ignored him completely. "—A culture in which discontent is almost never expressed when it encounters one in which it is celebrated almost daily, as routinely as we monks chant the divine office?"

"I begin to see the problem." Seamus leaned forward on his chair. "And the difficulty from their point of view is that, if our estimates are right, their culture has lost its drive. And ours, as far as we can tell anyway, has as much drive as it ever had."

"There are disadvantages in anarchy, as I of all people on this untidy, disorderly, contentious ship have reason to know, but it rarely runs down. On the other hand, their culture seems to be in acute trouble. Either it will be running down like a clock that cannot be rewound or it will have built up enormous energies of frustration that are ready to explode. Podraig thinks there is a fifty–fifty chance of violent disintegration within the year. Arguably both processes will be occurring."

"Will any of them know it?"

"Most will deny it—" she glanced at the blank screen "—but some of the more intelligent or the more lunatic will know it, of course. That will make the situation there very volatile, however serene and untroubled the veneer may appear."

"So with that kind of error margin, you need a human spy to second-guess that cheap thief of a computer?" he asked, sitting himself across from her without waiting to be asked.

The Lady Deirdre Fitzgerald sighed. "You know well, Seamus O'Neill, that you are under no obligation to go on this mission." She pointed a delicate finger at the map of Zylong that she had caused, by a mental wish, to appear on the small viewing screen. "Seamus, that may be the end of our pilgrimage. God knows, it is time to end it. You and I know more than most the costs that have been paid for it. We cannot afford another disaster."

There was silence in the heavily draped room. The Captain Abbess rearranged her plain brown robe, not the elaborate Celtic dress blue used on solemn high occasions, with its thin red fringe and the blue Brigid's cross. She was thinking of her husband and children, O'Neill knew. And he thought of his parents, slain ten years ago in the disastrous landing on Rigoon. None of the other pilgrimages, not even the fateful trip of the *Clonmacnoise*, had been so long or so tragic. He didn't want to talk about it.

"Moreover, as you are well aware, there is a faction within the monastery which thinks that it is time to change the Rules."

"Idjits." Seamus leaped from his chair, ready to battle with anyone who challenged Her Ladyship's wisdom and leadership.

"You're the idjit too." She pointed at the chair. "Restrain your temper and sit down. This matter is too serious for a display of your masculine pride." She readjusted her ivory cross and tucked a few strands of errant hair back under her veil. "Their dissatisfaction is understandable. We are, after all, in serious trouble. Yet if we become colonists instead of missionaries, convert makers instead of respectful visitors who come peacefully in response to invitation, then there will be violence and death. We may win at first, but in the long run we will lose just as surely and far more dreadfully than we will if we let this monastery become a lifeless space derelict."

"And you'll have no part of leading an invasion."

"I will not." She rested her hand gently on the desk in front of her, as determined as gravity.

"Nor will a lot of the rest of us. If it comes to that, they'll invade by themselves."

"Shush, Seamus." She sighed wearily. "It has not come to that yet. Mostly now it is talk. Yet I cannot be wholly displeased with mothers and fathers who do not want to see their children die slowly and painfully as we run out of food and air and water. The talk of mutiny is not dangerous, not yet."

"So I am to pop in and find out if the Zylongi would allow a monastery of the Order of Saints Brendan and Brigid to land and on an island in their great big river." He hoped his light tone would dispel the unhappy memories that haunted both of them.

The Captain Abbess played with the ruby on her finger. "As you know, Seamus, ours is not a missionary order. The *Peregrinatio* is an act of devotion and service in itself, needing no other justification. We convert no one to our Holy Faith by force. Ever since the great Columcile on the original *Iona*, our monasteries have been devoted to scholarship and prayer. If the example of our lives of joy, learning, and service attract people to the

Holy Faith, then well and good. We are not out to make converts."

It was the official party line. Deirdre repeated it as though reciting a lesson. Seamus knew she believed it; he believed it himself, more or less, and certainly his parents before him had believed it. Why else would a young couple have embarked on this crazy pilgrimage?

"But," Seamus added, with a faint touch of sarcasm, fleshing out the official version, "since there is a little bit of the gombeen man in all of us, we have the custom of ending our pilgrimages only when we find a planet where there is a good chance the natives will be attracted by something more than the quality of our poteen. If Podraig is right, the Zylongi are going to need someone to pick up the pieces for them in the very near future." He was backing her into a corner where she would have to trot out the whole truth.

Deirdre ignored his sarcasm. Fingering the sheaf of papers on her desk, she spoke: "You will remember that my sainted predecessor thought we would be received with open arms on Rigoon. It was only Carmody and the last company of Wild Geese that saved us all from extinction."

O'Neill remembered all right. A fourteen-year-old boy with a bloody pike in his hand, looking down at the mutilated bodies of his family, would not ever forget Rigoon or the sainted fool who led them into the trap. "So I am to observe how far along the line toward collapse the Zylongi are?"

"Something like that, Seamus O'Neill." She

sighed again and found on one of her summary papers something to hold her eyes.

She won't look at me, damn her.

It was time for Seamus to raise his real objection. "Why not just leave them alone? If the Zylongi have a happy culture, why take the risk of disturbing it? Do they care that they're not free?"

Rising from her throne, the Captain walked over to the viewer. "You've only known freedom, Seamus O'Neill. You cannot imagine life without it." She wasn't letting him look at her melancholy eyes. "We will not harm the Zylongi. You know me well enough to know that I will not take away anyone's happiness or contentment. I trust you on this mission; you must trust whatever decisions I have to make."

Whatever was on Deirdre's mind, it was making her sad and weary. Still, O'Neill knew it would come to that. The whole crew of the *Iona* worshiped the woman. Each year when she came up for reelection the vote was overwhelming. Even those who were muttering about a vote to change the Rules assumed—irrationally, it seemed to Seamus—that she would accept such a change. If the ill-starred pilgrimage of the *Iona* was ever to end happily, the Lady Deirdre was the one who could do it. Of course, the fact that she read the whole monastery, perceiving problems even before they arose, didn't hurt. He had seen Deirdre turn aside a large meteor when the safety shields were not functioning. "There is," Liam Carmody said once, "just a little bit of the witch about Her Ladyship."

It was not unusual for a woman to captain a spacecraft. Holy Brigid herself had presided over a monastery of monks and virgins long ago. Of course, the Captain Abbess was not a virgin; she had been married with three children before the disaster at Rigoon. If rumors were to be believed, she was not exactly pious in her youthful days on Tara before the pilgrimage. After Rigoon and the loss of her family, she chose to leave the Wild Geese and to join the monastic community in order to erase the great wound in her heart. She grew in wisdom and political skill, as well as piety, without losing the strength of her youth. So the slender figure of the Captain Abbess took command of the Abbot's throne on the bridge of *Iona*. She was neither young nor old but timeless beneath her veil, her long black hair covered now; the delicate face looking out clear-eyed and farseeing over a world she was already beyond. Trust Deirdre? The monks and the Wild Geese might complain mightily—that was part of being a Taran—but the pale, melancholy Abbess had absolute command of their fidelity.

One did not, of course, imagine the Abbess without her monastic robes. But she did swim in the *Iona*'s pool like everyone else—in a brown swimsuit with a crimson fringe—and one could hardly help notice that her figure was still, to put it mildly, presentable. That, however, was never discussed and certainly was far from anyone's mind when they were in her throne room.

Well, reasonably far.

Her sigh captured O'Neill's straying attention. He stood up and drew himself to his full height. "Woman," he said, "there's something you're not telling me."

"There is, of course, the matter of the aborigines," she said, gazing thoughtfully at the map, "creatures who were there before the Zylongi migrated to the planet. There are hints in the few reports we have from travelers that there is something unusual either about the aborigines themselves or with the Zylongi's relations with them."

"So that's another one of my jobs. I'm to keep an eye out for the aborigines. But rumors from space tramps are not enough to make you frown that way, Lady Deirdre." *Get to it, woman, stop beating around the bush. You'll drive me daft.*

"How perceptive of you to notice." She sighed wearily, rose gracefully from her throne, and wandered over to the observation port. "Some of the early travelers made crude drawings of the aborigines. There's one on the desk, as Podraig has reproduced it from his memory banks. Take a look at it, Seamus O'Neill."

He leaned forward, searched through the papers, and found a drawing of a creature that looked almost human.

"Sure, 'tis like one of them cute little creatures in the biology textbooks." He hesitated as he searched his memory for the right word. "Prehominid? What are they doing here?"

"Precisely, Seamus Finnbar O'Neill. I don't

know the answer and I may never know it. Removed from Earth aeons ago by a Great Exploration from elsewhere of which we know nothing? Perhaps. Evolving at a slower rate here because of a different set of environmental challenges? Maybe."

"Brigid, Patrick, and Columcile!"

"Precisely." She touched a button on the wall, and the thick damask curtains soundlessly closed over the observation port, much to Seamus's relief. "And all the other holy saints. Therefore, there is a reasonable possibility that the so-called dominant race has interfered with the evolutionary process of this species, which is in all likelihood conspecific with us and them."

"Ah."

"I'll tell you my gut instinct, Seamus." She placed a hand briefly on an admirably flat belly. "Where you find domination of conspecifics, you encounter sexual exploitation. A shortage of women, powerful men displaying their might with harems, organized prostitution. The races mix. Then the superior race, horrified at what it has done, denies the past, which means they deny the conspecific nature of the subordinate race. The result is even more cruel violation, exploitation, degradation—if necessary, of millions of creatures. Do you understand?"

"As yourself has said, even the Tarans are bigots."

"Even." She smiled wryly. "At least we know it."

She walked back to her throne and sat down in it, as elegantly as she had risen.

"You even say that the bigot distorts himself more than he does the target of his bigotry."

She smiled indulgently. "You do have a brain, don't you, Seamus Finnbar O'Neill? Leaving aside all social science predictions—" she brushed her report away impatiently "—I would bet, if it were permitted an Abbess to gamble the few jewels left on this ship, that the dominant race has done terrible things to itself and to the other race in the name of its supposed superiority."

"Whose side are we on? The poor little creatures', I hope."

"Everyone's!" she snapped impatiently. "We try to make peace, not choose sides in conflict. You know that."

"Ay," he agreed solemnly. "It just takes me a little time to remember the right Rule."

The Captain leaned back on her throne and said very softly, "We can't be precise, Seamus. We can't lock onto it. There is something bizarre about Zylong that doesn't fit our expectations. The culture is so different we can't process it. That's why we need a transceiver. . . ." Her voice trailed off.

"You mean a psychic bug? I'm not one of those!" he exploded.

"What makes you so sure?" Now the deep blue eyes locked in on him.

Somewhere in Podraig's memory banks was a notation doubtless dating back to childhood. Seamus O'Neill was low in psychic perception powers

39

but had abilities to transmit psychic energy to others. He was being dispatched to Zylong to soak up vibrations and send them back to others to interpret. Damn the woman! Still, there was more coming, those eyes were not ready to let him go. With resignation he slipped back into his chair.

"You'd better tell me all the bad news."

"Zylong may be the final planet." She put her hand on his shoulder. "Those who speak about changing the Rules do not really understand how bad our situation is. If they knew, their talk would be more insistent. We might well have a mutiny on our hands."

"The final planet? What do you mean, woman? The cosmos is filled with planets. Sure didn't Himself create more than enough to go around?"

"Seamus, I mean the final planet *for us*. The *Iona* is tired and old. It doesn't work as well as it used to. Ours has been the longest Taran pilgrimage; we don't know how long these ships can last. My own guess is that we'll be lucky to last another year or two without incapacitating trouble."

O'Neill was grimly silent for a moment. "Well, morale is still pretty good," he argued lamely. "Despite the complaints."

"Is it, Seamus? We Celts are a blend of fatalism and hope—that's why we go on pilgrimages. When the hope wanes," she sighed, "you have only paralyzing melancholy left. There are a few incorrigible hopers like yourself—" she smiled at him gently "—but melancholy is increasing on this ship. There's nothing we can do about it. How many marriages have there been among the young Wild Geese? I realize it may be a sensitive matter to raise with you, given Lieutenant Kavanaugh's choice."

"You mean it's like after the Great Famine on Earth? People just don't have enough hope to begin new families?"

Another sigh. "Too many failures, too many frustrations, too many defeats, Seamus, even for a crew of Tarans." She spoke slowly, heavily, as though she bore the weight of all the sorrows of the pilgrimage.

"If we don't land? . . ." O'Neill asked. *Damn it, of course I'll go. Why does she have to be so indirect about telling me the truth?*

Cardinal Deirdre smiled. "Then it was not to be, and it has been an interesting if overlong pilgrimage." She dismissed him with a wave. "Now, Seamus O'Neill, off with you. While I am not normally greatly pleased at anything, I would be pleased if you are able to send back good news."

It was arranged. Connor McNulty, the monk psychologist, prepared a mixture of drugs and conditioning to present O'Neill to the Zylongi as a harmless and hungry space minstrel. It was a role close enough to what he actually was so that, as McNulty observed, there was an eighty percent probability that the Zylongi probes would not break through the cover. The cover also portrayed O'Neill as having studied anthropology at the university in Tara before being expelled for drinking too much. ("Which of us doesn't?" said O'Neill.)

The Prior sang the farewell Mass. It was a nice touch. Had they never expected to see him again, the Abbess herself would have participated in his "last rites." If they thought he had a good chance, the Subprior would have celebrated; as it was, the Prior's Mass signaled that Seamus O'Neill's chances were neither bad nor good.

"Well, I suppose I had better get your blessing before I go," he said gruffly to the Captain Abbess after Mass and just before debarkation. "Sure it can't hurt." He knelt on one knee to kiss the Celtic cross on her abbatial ring.

She took his head in her hands. "Go with God, Seamus O'Neill. Come back to us just as you are now." It was her most solemn benedictory tone.

The peace that was reputed to be in the hands of an Abbot flowed through his person. Then Seamus Finnbar O'Neill's whole being was filled with joy and light and the warmth of overpowering love. *Sure it didn't seem right that a holy Abbess herself should feel such love for him. Still, what was wrong with it? She was human and she was a woman and he was kind of a son to her anyway.*

Besides, he loved her too. Like a son. Mostly.

He was jarred to notice that as she made the sign of the cross over him, she was weeping. The Captain Abbess was not known for sentimentality. His confidence went down considerably at the thought of the Abbess already keening for him. Tears rose in his own eyes.

Hennessey, his second in command, was waiting with his new wife just in front of the pressure chamber that led to the tiny spacecraft. *Ah, well, your best friend marries your girl on you and they both come to see you off.* He shook Fergus's hand and hugged Tessie, saying, "Sure, woman, you made the right choice. Never a doubt about that."

As he walked down the long ramp of the pressure chamber to his ship, O'Neill thought that Tessie probably had indeed made the right choice. No one would send the sentimental Hennessey off on such a wild mission. He strode by the great troop carriers *Kevin Barry, Thomas Patrick Doherty,* and *Daniel P. Moynihan,* past his beloved training ship *Napper Tandy,* the abbot's shuttle *Michael Collins,* the gunships *Bernardette Devlin, Eamon Casey,* and *John F. Kennedy* to the very end of the ramp, where his battered *Eamon De Valera* was docked. It was allegedly a craft with interstellar capabilities; in fact, it was a cranky, unpredictable tub as expendable as its pilot.

Through the sound system he could hear the monastery bells chiming vespers as he clanked the door of the *Dev* shut. Just before he pressed the signal to launch, Podraig, in the mindless singsong of a computer, intoned, "God go with you, Seamus O'Neill."

He replied by raising a number of pointed and profane questions about Podraig's ancestry, slamming off the communications input before the blatherskite had a chance to reply.

3

From a great depth O'Neill clawed his way back to consciousness. The Zylongi were bumping and jolting him down a jungle path. They had misjudged the dosage necessary to put him out. He almost wished he were unconscious; he was hot, sweaty, thirsty. The rough ride gave him a headache. Resolutely he kept his eyes closed and began to "read" the environment for the damn crowd up there in herself's throne room—bad luck to the lot of them.

With considerable effort and many brisk commands and gentle tugs from the medical woman, they got him into a small hovercraft vehicle that whizzed along a jungle path and then over a wide body of water—a lake or a great river, he couldn't tell which. Apparently his head was resting in her lap, a position that was intellectually consoling but in his present condition not much else.

The jungle was teeming with animal life: Kiernan's food chain. There were a lot of little critters, quite unrecognizable to Seamus. But among them were massive bears, some suspicious-looking medium-sized dinosaurs, a flock of mastodons, and some wandering cats that seemed to be exactly like the pictures Seamus had seen of saber-toothed tigers.

Just like someone has scooped up creatures from Earth long ago, deposited them here, and then forgot about them.

Seamus had the impression that there were degrees of jungle and that the wilder critters were way off in the distance. He also noted that his captors were scared stiff of the place and in a hurry to get out of it.

Then they cut across an intensely cultivated plain, in parts of which, sure enough, there were vast herds of furry cattle. As a product of a culture whose sagas dealt with cattle raids, Seamus was affronted by the furry cattle, but he was too sick and too uncomfortable to take much pleasure in being affronted.

There were only two or three kinds of crops, presided over by robots and human technicians, with other humans—well, kind of humans—running errands for the technicians. An old and highly sophisticated system of agriculture it seemed.

Then closer to the City he "saw" wagon trains, long processions of large carts being drawn by animals that looked like squat ungainly horses. These trains streamed back and forth across the plain, bringing in supplies of raw materials, stuff that looked like metal ore and lumber, and tracking back empty for more supplies. As they drew closer to the City, they met mechanical movers, heavy, slow, and clumsy, and an occasional rapid scooter like the hovercraft they were in.

The City itself loomed up in the distance, a giant manufacturing and commercial center, the throbbing core of life on Zylong, but to Seamus's psychic senses, a curiously lifeless place, seemingly with less human energy than the comparatively tiny *Iona*.

The planet was laid out pretty much the way the chart on the Lady Deirdre's desk said it should be: a single world island in the Northern Hemisphere—tundra on the very top, trailing off into steppes, and then the plains of which the City was the center. Beneath the City—as you looked down the island—was a massive snow-covered mountain spine with a rain forest on the left, on the fringe of which was Seamus's landing site, and deserts on the right. The precipitation obviously came from the east.

The City itself was on the bank of a meandering, sluggish river that originated in the mountains, flowed through the jungle, tumbled over a broad waterfall, and then flowed by the City into a vast delta land and then into the sea.

Sure I've spent my life on a titanium cylinder. I should be enjoying all these wondrous sights, and instead, I'm half-conscious and have a friggin' headache.

Finally they landed on a platform at the edge of the City—a place so dazzling physically that, despite its lack of human vitality, it was beyond Seamus's drowsy comprehension.

I'll come back for it later, he promised weakly.

An armed guard helped to transfer O'Neill to a monorail car that moved him first across a grassy meadow, then along the riverbank—above the wide and slow-moving blue sheet—and then into a deep dark tunnel, where O'Neill would have been perfectly willing to have left his consciousness if that had been possible.

The medical woman was fussing over him anxiously, now, to tell the truth, bothering him with her chatter and solicitude. *Can't you leave me in peace, woman? Don't you realize that I'm a sick man? Put my poor head on a pillow, would you please, and let me have a little bit of peace.*

Then the car arose from the tunnel and into the vast and splendid City, a mass of great buildings in light pastel colors, pink and blue and green and lemon, looming on all sides.

Despite his frigging headache, he read the City to be composed almost entirely of giant towers, forty and fifty stories high, made of a substance that was either rock or very hard metal, each one designed with a distinctive shape or rather in a series of distinctive patterns in which the shape of the building seemed to match the color in which it was painted. No, the colors weren't painted, they were somehow imprinted on the rock or metal.

They were windowless and even though it was now well into the Zylongian night, they gleamed in an artificial light radiating up from the ground at their base. There was no sign of vegetation in the City. Between the buildings were huge plazas, boulevards, and wide esplanades of an elegant, formal checkerboard pattern—all swarming with handsome people clad in a dazzling variety of garments in the style of those the police wore, some reaching to the ankles and others, in the case of young women, barely to mid thigh. Seamus was too sick to notice whether the thighs of the young women were attractive.

Dear God, he prayed, *put me out completely. When I am no longer interested in female anatomy, I am too sick altogether, not long for this world, at all, at all.*

Well, almost too sick. It was his impression that the thighs and butts that were displayed were a bit too thick for his tastes, not that he was in any position at the moment to be choosy.

In addition to the monorail on which he was now riding, O'Neill read tiny individual vehicles scurrying to and fro on the streets like multicolored bugs. There was also an extensive tunnel system into which the monorail plunged, though not, as far as he could see, the bugs. For someone like Seamus, born and bred on a spaceship, the City was dazzling, a glorious vista of civilized living, despite his monumental headache.

A decayed culture it might be, but, since I have to be here, I might just as well enjoy the decay—a little. Just so long as it doesn't change me much. And of course that couldn't happen.

The drug was beginning to wear off, and he

reconsidered his wish that the medical woman leave him alone. *If she insists on holding my hand and resting my head against her breasts, I'll just have to accept that as part of the mission. So the culture's degenerate. A little bit of degeneracy never hurt anyone.*

As he snuggled closer, still trying to act like a man in a trance, his monorail car plunged once more into a tunnel, deeper, it seemed, than before. Seamus thought he could sense running water, deep streams feeding into the vast river and perhaps providing the City with water. No engineering slouches, these folks.

The woman was very comfortable indeed. There were undoubtedly others in the car with him. He sensed their presence. But it was dark.

Ah, now, Seamus me boy, take things as they come. Remember you're supposed to be unconscious. Then the car ascended to the surface and docked in front of a huge complex of towers, pale lime in color and, his psychic sense told him, bustling with human activity.

His body must have somehow signaled his alertness. The woman's firm breasts were, after all, a distraction and a torment. It was hard not to move just a little bit. They were, he realized, about to carry him into this complex. Then there was no chance to reflect further. He felt an instant of pain and then nothing at all.

The Lord God had heard his prayers for oblivion.

*   *   *

49

"Good morning, Poet O'Neill. You seem to be feeling better today." The voice sounded as fragile as a tiny glass bell.

He was lying on a contour couch in a windowless room illuminated by diffused light. It was much like the dentist's quarters on the *Iona* and the woman looked much like a dental assistant in her soft white wrap with light blue jacket over it.

Where am I, he wondered, *and who is this cool person looking down at me with such curiosity? Am I dead? Sure I can't be in hell because it doesn't hurt. Maybe it's heaven, but I don't hear any harp music and this woman doesn't look like an angel, though she'll do till one comes along.*

"I've felt worse," he said, temporizing till he got the lay of the land. "A little weak to tell you the truth."

"That will pass quickly." She smiled. "You are a very interesting patient. It took six of our orderlies to hold you down at one point. We're . . ." She hesitated. "I mean no offense, but we're not used to someone of your size, Poet O'Neill."

My size, now what the hell does that mean?

"I hope I didn't hurt anyone."

"Only a few bruises. We must apologize for seeming to be rough. However, you surely understand that it is not every day that a spaceship lands in our jungle. The First Ones taught us always to be courteous to guests. If we have been discourteous to you, we sincerely apologize."

Jungle? What the hell?

Then he remembered. *Zylong. They must have*

played their mind-probe games. Well, he was still alive so they hadn't figured too much out.

"I see you have me programmed to speak your language," he said, feeling stupid as he spoke. Not very smooth for a master spy.

"That was no great difficulty, Poet. Our tongues have common ancestors. Yours . . . let me see . . ." she consulted a clipboard ". . . is related to Proto-English and Old Gaelic mixed with some unusual Teutonic features, while ours is of the Romance variety. We could have communicated without programming you if you had used the translator you carried on your belt."

O'Neill looked down. He was clad in a Zylongian kilt that matched the gray color of his tattered poet's gown perfectly. His translator was gone—probably being analyzed by some electronics technician.

Then he remembered the woman. The medical person. There were gold stripes on her white uniform, considerably more elaborate than her jungle dress, but still leaving little doubt about her attractions. The stripes spanned ample but neatly shaped breasts and then ran down her flanks, emphasizing, more than any Taran daytime fashion would have dared, the curves of her body. There was more gray in her hair than Seamus had realized, and more delicate lines at her throat. Still, she was more than adequate. Indeed, maybe even proper.

I've never been in love with an older woman before. It might be an interesting experience.

Seamus O'Neill, get your mind off such things. You're here to be a spy, not to be involved in ridiculous love affairs.

Go 'long with you. Having love affairs is part of being a spy, isn't it? Certainly your spies have a good time in all the books you've read in the monastery library. And herself didn't say no.

She didn't say yes, either. And you know what the Rules say.

Only if invited. But what if she invites me?

"I am sorry," the woman went on, uneasily fingering her clipboard, "that we may have seemed to be unconscionably, ah, brutal with you. It was necessary or . . ." she hesitated uneasily ". . . it was thought to be necessary. I trust you will accept my apologies, both official and personal."

"Well . . . Doctor?"

She nodded as though her title was unimportant.

"My mother taught me never to make a false move with a spear pointed at my heart." He tried his most roguish smile, but his lips barely parted.

She laughed, revealing teeth that were slightly but prettily pointed. *Carnivorous ancestors, indeed. Score one for the Lady Deirdre.*

"Poet O'Neill, we have very few visitors to Zylong. Three days ago there were mysterious energy forces at the outer rim of our sensor system. We did not know who or what to expect. Some of our more superstitious people remembered an ancient legend about a red-bearded giant god who would come to destroy Zylong. Even we scientists were disconcerted by the image we received of you when you landed. Yes, I am a doctor. My name is Samaritha and I am Director of Biological Research at the Body Institute."

So, they had sent the big brass out for me, gorgeous brass at that.

"I'm happy to meet you officially," he tried to respond in kind, "and to know that I have been in the care of a distinguished scientist."

She colored deeply, still abashed by him. *Well, that can't hurt now, can it?*

"I hope," she said, frowning, "that you do accept my apologies. I greatly regret what was done to you. It was most inhospitable."

She was serious. The apology was not just a formality. Had there been disagreement about his treatment? Did she represent a scientific subcommunity that was in partial dissent from whoever controlled this place? Or was this merely deeply ingrained courtesy?

So far two mistakes for Podraig and the Captain Abbess. The Zylongi had picked up traces of the *Iona*, and somewhere in their mythology lurked a red-haired giant. *Nice going, fellas,* he thought. *If you've made any more, you can forget about O'Neill.*

Aloud, he said, "I accept your apologies, Doctor Samaritha. If one is to be examined as I have been, it is at least consoling to know that it has been done by a competent and gracious woman."

She now was so embarrassed that she seemed ready to run from the room. "You do have a poet's skill with words, Poet O'Neill."

They're great ones for titles around here, aren't they?

"If you're a biologist, then you've at least discovered that I'm not a god—despite the red hair."

"You are interesting biologically ... I mean you are much like a Zylongi and yet different in some ways. My colleagues find your data fascinating." She had him at a disadvantage—after all, she had taken off his clothes and not the opposite (except, of course, in his imagination and that didn't count). But she still wouldn't look at him. Women had been avoiding his eyes lately.

"In addition to being biologically interesting, what else did you learn about me?" O'Neill inquired. "I have the feeling you didn't miss much."

The beautiful doctor flushed again. "I am sorry, Poet O'Neill, that the probe had to be so thorough. To violate someone's modesty without permission is a terrible offense. I must ask again that you forgive me."

"As many times as you ask—" he turned on all his Taran charm "—I'll forgive you, Doctor—and a few times extra for good measure."

She laughed, reassured, and actually sat down on the hard chair next to his couch. "Do you feel well? Sometimes the probe has uncomfortable aftereffects. Here, let me check your pulse."

She checked it by touching his throat rather than his wrist. *Wow,* O'Neill thought as she leaned over him, *if someone has to take off my clothes and inspect my biology, she'll do nicely.*

Still no hint of whether they had broken

through with the probe. "So you found that I was ungodlike. I hope you found that I was not about to destroy your world."

She glanced at a disk on her jacket. "A bit slow by our standards." Her fingers seemed to linger a tiny bit longer than necessary on his throat. "But apparently quite acceptable for your biology. . . . We find you to be utterly and completely harmless." She consulted her record board again. "Poet Seamus O'Neill, an exile from Tara—for certain infractions that need not concern us—space minstrel, wanderer from world to world, entertaining as he goes. Low on his luck, lower on fuel, and lowest on food. We welcome you to Zylong. We are sorry that our first meeting with you was inhospitable. We will try to make your sojourn here pleasing."

She finally glanced at him and smiled. O'Neill felt his heart do some odd things. She looked back at her record board and blushed. "I wonder if I may ask you a question that is perhaps inappropriately personal. It . . . it is not strictly within the limits of my professional discipline. But I fear that our students of behavior would never dare ask you."

"Ah, there's no harm in that."

"We noticed, we could hardly help notice that you kissed me in the jungle before I, ah, sedated you."

"Did I now?" *Seamus O'Neill, you're a damn fool. Violating one of their taboos the first thing you do on this heathen world.*

"Is that acceptable behavior in your culture?" She had turned a dusky purple. *Sure she's terrible pretty when deeply embarrassed.*

"Well, we don't think there's anything wrong with a little kiss. If it's not done here, I'm apologetic altogether."

"Of course we kiss, but in the privacy of the chamber, and only with our mate or our promised."

"We do that too," Seamus decided to temporize.

"But we had not been formally introduced. We are not mated or promised. Was it therefore appropriate by your cultural norms?"

"Well now . . ." *You might as well tell the truth.* "You seemed afraid of me and I wanted to let you know that I wouldn't hurt you."

"I see. That was very kind of you. I was frightened and you did, ah, reassure me—" She looked like Eve might have after she ate the apple: her averted face and her body, leaning inward in self-protection, hinted at a mixture of fascination, fear, and guilt. "—as well as astonish me. It was a disturbingly erotic experience."

Was it now? "Forbidden fruit?" he asked, thinking of Eve.

"I have been asked by many—" she was studying her clipboard intently "—what the experience was like."

"And . . . ?"

"I laugh," she laughed, and was radiantly beautiful, "and say that it was like being kissed in public by any red-bearded god."

What did Murtaugh MacMurtaugh say in their

ethics class? Nothing is more pleasant than violating mores in the search for truth.

"I'm sorry if I caused you any embarrassment," he said, meaning about half of what he said.

"In your culture, then, such signs of affection are permitted between doctor and patient?" She was making notes on her clipboard.

Now Seamus's big Irish tongue got him into trouble, big trouble. Most of the problems that would later arise resulted from the tiny, wee fib he told.

"Nothing would be thought wrong with it at all, at all. Sure doesn't the research literature show it facilitates the healing process, if you take my meaning."

A harmless exaggeration. He didn't expect to be taken seriously.

"Really?" she looked up from her notes. "I could see that it might. . . ."

"No more than two or three times a day, however."

After all, it was a very chaste kiss.

"Really!" She made another note. "How very interesting."

"Some of the scholar folk have done research which indicates that it helps the recovery process, speeds it up something terrible. . . ."

Well, if they haven't done it, they ought to have.

"How extremely interesting!" Another note, now with eyes anywhere but on him.

"How many days have I been here in your hospital?"

"We call it a Body Center." She finally looked at him. "Two days. This is the morning of the third."

"That means—" he was only joking, really only joking "—that you owe me four, maybe five kisses. I'll have to be catching up."

"How astonishing." She made more notes, scribbling rapidly. "That's fascinating. I must share this with my anthropological colleagues as soon as possible."

The devil made Seamus Finnbar O'Neill do what he did next.

He reached out from his couch, grabbed the woman's arm, drew her toward him, put his other arm around her waist, and brushed his lips against hers—briefly, but twice.

"Now you only owe me two." She wore some sort of thin but firm corset garment underneath her wrap. He permitted half of his hand to slip down toward her rear end; and delightfully solid it was too.

She did not resist or pull away.

"That is not our custom," she said blandly, her lips trembling, and delightfully solid lips they were too. "It is not, however, unpleasant." She drew several strong lines under some of her notes. "Ought I to thank you?"

"That depends on whether you liked it."

"Of course I liked it, Poet O'Neill. I am not immune to human reactions, even if I am a Research Director."

"Well, I'm glad of that anyway."

Careful, Seamus me boy. Your big mouth might be getting you into trouble. This woman loves sinning something terrible.

Time would prove that an understatement.

She scribbled frantically.

"And what would you folks be planning to do with me next, lock me up in a cage, where the common folks of Zylong can come and stare at the red-bearded nongod?"

"Of course not." Her dark eyes flashed dangerously. "We are not savages. You will be our guest until your machine can be repaired. We have no such machines here, so it may require some time." She tucked her note pad under her arm and edged toward the door. "Where you will be housed has yet to be determined. In a short time Technician Londrau will escort you through our Health Center. Is that acceptable?"

"Anything you say, ma'am." He sighed loudly and patiently.

She paused at the door.

"We will ask many questions, you should not think this hostile."

"I guess I am a questionable phenomenon." He smiled his most charming smile.

"Quite."

Swiftly and gracefully she glided back to the couch, bent over him, and touched his lips with hers, permitting Seamus an extensive, if very brief, view of her breasts. Twice.

"I believe we're even now, Poet O'Neill."

"For the last two days," he stammered.

"We shall see about the future." She vanished through the doorway.

I think I'm in deep trouble. I'm nothing more than a horny adolescent male. God won't hold it against her. But no good can come of violating your most powerful mores. Murtaugh again. Still, she wanted to do it.

Well, Podraig said the culture hereabouts was falling apart. Maybe I'll have to kiss every lovely woman on the planet as part of my spying mission. Sure she practically forced me into it. He pondered with satisfaction the possibility of Zylong being a vast harem for himself and decided that it was a fantasy he ought not to encourage.

The Lady Abbess would not be amused. No, decidedly not.

Technician Londrau was an enthusiastic young man with a voice as flat as the *Iona's* computer, if not a comparably foul mouth. However, the exhausting tour that he conducted of the Health Center took Seamus's mind off his lovely boss—more or less.

It was an enormous complex of buildings, housing various hospitals and research facilities with massive banks of equipment and a huge staff of workers, much larger, it seemed to Seamus, than the work required.

For the first time, he began to feel not only like a foreigner, but an uncultivated one at that. There were at least twice as many workers in the medical complex as the slightly more than five hundred monks, Wild Geese, and pilgrims on the

Iona. While, as far as Seamus could see, the Zylongi had no greater medical capabilities than did the tiny medical staff of the monastery, they put a lot more of their resources into health care.

Of course, he told himself, *they have more money and more people.*

The trouble with you, Seamus O'Neill, is that you're a peasant who has spent all his life with eccentrics, characters, oddballs, and other related peculiar types. Sure they've shown you the films and the pictures and made you read the books, but your world has been alloy hull and half a thousand people for the quarter century you've been around. Now you're in a great city of a mature and sophisticated civilization. You'll gawk every time you turn around if you're not careful. Once they become accustomed to your height and your great, terrible red beard, they'll see you for the bumpkin you really are. Especially if you keep kissing their mature Research Director types.

Ah, sure they weren't really that powerful kisses. Just little pecks, if you take my meaning.

"These are the hordi on which Director Samaritha is doing her most important research," Londrau droned on. "See how clean their quarters are and how well they are treated. The Director is teaching them to read and communicate. They are not the domestic strain who act as our servants, but the wild species from the desert and the jungle. Yet note how quiet and happy they are."

The hordi were diminutive creatures, a little more than four feet tall, and indeed looked much like the protohominids in the textbooks in Seamus's biology courses. About a dozen were eating and sleeping and playing with and nursing their young, huddling together in a large area that had been arranged to look like a jungle habitat. Indeed, they seemed placid and gentle, unperturbed by the four white-clad technicians who were monitoring them.

"We do not even need cages," Londrau boasted. "They are all very fond of Director Samaritha."

"That shows good taste on their part," O'Neill agreed. "Obviously they are an earlier stage of the evolutionary process. Prehominids." Probably the natives of the planet. They had managed to survive along with the colonists from Earth, the ancestors of the Zylongi. Of course, on Earth, the various pre- and protohominids had survived for aeons, side by side, if in different ecological niches. Till Cro-Magnon man occupied all the niches.

"Certainly not." The Technician fought to control his temper. "They are obviously unrelated to us."

"I see," said Seamus, who did not in fact see at all. There were enough traits of these docile, attractive little creatures in the Zylongi to leave little doubt that there had been cohabitation sometime in the past. Samaritha's faintly pointed teeth, for example. Nothing wrong with that, but why deny it?

The more fascinating question was why the prehominids on Zylong were so similar to those who had apparently once existed on Tara. Parallel and unrelated processes? Or had some prehistoric visitors brought species from Tara to this world, where they had survived long after their species had become extinct on Earth?

If the Zylongi had such hangups about their prehominid neighbors that they denied the mixing of the two species, they could hardly be expected to know the answer to that question—not that it was particularly important for Seamus's purposes to learn the answer.

"You perhaps have noticed that they are not naked?" Londrau's singsong voice interrupted O'Neill's reflections.

"Ah, aren't they now. Sure 'tis a good thing you called my attention to it. I wouldn't have noticed it at all."

This guy is beyond belief.

"It is very interesting. Once they have learned to communicate with us, they wish to clothe themselves. We permit it, of course. They seem to learn shame with the power of communication."

"Or maybe just imitation."

That stopped Technician Londrau cold. "What a very interesting speculation." He scribbled a note on his pad. "Fascinating."

Seamus considered whether he would want to engage in sex with the slender little female hordi, nervous darting creatures with pert breasts and slim hips. They were appealing enough, he supposed, if you didn't have your own women around or if you found excitement in brutalizing the frightened and the powerless. Since Seamus didn't enjoy the latter much, even in fantasies, he decided

that the little critters were not much threat to his
virtue.

Well, didn't you enjoy the doctor's fright?

Yeah, but she's not powerless. I am.

More or less.

As the tour continued, Seamus noted several
more interesting phenomena. First of all, only a
few members of the staff seemed to be working
very hard. The energetic types like Samaritha and
Londrau were far outnumbered by those who didn't
seem to be doing much at all, save for filling out
forms and sitting at desks watching what seemed
to be video monitors. They moved slowly and did
not seem particularly interested in their work. They
were, however, quite interested in him. An ever-
changing band of gawkers followed him through
the spotlessly clean, indirectly lighted pink and
beige corridors and rooms of the medical complex,
chattering away about him, just quietly enough so
he could not hear them.

"Begone, you curious rabble," he had shouted
at them once, more or less for the hell of it, waving
his arms in a mighty theatrical gesture.

That band of gawkers fled in terror, to be
replaced a few moments later by another crowd.

"That was very amusing," Londrau commented
in a tone of voice appropriate for an obituary,
making an inevitable note. "You frightened them."

"Just gave them something to talk about,"
Seamus sighed.

"Of course," said his guide, scrawling away.
"Fascinating."

Secondly, there were only a few elderly people in the Body Center. Either they were treated elsewhere, or Zylong had another way of dealing with the old. Seamus did not like the implications of that at all but decided not to ask about it, not yet.

Finally, while the Body Center was clean, neat, airy, and well illuminated, it didn't seem to work very well. Many of the lifts were not functioning. Banks of terminals were not lighted, the workers staring idly at the empty screens. Several large machines—for the making of blood and nourishment he was told obscurely—were also inactive. Each time it was explained to Seamus that these mechanisms were "temporarily waiting repair."

Now on the *Iona*, most everything was messy, as the Lady Abbess constantly complained. The Tarans didn't mind mess at all—not so long as they could take their three showers a day. In fact, the more mess the better: it was a sign work was being done. Sometimes when you were a little lazy, you'd make a mess just so your fellow pilgrims would think you were working, a technique at which Seamus O'Neill was, to tell the honest truth, extremely skillful. Yet all the machinery functioned, even if it wasn't needed. A Taran took any nonworking machine—even if it was a tertiary backup mechanism that had never been used in the whole pilgrimage—as a personal insult, a challenge to his or her integrity and honor.

Overstaffed and with broken-down equipment, he summarized for himself and anyone who might be listening on *Iona. Of course, they may have the resources to be able to afford both.*

"You benefited from the tour?" Samaritha demanded when she found him later, reclining, half-asleep, on his couch.

"Fascinating," he replied. "Incidentally, one question. What is the meaning of the metal—I'd call it silver—band many of you wear around your neck?"

"This?" She touched her band shyly. "It is our mating band. On the day my man—the Music Director—and I were formally mated, he put this link around my neck. And I a similar one around his. It represents—" she hesitated "—a chain of love which is to bind us together for life. Do you not have a similar custom?"

"We use rings, same symbolism, however."

"Interesting . . . you do not wear such a ring, Poet O'Neill?"

"When one is a space tramp like myself, how would one find a woman? And what kind of a woman would mate with me anyway?"

His self-pity was so convincing that he almost believed the story was true.

"Interesting." Yet another note. "And lamentable, of course."

"Terrible altogether."

"Now as to your residence during your sojourn with us." She became very official. "You may rest for several more hours. At sunset you may come to the living space of Music Director Ornigon and make your home with us. The Committee has decided that he and I will be your hosts. We will take refreshment there. Technical Student Horor, our son, may join us, and perhaps the Secretary and the Guide will visit us briefly. Some companions of our quarter will take nour- ishment with us. Afterward there will be a contest. Does this meet with your pleasure?"

She sounded like Podraig reading out a pro- gram. "And if it doesn't?" he said dryly and not too politely.

Her eyes locked with his again in the same vulnerable plea that he had seen at the landing site. There was a fleeting moment of shared desire. She looked away—more slowly this time.

So, I trouble you just as you trouble me? O'Neill thought. She was the kind of woman you wanted to take in your arms. He imagined the frightened, eager beating of her heart as his hands tightened around her. *Slow down, Seamus. This is a flirtation, nothing more. Remember that, you dummy.*

"I am afraid, Poet O'Neill, that I do not under- stand," she said slowly, as though quite mystified. "Perhaps we should postpone the scheduled events?"

O'Neill assured her that whatever events she wanted to have today were just fine with him. She left the room—or was it a cell?—still puzzled by the Taran's response.

The lovely doctor spoke formally. Was that the way the Zylongi always talked? She accepted that he was a down-and-out space tramp—at least she said she did. A "Director of Research" and a "Music Director" (her husband?—she had spoken of their son) were obviously important people. Why would they host a space bum? The "Secretary" and the "Guide" must be very important, too, otherwise why would a brief visit be described with such awe? Why would such personages waste their time with someone who was no threat? The first stirring of suspicion began to poke at the back of his brain. The good doctor knew more than she was telling.

He wondered if the refreshment had a bit of "the creature" in it. *Sure a wee touch of it wouldn't hurt a bit.*

4

O'Neill fell in love with Lieutenant Marjetta on sight. Not the way he loved his hostess, Sammy —a mild and, he hoped, harmless, if exciting, flirtation. Not the way he loved any of the objects of his crushes on *Iona*, not even the way he loved Tessie. *No, this is*, Seamus mentally insisted, *the real thing*. Marjetta was his fate, his destiny, the one great love of his life. It had taken him a long time to make that decision—slightly in excess of a half minute.

This conclusion might notably affect his mission to Zylong, if only by distracting him something terrible. It would certainly involve the eventual landing of *Iona* on the island in the river that Podraig had tentatively chosen. Marjetta would have to forsake her heathen ways. All these were minor details. This was the proper woman Seamus had been searching for all his long and hectic life.

Well, for the last six months anyway.

To begin with, she treated Seamus with total

contempt. He was, she implied by her tilted chin and stony brown eyes, a worthless derelict, a loud-mouthed braggart, a bit of a biological freak, a poseur who might deceive the older folks on Zylong but was transparent to the superior wisdom of her nineteen years (Taran time).

No one appealed to Seamus O'Neill more than a woman who saw right through him.

Moreover, she was devastatingly lovely, tall for a Zylongi, tall even for a Taran, lithe and willowy, short brown hair, a gently curved face, strong, expressive mouth, flashing eyes, absolutely irresistible legs, the confident shoulders of a competent military officer—*Ah, my dear Margie, you're the most proper of proper women. 'Twill be hard to win you, but that's part of the fun.*

She was not part of Sammy and Ernie's crowd, but rather a friend of their son, Horor, and his "promised," a cold, rather hard-eyed young woman named Carina, both of whom seemed to be students somewhere and neither of whom would give Seamus O'Neill the time of day—behaving, in other words, the way he had toward his elders only a few years ago. If the older generation on Zylong found him fascinating and interesting, the younger generation clearly found him boring if not disgusting. Red-bearded giant space tramp? What could be more deadly dull?

At first Seamus was annoyed. After all, didn't his program claim he was a bit of a rebel? And shouldn't young people identify with a rebel? Besides, didn't he have a quick smile and a quicker tongue? Didn't women invariably find him charming? Why, then, did Carina and especially Marjetta turn away in disgust when he would pay a certainly not undeserved compliment to one of the older women guests as they ate the candied fruits that apparently played the same preprandial role on Zylong as the poteen, straight up, did among Tarans?

(The "candy" in the fruit, or maybe even the fruit itself, contained a chemical at least as powerful as the poteen—loosening O'Neill's admittedly loose tongue even more.)

Anyway, they didn't like him, which was a challenge to O'Neill. He almost forgot that the space-lout mask he wore concealed the real O'Neill, whom, of course, Marjetta would find irresistible. Didn't everyone? Why should he feel defensive about a *persona* which wasn't his anyway?

"And so what do soldiers do on this planet?" he had inquired, harmlessly enough.

"Protect it from invaders," he was told tersely, with a slight shrug of absolutely glorious shoulders.

"How many of those have you had lately, not counting myself of course?"

"None."

"Ah then, there can't be much work to do."

"We manage to occupy ourselves."

"Sure I suppose there are scores of you assigned to watch me and you'll be my constant escort—to keep an eye on me, of course."

"It would appear that no one believes you are much of a threat."

"But you don't agree?"

"I would not worry about a thousand red-bearded space tramps." A contemptuous twist of her lovely lips. "Nor red-bearded gods of hordi legend who are supposed to return to redeem them."

"Kind of confident of your military capability, aren't you?"

Another pretty shrug. "It is adequate for our needs."

"Where did the hordi get this legend?"

"Ask them. Perhaps it is a memory of the species which brought them here before we came."

"Ah, is that what happened?"

"What do you think?"

"I think it is an interesting question of whether there is hordi blood in a lot of you folk."

He waited for an explosion.

"Are you trying to shock me by challenging the official wisdom? Come now, Space Tramp O'Neill, surely you have noted the slightly pointed teeth?"

"Not on you. . . . And why did a lovely woman like you become a member of the officer caste?"

"My family has always been in command positions. I was assigned to my role."

"When you were a wee lass."

"When I was born. Were you assigned to be a wandering minstrel?" In a tone of voice that couldn't have cared less.

"Ah, no. I chose it of my own free will."

"How degenerate."

"Would you want to be something else, I mean not a soldier at all?"

"That is an absurd question."

Ah, thought Seamus proudly, *I'm making great progress—well, maybe I am at that. There is contempt in some of them for the party line. And anger, lots of anger. . . .*

The relationship between Horor, the son of the house, and his "promised" mate was strange. They snapped unpleasantly at one another and argued almost every time they opened their mouths. He treated her like an empty-headed flake, and she reacted to him like he was a stuffy dullard. Yet, later on they left the apartment, following the gorgeous Marjetta, hand in hand.

Sammy whispered a hasty explanation in his ear. On Zylong young people were assigned their spouses and their careers shortly after birth, based on a careful study of their antecedents, so that the best possible genetic combinations would result. Sometimes they resisted this sorting process and refused to mate with their "promised." This was possible. Marjetta, a truly remarkable young woman, Sammy declared nervously, had insisted in delaying indefinitely her mating with the soldier to whom she had been promised. This could mean a life in which one did not marry, though sometimes the Committee would make exceptions, particularly if the petitioner was more humble than Marjetta was ever likely to be. Other young people would accept their fate but never become emotionally attached to their mate.

Yet others would find love after they had been mated for some time. Carina and Horor, the Most High be praised, were falling in love now, though they had to pretend to hate each other because that was the way with young people.

"They will be happy, we now know it with certainty," Sammy concluded breathlessly.

"This is the way you and himself got together," O'Neill nodded in the direction of his handsome, cultivated, gentle host.

"But of course. And you see how well we are matched. The Committee is very wise, is it not?"

O'Neill didn't think that this intense, almost manic woman was at all well matched with her reflective, melancholy mate. Whether they loved each other or not was less clear. Sammy was, however, a Zylongi Panglossa, the kind of enthusiast who had to persuade others and herself that everything was for the best.

"Marjetta is a lovely girl," he commented carefully.

"So you are of the same humanity as we," she grinned, almost wickedly. "All men think that. Perhaps someday she will find a man for herself. She may have to pay a heavy price, however."

O'Neill did not want to know what that heavy price might be. "And her parents are both dead."

"Yes," Sammy said, with a sad shake of her curls—and there was even more gray in them than O'Neill had noticed before, "both killed in battle."

"I thought there were no invaders here. Who is there to fight?"

Sammy looked around nervously, fearful that other guests might hear them. "It is not wise to discuss that."

Aha. It's matters like that you're supposed to be investigating, Seamus O'Neill, not taking off Lieutenant Marjetta's clothes in your imagination.

Well, you can do both, can't you? After all, you're young and the juices are flowing like they're supposed to.

So the party went on, and Seamus Finnbar O'Neill found himself even more puzzled by his strange hosts. On the one hand, they purported to kiss only their mates and them only in the "private chamber"; on the other hand, they seemed to be preparing to turn the party in his honor into an orgy. If they were going to be decadent—and at the moment Seamus was prepared to be tolerant on that point—why couldn't they be consistently decadent?

Then the event for which everyone had anxiously waited—the arrival of the Guide and the Fourth Secretary. The former was a doddering old man who smiled politely, nodded in answer to his own routine questions, and fluttered around shaking hands with everyone. He apologized to Poet O'Neill for any discourtesy. The First Ones and especially the Founder had strictly forbidden discourtesy. Before Seamus could praise the courtesy, the old man went on in a singsong voice, "You are welcome. Strangers are always welcome. We are honored. Enjoy your stay. Tell good things about us. Thank you thank you."

"If it's all the same to you," Seamus whispered to the Deity, "I'll keep the Lady Deirdre if you don't mind."

The Fourth Secretary was something else, a gombeen man if Seamus ever met one—short, fat, oily, leering at the women (which no one else on Zylong did), patronizing the men with false geniality, reveling in the power he obviously had over their lives.

He especially offended O'Neill by his frankly lascivious fascination with Marjetta—who in her turn treated the Fourth Secretary with the same contempt she had turned on Seamus.

I'm not that type at all, at all, he protested in his head.

"Well, I see the red-bearded god has come at last," the Fourth Secretary smiled at Seamus. "You are, of course, most welcome."

"Only if impoverished space travelers without fuel or money can be considered gods," Seamus replied evenly.

"You are too modest. Our probes reveal that you are a man of many talents."

"All which pale before the talents of the population of this astonishing civilization."

"You speak well." The Fourth Secretary did not seem happy about that fact.

"Poets do."

"So do you like our planet? What about our women? Have you seen anything like them in the universe?"

"There is much beauty in the universe. Zylong is especially rich in it."

Sure did Margie actually smile a little at that?

"You will stay with us long?"

"Only till my vehicle is repaired or till you grow tired of me."

"Oh, we never grow tired of giant red-bearded gods."

"Don't you now?"

If you're listening up there, Your Ladyship, this one is the Enemy.

With a crude guffaw, the Fourth Secretary took his leave. Everyone seemed to unwind; the worst was over.

The three young people wanted to leave a few minutes after the politician, but Sammy demanded that they stay while Seamus sang for them.

"Space bards are noted singers," she said primly.

The three kids made faces of resigned disgust. Seamus chose to ignore them and to concentrate on the lovely Lieutenant while he sang.

It is well for small birds that can rise up on high
and warble away on the one branch together
Not so with myself and my millionfold love
that so far from each other must rise every day.

She's more white than the lily and lovely past Beauty,

more sweet than the violin, more bright than
  the sun,
with a mind and refinement surpassing all
  these . . .
O God in Your Heaven give ease to my pain!

"Good-bye, Honored Guest," Marjetta said with
what in someone else would be described as a sneer.
"I'm sure we'll not meet again."

*Not a word about my song, even though I did it
just for you?*

"That would be a tragedy for me. Don't I get
a little credit because himself doesn't like me."

"A very little," she said, blessing him with a
grudging smile.

"Not enough to say you'd like to meet me
again?"

"Certainly not."

Women, they're the devil.

A half hour later he was telling himself—in
mental tones of vigorous warning, not unmixed
with anticipation—that if the woman reclining next
to him brushed her hair against his shoulder once
more, he would go to pieces altogether. He took
another wee sip of "refreshment" to calm his nerves
and contemplate the torso of Energy Supervisor
Niora, which was hardly an inch away from his
face.

It looked like he had gotten himself into a
Zylongi orgy all right, a cultivated, civilized orgy
indeed, but then those might be the worst kind.
From wondering which of the women he might be

supposed to sleep with, he had turned to fearing that he might have to sleep with them all.

A fantasy which, for all his self-image as a horny young male, scared the living daylights out of Seamus Finnbar O'Neill.

And for all his talk and fantasy about love, when it came to action—Seamus O'Neill was prepared to admit to himself at the moment—he was not particularly experienced or confident. Not when faced with these mature and certainly practiced beauties who lolled around the table, blatantly flirting with him while their husbands watched with no stronger emotion than amusement.

Brigid, Patrick, and Columcile, save and protect me, he pleaded with considerable fervor.

Soft light glowed from the lemon-colored walls of the "living space." Matching music and odors filled the air. The bodies of the guests were languid. Hairless male chests and soft female shoulders crowded around the table. Hemming him on either side, the relaxed forms of Energy Supervisor Niora and State Painter Reena were almost enough to keep his mind off the legs of his hostess as she padded around the table serving food with the aid of a chimpanzeelike hordi.

Research Director Samaritha, he mused, *you have as satisfactory a pair of legs as I've ever seen, save for Marjetta's, of course, but that was another matter. No, your legs and thighs are not too stocky at all. And the rear end is practically perfect.*

All you can think about, O'Neill, is women.

Well, under the circumstances, how can I think of anything else?

"You think it strange," Niora said softly, "that we do not try to improve on Mozart?"

O'Neill tried to focus his attention. He had matched the other guests drink for drink. They apparently were able to drink a good Taran under the table. Not that la-ir, a pink ice cream concoction, was all that weak a drink; it reminded Seamus of a twenty-third-century beverage he once consumed called a stinger. "To tell you the truth, lovely lady, I'm not sure what to think just at the moment."

His eyes followed the curve of her throat and the slope of her shoulders to the top of the thin blue wraparound that was evening dress for Zylongi women. He fantasized about the corsetlike affair that was presumably under it. The garment, he had learned, was called a lentat, the same name as for his undergarment, but presumably of rather different structure and purpose, given the strapless gowns and flowing but disciplined charms of the Zylongi women.

How would one go about removing it? Ah well, you can figure out anything if you have to. Who cares about Mozart?

"Your Guardians permit complete license in music, Honored Guest O'Neill?" Niora asked, seductively caressing her goblet.

"They don't see any harm in it. We let men like Music Director Ornigon compose their own music and interpret other composers any way they want."

"But that is very strange, Honored Poet. Does it not make for great competition?" Her lovely brow furrowed.

Are all the Zylongi women so sumptuously beautiful? And are there others around like Marjetta?

That would be something terrible altogether.

He paused before answering. Why had there been only a few polite queries about his trip, his background? Maybe they weren't interested, or maybe courtesy or orders forbade them to ask. Finally he replied cautiously, "We believe that competition makes for excellence." Niora began to say something but then sipped her drink instead.

He tried to concentrate on the creamy food, of which he was eating too much. It puzzled him—the extremely formal talk combined with the disconcerting sensual atmosphere.

Niora interrupted his thoughts. "Was not the Honored Music Director's recording of Mozart that we heard before the nourishment excellent? There are many paths to excellence within the official interpretation." Seamus shifted his weight to put a little more distance between his lips and her shoulders.

He thought it had been a clever but stilted and wooden Haffner symphony, but one that fit the atmosphere perfectly. He dug into the cream thing again. *You're making a pig out of yourself, O'Neill.*

Niora moved her body closer than ever. "Do you not find me attractive, Poet O'Neill?"

He choked on the cream. "Sure, I'd have to be a hunk of stone not to think you're one of the most lovely women in the cosmos."

"Now you exaggerate, Honored Poet," she scolded him. "But you often do not look at me. During formal nourishment we are to enjoy one another's bodies. It does not mean violation. Does it in your culture? I find your body very attractive."

Brigid, Patrick, and Columcile, what have I gotten into? Here she is sitting next to her husband, Secondary Principal Gemmoff! "I've been wandering through space alone for such a long time, I guess I'm numb," he said weakly.

"But please enjoy me while we eat. It is good to be admired by an Honored Guest." She lowered her eyes, smiled shyly, and began eating again. "Is admiration a prelude to violence in your world?"

"Uh . . . no, of course not. I guess we . . . well, we are a little more restrained in the way we do it."

"And less restrained in your violence."

"We don't believe in violence to women," he said firmly, noting to himself that practice didn't always follow theory.

"How unusual. Does admiration mean that you will enter a woman's body?"

"Of course not!"

"Well then, neither does it for us." He took another strong drink of their poteen and decided that he wouldn't do anything until someone else did. What if they were all waiting for him? He slopped up some more of the thick black cream.

"I see you like our dark cream, Poet O'Neill," said the Music Director, a thin man with iron-gray hair and a warm, lovely smile.

" 'Tis wonderful altogether. I suppose it comes from your heathenish furry cattle."

"Heathenish?"

"Ah, just a manner of speaking." O'Neill turned his attention away from the languid form of State Painter Reena.

"All our food comes from the same common crops and from the milk of our cattle. Our scientists, like my Honored Mate, have developed many ways of synthesizing these simple staples into a variety of foods." He talked briskly, like a gombeen man trying to make a sale. O'Neill didn't think his heart was in it, though.

"And of combining them into delicious meals." A wee compliment for the cook never hurts.

His host smiled proudly. "Ah, my mate has many gifts."

It wasn't what one would expect from a man contemplating swapping wives for an evening. O'Neill turned back to his own dinner companion, lying quietly next to him, delicately chewing on a small piece of pastry. "Am I supposed to pay compliments or would that be rude? You're so pretty that my voice gets caught in my throat when I try to talk with you."

A pleased rose glow spread over her dark skin. Her smile accepted him. "That in itself is a very nice compliment. To look is all that is required— really all that is proper."

"I wouldn't want to be improper. But I won't take back the compliment," he insisted.

"Certain exceptions are made for visitors, especially if they are poets." She lowered her eyes modestly, now very satisfied indeed with her dinner companion. O'Neill relaxed. He was relieved altogether. No orgy.

Well, it might have been fun. No telling what I could have learned.

Looking was all that was expected. The guests reclined in intimate and proximate positions, but none of them touched. You had to be very observing of your partner's moves to maintain the few inches of space that separated you. When her gorgeous little ass shifted too close to your thigh, you simply moved a fraction of an inch. Skillful, but what a waste of energy.

He managed once to "accidentally" brush his shoulder against Samaritha's thigh as she leaned over to serve him what seemed to be the tenth or eleventh course. She jumped back, a look of anger and horror on her face. Seamus mumbled an apology about Tarans being a clumsy people. It was graciously, if formally, accepted.

To distract himself from Niora, he asked about the hordi. The subject was one on which everyone had an opinion—all of it spoken much the way children recite memory work at school. The hordi, Samaritha told him, were obviously not hominid; probably they were not even related to hominid ancestors. Their evolutionary progress was very slow, if it had not ceased altogether. They were quite savage in their native habitat but could be domesticated if captured early enough or born in captivity. They made pleasant pets and useful if dull servants. Some of Samaritha's most important work was the selective breeding of the hordi to upgrade the strain of the domesticated type. It was a difficult and frustrating task, as there was so little in the hordi gene pool with which one could work.

Now all of this was patent nonsense. The tiny female hordi—four feet high—who waited on them clearly had a hominid body under her plain brown wrap. She was not anything like an ape. Her speech was rudimentary, clicks and grunts, but her hands were almost human. She was made for upright rather than quadruped movement; furthermore, one look at their pointed teeth showed where the Zylongi had acquired their "interesting difference" from the Tarans. The hordi could crossbreed with humanoids; at one time in the history of the Zylong planet, they had done so. Presumably such breeding was stopped, and now there was a cultural need to deny its possibility. O'Neill wondered how a scientist like Samaritha could talk such nonsense. He also found that the little creature could smile back at him, with a kind of knowing complacency: We both know they're pious frauds, the servant girl seemed to be hinting. And we both survive by exploiting their fraud.

Was the domestic hordi attractive when she smiled, a young body, tiny but neat breasts, quick appealing motions? *Sure she is attractive.* O'Neill revised his opinion of the aborigines upward. Men without women could easily be tempted to make love to such creatures. Had it been that way with parallel species on Earth?

Once we evolved beyond the monthly "heat" phase, why the hell not?

So that's what our ancestors were up to. The dirty things.

The last course finally came. Ornigon suggested that they must not keep the contestants waiting. The sensuality of the dinner ended. Niora's gloriously relaxed charm became formal again—to both the relief and sorrow of O'Neill. Even the room temperature, which had risen to almost jungle heat during the meal, seemed to fall abruptly. *Party's over, kids,* O'Neill thought. *Off to the "contest"—whatever that is.*

The arena was in the same quarter of the City as the apartment building in which his hosts lived. They descended in an elevator and walked across a brilliantly lighted and crowded plaza. Once more O'Neill felt like a bumpkin come to the big city—which of course was precisely what he was.

I wonder how long you can sustain this cosmopolitan pace, Seamus me boy. Soon they'll smell the aroma of cattle on you and know what you really are. The descendant of a people whose great epics are about stealing bulls from one another.

Outside, the night air was balmy and pleasant. Thousands of people crowded toward a tall pink tower located at the end of a short street that angled off the plaza. They entered the building, took an elevator down, and emerged at the edge of a vast arena that appeared to be part gymnasium and part swimming pool. The audience sat on tiers made up of deeply cushioned contour chairs. *You watch your sports in comfort on this planet*, O'Neill observed to himself.

The contest was between the Northeast Quarter —where Samaritha and Ornigon lived—and the South Central Quarter. His hosts had pinned small red and white ribbons to their coats; the other side wore yellow and blue. There was no attempt to segregate the supporters of the two teams.

The contest began with a formal ritual that made him think of the Japanese No plays he had seen on the *Iona*'s video screens. Then the contest began in earnest: a combination of volleyball, water polo, and field hockey, played by superbly conditioned young men and women with grace and skill—almost like an elaborate ballet—their strong young bodies covered only by lentats, the minimal undergarments worn by Zylongi of both sexes. (*I still don't see how you get them off a woman without tugging*, he thought.)

It was a vicious and violent ballet. O'Neill never cringed from working mayhem with a hurling stick on the *Iona*'s playing field, but he knew he could never slash at a woman with the stick. The young Zylongi males had no such compunctions, and the young women were not reluctant to fight back.

Even worse, it seemed to O'Neill, was the contrast between the destructiveness of the contest and the demeanor of the audience. Calm and controlled to the point of blandness, they applauded skillful play and showed no reaction at all at the sight of a broken limb or lacerated face. The whole wild enterprise seemed only faintly amusing to them. It was hard to tell if they even cared about whether their team won or not.

He tried his best to remember his anthropological manners, but when a tiny girl was carried off the floor with a broken arm hanging limply, blood pouring from a wound in her forehead, he gasped in disgust. Leaning in his direction, Samaritha quietly reassured him. "Do not worry about her, Honored Poet Guest. The contest surgeons are very skillful. In a day or two there will be no trace of injury. She will play in the next contest."

"But how does she feel now?"

"Perhaps pleased that she has played well. Much worse happened to me when I was in the contest. I was proud to have played well." She drew back into her couch.

The bloodshed ended with a victory for the home team. Secondary Principal Gemmoff was congratulated—it was his school's team. The glory of the Northeast Quarter was preserved. The other two couples, who lived in another tower, went home. O'Neill and his hosts returned to the family living space for yet more refreshment and more music.

"Do you have anything like the contest on Tara, Poet Guest?" the Music Director asked formally, as though it were now time to begin the "serious conversation" again.

O'Neill tried to describe hurley and Gaelic football. He was not at all sure, though, that the interest his hosts indicated meant either comprehension or appreciation. Both wild games were apparently too tame for their tastes. Samaritha was offended that young women were not permitted in the same contests as men. She seemed not to understand Seamus's explanation of fear of injury.

He changed the subject. He asked whether the Music Director had played in the contest when he was in secondary school.

"Alas, it is not permitted to us who are programmed for the arts to participate in the contest. The Research Director brought glory to both of us. In the quarter there was much pride in her skill." There was a curious melancholy in his voice.

"Well, when she gets mad at you, you must be careful to avoid letting her get hold of a stick." The joke, which he would not have tried had it not been for the poteen, fell flat.

"But the Research Director does not grow angry with me. We are mates," said Ornigon, obviously astonished and perhaps a little pained.

Samaritha's blush was fiery red. "One does not hit another with the stick, save in the contest!" she exploded. "To use the stick outside the contest would be savage. I do not understand what you are saying."

So there it was. Stylized but rigidly controlled violence and stylized but rigidly controlled sensuality were both enjoyed by the Zylongi in the lower depths of their personalities but kept under rigid social controls in their conscious lives.

It's a way to live, thought Seamus O'Neill as he drifted off into a sleep crowded with voluptuous brown bodies and bloody sticks.

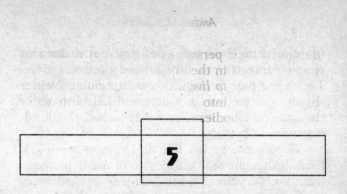

5

The back of his neck twitched again. Seamus O'Neill whirled around. There was nothing behind him, the bridge was empty, the winding street behind it dark and deserted. There was no sign of life in the buildings on the other side of the bridge. Yet someone had been watching him. All day long they had been spying on him ... spying on the spy. *Well, that's fair enough.*

It was, he had concluded earlier in the day, a planet that had been dominated by terror for centuries—the terror imposed by those determined to do good and to constrain others to do the same. Fanatics. No one worse than a good person, herself had often said, than a good person who knows he's good.

"Or she," he had added.

"Ay," the Cardinal touched her ruby ring of office, "we women are superior even in fanaticism."

And now the terror of the fanatic was right behind him. He rubbed his neck and turned back to the stream. There was a network of such streams running through the City toward the great river. They were part of the City's sanitation and water supply system, with bottoms and banks made of the same rocklike substance out of which the buildings were constructed.

Once more he felt like an ignorant bumpkin. He had thought that the system of waste management and recycling on the *Iona* was sophisticated. It was a primary-grade student's childish drawing compared to the immense and sophisticated Zylongian scheme for recycling waste so that it could be used again and again and generate energy in the process. Moreover, the abundance of natural resources on the planet seemed to make this recycling system unnecessary. The natural process of the swift-flowing river would have cleaned the City's waste in an hour or two. And the river itself could easily have been channeled to provide hydroelectric power. The Zylongi knew about such things because they had power plants up in the foothills of the mountains; you respected the forces of nature and did not violate them, as the First Ones and the Founder had taught, but you made up the rules as you went along about what constituted such respect. In the mountains the River was not sacred. Near the City it was. If you began with such definitions, it was all easy.

He began to spell "River" in his own mind with a capital *R* because it was obviously sacred by the time it reached the City. You did not pollute the River either with waste or dams and generators. Why not? Because the First Ones had taught that you must respect the great powers of nature. They contained the Most High.

Fair enough, except they were not a religious people, as far as he could tell. And recycling waste was interfering with the processes of nature too.

But his task was to observe, not to argue. Nor to look for consistency. A visitor would doubtless find Tarans inconsistent too—though, he hoped, more honest with themselves and others about their inconsistency. When caught in a seeming contradiction, the locals here would either argue passionately, like the good Sammy, or sneer like the good Margie. Tarans would simply laugh and say, "Ah well, we never did claim to be logical, now did we?"

He had spent most of the last two days in the "Resource Center" of Zylong, leafing through their various historical documents. The Resource Center apparently had a large staff (which had been instructed to bring him everything he wanted, no questions asked) but almost no clients. For all the piety in references to the Founder and the First Ones, there was little interest in their lives or the time of their "Arrival."

Earlier that day, his library search mostly complete, Seamus had slumped over his terminal in the Resource Center, head in hands. He had seen evil during the years of his pilgrimage on the *Iona*, but he could not have imagined the barbarism of Zylong's millennium of history. And he probably didn't know the half of it. No great psychic, Seamus Finnbar Diarmuid Brendan O'Neill, he still felt the terror of Zylong in every nerve ending of his body. He had to get out of here and bring his woman with him as quickly as possible.

Still, he told himself, *if this place can produce someone like Margie it's not all bad.*

He uncrumpled his notes on *Sayings of the Founder* and considered them again. "I hope to hell you folks up there are keeping track of this cow dung," he whispered to the readers on the monastery.

His translator was revealing the sayings in Spacegael, but even in translation it was obvious that they represented different times, different situations, different authors. Some were flat and harsh:

Have no congress with beasts. Eliminate those
who do.
Every woman is a walking womb.
Slay them who turn away.

Others were more paradoxical:
The woman is for the man. Man is for the
woman.
Food for everyone. Women for everyone.
Let them who eat too much, starve. Let them
that bear too many be made barren.
Destroy those who would make peace. Make
peace with those who would destroy.

Still others made no sense at all:

> Beware the time of the wind. Beware the word of the prophet. Beware the body of the tempter.
>
> Let not sex interfere with your manliness.
>
> Let those who disturb go to Zylong to learn peace.
>
> Love him who punishes your needs.

Yet others were reasoned and occasionally moving:

> In our world we must have only those rules which free the natural human propensity to goodness.
>
> Sex is joy for all who will enjoy it.
>
> All are equal, men and women, old and young; let there be no distinctions. Treat all life with respect.
>
> No power should endure, lest it corrupt.
>
> Reverence all who share this world with us.
>
> We must be equal to be free and free to be equal. No freedom which threatens equality.
>
> No equality which threatens freedom.

There were finally a larger number of sayings that described women, of which the mildest was: "He who kills a male child does a great evil. He who kills a female child prevents a great evil."

It was possible, Seamus thought, that if anyone had the stomach for it, he could find the times in the history of the Zylongi settlement—now 1119 Earth-years old—for most of these sayings. The reasonable ones went back to the fervent idealism of the Founder, who believed in natural, human goodness, commonality of property, respect for nature, and complete sexual freedom.

Reading between the bland and pious lines of official history, Seamus was able to piece together much of the story in rough outline.

It soon turned out the sexual freedom was for men and not for women and it meant that men had the fun and women did the work. "Sexual freedom = sexual slavery for women after two generations at the most," Seamus had scrawled on the paper.

There had been a revolt of women that was mercilessly put down. The Great Lords then took hordi females as wives and built great cities all over the plains. In violent and bitter wars, they destroyed one another, tearing down great settlements and destroying much of the machinery they had brought with them. Then came the time of the "First Reorganization"; sobriety and frugality were imposed by the "Reorganizers," who pitilessly destroyed all who seemed to have hordi genes in them and began to rebuild the central city where the first settlement had occurred. They extirpated every other town from the world and forbade all but the outcasts and "degenerates" to live in the country.

Sexual freedom returned. An attempt was made

to exterminate all hordi as "evil ones." There was no explanation of why it had failed.

There then followed a time called the "Terrible License" in which morals degenerated and, according to the sources from that era—maybe four centuries ago—every vice was practiced, despite the warnings of occasional wise men about the evils of "yielding to the body." Then came the Second Reorganization about two and a half centuries ago in which a "Guide" and a "Committee of Secretaries" and "Order of Guardians" had been established to maintain "order, discipline, probity."

"A very wise plan, the Second Reorganization," one of the sages had remarked.

Well, Seamus thought, *it seems to have kept them from slaughtering one another for two hundred and fifty years, so it can't be all bad.*

What's next? The Second License?

As much as he was shocked by the stories of torture, massacre, and near genocide, Seamus was impressed by the durability of the original vision and the sincere commitment of the Zylongi, however twisted their methods, to that vision: an orderly world of equality, commonality, and publicly approved virtue. If women and hordi were often attacked, the reason that was given was that they were a threat to virtue. If sex was often denounced, the reason was that it was seen as an obstacle to a sober and rational life of civic responsibility. If personal freedom was constrained, it was in the cause of justice for all.

So a thousand years of destruction, tyranny, and death. What had been accomplished? Well, for the last quarter of a millennium they had created a successful illusion, which maybe was an impressive accomplishment. Now the illusion was fading, still powerful for Sammy's generation but not for her son's or for Margie's.

And the illusion was maintained by a terror that at times on Zylong, even in the crisp, quiet library, was palpable. (Here Seamus was certain, though he could not explain yet why or how.)

Ought that not be enough for the geniuses up on the *Iona*? Probably not. They'd want details of the terror today. *Get with it, Seamus.*

So here he was risking the terror by breaking the local rules and walking along the side of the sanitation system after the "advisory" curfew hour and in a section of town which he had been warned by Sammy was not "suitable" for walking. *So what?*

Seamus was never one to take such rules very seriously. Besides, the disturbing presence of his host and hostess had begun to overwhelm him. Their relationship was baffling—especially since they slept in separate rooms, as it would seem did all Zylongi couples. He needed a few peaceful moments in the clear night air to try to make some sense out of this weird world into which he had been set, much against his will and, as he was saying now, against his better judgment too.

He had been walking through the Old City of Zylong, whose narrow streets followed the paths of the first settlers and whose low buildings commemorated the era before skyscraper apartments. At the end of the street leading to the bridge, he saw the glow of the great Central Plaza. Drinking in the colors and sounds, he had ambled across the plaza, filled with elegant, brightly dressed bodies, walking, talking, sitting at tables, listening to strolling musicians. Their voices were soft, their manners discreet, their greetings to him elaborately civilized. His host and hostess saw no problem with his "taking a bit of air," though they only dimly knew what he meant.

Zylong City at ten-thirty at night was a pulsating, shining, glowing place. Seamus drank in its charms—which included most notably the greatest collection of shapely female forms he had ever seen. It was a great place, it was . . . with the most lovely women in the cosmos, though none—his question was now answered—as lovely as the fair Marjetta, whom he had alas not set eyes on since the fruit-nibbling preprandials.

If only they weren't spying on me . . .

Then the lights flickered, warning the folks to go home. Without reluctance or protest the crowds slipped away and left the center of the City deserted in less than a quarter hour. Then the lights went out, leaving Seamus alone, or so it seemed, in the total darkness, broken only by the frail light of one of several tiny and unimpressive moons.

Alone except for the spies.

He frowned at the black waters of the stream. It looked pretty deep. Of course they weren't telling him the truth. Or rather they were telling him so much which was true that he was not really getting the truth, not even the truth of why they were so eager to give him a crash course on Zylongian life. Somewhere something was very wrong.

Again, the twitch in his neck. *Damn it, still no one there.* "Come out in the open and fight," he said in Spacegael. There was no one willing to respond. Back again to the flowing waters. Deep and rapid, doubtless some kind of sewer.

I'd sure hate to get pushed in.

In the morning everything had been straightforward. Technical Institute, Computer Institute, Body Institute—he got the full official tour of each one. He saw the great Central Plaza with the sprawling complex of Central Building, computer center and military headquarters. He walked some of the curving little streets of the Old City behind the plaza. His questions about politics were answered in great detail: they were governed by an elaborate structure of Committees that made all the decisions at every level in the society—unanimously, he was assured.

He had to ask very few questions. Most of his queries were anticipated. Someone had sent the word to tell him everything—so much of everything that he would be drowned by detail. If you keep pointing out the technical name of each tree, you don't give anyone time to focus on the forest. He had heard everything and learned virtually nothing.

At the sternly antiseptic Body Institute with

its pastel green walls, O'Neill was surprised at the relationship between Samaritha and her staff. He expected the Director of Research to be stiff with her juniors, but she actually unbent and relaxed. Her gang seemed to like her; their banter was mild compared to what went on aboard the *Iona*, but in this uptight place it was almost disrespectful. She actually smiled once or twice, even managing something which by Zylongian standards must be considered a laugh. When she laughed, the urge to hug and kiss her was strong again. He had to watch himself.

The Zylongi, he learned from the doctor and her staff, lived in close harmony with their environment. At the time of the Reorganization, it had been determined that population expansion was to cease and that the rest of the continent would be left to its natural inhabitants. Jarndt, their main crop, was the source of their food and clothing. Rock and metal ore quarried beyond the City provided them with materials for their buildings. Research was required merely to develop new and drought-resistant forms of jarndt and new techniques for exploiting its bounty and, in Samaritha's case, for the better understanding of the inhabitants with whom they shared the planet.

All reasonable enough, he supposed, until they got to the genetic engineering part of the story. Young people were mated in infancy after a computer examination of their genetic potential. Random mating, he was told, was undisciplined and socially dangerous. The Body Institute staff were astonished that O'Neill was pledged to no one and that if he wished to marry, he could choose anyone he wished.

After the Body Institute, Samaritha walked with him to the Music Center, where he was to listen to her husband conduct a rehearsal. He sensed disapproval and anxiety in her tense, voluptuous little body. "You truly have no pledge to a woman, Poet O'Neill?" she asked dubiously, a frown on her face. "Does that not lead to promiscuity?"

"Well, I usually manage to keep my animal instincts under control, though it's hard when I'm walking with beautiful women. . . ."

Her frown deepened. "You must try to understand our culture and not to dislike it," she said primly, ignoring the compliment.

She said a formal good-bye to him at the entrance to the Music Center and turned to walk back down the street. Seamus enjoyed the sight of her swaying buttocks as she melted in with the crowd. *Lord save you, man, she's twenty years older than you.* He still watched until she was lost from sight.

He thought of her swaying body again as he watched the sewer water glide swiftly by him. The Central Plaza was as dark, according to the Taran saying, as a Cardinal's heart. He should hurry back to the living space. They might worry. Sammy and Ernie were merely doing their duty of hospitality. They had been told by the Committee to provide him with answers to all his questions. They may have suspected something else was happening, but they were either afraid to know or too wise to ask.

Did they know about the shadows that had been on him all day? Probably not. For Sammy it was essential that he not only know the answers to questions he really had not got around to asking but also that he accept the wisdom of Zylong's cultural decisions. Did that mean she had her own doubts?

This time he was sure he heard sounds in the street. Still no one there. Sammy was a true believer, though; her husband apparently less so.

"My mate is a virtuous woman," Music Director Ornigon had said that day. "She is not able merely to explain and accept, she must also defend. For an Honored Guest, that can be tiresome." Again there was a deep tinge of melancholy in this gifted man's voice.

O'Neill observed that such a splendid woman could never become tiresome.

Ornigon continued. "The Honored Research Director has been very popular since her youth and very enthusiastic. Such traits are admirable in a scientist, I think. As an artist, I may be excused, perhaps, for being more cynical." He shrugged his shoulders ruefully.

It was after the rehearsal, a mechanical Haydn played with instruments that looked like caricatures of the symphony instruments he knew. The horns, violins, even the wind instruments were almost half again as long as they were in the prototypical Taran orchestra. There were also a

103

couple of super bassoon-type things that made a deep and haunting sound.

O'Neill and his host stood on Reorganization Bridge watching the fading sun color the big stream scarlet as it rushed through the City toward its confluence with the great River in the midst of the vast sandy banks beyond the walls.

They sipped companionably from a container of la-ir that Ornigon had managed to find in a back room of the concert arena.

"Is it true that mates are chosen here by a computer?" O'Neill asked, leaning casually against the bridge.

"Oh yes, it is true. I know of no evidence that it has notably improved our species, save perhaps in some physical ways. I do know that it produces certain divisions in our society. Mates are chosen according to principles which lead people to mate within their own groups. Thus the Honored Doctor and I are both from families of important people in the country. Our son's mate, the Military Student, is the daughter of important officials. The goal of a society without classes seems to be in conflict with the goals of a genetically improved society." He spoke gently, but the empty paper container crumpled in his hand.

"But how does someone like Dr. Samaritha explain that conflict?" O'Neill drained his paper cup and filled it again.

"She says that our society exists in its essence during the planting and harvesting of the crops— which reflect our origins, after all. The Festivals that come after are times when we return to primitive equality. Whether that satisfies those who think we have rigid social division and that they are the victims of it, I am not wise or informed enough to say. The Committees have thought so; one hears very little complaint. Of course, those of us at the top would not complain, would we?" He shook his head negatively to Seamus's offer of more drink, noticing with surprise what he had done to his cup.

"Social divisions?" O'Neill asked, not bothering to hide his curiosity.

"A small matter." His host regretted his quiet outburst almost at once. "It is rarely discussed."

O'Neill emptied the container into his own cup and glanced at the glorious skyline. *Heaven save us, it is beautiful. Not worth the price that's paid for it, but still beautiful.* A pastel symphony against the serene blue sky, much softer and more flexible than the concert piece he had heard.

Who was in charge here? What shadowy forces if any made the real decisions? On the *Iona*, you knew what the factions and the parties were and who dominated the Captain Abbess's council this year and who had the ear of the Abbess and the Prior and the Subprior and whom to see when you wanted something done. But here it was impersonal, mysterious, secret. "Committees," "Guides," "computers"? Nonsense. Someone had to be in power.

Didn't they? Or could a cultivated civilization become so rigid and so old that no one was in charge? At least a third of the recycling units did not seem to work and two of the streams were bone-dry, their artificial stone beds harshly stained in the sunlight. They would be repaired "shortly," he was told. But the word sounded more like an approved cliché than a confident assertion that the repairmen were on the way. One of the two lifts in the Ernie/Sammy skyscraper would also be fixed "shortly"; but when he demanded how long it had not worked Seamus learned that (a) he should not ask such questions and (b) for several months.

"The Repair Committee is very busy. There is much to be done. It assigns the proper priorities. We who do not understand must wait patiently. It serves no purpose to complain."

Which O'Neill interpreted as meaning that the efficient Samaritha wanted to complain and repressed her urges, even to herself.

In a society with the wealth and resources this one possessed, there was no reason for anything breaking down for a long period of time. Save for bureaucratic incompetencies, about which Seamus had read, but which, heaven knows, he had never experienced in the small contentious world of the monastery. If the repair crews didn't show up in fifteen minutes, you sought out the responsible person and posed numerous questions about his ancestry, his sexual preferences, and the advisability of propelling him instantly through the space lock into permanent individual orbit. He responded in kind but then came with his surly crew and did the job; after which, a bit of the drink was always happily taken. No waiting for months.

"Does the computer decide when you can have children too?"

"Pregnancies are authorized by the Pregnancy Committee," Ornigon responded slowly. "Only after careful tests do they approve it. The most any family is permitted is three pregnancies; the normal is two; many have only one. Sometimes none are authorized. In addition there is a test the infant must pass to qualify for life. Should he fail, he is disposed of. It is very difficult to get permission for a replacement pregnancy." Ornigon paused. "We had a second child . . . a daughter . . . she had a slight defect. . . ." Brusquely he added, "It was a pity, but there is a social cost in such defects that a society like ours simply cannot afford. The child would not have been happy in any case."

"Is this same thing done to old people?" O'Neill inquired, beginning to suspect why he had seen so few.

"All careers are 'terminated' at the age of ninety—about seventy-two of your years, I understand. It is possible to apply for an earlier termination; sometimes, in cases of illness, termination orders are issued before the officially designated date. You wonder how we 'terminate' careers, but you are reluctant to ask?"

O'Neill nodded, draining the last drop of la-ir and hoping his own horror did not show.

"Well, at Harvest Festival," Ornigon explained,

"they 'go to the god.' They become one with Zylong."

"Human sacrifice?" O'Neill gasped, his own paper cup now crumpled into a tight little ball.

"It may have been once, Honored Guest. Now, of course, we are too civilized to do such a thing. It is all quite painless, not frightening at all—an easy way to end one's career. At least it is said to be easy. We have no testimony from those who have been terminated." Noticing that O'Neill was gripping the bridge railing tightly, Ornigon smiled wanly. "You are shocked at our customs. They are perhaps different from yours? Our motives are humane; no one wishes to be a burden on the rest of society. It is always said they would not be happy alive. . . ." His voice trailed off. The two of them silently watched the sun disappear from the sky.

Later that night, leaning on a smaller bridge over the swiftly moving sewer, O'Neill thought that there was much repressed cruelty in this graceful and cultivated civilization. But it all seemed to work. There was no reason why everyone in the cosmos had to be Celtic anarchists like the Tarans. He turned away from the bridge to begin his walk back to the living space, hesitating as he tried to figure out which direction he should go.

Yes, there was. The Tarans were crazy, but they loved kids, even handicapped ones, especially handicapped ones. And they treasured the old for their wisdom and their storytelling and their goodness.

It's not just a difference of opinion, he told

himself firmly. *These folks are civilized and we're barbarians, but we're right and they're wrong, damn it all.*

His neck twitched dangerously. And a little too late. A foul smell filled his nostrils as a dirty rag was pressed against his face; hands were grabbing at his shoulders and ankles. Violently he thrust the hands away, but they persisted, slowly dragging him to the ground. He felt nauseous; his strength was failing him. His head spinning, consciousness slipping away, he tried to continue his struggle, but his muscles grew lazy and sluggish.

He was roughly hoisted to the rail of the bridge and pushed. He floated in space and then abruptly hit the water. It was cold and dirty. *A sewer indeed,* he thought absently as he went under. He made a vague effort to swim, but his lazy body dragged him under again. He surfaced once more, one hand grasping for something to hold. It hit a projection on the stone riverbank. He clung to it. The current ripped at his arm, tore him away from his grip on life and bore him under in the darkness. His head was beginning to explode; so were his lungs. He wanted to pray.

A hand grabbed his arm, a firm strong hand. He yielded to its strength. In total darkness he was pulled to shore, hauled laboriously up on the bank, forced to stand on unwilling feet, and then, smelling of sewer, dragged into a building, up a short flight of stairs, into a room. He collapsed on a hard bed.

After a time he opened his eyes. The room was

a yellow blur. The sickness was passing. The effects of the drug wore off quickly. *That way they don't find any traces in your body.*

"Our la-ir is too potent for you, Taran Visitor," said a woman's voice reprovingly. *Ah, it couldn't be herself now, could it? Was she the guardian angel the good guys had sent to protect him?*

"La-ir, hell, woman," he replied weakly. "I was poisoned." He tried to focus his eyes. Was it really her?

"Oh," said the voice skeptically, "how interesting."

'Twas indeed herself. Seamus Finnbar O'Neill's heart began to beat rapidly. He opened his eyes.

The room was small, barrackslike in its simplicity: a bed, on which he was sprawled, a chair, a table, a video screen, a small bathing pool, lemon-colored walls, diffused light. Somehow it was an intensely feminine room, in part because of the intensely feminine presence in it.

"I should at least know the name of the lovely lady to whom I owe my life," he said, rubbing his aching head.

Strong brown eyes regarded him critically. "You know very well who I am, Visitor; you made a fool of yourself ogling me at the Research Director's living space. I am Lieutenant Marjetta of the Zylong army, Visitor. I'm not sure your life is worth saving."

"Well," said Seamus weakly, " 'tis yourself that's worth ogling."

"You can watch to your heart's content now,

not that it makes any difference to me." She had already tossed aside her robe. Now she slipped a practically invisible zipper and discarded the top of her lentat.

Ah, that's how they work, in two parts, is it?

He also settled the critical issue of his daydream world about the most desirable variety of breasts; in this area too, the exquisitely flowering Marjetta was perfection.

Quickly, but not rushing, she slipped into the pool. "I don't care whether you wish to continue to smell like a waste-disposal unit. If you don't, you may use the pool. You will not disturb me."

"If it were the la-ir," Seamus defended himself, "if I'm drunk, how come I've come out of it so soon?"

"Come here," she ordered briskly.

He obeyed, as he would a command from the Lady Deirdre, with whom she could fairly be compared, Seamus realized with a touch of unease.

He put his feet on her soft carpet and stumbled toward the pool. She had sunk low enough into its opaque waters to serve the basic requirements of modesty but still suggest enough womanly attractiveness to threaten his self-possession.

She peered intently at his eyes. He tried to look innocent, though his heart was beating rapidly.

Dissatisfied, she pulled his head toward her face. "Let me look at you. I'm not going to rape you. Hmmm. So it would appear that you were assisted in your evening swim. That is no concern of mine." She released his head and sank lower in the water. Despite her words, she was puzzled and perturbed. Maybe she was only a chance, not an official guardian angel. "So, as I suspected, the Fourth Secretary did not find your god legend amusing."

"It was him, was it?"

She shrugged her strong shoulders indifferently. "Who else has power in this chaos? There are others who might have done it, but they hardly know of you yet."

"Others?"

"If you stay in our city long enough, you will learn of them."

"Maybe it would have been safer for you just to have let me go under," he said, probing for her reaction.

Her brown eyes turned hard with anger. "Don't be absurd. I am commissioned to protect life. . . ." She hesitated, wondering perhaps who had other designs. "Poet O'Neill, for so I am told you are called, you smell of the foul stream. Would you please remove your garments and step into this pool. I will look the other way while you undress, lest I offend your strange outworld prudery. After I have bathed, you will remain here, looking at the wall, while I dress. Then I will leave the room while you do the same. Then I will escort you to the living space of Samaritha and Ornigon."

"Sure, in my condition, even your great beauty would not stir me up." He tried to laugh as he stripped off his clothes and slipped into the pool, careful to stay as far away from her as he could.

Still, his eyes sought out her breasts, just beneath the level of the water and not altogether invisible.

She gripped his shoulders and turned his face firmly to the wall. "You will do as you have been told." No sense of humor at all. He was still dazed. He tried to think it out. His body ached.

"Ah now, 'twas a very fortunate thing for me, wasn't it, Lieutenant Marjetta, that you just happened to be coming down the street when I was going under," he remarked amiably to the wall.

The discreet splashing of water at her end of the bathing pool stopped. "You're quite right, Poet O'Neill. I might also have been the one who pushed you in. You will just have to take the chance that I am not, won't you?" The voice was firm but not hard, the womanly laugh that followed made him forget he was still dizzy. He clenched his fists, grimly determined not to look away from the wall.

"You're a terrible woman altogether," he complained, causing another laugh.

She's enjoying this. She's got me in an awkward and embarrassing situation and loves every second of it.

"Well, just for the record, I want to say thanks for saving my life. It may not be all that much a life—" a plea for pity "—but it's the only one I have."

"It is indeed not much of a life, to judge by the reports about you, which I do not altogether believe," she said in a terse, hard voice, "and all I did was my duty. I would do it for anyone." Then the voice softened, becoming almost maternal.

"Still, I accept your gratitude and am happy I could save your life. You are not—" she gave a small, only faintly disapproving laugh "—a light burden to pull from the sewer."

There was a splashing noise indicating that she was climbing out of the pool. Seamus did not dare look.

"This cloak will probably cover you adequately until we return to the living space of the Research Director." She threw a huge brown sacklike garment on the couch. "It is a mountain robe. It may be a little warm," she actually giggled. "But you do not come in any of our regular sizes. Now I will leave the room, so as not to offend your male prudery." Silently and unsmilingly she left.

After O'Neill, thoroughly humiliated, had dressed, they left her room and walked down the steps. *A cruddy old place for someone like her,* he thought. Then without reflection he muttered the age-old Gaelic benediction. "Jesus and Mary and Brigid be with this house."

"Who are they?" Marjetta demanded.

"Ah, holy people."

"What does that mean?"

"Well, special friends of God."

"I see," but in the darkness she sounded like she did not. "Your god has special friends?"

"Well, kind of. We pray to Him through them. We sort of hope they'll use their influence with Him."

"How consoling. A kindly god then?"

"Sometimes too kindly by half. Won't leave us

114

alone. Head over heels with us. If you take my meaning."

"Extraordinary. And yet somehow not unreasonable. I should like someday to know more about him. It is him, isn't it?"

"Sometimes," O'Neill answered. "Well, the Old Fella has the characteristics of both."

"You do not deceive me?"

"Why would I do that?"

She conducted him back to the quarter of his hosts. They said not a word to each other till they came to the small parklike plaza in front of the Sammy/Ernie skyscraper.

"Thanks again." He reached in the darkness for her hand. "I owe you one."

"What nonsense is that?" she demanded imperiously.

"You've saved my life, so I am, uh, well, not in debt to you—" he searched for an explanation "—but, well, at your service if you ever need me."

"That is very beautiful," she said, her voice choking up. "I may well need you. And I will call upon you gladly."

Now that was a change of tune, O'Neill thought uneasily.

"How can I help?" he asked spontaneously.

"No one can help." She sounded close to tears.

Then they were, unaccountably, in each other's arms, locked in as furious an embrace of love as O'Neill had ever known, her breasts pressed against his chest, his hands digging into her rump, their lips glued together, their bodies twisting in

115

the preliminary motions of passion. His cloak fell off him, her robe slipped away with a simple touch of his hands. He felt her body stiffen in resistance. "Please . . . ," she begged.

O'Neill was an expert on no's. This was a real no, reluctant, sad, but definitive. She didn't expect him to honor it, which was, his instincts told him, all the more reason to do so. It would be much better eventually when she said yes.

Besides, the pavement was awfully hard.

Then in an instant Seamus Finnbar O'Neill discovered what love was. Her fragility became more important than his passion, her fears more important than his need. His lips and hands became instruments not of conquest but of reassurance, his embrace not an imperious demand but a tender offer of protection, his kiss a delicate and sensitive tribute to her goodness.

She melted in his arms. He released her. She leaned against him for a few seconds and then pulled back.

He reclaimed his coat and her robe in the darkness and arranged the robe around her trembling shoulders.

"You stopped," she said, her voice shaking.

"You wanted me to."

"Most men wouldn't. It was my fault. My emotions are more undisciplined than I thought. Now I owe you a favor."

"Don't mention it."

"You may be a space parasite, Poet O'Neill,

but you're still a good man." She paused. "And a fine lover."

"I'm flattered." He tried to laugh. "At least I think I am."

"You kiss Dr. Samaritha that way?" she asked curiously.

"I've never kissed anyone that way in my life."

"Why not?"

"I've never quite loved anyone like I love you."

When we finally know what love is, the Cardinal had often said, we know what God is like.

"Now I am flattered. But enough. I must take you home. Here is my hand," she laughed, "for guidance purposes. Follow me."

His heart sang within him. She felt the same way he did. She needed to be saved from this terrible place and he was the man to save her.

"Poet O'Neill found our City so fascinating that he became lost," she sternly told the four people who were anxiously waiting, Horor, the slender, intense son, and Carina, the diminutive hard-faced future daughter-in-law, having joined his host and hostess.

The kids were impassive; Ernie and Sammy were obviously relieved. "You folks certainly provide charming guides." He smiled expansively, going along with Marjetta's lie.

"A happy event which brings the good Lieutenant to our living space," said Sammy warmly, taking the girl's hand.

Everyone in the room seemed delighted by the trim soldier's presence, the young people especially.

For a kid not yet twenty, she was very well known. *Ah, woman, I've got to get to know you better.* Still he was more than a little afraid of her. She was almost as tough as the Lady Deirdre. *Come to think of it, Your Ladyship, who the hell tried to kill me and why?*

When she left the apartment, she said, with a glance at O'Neill, "Jesus and Mary and Brigid be with this house."

They stared at her in astonishment.

"It is one of the Poet's blessings." She permitted herself a small smile. "Friends of his god. I find it consoling."

Glory be to God!

Later O'Neill was luxuriating in the fragrant waters of his bath. The jungle smell that filled the room had chased the last memories of the drug and the sewer. The Zylongi were bathing freaks, worse than the Tarans, if that were possible. Even the Technical Student—in whose quarters he was staying—had a vast bathtub, set into the floor, in which many-colored pulsating waters created a feeling of deep tranquillity. Then he thought about the simple almost harsh quarters of the Lieutenant. Not everyone was equal in this world, not by a long shot.

He splashed some water on his face and sank lower into the tub, fantasizing about the long trim legs of Lieutenant Marjetta. His door panel slid open and Dr. Samaritha entered.

"I am concerned about your health, Honored Guest." She leaned against the door, slightly and becomingly out of breath. *Oh Lord, now two women on my mind.*

"Not a thing wrong with me," he boasted. "Just a long hard day in the most pleasant possible company."

Dr. Samaritha smiled. Then she asked, "Honored Poet Guest, may I ask you a question?"

O'Neill nodded.

She blurted out, "Do I displease you completely?"

"Of course not. What would make you think that? Sure, I doubt any space tramp has ever had a more gracious and considerate hostess." He again splashed his face with water, trying to hide his unease.

"Poet O'Neill, you are a strange man. Sometimes you joke, sometimes you say improper things, sometimes you are kind and considerate, sometimes you look at me very suspiciously. It is . . . it is most disconcerting." There was a muscle in her throat that twitched bewitchingly.

She was at her best when she was vulnerable. He pressed his hands against the bottom of the tub to restrain his impulse to jump out and embrace her. "Well, lovely women always throw me off balance, I guess. Besides, sometimes I get the impression there are many things I don't understand."

"Must you understand everything?" she pleaded, extending her lovely arms. "It is not too good to be too curious. The Music Director and I intend you no harm. You should allow us to please you. But

. . . I have said too much." She turned and fled, as though some emotion were too powerful to contain.

Uh, oh, O'Neill, you may just be in really serious trouble. You've been here a couple of days and already you have two beautiful, vulnerable, fragile women on your hands. This wasn't supposed to be part of the program.

At all. At all.

6

The next day O'Neill was to hear, much to his disgust, substantial clinical details about the fragile and vulnerable Doctor Samaritha—Sammy—in bed. Only she was described more like a beast in heat than a woman who needed to be treated with the utmost tenderness. He and Ernie were "engaging in exercise" in a local "exercise" center. He did very badly in a kind of team handball—a melee in which every man was for himself. Though he was a half-foot taller than the Zylongi males and thirty pounds heavier, they were in much better condition and more agile than he. Every muscle ached—too much dark cream and la-ir, he judged.

The locker-room conversation afterward was a shock. All five of his fellow exercisers had made love to one another's wives and all felt free to discuss it. Their collaborative description of Sammy in advanced stages of passion revolted him. They made her sound like a sow, a grunting, howling, disgusting animal.

There was locker-room humor on the *Iona*, too, heaven knows. And Seamus was not above engaging in it, all the time wondering what the conversation was like in the women's locker room—and never of course having the nerve to ask. It became pretty clinical and explicit at times, but while it treated women like things (something a Taran male would do in the real world only at peril to his limb and life), it was not deliberately cruel and it would certainly never be done in the presence of a woman's husband.

The Tarans, in their own bumbling, incompetent, shy, and often prudish way, liked women, enjoyed them, feared them, worshiped them, and more or less respected them.

The Zylongi men seemed to hate them with a pent-up rage and frustration which suggested that sex was messed up more on this planet than even among the Tarans, where it was, Seamus thought, notably messed up.

One of the Zylongi, with an uncharacteristic bluntness, asked for details of his conquests. O'Neill told him they were far more relaxed about sex on Tara than on Zylong. "I can make love only a hundred forty times in twenty-four hours, so you can see my romantic life is quite undistinguished."

He saw a flicker of amusement on Ernie's melancholy face. *You don't like this custom either, but it's too strong for you to fight.*

Later he and his host were sitting at a sidewalk café eating the wafers that were supposed to be lunch. Ornigon began somewhat hesitantly. "I am very sad, Honored Guest, that our conversation this morning upset you. If I had known, I would never have permitted it. Surely you understand that in every society there are traditional ways of expression that hide as much as they reveal. It would be a mistake to take those ways of expression as literal truth."

"Ah, it's a powerful passion, sex is," Seamus agreed tentatively. "It's lots of fun, but it can get out of hand, if you take my meaning."

"That is why," Ornigon replied evenly, "sex is limited to the Planting and Harvest Festivals. If it happened at other times, it would destroy us completely. It is difficult even then. We have special energies during the Festival; even so, the business is greatly wearing."

Seamus held on to the table. His head was spinning. *Glory be to God, he couldn't have said what I just think he said, could he?*

"You limit sex to two months a year—at the most?" he asked, his voice tight with the effort to keep it under control. *Ah, that would be worse than being a monk. Altogether.*

"It is our way. Obviously, it has its limitations and . . . uh . . . frustrations." The man gestured nervously with his thin expressive hands. "The Guardians thought it was the proper method for maintaining the ideals of our society. Our fertility should come only to celebrate the planting and after the harvest is reaped. There are ways of relieving some of the consequent strains, as one of your acuteness has doubtless noticed."

When the ancestors of the Zylongi came here from Earth, they were utopian communitarians, firmly opposed to marriage, pledged to "complete sexual accessibility." However, in the pioneer years of clearing the jungle, fighting the hordi, planting the crop, building the earliest city, permanent pairing began to reemerge. It was convenient on the scattered pioneer farms and outposts. There was evidence that such tendencies began to develop on the space flight that brought them here. "Logistically and emotionally it seems to create less strain," Ornigon said, his voice tinged with its frequent melancholy. "Women are reputed to favor it more than the men at first; later, men came to find it more convenient to be concerned with only one woman.

"To maintain the illusion that the ideology was still being honored—and ideology has always been important to us—" Ornigon emphasized, "there was a period at planting time and another one at harvesttime when our ancestors returned to a more communitarian style of sexuality. One-month periods for the release of tension—something like the Carnival or the Oktoberfest on ancient Earth. Also it likely served a superstitious function of blessing the fertility of the fields. However, with the passage of years, the Festivals became quite tame until the time of Reorganization.

"The Guardians were faced with a dilemma. The primitive practice of universal sexual accessibility had to be honored, yet the disruptive social impact of random coupling was intolerable. Since

124

they were also committed to genetic engineering, they couldn't allow unplanned pregnancies. They limited the expression of sexuality to the two months of Festival—just after planting and just after harvest each year. For the first fifteen days of each period, coupling is indiscriminate; the second fifteen days are limited to couplings of mates. Pregnancies, to be 'valid,' must occur during the second period. For the rest of the year, the irrationality of sexuality is not permitted to interfere with the running of an orderly society. No one is sexually available to anybody except during the Festival, and then only until after the mating ceremony. Some cheating is possible, but offenders are punished severely."

"Those Festivals must be something else." O'Neill shook his head in wonderment.

"They are, Honored Poet, very unusual times. Some look forward to them with great longing." His face now a tragic mask, he shook his head sadly. "It is a period when many energies that are pent up are released. In that release there is satisfaction and pleasure; often it is violent and irrational. We exhaust ourselves physically and morally. Few are sorry to see the Festival end. The Festivals vary from year to year—sometimes they are especially terrifying. In recent years they have gotten worse; it is as though we are demons. I think something else besides sexual hunger takes possession of us. There are those who understand such things who contend it has something to do with the physical effects of harvest. A biological reaction to which we have become sensitized either by evolution or by repeated exposure."

"And no one cheats?"

He considered O'Neill very carefully.

"What do you think?"

O'Neill thought of the two overwrought women the night before. *Of course people cheat.* "Well, you said that you are severely punished if you're caught."

"To my knowledge no one has been caught in my lifetime."

"Ah. Then I'd say there are ways around the rules."

"Dedicated citizens like my wife would tell you—officially, I assure you—that no one breaks the rules. The cultural controls are strong enough that no one talks about it. The pretense is maintained. Perhaps it always was merely pretense. Yet it is a powerful conviction in our society. So it is necessary, even if there is cheating, that we maintain the facade of obedience. As to how much occurs, I cannot say."

An elaborate nonanswer worthy of a Taran, worthy indeed of an Abbot. He had said that he and Sammy didn't cheat. No, he didn't quite say that either. How could you live with a woman like that and not . . .

Still, the norms of a society, he had learned in the monastery school, can impose almost any kind of behavior.

"I suppose that in recent years there has been more cheating?" O'Neill asked cautiously, thinking of those who were listening up on *Iona*, now probably with open mouths and incredulous faces. The Tarans might be messed up on sex and they might not know quite how best to do it, but they certainly did it a lot.

"Everyone says that our society is deteriorating. I suspect that it is said always. I am not skilled enough to understand these matters. I direct music, as you no doubt have perceived, somewhat woodenly. I do know that when the Research Director and I were promised but not publicly mated, it would have been unthinkable for any of our group to think of sex with our promised. Today, I understand, such practices are widespread. The juices are strong, I am told, though they were strong in our time too. I am convinced that Horor and Carina have performed the act together. For my wife it is impossible even to consider such a possibility."

You got all that down up there? You should have sent a monk here instead of a twenty-five-year-old bachelor with a wild imagination and a horny body. Your Ladyship can take me out now.

He didn't expect a reaction and sure enough there wasn't one.

That evening the three of them were sitting quietly, listening to a new Bach recording made by Ernie's orchestra. O'Neill was deep in thought. Enough of the pieces were fitting together. Repression, license, then repression again. Strong social bonds, weak personal freedom. Yet the individual personalities were sharply etched. Ernie, Sammy, the handsome and enigmatic Marjetta were not merely cogs in a vast social wheel, nor docile ants in an ant hill.

Your Blessed and Holy Eminence, I haven't found out anything yet that you couldn't have figured out with our dirty-minded computer. There must be something else that I've missed. Still, how do you like the part-time celibacy? Wouldn't work at all among us, now, would it? Besides, they're still shadowing me, if I'm to believe the twitching in my neck.

"Were you pleased with Officer Marjetta?" Samaritha interrupted O'Neill's thoughts.

"Yes, indeed. She seems to be a very competent and intelligent soldier," O'Neill said noncommittally.

Speaking of celibacy, was I? And herself brings that one up.

"She is very independent," added Ornigon. "Too independent for many. Her delay of the mating ceremony with Captain Pojoon has upset many people. Captain Pojoon could seek destruction of the agreement, and that would be very bad for Lieutenant Marjetta. Ways can always be found for the aggrieved party to find another mate, but the offending party will not be allowed to mate. Such people often leave the society altogether rather than suffer such disgrace. They are no longer with us."

A whole new category of people, and Ornigon had no intention of telling him any more. "Doesn't she . . . is not the Captain pleasing to her?" he asked, trying to sound innocent but his heartbeat picking up.

"She says he is very pleasing," Samaritha answered disapprovingly, "but that she is not yet ready to mate. He cannot be expected to wait until his career is terminated." Her frown suggested some deep unease. They listened in silence to what Seamus thought was a very dull Second Brandenburg.

As the last strains of the music died away, Samaritha stirred restlessly on her couch. "Is it now permissible to ask him the question, Honored Mate?"

"If you wish," said Ornigon, somewhat nervously, turning off the switch on their sound system.

"If it gives offense, Honored Visitor, we will talk of other things. My Honored Mate and I have noticed that sometimes you call us by strange names. For instance, though my name is 'Samaritha,' sometimes you call me 'Sammy.' Ornigon says you have called him 'Ernie.' You even addressed the excellent Marjetta as—I believe the term was 'Marj'?"

"Margie."

"We are curious as to why you do this."

"Ah, well, but they're nothing but little nicknames. Why was that so difficult a question to ask? It's a short name we Tarans use with our friends—a sign of friendship and affection. Sure it means no harm at all."

Strange to see, Samaritha was weeping. "Poet O'Neill, how is it possible for you to consider us friends? You hardly know us." She sat up on her couch, leaning forward so that the tops of her breasts were distinctly visible. She was intensely interested in his words.

"Maybe we mean different things by 'friendship.' I mean . . . well, someone you can trust when the lights go out is a friend." He was stumbling, trying to figure out what kind of deep waters he had blundered into.

The barroom reference was no help. Both husband and wife seemed baffled. Seamus tried again. "A friend is someone you can be yourself with, someone from whom you don't have to hide and who won't let you hide when you try."

Sure, it's nothing more than a cliché I learned in school.

"Extraordinary," murmured Ornigon. "It means much the same to us, I think, although we would not put it so well. My mate and I are overwhelmed that you think of us this way. We were mates for many years before we became friends . . . it was not an easy struggle. . . ."

"How can you see all the anger, ambition, and selfishness which makes me such a vile person and still want me for a friend?" Sammy demanded, tears streaming down her face.

The situation was getting out of hand. *Dear God in heaven, and I wondered whether these two loved each other. Now what do I do and say?*

Running on pure instinct, O'Neill rose from his couch, his fists shoved together to keep his own emotions under control. "Damn it, Sammy, where

I come from," he said gruffly, "if a beautiful woman speaks that kind of nonsense, you take her in your arms and hug and kiss her until she laughs it all away."

She lifted her head slightly and looked at him with liquid brown eyes.

"If I may," said Ornigon, deeply moved himself, "we have an approved, though perhaps not so satisfactory a sign as the 'nickname' or 'hugging' or 'kissing.' One extends one's fingers like this." Ornigon reached out toward Samaritha, who extended her hand toward his. "The friends touch like this." Ornigon and Samaritha gently touched fingertips, then intertwined them slowly. It was a painfully beautiful moment. They then extended their free hands toward him, forming a circle of friendship.

Later, as he tried to sleep, O'Neill wondered what he had gotten himself into. His neck twitched. There was no one at the door.

Damn, I hope you folks up there are protecting me. Hey, are you responsible for that girl being on the bank when I drifted by? That was a nice thought. But what am I going to do about these two?

Sammy and Ernie's literal-mindedness led them to treat his casual use of the word "friend" as something of immense importance. There was so little friendship here on Zylong that it was a desperately serious thing. They were now deeply involved with him. He was systematically deceiving them about who and what he was. On both Zylong and Tara, you were not supposed to deceive your friends.

7

Slowly, with dignified and solemn rhythm, like a *Corpus Christi* procession, the crowd moved down the narrow old street. Hundreds of portable lanterns in the hands of devout worshipers cast an eerie light in the predawn darkness. *A hell of a way to go to church. What am I doing here with all these heathens?*

It was not like a procession in the monastery, however. There was no center to it, no Blessed Sacrament to be carried, no Abbot or Prior walking at the end, no acolytes or thurifer in front. The crowd simply formed and processed on its own, as though it were animated by a single soul.

They loved processions and Holy Days on the *Iona*. Festivals broke the often monotonous routine of the space pilgrimage. But Tarans were quite incapable of spontaneously forming themselves into a procession or a festival celebration. Someone, normally the Ceremonialist, had to make plans and give orders. Even then, and even with the cool eye of the Captain Abbess watching every move, the processions were likely to be ragged, chaotic affairs. When Tarans were having fun, they were quite incapable of self-disciplined ritual dignity.

So Seamus thought that the early morning ceremonies in the great City were just a little bit creepy. No, more than that, they were creepy altogether.

It was Zylongday—the first day of the ten-day Zylong week. There were three weeks, he had learned, to the month, ten months to a year, so you multiplied by 0.8 to get an Earth estimate of Zylong age. Sammy had said it would be thought "strange" if they failed to honor another day of worship. There was, she said, no obligation, but people were expected to go to religious service at least several times a year. Since she and her mate had major responsibilities in the society, it was their custom to go to the "Worship Plaza" just behind the Central Plaza rather more often. O'Neill understood. It was expedient not to break long-standing patterns. The Committee tended to "notice" such things.

Whoever the Committee were.

Approaching the main Worship Plaza (other smaller ones were scattered throughout the City), O'Neill saw that the square was elevated five or six steps off the ground. In the center of it was a large translucent globe that emitted a soft glowing light. In front of the globe and behind a raised platform was a big opening from which a few wisps of smoke could be seen. It was into that pit that people "went to the god" at Festival times. Probably some kind of natural underground thermal activity beneath parts of the City caused the smoke. Perhaps the pit contained quicksand. Sacrificial victims sufficiently tranquilized would go into the mud without protest. Since the god was equated with the planet—as well as the society—sinking into the earth could quite literally be thought of as "going to the god." Those who died of natural causes before their careers were terminated were thrown into the hole at a private funeral.

As the Worship Plaza filled with people, the light from the lanterns shone against the plain white worship togas worn by the assembled congregants. Each person held a little cup of something that looked like wine.

A deep chime rang out once just as the first light appeared in the sky. Complete silence fell on the crowd. Lights began to flicker and swirl within the globe; a line of hooded figures clad in exuberant red and gold togas approached the globe from one side of the plaza. They moved slowly, murmuring a chant that increased in volume as the worshipers began to respond. This antiphony of "priests" and "congregation" grew louder and louder, gaining in intensity of rhythm and emotion.

No, I don't like this at all, at all, Seamus told himself. *Her Ladyship would be profoundly offended at what they've done with the memories of our liturgy.*

After each verse they sipped at the little cups of liquid. Seamus managed to spill most of his. In the darkness, no one noticed.

The light in the globe changed colors rapidly. The singing, the lights, the swaying motion of priests and crowd were hypnotic. O'Neill struggled to maintain his equilibrium. The strange liquid, even in small amounts, seemed to be more of a liquor than a wine—sweet and soft. It had a powerful and immediate effect. Ugly images raced across his mind; he was hard put to control the terror they evoked in him.

Images of the *Iona* blowing up, the Wild Geese being slaughtered, the Captain Abbess being destroyed by a satanic serpent, rape at High Mass in the chapel, inundated him. Then, replacing all the others, an image of God—nothing.

For a few desperate moments that seemed like the whole of eternity and more, these terrifying pictures became the only reality in his existence. They were true and nothing else was. He fought to break from them, but they would not let him go. They absorbed his mind, permeated his imagination, filled his soul. It was the end of all he believed in, all he wanted, all he was willing to die for.

For several terrible seconds he was captured by a compulsion to dash up on the worship platform and throw himself into the pit of fire, to obliterate himself as all his hopes and loves had been destroyed. Then the full rays of the sun flooded the plaza. It was all over. There was a loud exclamation of joy from the crowd, like the *Deo Gratias* at the end of Mass. They began to file out of the Worship Plaza, just as calm and normal as when they came in, chatting pleasantly with their companions. If anyone knew they were in a drug-induced ecstasy, they didn't show it. Whatever it was, O'Neill realized, its effects subsided quickly.

Sweating and trembling still, O'Neill puzzled it out: *if you're not sensitized to the stuff, it's an ecstasy of terror. Maybe it's like that for the others, too, and they're so used to it that they don't notice. Maybe it's like hitting your head against the alloy wall of the monastery. It feels so good when you stop you don't remember what the pain was like.*

"Is it not a beautiful and refreshing ceremony, Honored Friend?" asked Sammy briskly, as they threaded through the crowded streets toward their tower. "It is so peaceful. You are at one with Zylong, with your family, your friends, with the people, all the universe. You see what everything means and how tiny you are in that meaning." She seemed in fine fettle. (Just like Deirdre on Sunday morning.)

"What *does* everything mean?" he asked innocently.

"It is inexpressible, Honored Friend," responded Ernie. "Perhaps you have to be a Zylongi to understand."

There was an unexpected benefit of Zylongday. Ernie referred to it as a "mild diversion" for a Zylongday afternoon. To O'Neill it was a picnic. After the worship service the City atmosphere was relaxed—a holiday spirit pervaded the air. Small wandering bands and orchestras played in the plazas and the squares. The sidewalk cafés were crowded. Streets were filled with people in brightly colored clothes, strolling together and chatting. Whatever was in the "communion" drug seemed to relax the formality and tensions of Zylong life. His hosts were more cheerful than usual. Sammy hummed a tune as she bounced around the living area preparing for their "diversion." When they left their tower for the "short" walk to the wall, she changed to another tune and compelled O'Neill and Ernie to hum with her.

The woman's idea of "short" was not the same as Seamus's. After the first half hour he began, Taran-like, to complain.

"You are young enough to be my son and strong enough to be a god." She poked a finger at him. "Stop your complaining."

"I'll complain as much as I want, woman." Seamus put his hands around her waist, lifted her into the air as if she was a child, and spun her around, shouting and sputtering, and then, when he thought she'd had enough of her carnival ride, deposited her unceremoniously on the ground. Ernie and the other folks walking toward the wall seemed to think this was hilariously funny. Taran savage doing his Zylongday thing.

Sammy was red-faced, dizzy, flustered, and exorbitantly pleased, truly the little girl-child he had for the moment made her. "You do strange things, Poet O'Neill, very strange things."

"You keep a proper tongue in your head, woman," he laughed at her, "or I'll do even stranger."

Everyone thought that was uproarious too.

"Well, you need complain no longer." She was breathing deeply still, wonderful breasts moving up and down rapidly. "We are almost at the wall."

" 'Tis the walk home that worries me," he protested.

"We will ride home, Honored Guest." Ernie didn't quite understand it was mostly a game.

"Almost" meant fifteen more minutes on his now aching feet. He complained. Sammy made little faces at him but did not take the risk of another ride. Too bad, he'd enjoyed it. *Ah, sure nothing but a harmless little game*, he told the Lady Abbess, just in case she was listening.

The wall of the City was what Ernie called a "symbol," a waist-high slab of gleaming pink alloy that circled the City (doubtless produced in one of the mills of the spanking-clean factory center which O'Neill had visited earlier in the week). Panels swung open when you touched them. In time of conflict an electrical energy was released to make them effective barriers; now one could easily leap over them—which he did, to the mingled dismay and amusement of his hosts.

"When do you shoot the current through it?" Seamus tried to sound innocent.

"In times of conflict," Ernie said calmly.

"And when do you have conflict in this well-ordered and peaceful place?"

His hosts were silent.

"We don't, of course." Sammy began to walk

along the wall, not looking at him. Her husband followed as he usually did when she led.

"It is merely a precaution," her husband added lamely.

"Ah, indeed." Seamus lifted his picnic basket, the heaviest because, as Sammy had explained, "you are by far the biggest," and followed along, docile and dumb.

At the nearest gate, an opening in the wall, at which two sleepy cops with rusty pikes stood guard, they entered a blockhouse and descended by elevator to one of the huge underground chambers that lay beneath the City. It was the end of a monorail line. Next to the terminal there was a garage filled with the small electric cars that scurried through the City. Ernie's status entitled him to the use of a car. He handed a token to the bored attendant. After trying two cars that refused to work, they found one that, with considerable effort, was persuaded to sputter into action.

The bowels of the City, Seamus noted before he was distracted, were also the seamy side of the City. The obsessive cleanliness that was required aboveground did not seem necessary underground. The monorail station and the car park were littered with torn scraps of paper and unidentifiable rubble and permeated with a strong smell hinting broadly at human sewage. The monorail that arrived just as they were leaving seemed to limp wearily into the station. Even the docile Zylongi muttered angrily at what Seamus took to be the late arrival of the train.

Underground you don't even have to be patient and polite: even mine host and hostess are churlish with this dummy that can't find a car that works.

Then came the distraction.

Seamus saw the Lady Deirdre herself get off the monorail train.

At least it looked like her, a tall, slim woman with black hair tinged with gray and a thin ascetic face, gentle yet determined. Like Marjetta might appear in, well, fifty years. Before Seamus could be certain, the woman slipped away in the crowd.

It couldn't be her, he told himself uneasily. *Just my guilty conscience.*

Yes, it could. You know very well that like some of the other "sensitives" up there, she can project an image of herself that is almost as good as the real thing, almost anywhere she wants. Isn't she after doing it for laughs on the great festival days?

And isn't it after wearing her out too?

And what should she be doing down here?

Spying on her spy, you idjit, what else?

And why does the Lady Cardinal remind me of Margie?

Because they look a little like each other, you idjit, even if you never noticed that before.

"Is there something wrong, Honored Poet?" Sammy asked anxiously.

"Ah, I thought I saw someone I knew, but sure it couldn't be?"

"The Honored Lieutenant Marjetta?"

"Not exactly. Someone maybe sixty years older. But sure it wasn't her at all, at all."

She doesn't have lithe swelling breasts like my Margie. Well, not that I've let myself notice anyway. And herself a Cardinal.

The car started then, and they chugged up the ramp, out an opening beyond the City walls.

"The day is so pleasant," Ernie said, a broad smile on his face, "that I thought it would be diverting to leave the City."

The air was warm and dry, the sky completely cloudless, the sun a deep, rich rose. The scent of flowers was everywhere. Since there weren't any in sight, the odor must come from the low grass-like plant that grew on the narrow plain which ran between the City and the great River, beneath the sweeping sandbanks that were upriver from the City.

It is not paradise, but it will do. Sure, it couldn't have been herself.

You have a guilty conscience, that's what you have.

I haven't done anything to be guilty about.

Not yet, but you're fixing to.

Their car actually was a small hovercraft, bumping along on a cushion of air. Its motor needed a good tune-up. Doubtless the Repair Committee had assigned it a priority. *Well, if it breaks down, I hope they don't expect me to fix it. I'm a poet, not a mechanic.*

Of course, the woman could have something else going on down here besides me. Maybe I'm a pawn.

The thought infuriated him.

141

Ah, but you've known that you were a pawn from the beginning, why let it upset you now and ruin your day?

The woman was up to no good, you can bet on that.

They sped over the plain to a small gravel beach on the riverbank. The Island (it had no other name) lay in the River, roughly parallel to the City, perhaps two miles from it.

So that's where she wants to land, is it now? Well, it's not a terrible bad place, I suppose. It sure beats the blackness of hyperspace.

Despite the beauty of the afternoon, there were only occasional small groups of Zylongi wandering around on the plain or sitting at the edge of the River. They seemed to keep close to the City walls when they ventured out for their Sunday, oops, Zylongday, picnics.

Their hovercraft left the bank and sped across to a small cove on the Island. It was unusual in the topography of Zylong—a low mountain rearing its head far away from the planet's main chain. Some five miles long, it had hills, valleys, some flat meadows, tiny forests, creek beds, and wide orange sand beaches on every side.

No, it's not bad for a monastery at all, at all. Why don't we just take it over? We can tell these folks that the red-bearded god took a fancy to it.

"May Jesus and Mary and Brigid be with this island," Sammy said devoutly as they climbed out of the rickety hovercraft.

"What did you say?" Seamus could hardly believe his own hearing.

"It is your blessing we learned from the Honored Marjetta," Ernie remarked apologetically. "You are distressed that we use it? It is sacrilegious?"

"Ah, no," Seamus sighed loudly. *Sure I should have thought about blessing the future site of the Iona.* "The question is whether they would object, and they're a lot more tolerant than we are."

"It is beautiful that your god has friends," Sammy murmured piously.

"Ah, lots of them, too many altogether."

They swam in the warm, buoyant River, drank la-ir in copious amounts, ate the nameless delicacies that Sammy had prepared, and lay on the soft sand. O'Neill had a hard time keeping his eyes off Sammy since she handed him her toga almost the moment their skiff pulled up on the beach. The scanty lentat merely emphasized her seductive charms. Sammy was richer and fuller than Marjetta, though not so perfectly sculpted. Marjetta's athletic grace challenged you, Sammy's flowing figure invited you to the warmth of earth.

Sure there's room for both, isn't there?

Near nakedness for her culture meant only friendship—before the Festival anyway; she seemed to feel no shame lying on the hot sand, her heels digging little holes in the beach, between her husband and her friend, both of whom were as unclad as she.

Ernie went for another swim. "Do you find my

143

body pleasing, Honored Friend?" she asked, laughing softly.

He had been staring too intently. "I find *you* pleasing, Sammy," he replied truthfully enough. He wondered what Marjetta would look like in a brief loincloth and banished the image. It came right back.

"As always, you speak the beautiful and the mysterious." The grip of her fingers tightened. "You are far behind in your kisses."

"What do you mean by that?" He wondered about pulling his fingers away.

"You said that patients and doctors exchange kisses twice a day."

"I never did."

"At the Body Center, you most certainly did."

"Ah, but that's our custom, not yours."

"It is a good custom."

"I like this one better." He repeated his spin-the-dolly-in-the-air routine.

Kissing, he decided as he whirled the delighted Sammy above his head, *might be safer than this. Sure she might just as well have nothing on at all.*

So he laid her back down on the beach, laughing and gasping, and kissed her lightly, twice for good measure. O'Neill decided he needed a swim too.

When he returned, his friends asked if he would permit them a brief stroll down the beach.

"I think I might take a wee nap." He yawned and stretched. "The woman wakes me up while it's still dark and now makes me hike halfway across this planet. The least she can do is let me catch forty winks."

That should convince them that I have no idea they're going off somewhere and breaking the rules, the dirty things!

"Forty winks?" Despite the softness of anticipation in her eyes, Sammy had to ask the question.

"An idiom for a brief rest."

Sure I'd never have thought herself would break the rules. I bet they haven't been doing it for long, either. Do you have to come over here or do you risk it late at night in your tower?

He was willing to wager that the security system shut down in Zylong when the lights went out, just like everything else. The Guardians probably did spot checks of bedrooms to keep everyone honest. You took your chances of ending up in the fire on Zylongday when you made love, so you did it rarely. But you still did it. There were probably a lot of things the Committee did not want to know, because it couldn't do anything about them anyway.

Sammy and Ernie, however unsuited for each other they may have been when they "officially mated," were now, it seemed obvious, deeply in love with one another. How could anyone expect them not to play with each other's bodies?

He had learned in the monastery school about the Shakers, mostly because they composed such wonderful songs. Despite their music, they did themselves out of existence because they believed in celibacy not only for monks—which Seamus supposed was all right as long as it was your vocation, God knows it wasn't his—but for married people too.

And they made it work till there were no more Shakers and no more songs. They probably did shake because of the way they lived. It'd be enough to make anyone shake. The songs were joyous enough, though, weren't they?

He hummed "Simple Gifts." And then sang it for his hosts. They loved it. He taught them the words in their own language and they sang it with him.

"It is indeed a gift to be free," Ernie sighed wistfully. "A great gift. Almost as great—" he took her hand "—as a good wife."

Sammy blushed happily and clung to his hand. "We must take our walk now, Honored Poet."

"Have a nice walk." Seamus could have kicked himself for that smart-aleck crack. They both blushed and turned away.

So you can live like a Shaker if you have to and want to and your society and culture make you.

Yeah, but most people can't.

But they've been doing it here. Or rather not doing it for a long time.

All right, so it is possible. But it's silly.

Since Seamus was an orphan, Carmody had provided him with his sex instruction—God knows the monks wouldn't mention a thing like that. The Brigadier was a good teacher. It was said of his wife, Maeve, that she became more beautiful each /

year and, with a knowing wink, "You know what that means!"

The power of sexual attraction, Carmody had explained, is that it keeps man and woman together, even though "they have no business trying to live in the same house and sleep in the same bed. Can you imagine a more difficult thing for two human beings and themselves as different as can be?"

Seamus admitted that he could not.

"And sure," the huge, grizzled Brigadier went on in his rich mischievous baritone, "just when you're ready to murder the woman and long after she's made up her mind to poison your coffee, you fall in love again and it's the most glorious thing in all God's world."

That seemed reasonable enough.

" 'Tis just like God feels about us," Carmody observed, echoing the theories of Cardinal Deirdre, after he had laid out some of the more graphic details for a fascinated Seamus.

"Ah, He's not that way at all, at all," Seamus protested. "God is a spirit."

"Are you letting those gombeen men in the school teach you that nonsense? Whoever said spirits don't have passions? God is daft over us. That's what herself means when she preaches that marriage is a sacrament—it gives us a hint about what God is like. Sure, He's even more crazy in love with us than we are with one another when we're turned on."

"Go 'long with you," Seamus said, dubious but delighted. "If God were like that, well . . ."

"Would I be misleading you now?" Carmody had demanded.

Sure he would not.

Sex is a hint of God? 'Tis a nice idea. I'll have to tell Marjetta the next time I see her. She seems kind of interested in our god.

And when will I see her again? It's all right for the two of them to go sneaking off into the woods so they can lollygag with each other. Here I am, an enforced celibate, and myself not even a monk.

The Tarans did not try to regulate the sex lives of their members. "We did try long ago," the Abbess said crisply, "and it didn't work."

Premarital experimentation was frowned upon officially, but when it happened, there were sighs and comments like "Ah, the boys won't leave the girls alone." Or vice versa. "The blood is hot at that age," the Abbess would say.

"And 'tis herself that would know about it," some of her contemporaries would mutter behind her back.

Extramarital sex was taken much more seriously because relationships were tough enough in the close quarters of a spaceship monastery on a pilgrimage that could last for decades. Men and women knew this and generally avoided complicating their own lives and other people's. Not that nothing ever happened by way of adultery, but the participants were careful not to get caught.

And when they were caught—"Sure they

wouldn't have been caught unless they wanted to be," the Abbess would complain—the emphasis was not on punishment or retribution but on "working things out."

Not that the Tarans had figured out how to make sex work. "The species has never done that at all, at all," Carmody complained. "But at least we don't have too many hang-ups and some of us—" he smiled complacently "—even manage to be good enough at it to enjoy the game now and again."

"Do you now?" Seamus decided that he would be one of those. If only he could find the proper woman. Which had turned out to be a more difficult task than he had expected.

Until the shapely shoulders of Marjetta had thrust themselves into his life.

Shapely and strong, he thought, remembering; *after all, she pulled me out of the sewer.*

Sammy and Ernie came back, arm in arm, glowing with satisfaction and complacency. *So they, too, were good enough to enjoy the game. Good for them.*

Seamus pretended to be asleep so as not to embarrass them. Or himself.

Finally, he made a great show of waking up and, without looking at them, announced that since he'd been promised that he would not have to walk back to the tower, he would exhaust himself altogether with one last swim.

The sun sank slowly into the horizon beyond the towers of the City, bathing it in gold and purple. The long haze of twilight settled peacefully on the River and the Island. After what must have been the fifth swim and their tenth round of la-ir, O'Neill and his hosts were collapsed in satisfied exhaustion on the sand by their skiff.

Sammy spoke finally. "Good Friend O'Neill, we must ask you another personal question."

"All right . . . I guess," he agreed reluctantly.

"You ask it, Gentle Mate. I have already said too many impulsive things." She dug her tiny heels more deeply into the sand.

"We like the 'nicknames' you have chosen for us. What do your good friends on Tara call you?" the Music Director asked hesitantly.

Images of Tessie and Fergus Hennessey flashed across his memory. "Ah, well, I suppose you must know that my very best friends, the people I grew up with, call me 'Jimmy.'"

Sammy clapped her hands. "Geemie—what a marvelously funny name. Oh, it is perfect for you."

Maybe by the end of these holidays all Zylongi get a little slaphappy.

The day was over. Reluctantly "Geemie" and his hosts gathered their clothes and their picnic equipment together and lumbered their way back toward the other side of the River. He handed Sammy her robe. She smiled a bit wickedly, for her, as she slipped it around her body. "Yes, I must wear it, but modesty is tiresome with one's friends, is it not?" *Glory be to God, can you imagine what would happen if I said that up there?*

He muttered a prayer to his patron St. James

(the Greater, of course) that it really wasn't herself lurking over at the monorail station. Not that there was any way of hiding from her when she wanted to keep her eyes on you.

They were late returning to the City. Sammy and Ernie, perhaps reluctant to face the rigid, formal style of their City life, delayed on the riverbank, treating each other with exaggerated gentleness. O'Neill supposed he should have been embarrassed. That Sammy and Ernie could turn the words of ordinary conversation into caresses didn't seem to fit the Zylongi personality.

By the time they got to the garage, the attendant was gone, the underground lights were dim, the monorail station empty. Seamus was so sleepy from the exertions and emotions of the day that he paid no heed to his hosts' nervousness as they waited for the monorail to respond to their signal.

An ugly, hoarse cry; then O'Neill felt his arms pinned behind him and saw a knife slicing toward his throat.

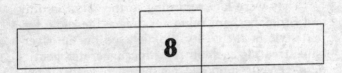

8

Seamus was out of condition, weary from the day's exercise, and long unpracticed in the skills of hand-to-hand combat. On the other hand, in addition to being a perhaps second-rate poet, he was one of the Wild Geese, the most respected warriors in the galaxy. "We Only Fight When We Have To" was one of their many mottoes. And another was "Don't Make Us Mad."

Well, he had to fight now. And he was very mad indeed. These shitheads had been sneaking around behind him long enough.

He quickly shifted his shoulders, ducked the knife, twisted it out of the hand of his assailant and threw him into the path of a second attacker. As the man crashed into the floor, Seamus heard a sickening thud. *Ah, that's the end of him, poor fellow.*

The second one rushed at Seamus with a big vicious pike, aiming straight at his chest. Seamus ducked. The man turned, backed him into a corner, and charged again. Seamus had no choice but to plunge the knife into his heart and twist it out again savagely.

That was that.

In less than half a minute, two black-hooded figures were dead on the station platform. O'Neill, panting for breath, stood over them, a knife dripping with blood held tightly in his hand.

These idjits with the hoods made the mistake of taking on someone trained to kill if he had to.

Sammy was screaming. Another hooded figure had her pinned to the wall, and a fourth had torn off her robe. Ernie lay unconscious, his head bleeding badly. O'Neill kicked an oncoming Hooded One in the stomach and sent him sprawling against the monorail car, which had appeared silently in the midst of the fight. He grabbed the two who were assaulting Sammy and cracked their skulls together. A quick knife thrust at the reviving attacker and there were five dead bodies on the platform. Ernie was still unconscious; Sammy's back was pressed against the wall, her body shaking with shock.

O'Neill grabbed her by the shoulders and yelled, "You look at Ernie, I'll find the police!"

Sammy willed herself calmer. "No, not the police. It will be the end of us all. You must do exactly as I say, Geemie. I will explain later."

She bent over Ernie, touched his head, lifted his eyelids. She steadied herself against O'Neill's arm. "It is bad, Geemie. If I don't get life serum he will not survive—my beloved. Quick, or he will die!"·

They pried open the door of the monorail car and lugged Ernie inside. They propped him up in the seat behind the control panel. "They are automatic this time of night," she panted. "I think I can make it start. Get rid of those monsters. No, bring them on the car. And clean up the floor."

"Yes, ma'am."

Seamus hopped to it, as he always did when a woman gave an order.

He dragged the five Hooded Ones into the car, used the remnants of Sammy and Ernie's clothes and a spray container from the station wall to clean up most of the blood, and buried the blood-soaked garments in the bottom of an overstuffed trash container.

Inside, Sammy was desperately pushing at buttons. O'Neill watched helplessly. Ernie was hardly breathing. *A goner*, Seamus thought to himself.

Then the lights went out, the vehicle leaped forward. "I think I've turned the override key for emergencies," she shouted over the roar of the lumbering train. "It will take the car directly to the Body Institute; no other station can stop or divert it."

"Isn't that nice now?"

The car plunged through the pitch-black tunnels, speeding by dimly lit stations, until it swerved to the left off the main line and entered the Body Institute's underground complex. Using manual controls, Sammy guided the car through a number of sliding doors that opened automatically when it approached. When they stopped, Sammy jumped out into the darkness and pressed a button on the wall.

A panel slid aside to reveal a large, low-ceilinged chamber illuminated by a pale green light. Save for a walkway around its perimeter and what appeared to be a loading platform in front of the door, the entire room was a vat of thick, slowly bubbling liquid. It had the hideous smell of death.

Sammy didn't hesitate. "Quick, Geemie, our lives are lost if anyone sees us!" She began to pull one of the Hooded Ones toward the seething rolling substance. Seamus tried to remove the hood; she stopped him. "We do not want to know who they are. That would be too much."

As the first body struck the surface, a hissing vapor arose and partially obscured the disintegration of skin over muscle, muscle over bone, and the skeleton itself in the caustic action of the acid. As each body followed the last, the vapor rose higher. When Seamus dumped the last body into the vat, the surface was frosted by a thick layer of sickly greenish cloud.

Sammy rushed around the edge of the vat to a panel halfway across the room, exclaiming, "I'm going to get serum for my mate!"

O'Neill spent interminable minutes in the dank underground chamber directing prayers to Yahweh, Brigid, Patrick, Columcile, Finnbar, James, Brendan, Kevin, and any other Celtic saints who might have been listening, sparing just a few moments to point out to Yahweh's local representative, Deirdre Cardinal Fitzgerald (a title to be used only when one wanted special psychic assistance) that help in this particular instance would be most appropriate. No answer from any of them. Ernie's eyes flickered dangerously; his slight breathing became more labored.

Not long to go. Seamus prayed all the harder.

Sammy returned breathless with a large syringe in her hand. She plunged it into her mate's chest. O'Neill watched anxiously as the fluid level went down. Sammy listened to his heart, her ear pressed to his chest. Seamus could see the movements in Ernie's thin brown chest slowly become more regular; the blood which was still reddening his iron-gray hair stopped flowing.

Sammy stood up. "He lives, Geemie," she said wearily, and collapsed sobbing into O'Neill's arms. Slowly and gently he caressed her to peacefulness. After a moment's relaxation, she dashed back into the chamber and pulled out fresh robes from a closet. Sammy quickly and skillfully guided the monorail car back into the main tunnel.

So the Honored Poet and his hosts returned to the living-space complex after a pleasant if slightly prolonged Zylongday outing on the Island. "A small accident with the car," Sammy explained to a station attendant as they helped the now conscious but groggy Ernie out of the car and into the elevator of their living tower.

"It is well that the trains run this late on Zylongday," he replied with mild reproof.

As they left the elevator, Sammy muttered,

"He will report us, of course, but no one will know what happened."

Lots of spies around this place, aren't there?

Later, in the privacy of their living space, while his mate began her ministrations to his skull, Ernie painfully filled O'Neill in on their attackers. "The Hooded Ones," he said, "are not the same as 'those who are no longer with us.' They are anarchists, not dissidents. They rarely appear in the daytime, although they have been seen more often at that time recently, it is reported. They attack after dark, then usually only isolated individuals or small groups like us. Recently the attacks have been both more vicious and more frequent. Their attacks are usually on the fringes of the City. Tonight's attack, so near the main gate, was very unusual. Few people dare to go out after midnight because they fear attack. We were late coming back; still, it was before midnight."

Those who are no longer with us, mused Seamus. *There's more damned categories of baddies around here than a poor space bard can keep straight.*

"Why didn't we go to the police? Why were we so afraid of being seen? Why did we cover up traces of the attack—as if *we* were guilty?" O'Neill was baffled.

"The Hooded Ones," said Sammy, carefully stitching her mate's wound, "do not exist officially. Some of them may live as ordinary citizens during the day, but many more live in the caves beneath the underground system—which also do not exist officially. It is not wise to talk about what does not exist in public. If one reports an attack from something that does not exist, one is causing trouble for the City. If the police are forced to encounter something that does not exist, whoever is responsible is an enemy of the City. They will likely end up in a vat like the one you saw. Geemie, we came very close to being there ourselves tonight. I was running down a corridor in the Body Institute with the life serum when something seemed to tell me to turn into another corridor. It was lucky I did. There was a police patrol in the first one. Now, beloved, the stitching is over." She touched his face with gentle affection.

Seamus took a blind-leap guess. "Are the Hooded Ones the same as the Guardians?"

Sammy paused with a medicine bottle in her hand. Ernie spoke: "We do not think so, although it is said that the Hooded Ones think of themselves as 'Guardians of the Next Day.' Of the 'New Reconstruction.' "

"Do they now?"

"Still," added Sammy, "they might occasionally cooperate—especially if there were a plan to eliminate an intruder who was no longer welcome."

"It is better not even to think that," said Ernie very slowly. "Not at all, at all."

PART TWO

THE COUNTRY

9

Seamus O'Neill, carbine at the ready, prowled the low hill just above Captain Pojoon's encampment. There was no moonlight yet, only shadows against the stars. It was like blundering through the storerooms in the deep hold of the *Iona*, except that the only folks who lurked there were ghosts, so there was nothing to be afraid of if you didn't believe in ghosts.

The "carbine," as he called it, was a light weapon which fired electrical charges that were strong enough to kill you if they hit you in a vital spot, not nearly as deadly as the automatic weapons or laser rifles the Wild Geese carried, but deadly enough.

Seamus, of course, did believe in ghosts, but not in the same way that he believed in enemies lurking in the hills behind them. Ghosts could scare. The folks up in the hills might kill you.

The Zylongi were too inept to set up camp in a proper place and too dumb to put out a proper system of guards. *What a rotten bunch of soldiers. Herself was right: this society is falling apart.*

Sure they need help bad. And if it's all the same to you, now would be the time to come and help them. And meself in the process.

No word back. Not that he expected any. They'd forgotten about Seamus Finnbar O'Neill. The woman had other irons in the fire. So they'd sent him on a suicide mission? Well, Seamus always was a good one at taking care of himself. He would have to assure his own safety.

The camp was a few feet below him; he could barely see the outline of the small tents that housed the troops. He yearned for the silver light from the tiny Zylong moons, billiard balls that bounced fretfully across the sky. The horses were invisible beyond the camp, but he could hear the nervous stamping of their hooves. Everyone but two guards was sound asleep. Nervously he fingered his gun.

Perfect targets for an attack. An exposed camp with no pickets and no preparations for defense. "There are no dangers here at the foot of the mountains," Pojoon said casually. "It is better that we get some sleep for tomorrow's march." Marjetta had no word of disagreement. Her attempts to turn the ragtag band of adolescent recruits into a marching column were cautious and discreet; she did not want to embarrass her future mate by suggesting in front of the Honored Guest that he was not much of an officer.

Pride, woman. That's what it is. The terrible sin of pride. The sin of Eve.

No, he got it wrong. Who was it that was guilty of the sin of pride? He couldn't quite remember. Well, it doesn't matter. Pojoon is a bum. No match for Seamus O'Neill at all, at all, even if she pretends I don't exist—and bad luck to her for doing that.

He considered carefully and asked leave to revoke the final wish. *Nothing but good luck to the poor girl. Sure, she's had more than enough bad luck for one life.*

O'Neill had tried to sleep in the stuffy little tent, but his psychic sense and trained military brain told him that tonight danger was very near. He didn't have much psychic ability, but at least he could sniff danger. "A very useful trait in a Commandant," the Lady Abbess had said dryly when she gave him his gold oak leaf badge of office—to be worn next to his tiny silver harp, of course.

There was menace in these foothills whether the Zylongi proclaimed them officially safe or not. If an attack came, he would be ready for it, no matter what they did. Save Margie if no one else. Every noise among the rocks, every shift in the slight breeze increased his nervousness. He fingered the illumination grenade he had stolen from a store's tent; he hoped it worked. The carbine that Marjetta gave him when they were switching from hovercraft to horseback at the edge of the desert was old but well maintained. It had been her responsibility, she'd told him curtly when he examined it; it would work well.

She won't look me in the eyes. Is she after blam-

ing me for what happened that night? Sure she was into it as much as I was.

Seamus cautiously reopened the weapon to make sure it was not jammed. *The woman told the truth. Sure she'd be a good housewife, too, much better than those slatterns up on the Iona, worse luck to them for leaving me down here to be murdered in this terrible desert.*

Well, when whatever was going to happen did, he wasn't going to have a jammed carbine on his hands.

The Zylongi troops were young, most of them new recruits. Many had never been on a horse (not that he had ever ridden one either—St. Patrick, how he ached!). They couldn't maintain a line of march for more than a half hour; they had a hard time setting up their tents; they went to bed even though they were in a dangerous situation; they probably couldn't fire a gun to save their lives— which they might have to do.

Washouts, Seamus suspected, *that the high command wants to eliminate. Along with Honored Poet Seamus Finnbar O'Neill, God be good to him.*

They had left the Military Center, just down the street from the main square of the City, while it was still dark, arriving at the departure station at dawn of the second day. Though all the baggage had been prepacked, it still was well into midmorning before Pojoon, Marjetta, and Retha, a frightened little-girl Cadet who looked like she was about eleven years old, managed to get the horses loaded. They proceeded out the Gate of Departure in something less than a trim line, with a small chorus of lame farewells from the garrison sounding behind them.

They would not make the trip to Fort Hyperion by hovercraft, first because there were only a few such vehicles and secondly because none of them had the range required for the trip to the other end of the World Island.

Seamus wasn't sure he believed either claim. He suspected that those who ruled Zylong wanted to keep control of all the long-range transportation on the planet.

The ride across the desert was hot but uneventful. By sunset of the second day, the weary and dispirited troopers arrived at the foothills of the vast mountain spine of Zylong. They saw the snow-capped peaks at the lower end of the chain far off in the distance. Although sunset behind the mountains was glorious, O'Neill paid little attention since he was preoccupied with the hapless efforts of the three officers to get their expedition settled for the night. They were not much of a command staff—a stupid Captain, a Lieutenant preoccupied with problems of her own, and a terrified girl-child Cadet. Seamus wondered who she had offended.

If the Committee were sending out an expendable expedition, they didn't have to make it so obvious. Of course, they didn't know they had a Commandant of the Wild Geese on their hands. Or did they?

The heat lessened as dusk settled. Everyone

continued to wear the hooded flowing garments that replaced the wraparound robe on desert marches. While it protected one from sun and sand, it gave little freedom of movement in a fight. *These folks know nothing about fighting. Then why have an army?* O'Neill left his cloak in the tent and went out to prowl in his lentat, a knife stuck in its belt.

The moons began to edge over the horizon. Marjetta was so unlike Samaritha. The latter was tense and businesslike on the surface but warm, sensuous, and yielding underneath. Margie was apparently pure rock all the way through, though delectable rock.

There must be some kind of military tradition in Zylong. She was every inch a sophisticated, tough, and resourceful soldier—high-quality officer material even by Wild Geese standards. He wondered what she thought of her own army.

The first news of this trip to the desert came two evenings after the fight at the monorail station.

Seamus was trying to talk with the young serving hordi. She could understand him, but he could get nowhere with her clicks and grunts. Like most women, however, she found him hugely amusing.

"You admire the good Dr. Samaritha?" he began the conversation.

The little creature clicked and grunted enthusiastically.

"All these people?"

She shook her head in a vigorous negative.

"Uh-huh. They kind of push around your people, don't they?"

The small one looked anxiously to either side, bowed her head and clicked once.

"The day of the hordi will come, won't it?"

The servant chattered with terror, pointed at him, and ran from the room.

The legend again. Why is she afraid? Of course, when the wild hordi come in from the desert, it may be rough on the collaborators. This scene gets worse and worse.

The normally dormant video screen in his room crackled and came alive. There was Marjetta on the screen, looking coldly at him. "Poet O'Neill," she intoned, "the Committee thinks it proper to offer you the possibility of a journey to our mines at Fort Hyperion. My senior officer, Captain Pojoon, will lead a convoy there in three days. It should give you an opportunity to observe the countryside of our planet before the time comes for you to leave. Will it please you to accept the invitation?"

It didn't please Poet O'Neill very much at all. The Committee was serving notice on him that his days on Zylong were numbered. Also, it was sending him out on a dubious expedition only two days after someone had tried to kill him. The Committee was issuing an order, not an invitation.

If Marjetta noticed his suspicion about the journey to Fort Hyperion—*Odd name. Greek, wasn't it?*—she didn't comment on it. "You will come to the Military Center tomorrow at the third hour after the zenith and ask the guard to conduct you to my office for a preliminary briefing. Try to be punctual."

"Bitch," sighed O'Neill, as she signed off. "But so lovely." He had gone at once to seek Samaritha's reaction to the invitation.

He found her reading on a couch in her own room, the water steaming in the bath next to her. O'Neill was still not able to get used to seeing the good doctor naked to her flat luscious belly. Every time he saw her he felt he wanted to run—though he wasn't quite sure whether to run toward her or away from her. Her body invited him into the depths of her selfhood, an invitation that attracted and frightened him. She luxuriated in his admiration. "Ought not one to enjoy friends?" she had asked him once with a mixture of naiveté and coquettishness.

"Is there something wrong with me, Geemie?" she asked, putting aside the book.

"Uh . . . no, nothing at all." If only his eyes wouldn't widen embarrassingly every time he saw her.

"Come, Geemie," she said invitingly, extending the tiny fingers of her right hand, "join me in a serenity bath. You will find it most restful. I think you're afraid of me. You must know me well enough to realize I would do nothing improper. My mate himself suggested that you might need the relaxation." She peeled off his robe and led him unresisting into the warm waters of the pool. "Is it really true that on Tara you hug friends instead of holding their fingers? It would surely be proper for you to hug me, would it not?" She laughed merrily and put his arms around her. She fit nicely; there was surrender in her body. *Glory be to God, Deirdre, the woman's trying to seduce me!*

Though there was no reply from Deirdre, Sammy wasn't trying to seduce him. The serenity bath had the same effect as la-ir. It produced intimacy from which all passion was drained. The temperature of the bath varied subtly, shifting patterns of coolness and warmth over his body— passion fulfilled rather than passion aroused. One more of the Zylongian techniques for sexual control.

"Geemie," she said after a long time. Her eyes were filled with tears.

"Musha, now," he said. "There's nothing to cry about."

"Why don't you take Marjetta with you and leave this planet? Go back to Tara. Have a life of joy and peace with your own people." She buried her head against his chest.

"Well now, to tell the truth, that's not a bad idea, but I don't think the young lady would be all that eager to step into my battered spacecraft. Sure, the old *Dev* is not the sort of thing to attract a woman with a career ahead of her like Marjetta." He didn't want to get mixed up with that one. Besides, had she dragged him into the intimacy of her bath to sell Marjetta?

"No, you are wrong, Geemie. She will go with you. I know she will. You two would be very happy. You would find love much younger than I and my dear mate did. You must go. You must go soon."

She dug her fingers into his arms, desperately pleading with him to leave.

While she spoke to him urgently, she was holding his head on her breast, gently stroking his hair. The rest of the universe slipped away; there was only himself and this beautiful woman who had admitted him into the sanctuary of her love. He touched her face; the jaw muscles were still stiff, but under the gentleness of his fingers they became soft. He was falling, falling back into childhood. He was a little boy and she was a tender and loving mother.

On the low hill in the desert, O'Neill realized he was perspiring despite the cool night air. There had been no aroused passion while he was in her soothing embrace but the memory of it made his body twist in pain. *I am going to pieces. Wild Geese do not fantasize about women when they're on battle alert.*

There was a sound down the hill from him. Instantly he tensed his finger on the gun. Perhaps only a stone sliding into the plain.

The plan for the journey to the desert was straightforward. A transport column of forty rather stodgy horses (their ancestors, probably not thoroughbreds to begin with, must have come here with the original settlers) and twenty soldiers with supplies would be conveyed to the edge of the jungle beyond the cultivated region by large transport (bigger versions of the hovercraft on which he had been brought out of the jungle). They would move out across the desert to the mountain foothills, following them around to the fort on the southern tip of the continent. There they would unload the supplies, rest for a few days, collect the concentrated minerals used in alloy construction, and retrace their route home. The whole journey would take no more than two weeks—three at the most, should there be storms on the desert. Which was the first O'Neill had heard of any storms. *Podraig, you goofed again*. The trip could be completed several weeks before the harvest.

It was simple enough—especially in a society which deliberately but capriciously limited its technology. On the one hand it used computers that were as good as any on the *Iona*, and provided electricity for the City from an old-fashioned nuclear reactor in the Energy Center; it could produce an elaborate monorail system inside the City and alloy metals, rock-hard, for buildings and walls. But it brought in raw materials and supplies on horse-drawn carts. The only large hovercraft, capable of any distance, belonged, he had been told, to "the Committee" and was used only for "official purposes."

Ernie explained that it would "violate" the harmony of the land to use big machines outside the City. The explanation was delivered in what Seamus had come to recognize as the "civic" tone of his host's voice—a tone reserved for the "party line," which the good Musical Director did not necessarily believe.

Seamus guessed that banning technology from the country kept its resources under control of the

Committee and protected ordinary Zylongi (*For their own good, of course,* he thought bitterly) from contact with the wild hordi or the other "monsters" (Carina's word, spoken in the only sentence that Sammy's sullen little future daughter-in-law had spoken to O'Neill) who lived in the wilderness.

"And Narth!" the angry little child had added.

"Who's he?"

She shook her pretty head disdainfully and walked to her impatiently waiting young man.

The day after the "invitation" he went to the Body Institute for inoculation against diseases on the trip. The Zylongi had brought disease under control in the area around their City and in the cultivated region; in the desert it was another matter. Sammy was very businesslike. She had no idea what the diseases were; the Inoculation Department was not connected with hers. Their research was not published. Still, everyone knew the serums were very effective. There was no need to worry about infection on the journey.

"Do people like you and Ernie really like the Festival?" he asked abruptly, remembering that he was supposed to be on an intelligence mission. "Don't you hate sharing your mate with others?"

Sammy turned her back and put one of the bottles of vaccine into the refrigerated wall safe from which she had taken it. She stood ramrod-straight.

"Of course we hate it. Do you think I like to feel the crude hands of the workers paw me? Do you think I enjoy those foolish young women . . .

who take my mate? It is unbearable. It happens. There is nothing to do. The Festival is part of our culture. It is in our bodies; we are prisoners to it. We must endure it."

She whirled around, her eyes blazed with fury. "Are you satisfied now, Seamus O'Neill?" she screamed at him. "Do you know everything about us that you wanted to know?"

Relentlessly he probed on. "Then the time you have with one another during the second half of the Festival must be very unsatisfying. People like you and Ernie, who really care about each other, will cheat. I bet you break the rules no matter how virtuous you claim to be. I bet you broke them the night I saved your lives down in the underground."

She threw the empty syringe at him and ran sobbing from the room. Seamus sighed. *Well, it does indeed look like they are coming apart at the seams. I hope you folks up there with Her Ladyship are happy about finding that out. I hate myself for doing it.*

Sammy and Ernie were mournful when it came time to say farewell. "They cannot do it," she wailed. "We had an agreement...."

"They can do what they want, my dear," Ernie replied grimly, wiping his hands nervously against his robe. "You know that."

"Ah, don't be after worrying about me." Seamus waved his hand airily. "Sure this space tramp can take care of himself. Why, did I ever tell you about what happened in the bar on Halley Number Three when the wee gombeen man ..." He went off on another one of the stories, utterly fictional, like the one with which he had calmed his friends after the rumble in the monorail station.

"You certainly displayed your ability to defend yourself the other night." Ernie raised his la-ir glass respectfully. "I was not, ah, in a condition to observe, but from what my Honored Mate tells me, you are not without warrior skills."

"He is a fearsome fighter." Sammy eyed him keenly. "Are poets also warriors in Taran culture, Geemie?"

"Not at all, at all," Seamus lied flatly. "I'm not much of a fighter. You should see our real warriors. They're called Wild Geese. There was a time when one of them and I were in a tight spot on Kerry and . . ."

So it went.

He had been quickly forgiven for the scene in the Body Institute. Sammy embraced him fiercely and kissed him passionately when she dropped him off at the Military Center. "If you are gone three weeks, Geemie, I will owe you sixty kisses when you return."

"At least. In our culture, the rate goes up when the patient is away from the doctor."

She doesn't believe, she never did. She merely likes to kiss me. Well, isn't that interesting.

His reflections were abruptly ended when he realized that a grimly frowning Marjetta had watched the farewell embrace.

Well, it's your own fault, woman, for not staying in your office, like you said you would.

He covered up his embarrassment by striding over to the younger woman and demanding the "truth" about the dangers in their trip.

"There are no dangers." She would not look at him. "It's a routine mission."

"Wild hordi?"

"Some. They are not a threat."

"How many?"

"Officially there are only a couple of thousand of them in the whole world."

"I don't want the official line." He grabbed her arm roughly. "I want the truth."

"Most of them are unarmed and afraid of us." She wrenched away from him. "I suppose that there may be tens, even hundreds of thousands of them, but they are not dangerous, save to cowards who are afraid of the child's tale that they eat humans."

"And monsters?"

"Who has been talking to you?" she glared at him contemptuously. "A few harmless mutants."

"Armed?"

"A couple of old-fashioned weapons."

"Zylongi?"

"You have no right to question me, Poet O'Neill. I will protect you. Let go of my arm. I thought I made it clear that I found physical contact with you distasteful."

"That's a new song."

"Very well, there are some exiles out there and some descendants of earlier civilizations. I do not discuss such matters. Now if you'll excuse me?"

"After you tell me who Narth is."

"He does not exist." She turned on her heels and strode away.

All of it, Seamus told himself that night in the desert, while he tried to guard the camp, *was lies. She had lied to me and did not even bother to hide the fact that she was lying.*

Lulled by the images of two beautiful women, O'Neill dropped off to sleep in a small ravine on the hillside. Something like an alarm bell sounded in his head. He woke with a start and threw the illumination grenade. The scene that was revealed in the split second before he began to fire the carbine was like a stop-action film. The hordi band and their Zylongi allies were caught just after the moment of attack.

The startled aborigines, clicking and grunting in terrifying rhythms, raced toward the camp, waving long, deadly spears as they charged. Behind them rumbled huge hairy creatures, bent, misshapen, terrible, with big flat broadswords. The monsters moved slowly but they were so large that one blow could wipe out three or four Zylongi kids.

Behind them came the cavalry, smartly uniformed soldiers on excellent horses carrying long, heavy lances, right out of one of the very old films about the West from the Earth film museum.

What the hell are these troopers doing out here? The woman didn't tell me a bit of truth.

Exploding light and O'Neill's rifle fire surprised the attackers. The lancers turned tail immediately—under orders, no doubt, to avoid organized conflict.

The hordi raced into the fringes of the camp, where they were met by a devastating volley of carbine fire.

I woke them up, O'Neill thought grimly. In the nick of time. He tossed another illumination grenade and continued to fire into the ranks of the attacking warriors. He was sympathetic to their cause, but such attacks would not bring peace to Zylong. Besides, somehow, the troops in the camp were *his*, almost as much as was his squadron of Wild Geese. Disoriented into panic by the flaring lights and the unexpected resistance, the hordi fled, leaving their taller and more frightening allies to withdraw in slightly better order, carrying off armloads of equipment from the camp. The carbines of the camp were silent.

"Carbines!" exclaimed O'Neill in despair. "The fools are letting them get away with the guns!" He ran down the slope toward the camp. By now the light from the grenade was gone. The camp was in a shambles. Soldiers were milling about in panic. Retha, her cloak ripped to shreds, was crumpled up on the desert floor by the tent she shared with Marjetta, sobbing hysterically. Sergeant Markos was holding onto his bloody arm, swearing with greater skill than O'Neill would have expected from a Zylongi, even a Zylongi noncom.

He shook the man. "Where's Pojoon?"

"Dead," grimaced the Sergeant, obviously in great pain.

"Marjetta?"

"They've got her."

"You must have shot the one who had me," sobbed the hysterical Cadet.

"We're finished," moaned the Sergeant. "Destroyed. They got every gun but mine."

"What will they do to Marjetta?" O'Neill hardly dared to ask it.

"They'll cook her. What else do you think hordi do with captives? They're cannibals." Sergeant Markos was desperate with pain and anger.

Retha's wails reached a nightmare pitch. It had been a stupid mission from the beginning. Now O'Neill had to deal with a wounded Sergeant and a hysterical junior officer. He picked Retha off the ground and clobbered her.

"Look, you little coward, you had better forget that you're not qualified to command, or none of us will ever get back to the City alive. You're the commanding officer of this unit now. If you don't have the kind of defense perimeter you read about in the textbook when I come back, I'll personally boil you slowly in oil!"

He then dumped her on the ground. Much to his surprise he heard her barking orders in her tiny voice behind him as he started up the hill. *Poor kid. How do you arrange a defense perimeter when all you have to fight with are carbines and some discarded spears?*

O'Neill did not use his light as he stumbled up the steep barren hills. He trusted to his dubious psychic instinct to discover where in the vast night

Marjetta was being held. Just when he needed it, of course, this sensitivity stopped functioning.

After hours of desperate searching and uncounted curses aimed at the Lady Cardinal, he collapsed, cold, tired, and discouraged. He had climbed well into the foothills now and found no trace of hordi or their companions, those big ugly hairy monsters he had glimpsed in the glare of the illumination grenade.

Marjetta is gone. I'd better give up and go back. Why did she, a competent officer destined for responsibility, come on this expedition? O'Neill shook his head. *Did she know that her chances to survive this trip were nil? Did she seek such an end?*

Probably. She sounded like she valued neither herself nor her life that evening in the room, almost as though she didn't care whether I raped her or not. Perhaps the woman didn't want to live.

He sighed. *And she was still the proper woman.*

People die on pilgrimage. You mourn them. You remember them. And you go on. Someday you'll meet them again and have a drink and laugh over it all— Seamus was not one of those who thought that the drink or laughter would be excluded from the kingdom of heaven.

He said a prayer for her and asked her to forgive him for giving up. He was a soldier and he had his duty—*Even if those idjits on* Iona *have forgotten about me.*

As he started down the depression reaching back toward the ridge that pointed to camp, O'Neill stopped for a moment and looked along the slight valley. For a fleeting moment he thought he saw a light flicker. A camp fire?

He eased himself back up on the ridge. Careful not to dislodge any loose rock, he crept along the top. At the end of it, where it linked to the next ridge, the valley below deepened into a steep ravine. At the bottom was the mouth of a cave obscured by a rock at one side.

Gingerly O'Neill slipped down into the ravine. Edging around the rock and peering into the eerily lit cave, O'Neill saw two naked hordi women tending a fire. A male was using a crude stone knife to prepare a spit. Outlined against the wall were a number of childish heads. At first, no sign of Marjetta. *I could wipe out the whole bunch of them, but that wouldn't bring her back. Besides, I don't know if they're the ones who attacked us.*

Then he saw her. At the back end of the cave, stripped, bound and gagged, and suspended from a rock outcropping, like a slaughtered steer. *Is she still alive? They haven't skinned her, have they? Well, there's only one way to find out.* The hordi were babbling away softly to one another, expecting, no doubt, a very succulent meal. He could smell the hot coals on their camp fire.

If he fired into the cave he could easily kill Marjetta with a ricocheting bullet. He reached for the knife that was a souvenir from the monorail incident and reversed the carbine to make it a club.

I kind of outweigh them all, if I don't exactly outnumber them. Taking a deep breath and mumbling a short prayer, he plunged into the cave, screaming like an angry and injured banshee.

The hordi were terrified at the sight of a red-bearded giant. Two quick shoves with the rifle butt and the females were cowering against the wall, their bodies protecting the children. The male hordi was braver; he turned toward O'Neill with the stone knife in his hand. O'Neill felt a moment of sympathy with the little creature; he stood his ground in defense of his home, family, and provisions. One fast swing of the rifle knocked the stone from the hordi's hand; a solid poke with the right fist and Marjetta's captor was out of action for a couple of hours.

He slashed the coarse rope that attached her to the rock, tossed her over his shoulder, grabbed a carbine and a heavy sack that lay on the floor, and left the cave. Marjetta was conscious. Her struggling body impeded his progress as he ran through the ravine and up to the ridge, stumbling and staggering as he went. Her muffled shrieks suggested that she might want to say something; so, at a safe distance from the cave, O'Neill paused long enough to pull the gag from her mouth.

"Put me down you fool. Untie me!" she ordered. "Where have you been? Why did it take so long for you to find me?"

"Well, that's gratitude for you." In exasperation he dumped her rudely to the ground. "We don't have time to stop. They'll follow us or raise the alarm and get the whole tribe down on us."

"They will not, you idiot. I know what the

she-demons were screaming. They think you are some great red god. It will be days before they dare leave the cave. We can go much more quickly if you are not carrying me."

Then softly she added, "You need not feel obliged to tell me about the Captain. I saw him as they were dragging me out of the camp."

Should I offer sympathy or congratulations? O'Neill wondered.

She stumbled on, her voice wavering, "He was a good man, O'Neill. He . . . he deserved better than me."

Not knowing what to say, O'Neill coldly suggested they climb the next ridge. From higher ground they could get a view of the desert in the now gray night just before dawn. Silently Marjetta stumbled up the slope behind him on legs stiff from the lack of circulation.

At the top they could see the lower hills leading to the desert. O'Neill pointed silently toward where he thought the camp was. Marjetta nodded.

"But, O'Neill, what is that light behind us?"

He turned and saw a glow rising from the other side of the ridge, perhaps two hundred yards away. They picked their way cautiously through the boulders around a great rock to peer into the next valley. Marjetta clutched his arm.

The valley before them was a wide circular hollow more than a mile in diameter, reaching deep into the earth. Almost every inch of the hollow was occupied by a tent city, illuminated by many glittering camp fires. Though most of the occupants were apparently asleep, O'Neill and Marjetta could see occasional armed bands of hordi and Zylongi patrolling the perimeters. This was a serious military position, commanded by tough-minded professionals. In the center was a compound of larger tents. Here a large armed guard was posted, their spears angled away from their bodies ready for action. O'Neill estimated that there must be at least seven thousand warriors, maybe ten thousand.

Later, preoccupied about other problems, he would forget the existence of this army, not that when they finally intervened there was much he could have done about them.

Marjetta leaned against a large rock. "Narth's camp," she murmured, "not more than a day's march from the cultivated regions. Only three days from the City itself."

Although it was hardly the place for a lesson in Zylongian history, nevertheless O'Neill announced bluntly that he would not take one more step until he knew exactly what was going on.

10

"I am unclad," Marjetta protested.

"That is unfortunate, but it's dark, and just now I'm not interested in your body, as admirable as it may be and as delightful as arguably it could be under other circumstances." That should put her down. "Right now all I want is the truth. And if I don't get the truth, all the easier to put you over my knee and give you the spanking you've been asking for since . . ."

"Since I saw you kissing the Research Director." The woman actually had the audacity to laugh at his threat. "Very well, I will tell you what I know. I warn you, however, there is much that I don't know. Even the highest officers cannot be aware that Narth is so near."

"Talk," Seamus ordered.

So she talked, concisely, lucidly, like the good soldier she was. Seamus was almost prepared to forgive her for her ingratitude.

The Zylongi, it seemed, had various ways of

dealing with those who threatened to disrupt their civilization. Some "went to the god" at the Festival —those who were defective, mentally ill, or too old. Others—those considered socially disruptive— disappeared into the acid vats. Some were too important or too well known to suffer either fate. They were publicly thrust out of the City in a solemn ceremony. They were what Sammy and Ernie had called "no longer with us." Those who didn't die in the desert or the jungle survived in small communities that struggled to exist off tiny patches of cultivable ground and an occasional meat hunt.

The hairy creatures O'Neill saw during the attack on their camp were mutants, the result of mistakes in the computer-programmed genetic manipulations. They were exposed to die outside in the cultivated areas. The hordi, however, considered these deformed creatures to be sacred and saved as many as they could, producing another race of humanoid type on the planet. They were smarter and stronger than the hordi but intensely loyal to their foster parents.

The wild hordi, once considered numerically depleted to the point of extinction, seemed to be regenerating. They hated the City folk and killed them whenever possible, then ate their flesh in the hope of absorbing their strength.

"A fate from which you bravely saved me."

"Uhm. Keep talking."

The hordi preferred the wetter, hotter, and lush regions on the other side of the mountains and existed in uneasy truce with the exiled Zylongi, who lived on the side of the mountain facing the desert. Both groups sometimes combined to make forays into the desert to raid ore trains, though they never crossed the banks of the River.

Five years ago, Marjetta told him, a brilliant Zylongi General was sent into exile for plotting revolution. "He was one of my teachers, a demented man, but one with a vision that many of us found attractive. He wanted to clean away the Committees and make himself Emperor. Then he would restore all the old freedoms."

"You want an Emperor?"

There was silence in the darkness opposite him. Then a tentative answer. "I don't expect to live long enough for it to matter, but no, an emperor, especially one like Narth, would merely exchange one form of tyranny for another. I want freedom."

Do you now? So after all these years, people down here know what it is. I hope you're listening up there, Lady Deirdre, and admiring my taste in women at that.

Aloud he said, "Keep talking."

Narth was not docile at his exile ceremony, but threatened to come back and destroy the City. Since he had left, it was rumored that he had rallied the three outcast groups under his single command. The existence of such a union (indeed the existence of the groups themselves) was officially denied. Most Zylongi went about their daily lives convinced that the legends about Narth's "em-

186

pire" were not to be taken seriously. Thus, poor
Dr. Samaritha kept trying to breed more domestic
hordi in the quaint conviction that the savage variety was virtually extinct.

"Does the Committee know that Narth's army
is this close to the City?" O'Neill asked, trying to
absorb all the startling new information.

"Of course they know it. You do not think
those sensors at the departure point would miss
such a mass of people? That is why they sent us on
this expedition. They knew that Narth would go
after our carbines. They expected we would all be
killed."

"They were after me?" He leaned against the
rock too.

"Surely a man of even your meager intelligence must have perceived that they were after
me. There is a lot of unrest in my generation. You
saw Horor and Carina. Well, there are hundreds
like them. The Committee knows I have not joined
them. Not yet.

"The Committee also knows that if I overcome
my hesitation, I might be a dangerous rebel. So I
had to die—and Pojoon, and Retha, and you and
the rest as well. They were just as happy to get rid
of you, too, but could have done that much more
easily. Since I do not care about life, I came. They
may even have sent word to Narth about the opportunity. What are a few carbines in exchange for
one potential revolutionary leader whose family
background protects her as long as she is in the

City?" There was no bitterness in her voice, rather she spoke with something close to despair.

"You're risking the back of me hand, woman, with those comments on my intelligence. But tell me now, if Narth can never hope to capture the City, why does he come so close?"

How did I ever get mixed up in this mess? Get me out of here. This isn't our war. Of course bring the woman with me, we'll give her more freedom than she ever dreamed of, too much freedom altogether.

"Perhaps he thinks that during the time of the Festival the laser weapon controls in the Energy Center will be immobilized. They are the only serious defense we have against all the Outsiders, not that I am confident they would work if we were forced to use them. I know you didn't see them; no one except the fools who command the army are supposed to see them. They are buried behind the wall and are supposed to break through the ground and begin firing at the touch of a button."

"And you've never seen them tested."

"Only pictures. They appear to be devastating. The Outsiders fear them greatly. However, the Festivals have become much wilder in the last few years. Maybe the Hooded Ones are in league with Narth; they could destroy the lasers. Narth must have the Committee very worried. I do not blame them; he is a fierce and terrible man." Marjetta shivered.

"He'd be after wanting you?"

"He would."

"Well, he's not going to get you, do you understand that, woman?"

"I'm much more afraid of you than of him."

Now what does that mean? It doesn't sound like a nasty crack. " 'Tis a wise and prudent attitude."

O'Neill considered. His war was not with Narth or with Zylong. He was a spy for the *Iona*, which he hoped was still orbiting around up there planning emergency procedures to extricate him and Marjetta from this sinister planet. His first and principal loyalty was to his regiment and the pilgrimage.

Marjetta interrupted his thoughts, clutching at his arm again. "O'Neill, look! A raiding party."

He could see in the increasing light a group of six big, grotesque, hair-covered monsters moving single file along the ridge. They were laden with guns and coming right toward them. "Our carbines," he said, flipping the safety switch on his own. "Does the silencer impede the efficiency of these relics?"

"Not at the range we are going to be shooting," she replied tersely.

"I'll start at the back, you take the front. Shoot fast. Those creatures seem to react slowly, but we can't take any chances. When I say shoot, you'd better do it or those young troopers will be dead before another sunrise. Retha will be a tasty morsel for some hordi."

She shot, all right. Her bullets were as accurate as O'Neill's. The monsters died quietly. *Poor things*, O'Neill thought compassionately. *I don't*

*like killing you. I'll buy the drinks when we meet
further on. Well, the first round anyway.*

They quickly collected the carbines and climbed
back across the hills toward the camp. When they
arrived at the last low ridge just above the Zylongi
camp, Marjetta whistled. There was a faint response. "It is all right," she whispered in his ear.
"Retha knows it is I."

The young soldiers, grimly holding their spears,
were deployed behind a small rise of rocks above
the camp. The Sergeant was patched up but still
looked badly battered. Retha was cool, competent.
As soon as she saw the two of them appear in the
early light of dawn, she rushed forward to throw a
cloak around Marjetta's bare shoulders (at which
O'Neill had resolutely refused to look, to say nothing of looking at the rest of her—well, maybe a
wee glance) and take the heavy sack of carbines
out of her arms.

The troops were ready for battle, and though
they could never have lasted long against any kind
of effective attack, they looked like they would
give a good account of themselves. Retha's disciplined air wavered for a moment when it looked
like she would hug her commander. "It is good
that you are back, Honored Lieutenant."

"It is not unpleasant to be back," Marjetta
responded with equal formality.

"And not me?" O'Neill demanded.

Retha turned away, flustered and ashamed.
"Of course, Honored Poet who saves everyone. What
would we do without you?"

"Well, at least someone around here shows gratitude."

Damn inhuman people.

Forgetting that he was supposed to know nothing about military matters, O'Neill suggested that the now rearmed Zylongi troopers deploy themselves on the low hill. With fires burning at the campsite, they would be able to trap the next raiding party before it knew what hit them.

Marjetta fixed him with a long, inscrutable stare, then nodded. "Those are excellent tactics, *Poet* O'Neill."

At high noon Narth sent a good-sized unit to wipe them out—a troop of monsters mounted on horses and a company of hordi armed with spears. The cavalry was inept. They allowed their mounts to bolt at the first volley, leaving the hordi at the mercy of the Zylongis' concentrated fire. At the end, thirty to forty dead and dying hordi lay inside the encampment with not a single Zylongi trooper wounded.

Narth himself appeared on the ridge just out of carbine range. He was clad in a flaming crimson robe, surrounded by a crowd of horsemen. O'Neill bet they were the pick of the exiled families—Narth's Imperial Guard.

There was a wide space of open ridge between him and the Zylongi troopers, who were now exhausted and let down after their success. A classic cavalry charge would have cut up the Zylongi. O'Neill could see Narth's fist raised in defiant fury and imagined the contorted face beneath his full black beard. Unwilling to risk further losses, the Emperor Narth turned and rode off down the ridge into the light of the risen sun.

Chicken, thought O'Neill contemptuously. *No match for the Wild Geese.*

Acting very much like a commanding officer, O'Neill called Retha, Marjetta, and Sergeant Markos into conference. "Margie," he began briskly, giving up all attempts at Zylongi formality, "you told me last night that the hordi don't venture into the desert. Are they afraid of it?"

She nodded.

O'Neill continued. "Our only chance is to run for Hyperion . . . to try to get back to the departure point will bring us much closer to the mountains, where they might be able to give us a taste of our own ambush medicine. We have to change our route, head directly for the ocean, and then follow its shore around to the fort. It'll be longer that way, but we'll only have to watch one flank. The hordi won't come that far out into the desert. If our friend Narth comes after us with his pony soldiers, we'll be able to see him coming." He turned to Marjetta. "How long before we reach the fort?"

"Two days on horseback," said Marjetta.

"We have no horses," said Retha, timidly.

"So we'll have to walk. That should double the time. Add two more days for safety and we have six days, right?" All nodded except Marjetta, who sat very still and looked at him suspiciously. O'Neill knew he was causing warning lights to go on in her head. The woman was no fool. Not at all, at all.

"Pack enough food and water," he continued, "for just six days, and enough ammunition for two long firefights. Destroy everything else. If there's any room for more in our packs, make it water. We should be moving in two hours." O'Neill stood up. The others sat for a moment confused, not knowing whether to obey his commands or to defer to Marjetta, their commanding officer.

Marjetta repeated, "We move in two hours, as Captain O'Neill suggests."

Major if it comes to it. Aloud he said softly, "Thanks for the promotion, Margie, but Poet O'Neill will do."

She looked like she didn't believe a word of it.

That night, when the camp had settled down except for the alert watchers Marjetta had stationed on the high ground, O'Neill was stirred from a deep sleep by a most unpleasant sensation. The long march through the desert had exhausted him. A man had a right to his sleep, damn it. He ignored the unpleasantness—until he heard a voice saying coldly, "Wake up, O'Neill, or I will kill you in your sleep."

It was enough to wake a man, all right. He tentatively opened one eye. Marjetta's cold, angry face was outlined in the glow of the portable light that hung from the tent pole. Her carbine prodded his stomach.

"Musha, woman, a man needs his sleep. Put that thing away. We'll worry about whatever's on your mind in the morning." He closed his eyes and rolled over.

"Oh no, we will not. You are going to tell me the truth now or I will kill you," she told him, sternly. "I do not like to kill, but I have done enough of it today not to mind one more."

The girl meant it. Seamus stirred himself to full consciousness, looked at the long steady line of the gun barrel and muttered, "Woman, you've taken leave of your senses."

"You told me when we first met that you were not a soldier, only a wandering poet. From the moment you came into the MC you acted like a soldier, you kept a soldier's lookout at the camp last night, you organized a soldier's ambush this morning, you laid out a marching plan that only a soldier could have thought of. An experienced and able soldier at that."

Oh, Lord, is she mad! "Well, now, that's a mighty conclusion you've jumped to," he tried to get her off the track with an argument, "if you take my meaning."

"You are wasting my time, O'Neill. You do not have much of your own left. What are you doing here? Why did you lie to me? To Samaritha and Ornigon? I want the truth this time." She jabbed him again with the carbine barrel.

He rubbed the sleep out of his eyes. There were so many better things to be doing with a proper young woman like her at this time of the night.

"I didn't want to tell you that I had been an officer because then I would have had to explain why I wasn't one anymore. I guess I was afraid that you would feel contempt for me. I didn't want you to know I was cashiered." *I'll appeal to her sense of compassion, that's what I'll do, though I haven't noticed her having much of it.*

"Why were you cashiered?" she barked at him. *No compassion there.*

The next question would be why the original mind probe at the Body Institute had not found out about this supposed disgrace. He answered the unspoken question first to throw her off stride. "I don't know why your mind probe didn't pick it up. Maybe because on Tara when they throw you out of the officer corps, they deprogram you. You remember some of your training but you forget your career completely." The gun went down a fraction of an inch. *Good, I've got her curious.* "It had something to do with the safety of my men. Friends tell me that it was a political thing, that the trial was rigged. There was nothing I could do about it. I was a Commandant, by the way. A Major."

Well, a man was entitled to a little vanity, wasn't he?

Sure you just want to impress her.

And why not?

"Do you work for the Committee?" The muzzle of the gun was back in his stomach.

O'Neill was stunned. "Glory be to God, why should I work for those Amadons?"

195

"The Hooded Ones?" she persisted. "The anarchist hooligans?"

"Didn't Sammy tell you about the fight on Zylongday?"

"Yes, a little," came the grudging response. "The Young Ones?"

"The who?"

"The student and military radicals—Horor, Carina, Yens, and others. You seemed friendly with Horor."

"Not all that friendly," protested O'Neill. "I never felt overwhelmed with his friendliness toward me. Who's Yens?"

"Retha's programmed mate. He is one of the Council of the Young Ones."

"Do I look like someone who would get mixed up with a bunch of half-baked kids?" He tried to sound angry and in the process he found himself getting very angry indeed. *The damn bitch.*

"The Fourth Secretary—he is the Committee for all practical purposes—is very much afraid of them. They are the Technicians who will administer the City in a few years."

"I don't care what that gombeen man fears. I'm not involved in any of your nonsense."

"So you are not part of any of them?" The carbine was almost in a position where he might survive the first shot.

"I hate to mention it, but I did save you from the hordi supper table last night—a fact that seems to have escaped Your Ladyship's attention."

"That could have been part of the plot," she responded stubbornly.

To hell with it. "Okay, Margie, me girl, maybe it is all a plot. You're either going to shoot me or not. Decide for yourself. If you think you're going to be able to bring these kids of yours down to Hyperion with just the help of a banged-up old noncom and a kid who should be in the classroom, you're crazy. Maybe you don't want to trust me; I don't care much, but you've got to trust someone. I'm the only one around who can be of much help. Now get out of my tent unless you have foul designs on my body—in which case, welcome. I need some sleep." He rolled over, moderately confident that she wouldn't shoot.

"O'Neill . . . ?" Her voice came plaintively from the entrance of the tent.

"What now?" he demanded impatiently. *Got her!*

"I am thankful to you for rescuing me from the . . . uh . . . supper table."

"Well, praise be to Brigid, Brendan, Patrick, and Columcile, it only took twenty-four hours to get it out of your mouth."

"May all those wonderful friends of your god be with this tent."

Well, now wasn't that nice.

And so poor Retha's on this crazy adventure because she's a dangerous revolutionary. I've seen more dangerous firebrands in the nursery on the Iona.

It was long after dark on the next day when

they crossed the line of dunes that separated beach from desert. The ocean water looked inviting, serene blue, topped by great white rolling surf. But it was bitter cold, so there was no refreshment there. O'Neill contemplated what lay before them. It was still a long walk to Hyperion. All they had to fear was the Committee, Narth, the Young Ones, the Hooded Ones, the hordi. How many other dangers were there that no one had seen fit to tell him about? Margie said the commander of the fort was a man of the highest integrity who would have nothing to do with an overt Committee plot. Maybe there would be respite there. Even if they made it, they were bound to return to the City. O'Neill yearned for just one small gunship, the *Tom Doherty* perhaps, a speedy and powerful craft, to help blast this whole planet into shape.

Deirdre, My Lady, how did you get me into this? . . . There's no answer. There never is. You've forgotten about me altogether.

The next morning he was in deeper than ever. Margie came up to him as they were breaking camp. "Come down to the shore with me," she said briskly.

"Ah, now, that's an invitation no man in his right mind would refuse."

"You were truly a Major on Tara?" she asked bluntly.

"Hmmm?" He tossed a clump of sand into the surf.

"I mean before you were cashiered. Or were you lying about that too?"

He had nothing against telling the truth when he could afford it. "Like I said, I was a Commandant. A Major. And," he added irritably, "I don't care, my bitchy friend, whether you believe me or not."

"I do not think I want to ask what a bitch is. How old are you?"

"Let me see, twenty-five of our years, that makes about thirty of your years."

"That makes you five of our years older than I am."

"Too much older?" he demanded.

"Oh, not at all—" *Was that a faint smile?* "—but isn't that very young for such a rank?"

"Customs are different," he said shortly.

"But still . . ."

"All right, have it your way. Yes, it was very young. The thought seemed to be that I was a very good soldier."

All of which was true enough, but it was poet he was meant to be.

"That's beyond a doubt." She nodded her head approvingly. "You are obviously a more experienced commander than I am. If you rose to such a rank so young, a much better one. I am going to trust you—as you said, I have no choice. You must be in charge. And one more thing, Major O'Neill . . ."

"Ah, musha, you'll find me a very democratic CO. You can call me Jimmy."

Tight-lipped, hands on her hips, she ignored his offer of friendship. "I am technically a widow now, even though Pojoon was only my intended

199

mate. I do not have to seek another; I do not intend to do so for a long time—perhaps never. I will not accept any suggestions in that direction. Do I make myself clear?" Her pretty face was hard, her brown eyes stern.

"What makes you think I'd even be interested?" he demanded.

She smiled faintly again. "That's right, I'm a bitch. I presume that in your world men don't mate with bitches."

She turned on her heel and strode back toward the camp.

"Well, as to that, it all depends," Seamus shouted after her.

She did not waver. *Ah, and the woman does have a lovely ass on her, doesn't she? Sure there's a lot better things to do with it than spank it. The threat will be enough.*

He then reprimanded himself for having such thoughts about a fellow officer in time of battle. The thoughts did not leave him however. Not at all, at all.

Giving him the command changed her attitude. Later that day she relaxed and smiled, and by the second day was joking with the troops, making them laugh. With him, however, she was deadly serious. *That's fine with me, woman. I want no part of the likes of you, wonderful ass and lovely legs and all.*

Well, not just now anyway.

Her good humor sustained the flagging morale of the sand-beaten, wind-stung, and heat-baked troops as they struggled along, falling more and more behind schedule. O'Neill ordered first half and then quarter rations of food and water.

They would never make it if they continued to march during the daylight hours when the sun scorched them and increased their thirst. O'Neill decided the troops should rest during the day and march at night, a decision that slowed the march still more. Some nights there were no moons to show them their way through the thick sand and rolling dunes. (But they were less visible to possible pursuers. Once, from the vantage point of a high dune, O'Neill thought he saw dust in the distance. A sandstorm? Narth's cavalry?)

Another torture was the sandstorms that struck without warning, forcing them to seek shelter in the lee of the dunes until they were over. Fortunately, they occurred during the day and seldom delayed a march. Seamus wondered how many of the carbines still worked.

On the seventh day, Marjetta and Seamus huddled together at the side of a great dune, hoods pulled down over their faces to protect them from the sting of wind-whipped sand.

"Tonight should be the last of it," he shouted over the wind.

Marjetta moved her hooded head so that their two cowls formed a tunnel. "It will if your calculations are right. Otherwise we'll be wondering where our next drink of water will come from." She was laughing at him. Maybe even with him. Her trust in his expertise was total.

He decided not to remind her that they had already marched beyond his calculations. Arrival time tomorrow was at the extreme of calculation, just before panic took over. He spread his robe over both of them so they could talk more easily. "Should I carry Retha in? I'm afraid the kid's feet are so bad she may not make it on her own."

"You told her back at the first camp that she was a bad soldier. She is determined to prove you wrong. She is one of those poor, foolish women, Seamus O'Neill, who feels a need to impress you."

"Well, 'tis a good thing you're not that way. Sure it might go to my head." Impulsively he put his arms around her. She did not try to fend him off.

Seamus kissed the sand-caked, weary face ineptly at first, then hungrily as his own weary mind let go in the face of urgent and long-suppressed emotion. He felt a surge of response in her, her breasts pressed against his chest. A flame leapt from his heart to hers and back again. With the flame came a strange dread. She turned her head quickly away.

"O'Neill, you are incorrigible. Kissing in a sandstorm." Her voice was severe but shaky. "I am not, after all, a stony-hearted bitch, am I?"

"Well, there's a time and a place for everything, like my grandmother used to say. As for the stony-hearted bitch, the adjective is yours. I'll reserve judgment on the rest." (Seamus never knew his grandmother, but that didn't make any difference.) He kissed her again. Gently she pushed him away.

"You're a good man, Seamus O'Neill, even better than you know yourself. Not many good men try to appear outrageous like you do. You are kind, gentle, and loyal; you would not hurt the smallest insect except in self-defense. I may never see you again after this mission is over, so I will say that I am glad my life had you in it for a time." Touching his lips with an affectionate finger, she slipped out from under his robe and ran back to the main body of troops.

Now does that mean I can have her if I want her?

He was fearful that it might.

He spent a dazed few hours when the march resumed at nightfall contemplating the afternoon's major event. *You heard her, I hope, Deirdre. I told you all along that you folks never really appreciated all my sterling qualities. Ah, but it's a good thing that we will get to Fort Hyperion before dawn tomorrow. Heaven only knows what that young woman will do for an encore.*

And thus, O'Neill walked through a long night, the last hours with the weight of the sleeping Retha in his arms. She had finally collapsed, her feet bleeding, her waiflike body dropping with exhaustion.

He picked her up. She seemed like a baby in his massive arms, a baby however with very pretty little breasts. *Yens, or whatever the hell the little idiot is called, has got himself a good woman.*

"I can walk," she protested weakly.

"You'll follow orders if you know what is good for you," he said gruffly. "Besides I want to walk into the fort tomorrow with a beautiful woman in my arms, and herself is a little heavy if you take my meaning."

The young officer giggled happily and snuggled into his arms.

Shortly after dawn Major Seamus O'Neill led his battered, hungry, and thirsty expedition through the open gate of Fort Hyperion. Most of them collapsed as soon as they were inside the walls. He put the waiflike child with the bleeding feet on the ground, tenderly wrapping a cloak around her, and kissed her soundly.

"You're a good soldier and a superb woman," he whispered into her ear. She smiled at him through tears of self-satisfaction.

It's all your fault, Your Eminence, ma'am, if I fall in love with every woman on this planet.

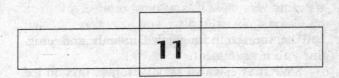

11

O'Neill pounded his fist with rage on the map table. "Damn!" The maps fell on the floor. Wearily he picked them up and rearranged them. Spread out before him was the map of Zylong with detailed drawings of the fort and its location. Hyperion was the perfect place to stay until the *Iona* crowd either landed themselves or gave him the signal to return. The food was good, quarters were comfortable, the garrison friendly; he saw Marjetta every day. What could be better?

The fort was at the end of a spit that jutted into the ocean at the very bottom of the continent. The ground inside was covered with a green, grasslike growth immune to the action of salt water and air. On one ocean side, large greenhouses enclosed flowering plants and acres of jarndt. A desalinating plant kept the fort and its produce well supplied with water. Hyperion could get along without the rest of Zylong very well.

Beyond the fort, on the opposite side, were the

metal mines that Hyperion was supposed to protect, staffed, O'Neill was told, mostly by some hordi.

"Slave labor," he had muttered.

"Who isn't in this sick world," his woman, standing very close to him now, replied.

" 'Tis a powerful place you have here," O'Neill had commented to the fort's Commander after his tour of the settlement.

"We may have to survive for a time on our own." Quars, the genial Commander, a handsome man in his middle forties with a big chest and a trim waist, waved his hands in a gesture of indifference. "As a man of your cultivation and experience must have perceived, the City is on the edge of anarchy."

"Indeed," Seamus murmured. Quars was a lot like Carmody, playing the bluff-soldier role, but shrewd and well educated.

"Whoever wins up there, and I hope it is someone more competent than the superannuated ninnies who are now in charge, will need this post. Our minerals are essential. They will, if it comes to it, have to deal with us on our terms."

"So that's why a man of your experience and intelligence accepted assignment here at this distant command?" If it came to flattery, Seamus was as good as the best of them.

"With relief. I did all I could to get it." He filled Seamus's la-ir goblet. "I had no desire to follow in Narth's footsteps."

"They would have thrown you out?" Seamus sipped the drink contentedly. A proper woman and a proper bottle, what more did a man want in the world? Especially when, for all practical purposes, the TPS *Iona* no longer existed.

"I wasn't going to take the chance." The man's deep laughter boomed as he drained his goblet and refilled it. "Besides, I don't want to be an emperor. It would be a very short life."

"You may have to contend with him anyway." Seamus drained his goblet too. No heathen would drink him under the table.

"Only if he could capture this post, which he could never do." Quars waved his hands proudly. "No one could capture it."

"And when would you be after expecting this revolution?" Seamus was becoming a wee bit dizzy, but he was in better control than the Commander.

"The next Festival might be the time." He sighed negligently. "The frenzy is worse each year. Fortunately we are unaffected by it down here. Even if we didn't have . . ."

Quars's voice trailed off. Drunk or not, there were some secrets, probably the most important ones, the ones that Seamus most needed to know if *Iona* was ever to rediscover him, that Quars was not going to spill to the friendly alien visitor.

"What causes the frenzy?" Seamus tried to make the question sound casual.

Quars refilled Seamus's goblet with the lovely pink liquid, so much like ice cream with a kick to it. Seamus thought he could see a woman's image in it. *Margie, of course. Lovely woman, even if a bit too pushy. Ah, no, it couldn't be the Lady Cardinal?*

Sure what would she be doing, lurking in a man's drink?

"I think it's obvious, just what a man of your sophistication would expect it to be, a massive and dangerous allergic reaction. The fools developed a new strain of jarndt some years ago. It was supposed to produce much greater harvests on the same acreage of land. As if we didn't have enough of the stuff already. The Festivals were wild enough anyway. At first no one noticed that they became much wilder. Then we made ourselves so heavily dependent on the new strain of crop that there was fear of changing back. My theory is that with each succeeding year the population becomes more sensitive to whatever gets into the air at harvest time."

"An interesting theory."

"It's more than theory, man. We don't have the new strain of jarndt here and we don't have the frenzy either. Is that not the next thing to a controlled experiment?"

"Ah, 'tis. And you don't celebrate the Festival down here the way they do up in the City?"

The Commander swayed. "You mean the orgy? I put an end to that as soon as I came. Nonsense. The women hated it. Not while I'm Commander. One of the reasons they need us up there," he chuckled complacently, "is that we supply them with the antidote."

"Do you now?"

"We do. And keep a supply here, just in case the need arises, interesting chemical compound, the molecules of our little pills blend ... but I won't bore you with it...." And the poor man passed out.

Seamus stood up uncertainly. *Ah, 'twas a grand evening altogether.*

"You two are worse than two adolescent boys," Quars's lovely wife appeared on schedule. "Drinking and bragging and trying to impress one another."

She arranged her husband's body on the couch, more amused than angry at their antics.

Sure if she were mine, I wouldn't want anyone else pawing her. Not at all, at all. If I had a proper woman ... musha, I do have a proper woman; the only trouble is that just now I can't remember her name. And I think she's trying to give herself to me and I'm not sure I want her just yet.

"Sure himself is a grand man," Seamus eased toward the door with artificial steadiness. "But he's not the drinker I am. Wasn't I after drinking him under the table?"

"That's no great accomplishment. I can do it too." She smiled complacently. "Now you'd better get back to your Marjetta, before you're as unconscious as he is."

THAT is the woman's name.

"I don't sleep with the woman; mind you, she's a delicious morsel, but there's no reason to rush into anything."

"Yes." She sat on the couch and took her husband's head in her lap. "They say you don't sleep with her. You outworlders are a strange lot. We are supposed to practice celibacy and avoid it as much as we can. You don't have to be celibate, I gather, and yet you practice it. How do you explain that?"

There had to be something wrong with her logic, but Seamus's brain was not functioning all that well. Besides, marriage with a proper woman was a serious business, not something to rush into.

"Ah, we're all a little bit strange when it comes to sex, aren't we now?"

The woman considered him carefully. "I suppose so. . . . There, there my dear—" she patted her husband's skull "—you'll be all right in the morning. Well, in the afternoon."

Seamus beat a dignified retreat. To his own bed in the guest officer's room. Not to Margie's.

So, all in all, it's a good life. A lovely woman on the beach in the day—with all her clothes on, mind you, none of this heathen nude swimming—and good drink at night. What more could a man want?

There were problems, of course, but they were his fault, not the fort's. Margie was the most serious of them. From contempt for O'Neill she had turned to worship. Now that would have been fine, he supposed, but like a lot of other women in his life, she seemed to think that worship gave her the right to be amused at him. So now the woman laughed at him whenever they were together, even when he was not trying to be funny, which was most of the time.

"Yes, Geemie, I want to live now." Noisy laughter. "Yes, I've changed my mind. Is that not per-

mitted?" Great hilarity. "Are you responsible?"
More raucous sounds. "Well, who else would be?"

*You kiss a woman a few times in the middle of
the desert and she thinks she's as good as married
you.*

*She was still certainly the proper woman for my
life, but there was no reason for rushing, now was
there?*

*Scared of the woman? Me, Seamus Finnbar
O'Neill?*

Yes, YOU.

Well, she is quite a handful, isn't she?

See what I mean!

Furthermore, as though that delicious handful
of woman was not enough to have on his mind,
there was the problem of his troops.

The struggles on the desert had made them
"his," not quite like his platoon of Wild Geese
perhaps, but still a brave band of young warriors
for whom he was personally responsible. Yet they
were up to something, and that pretty little child
Retha was up to her lovely neck in scheming. They
hadn't told him about their plots, which was bad
enough, and they were probably going to inform
him soon, which was worse.

Still, both Margie and the troops were tolera-
ble problems, even enjoyable if you wanted to push
the point. At least he had people about whom to
be concerned again, people that unaccountably
seemed even to love him, one way or another.

*Ah, 'tis the way that's the problem, don't you
see? The woman wants to get me into bed and the*

*troops want to get me into a revolution. And all I am
is a simple poet and an occasional spy.*

*I could tolerate the uncertainty for a while longer.
Lounging on the most beautiful beach I've ever seen
with the most beautiful woman I've ever met eases
the pain of ambiguity. If you take my meaning . . .*

Just as Seamus was beginning to settle in and
get his thinking organized, the "Fourth Secretary"
appeared with his staff—to the ill-concealed cha-
grin of Quars. The staff were police types, obviously, despite their army uniforms. Quars's reaction
was one of frigid politeness. He wanted no part of
the Committee, but he had to deal with them as
long as they were the authority at the other end of
the continent. O'Neill wondered how he would
choose between Narth and the Secretary.

The point of the visit, O'Neill was informed by
the oily little gombeen man, was that the Committee had assigned him the great honor of "personally escorting the Honored Guest and the brave
Captain" (a promotion, O'Neill noticed) back to
the City after their "terrible ordeal." Lieutenant
Retha (another promotion) could lead the rest of
the troops back when they were fully recovered.

Quars didn't like the idea, not at all, at all.
But he knew an ultimatum when he heard one.
The Fourth Secretary was the first Zylongi for
whom O'Neill felt an intense dislike. The oily, genial man was a type the Tarans knew well—a
crooked, dishonest politician.

"What do you think?" Margie asked anxiously
as they looked out of the huge window of the Com-

mander's apartment and watched the blue-robed Secretary ride into the parade grounds accompanied by his forty heavily armed "staff."

O'Neill said, "I think they may have a hovercraft transport that is a little bit bigger than they're letting on. Those horses have come no more than a day's march."

"What do they want?"

"Us, probably."

So he was in the chart room trying to figure a way out. The alternatives were not attractive. Marjetta joined him at the map-littered table. Since the episode of intimacy he shared with her on the desert, he had adopted a playful attitude—patting whatever part of her anatomy presented itself, hugging and kissing her a couple of times a day, and leaving it at that. She did not seriously object, only routinely remonstrated, "Geemie, stop it." Then more of her laughter.

"Am I that funny?" he demanded.

"Yes, you are." And she laughed even more loudly.

On this occasion he swatted her delectable backside. After the "Stop it, Geemie" and some nearly hysterical giggles, she added, "One of our 'friends' is outside."

"Can't we go anywhere without them? Your Fourth Secretary is not my idea of a nice man," O'Neill said.

"It is said that he is the one who really runs the Committee." Marjetta shuddered. "I cannot stand the way he looks at me."

Seamus hadn't noticed that. *Look at my woman, will you? Well, we'll see about that.*

"Let's not give him time to look. Here, take a good look at this map." He pulled out a detailed map of the southern half of the continent. "Let me ask you something first. Are you sure you want to escape from these guys? It means you'll be outlawed. If they allow you to get back to the City, there might be a way for the condemnation to be neutralized by your friends in high places. But your chances of ever getting back to the City in the company of the Fourth Secretary and his henchmen are pretty remote. My way carries a lot of risk, probably more danger, and a slow death if it doesn't work."

"If it is your idea, Geemie, it will work."

I wish I had that much confidence. If only she didn't think that I was better than I really am.

"Look at the south," O'Neill whispered. "The continent tapers off to a point here at Fort Hyperion. The mountains are still high—you can see that snow-capped peak out the window of the Commander's office. There's a low pass that leads into the jungle just beyond the first set of foothills. The River flows north from close to where we are to the edge of the Zylong plateau, where it branches east at the Great Waterfall. We know the hordi won't cross the River even when it is narrow, as it is at this end. The jungle west of it, along the coast, should be clear of hordi all the way up."

"I see all these things, Geemie, but what are we supposed to do?"

"Sure, we'll be leaving here at sunset the day after tomorrow with the Fourth Secretary. By midnight we'll be about here, halfway to where I bet they've stored their large transport, just opposite the low pass. We'll take our leave of them and cut out for the mountains and the high jungle. It shouldn't take more than a day and a half or two days. We'll have to slog through a bit of hordi jungle to get across the River. I don't imagine Narth will have many of his hordi this far south; we can probably avoid the wild ones. Then we'll follow the River to the Great Lake, make some kind of raft and float across it up to the waterfall—you'll be one of the few Zylongi to see it. We'll manage to get down to the low jungle and across it to my spacecraft, then fix the radio so that we can broadcast to the City on enough frequencies so that the whole City knows we're out there. The Committee will have to bring us back heroes."

"Seamus O'Neill, you are mad," she said admiringly, her brown eyes shining.

"I've been told that, woman. The point is, will you do it?" he demanded.

"I will." She took his hand firmly and squeezed it.

Standing up, he took her other hand and drew her toward him. As their lips touched, she pulled away.

Now the woman is turning skittish on me. What's going on?

"Seamus, don't. Please." She meant it. Reluctantly he let her go. "Please, do not look so crestfallen. I did not mean to hurt your feelings. I like you very much—who would not? I will follow you to the end of this planet, but there can be nothing between us. I have made my decision. I must go back to the City and take command of the Young Ones. We have to save our people. I know they are not much, but they are eager to make things different. There are many more good ones, like Ornigon and Samaritha, who want new lives. They must be free. I do not want to lead. I have done my best to avoid it; now I have no choice. It is not your fight."

"Some people have made it my fight without asking me," he said hotly. "I've got nowhere else to go; I've got friends here—the only friends I've had for a long time. I'm staying."

What am I saying these things for? he asked himself. *They're all lies, except that I got caught up in a conflict I had tried to avoid. Sure the woman's turned my head altogether.*

"Do not say that just for me," she warned him stiffly.

"Woman, you're being an idjit. I'm not saying it just for you. I'm after telling you it's for Sammy and Ernie and Horor and the little girl those so-and-so's killed, and for Pojoon and Retha."

There was a long pause. "Are you sure?" she said softly.

"You'd try the patience of a saint, woman. Yes, I'm sure."

"I never thought you were a saint, Seamus O'Neill." She kissed him like no saint had ever been kissed. Her lips tasted much better than they had in the desert, her hair smelled like the jungle flowers. Her firm, young breasts were a torment to his body. He dug his fingers into the strong muscles of her buttocks.

Now might be the time to make her his own. Sure what was the point in waiting any longer? All right, the woman was a handful, but so what? Her breasts fit nicely into his hands too. She was much too strong, but Tarans liked strong women, didn't they?

No, there was no point in waiting at all. And it was cool and quiet here in the chart room. To hell with the spy outside. I want her.

He began to ease her toward a chair in the corner. The beach might be better, but the beach was far away and now was the time.

Drawing away, she whispered, "Will you help me steal the tranquillity pills?"

12

"Huh?" said Seamus, his romantic illusions shattered. While he was thinking grand and passionate thoughts, the woman was planning a theft. He released her and watched her modestly rearrange her robe.

"They keep them in the vault. They make them down here, you know. Quars is a scientist as well as a soldier. That's why they didn't feed him into one of the vats. He's too valuable. We will take only enough for one Festival day. We can't leave them without any. Horor and Yens pleaded with me to do it. I refused, but now I must. Retha has convinced me. She says that if you saved our lives it must be for a purpose." The words tumbled out recklessly, her passion turned from him to her newfound cause.

Retha, huh? That thin-shouldered little scamp is nothing but a great terrible troublemaker.

"You want to go through all that again?" said Seamus, now very much back down to earth. He let go of her and sank wearily into a chair by the map table.

"The Young Ones have a plan. On the first day of the Festival they will take the tranquillity pills and storm the Military Center. They have keys to the arsenal. With the carbines and explosives they will take over the Energy Center and the Central Building. They will liquidate the Committee and take command of the City. When the Festival is over, they will be running Zylong." Her brown eyes were glowing with excitement. "The Guardians, the Committee, the people at key forts like Hyperion, and the Energy Technicians use the pills to stay rational during the Festival. With pills, we can take over the City."

Seamus put his hands to his forehead and stared glumly at the maps. "Woman, you're pretty damn intelligent. What chance do you think such a harebrained idea has? Do you think two kids like Yens and Horor and a poor little tyke like Retha can overthrow an old and very established society?"

"They have about as much chance as we have of making it through to your spacecraft, the *Dove*, or whatever you call it," she flared back at him.

"*Dev*." Absently, he corrected her.

"Yes, *Dev*, then. Someday you must tell me who he was."

"He was too cute a man to get into something like this." Then he remembered some of the things De Valera had done and wasn't so sure. *Maybe this upcoming Festival day will be Zylong's Easter Monday. The woman has never loved you at all. She's scheming and conniving and pretending to love you.* He noted with considerable satisfaction that his heart was welling with self-pity. *What's the point in living anyway, if your proper woman is only trying to seduce you into a revolution?*

"All right, woman, I'll do it. When and how?" *It would be a great story to tell their grandchildren.*

"Late night. I'll come to get you when all is clear. It should be easy." She was beaming with happiness. Another damn true believer! Then she laughed at him again and hugged him fiercely.

So maybe she's not lost interest in you altogether. If they laugh at you, it's a sure sign that they still adore you, if only a little bit.

Although Marjetta looked as if she might kiss him again, Seamus O'Neill was no longer in any mood for romance.

Nor was his romantic mood revived when she shook him awake in the wee hours of the morning, even though he felt the warmth and inhaled the delicious odor of her skin. She had shed her robe for the night's enterprise. "It will only get in the way. Besides it's dark. You can't see me."

"Worse luck for me." He sighed loudly. His imagination did a quick flip at the thought of her lentat-covered body. The old dread she stirred in him returned quickly and cooled his fantasies. *Still, who knows what we'll both feel like when we get this stuff out of here?*

Taking his hand in her own, Marjetta led O'Neill down a jet-black, bitter-cold corridor. *They conserve energy here at Hyperion,* O'Neill thought as he groped his way through the dark behind her. *The woman's hand is warm enough, though. Ah, what would be wrong with that warmth next to you in bed every night?*

I'll tell you what would be wrong; you'd have to put up with that tongue and willpower during the day.

I could do a lot worse.

Given time you probably will.

I'm fated.

He abandoned the argument with himself because he didn't like its conclusion.

Margie seemed to know where she was going. They stopped suddenly. She pushed against a door that swung open slowly.

"The guard is asleep. I ... uh ... his drink tonight was a bit strong. No one has ever tried to steal the pills before—they don't officially exist," Marjetta breathed into O'Neill's ear.

"Shall we kick him to test it?" he asked ironically.

"Sssh." She pulled open a trapdoor, revealing a dark hole. "There is a ladder there. You go first. Be careful, it is a long way."

He had every intention of being careful. The ladder was metal and it was cold on his bare feet. The hole into which they were climbing was frigid and smelled strongly of seawater. An old tidal cave perhaps.

Here I am, he thought, *a latter-day Finn Mac-Cool, or was it Art MacConn or Con MacArt? I can never keep those shitheads from the old mythology* straight. *I'm searching for the Holy Grail on the planet Zylong. The magic cup is a box of pills, my magic princess is a half-daft conspirator, and I'm cold and miserable and lonely and the place smells and the woman doesn't love me and I've been abandoned by my friends and I might as well be dead.*

You go first, she says. So I can be the first one to drown in that seawater I hear roaring down there.

Lancelot du Lac, indeed. Galahad, for sure. Parsifal, of course. Maybe they didn't have to do much to program me into a no-account space bum.

The woman was right about one thing. It was a long way down. When he finally touched the slimy hard rock floor, he was shivering in the cold air.

"I am glad I could not see any of that coming down," said Marjetta nervously. "I do not like heights."

"You'll catch your death of cold in that thin thing," he warned her.

"Not when I have you to keep me warm." She started to giggle.

"None of that laughing-at-me stuff now," he said irritably. "I'm Lancelot du Lac in quest of the Holy Grail."

Her giggles turned into sniggers, then into laughter.

"What are you laughing at, woman?" he demanded. "You don't even know the myth."

"I think Lancelot is a very funny name."

"Ah, there's that. Anyway, let's find this Holy Grail of yours. Turn on your frigging light."

"What's frigging?"

"Never mind. Turn it on like I say."

She turned on the tiny handlight that was strapped to her wrist. The beam searched what appeared to be a small room, coming to rest on a cabinet against one wall. *We'll have a devil of a time getting it open.*

Marjetta pulled the drawers open one by one until she found what she was looking for, a tiny wooden box. It was filled with white pills. Holy Grail as anticlimax. No dragons to slay—when he was a kid, he'd always wanted to be a modern St. George and slay a dragon—no evil queens to fight off, no curses to escape, no sword battles with black knights. You simply climb down a long hole with your shivering magic princess and you find it in an open box. Easiest thing in the world.

Then the poet in O'Neill began to think about the symbolism of climbing down a long hole into a dark, sea-scoured cave.

Now isn't that interesting. What dirty minds those mythmakers had aeons ago. Well, sure I'm not climbing down anything more tonight. You're never certain whether you can get out of these cave things.

"A hundred of them—enough to free Zylong!" She was shaking with excitement. "Hold me tight, Geemie. When I think what this can do for my world . . . I am frightened."

He held her close to him, his hand fitting naturally into the concavity of her back. The pressure of her soft body against his chest was enough to make him almost lose his reason. He felt a sharp

223

stab of delicious pain in his chest, as though something were breaking. He wanted this woman; he was afraid of her; indeed, terrified of her. But he still wanted her. She was the proper woman if there were ever to be one.

Well, maybe you should climb down into some caves. His knees were shaking. *Tonight is the night to get her into my proper bed and begin my descent into the underworld. Ah, now that's a good image.* He held her closer and began to explore her body with his lips. *That's what the Grail legend is about, isn't it? Finn gets the magic cup and the magic princess? Two sacred vessels?*

"Let's get out of here before we decide to stay," he muttered into her hair.

This business of searching for the Holy Grail might have its good points after all.

O'Neill was back in his own room before he realized how easy it had been. He was in it now up to his neck. Stealing the pills was a kind of engagement with this society which the battles on the desert were not. Tricked into it by two women, one of them a wee slip of a revolutionary and the other someone who pretended to love him.

Of course, he didn't bring Marjetta back to his bed. She would have come. She was so happy and grateful that she would have done anything he wanted. Seamus Finnbar O'Neill wanted no woman on those terms.

"Shall we swim in the ocean, Geemie? It will be very warm after that terrible cave."

"Swim at night?" he exclaimed in horror.

"The moons will be out," she was laughing at him again.

"I think I'll pass it up tonight," he sighed. "We have a long trip ahead of us."

She kissed him at his door. "Brigid and Brendan and Mary be with you, my beloved."

First time she had ever called him that.

"You're picking up all the names," he admitted grudgingly.

"I don't quite understand how Mary and Brigid are different."

"My ancestors had a hard time with that too. Well, off with you, woman. You need your sleep too."

Seamus Finnbar O'Neill, the last great playboy of the western world—indeed, the whole western quadrant of the frigging galaxy—fell into an uneasy sleep in which he was pursued by dragons and demons who lurked in deep, cold caves.

He woke up with a start. It was still dark. Why did he feel frightened and guilty?

Then he remembered what had happened. *Dear God, I broke all the Rules. The Taran Code says you do not interfere in the politics of an alien world. That's exactly what I did. Without even thinking about it. Seduced by a terrible woman. Now I'm in the big muddy altogether.*

The farewell scene when they left Retha and their desert companions was a bad one. The little Lieutenant was tongue-tied with emotion and worried about her own task of bringing the troops back to the City.

"Rea, me girl," Seamus O'Neill tried to hearten her, "in one week I'll be buying you and your young man the biggest refreshment in the whole of Zylong. Now take care of your feet this time. I'd hate to have to come out and carry you in again."

She began to laugh. O'Neill bent down over her and tenderly kissed the small forehead. "Sure it's the truth you'll bring the troops back, girl," he whispered. He hated to leave them. They were a good troop after all—not like a company of Wild Geese, but given time and a good commander . . .

"Do you Tarans kiss every woman you meet?" asked Marjetta coldly, as they rode off into the dusk with the column of "staff."

"Only the beautiful ones, my dear."

"You think Lieutenant Retha is a beautiful woman?" Her control was slipping.

"Ah, well, we kiss them all back on Tara," he said teasingly. "Why, one day I even kissed the cheek of the Lady Deirdre. . . ."

"Who?" Her voice was edgy.

O'Neill froze in his saddle. *How did that slip out? How am I to explain Deirdre?*

"Ah, nobody important," he managed. "Well, she's kind of important—a religious leader of a sort," he amended.

"Is she beautiful?" Marjetta was stony-faced now. Good enough for her.

"Oh, no. She's an old woman now. I guess she never was anything much to look at."

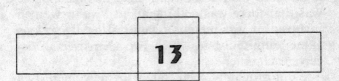

13

The midday meal which Quars had presided over before they left was pretty much like that last dinner at Ernie's living space before the journey through the desert, somewhat less cheery than a Gaelic wake.

The Colonel obviously never expected to see them again. Retha, her eyes intermittently filled with tears, hardly touched her food. Marjetta was charming but tense. The ugly, oily, heavy-browed Fourth Secretary radiated charming geniality, like an undertaker at a wake.

"It will be," he insisted, "a quick and pleasant trip. Nothing like the last one."

Babbling about music and poetry on Zylong, O'Neill matched him cliché for cliché. It was the kind of battle of wits Seamus O'Neill loved, especially since he was convinced he was smarter than the Fourth Secretary by several light-years. The contest would continue out in the desert, too, and Seamus knew he'd win there. *This little gombeen* man is no match for a commandant in the Wild Geese. At all, at all.

The nice thing about a battle of wits between a gombeen man and an officer in the Wild Geese was that there was nothing about love or women involved. It was merely a game, a deadly serious game admittedly, in which two men tried to deceive each other.

Unfortunately there might be a woman as a prize: the Fourth Secretary did not bother to hide his lascivious examination of Marjetta. He wanted her and proposed to have her before the sun rose again.

Well, we'll just see about that, my good man. She's mine, you see. And while I have no idea just now what to do about her, I'll not be after letting you have her.

So they were fighting over a woman, among other things, but the woman was only an object of the battle and not a person whose erratic moods, alternating between laughter and fury, both equally unexplained, had to be seriously considered. When it came time to act on the desert, she'd follow orders. *She's a good soldier, if nothing else.*

Go 'long with you, Seamus O'Neill. She's more than that.

Don't bother me with such considerations. I must worry about the game with this gombeen man here.

The Fourth Secretary announced that it would be appropriate for everyone to retire to their rooms for some sleep before their departure after sunset.

Marjetta stopped O'Neill on the way to his room. "How will we escape? Have you figured it out yet?" she asked, her voice strained by tension.

"Don't be so impatient, woman. We have seven or eight hours yet. I'll tell you what I'm thinking. We'll probably be safe until we get to the large transport. They won't try anything while we're riding and carrying our own guns. Also they won't try anything until we're beyond the range of Quars's monitoring system. So we should make our move sometime about midnight. I have stolen one of the good Colonel's maps; we'll be able to find our way with it. This clown thinks he's got us fooled. It's Quars he's worried about. If we seem dumb and innocent, they'll lower their guard. When I whistle like this—" he hummed the first few bars of the "Whistling Gypsy" "—you turn to the right and gallop like hell. I'll give them something to remember us by and follow after you."

She nodded. He didn't bother to tell her he had also filched powder grenades from Quars's arsenal.

O'Neill moved again toward his room, then stopped and looked at Marjetta. "You're sure that they'll not harm Retha and the rest of my . . . our troops."

"Of course not. She's now known to be a heroine. If all of us died, the Committee would not be able to prevent discussion. And if I disappear, perhaps into Narth's harem when the Secretary is finished with me, they will not consider her or any of the Young Ones a threat."

"We'll see about a few wee changes in that scenario. So they really are that impressed with you?"

"I'm sure that seems inconceivable to you, Major O'Neill, but yes, the Committee seems to think I am brilliant and dangerous. And myself a woman too."

She was even imitating his idiom.

"Women are all right in their place." *Dear Brigid, would he be in trouble for even thinking that on the* Iona.

"Well, you needn't worry about your little friend Retha. She'll be in her man's arms in a few days."

"Ah, sure you wouldn't be telling me that they're lovers. She's a mere child."

"You should see him." She smiled faintly. "He appears to be about fourteen of our years. I am certain she was the aggressor. They are, ah, quite passionate about each other."

"Breaking the rules?"

"As you must know by now, the rules have been discarded by many. They do not even receive nominal obedience out here."

"West of the Pecos."

"What does that mean?"

"A mythological reference. Why do they break the rules that young?"

"It is simple." She shrugged and made a distasteful face—at him, he supposed. "They are young. They love each other. They expect to die. Is that not enough reason to be in the same bed?"

230

"Well, I suppose so. I never thought it would happen here."

"Tarans are bigots," she snapped and turned to leave him.

Right enough, my dear. We know all there is to know about cultural diversity. Our Rules demand that we be tolerant of it and not meddle in other cultures, like I've been doing since you talked me into it. But still, there are only a few of us on a small planet and fewer still on our monastery ships. So we're narrow and tight and convinced that our ways are the best. Which they are. And we look down on everyone else as poor benighted heathens. Which they are. But you're a heathen, my darling, and I love you. I'm not going to let that greasy goat lay his hands on you, not at all. At all.

"Marjetta . . ."

"Yes?" She jumped as though she had been shot.

"Don't forget those pills." He swatted her rump.

She turned and faced him. "Will I like her?"

"Who?"

"Deirdre."

"Not at all, at all." He was in so much trouble now, what did a few more lies matter. "Well, maybe after a while. Sure you might become as thick as thieves."

The woman was already assuming that she was going to come with him. He'd never told her that. Not exactly, anyway.

"Will she like me?"

"Ah, now that's the question."

Dusk had already begun to settle at this end of the continent. Soon they would have to leave.

"Well now, I think she'll delight in you, Margie me girl. You're the kind of woman that Tarans of both sexes adore. The men will all fall in love with you, like I was after doing, and myself seeing you for the first time, and the young women will all identify with you, and the old women, even the real old women like the Lady Deirdre—" he mentally made a sign of the cross "—will want to mother you."

"Thank you very much, Seamus O'Neill, Poet and Soldier." He glanced to one side and saw her warmly smiling at him. "That was very nice. You are very nice too. Some of the time."

"A man tries." He turned away, stunned by the loveliness of her smile.

No, that greasy gombeen man isn't going to get one of his filthy paws within half the galaxy of you. Not if I can help it.

Later that night, Hyperion long since lost in the darkness and its scanners probably out of range, O'Neill gripped the reins of his horse tightly. For the tenth time that night, he cursed the Zylong moons.

They had risen early. He had not figured their rotation cycle properly. Now every grain of sand on the wide beach seemed visible as the silent column trotted across it. The high mountains toward which they rode stood out clearly in the moonlight, their snow-covered peaks gleaming.

Chances for a successful escape in this light were poor.

You were so besotted with the woman that you weren't thinking clearly. You're still not.

His throat tightened. He'd never played the game for such a prize before. It changed everything.

O'Neill's danger sense was much higher than it ought to have been this early in the ride. Maybe the Fourth Secretary's boys weren't planning to wait until they arrived at the transport. He was a more clever gombeen man than Seamus had thought. "Never, I repeat, never, allow yourself the luxury of underestimating the enemy": Carmody's first rule. And he'd broken it. Along with a lot of other rules.

So get ready for battle, he warned himself. *Shape up, O'Neill.*

But the problem was not so much battle as trickery. He was alert, ready, physically and mentally eager for battle. He sniffed the cold desert air, a soldier now, not a spy. But he wasn't able to activate the crafty part of his mind. Away from other Tarans too long.

Well, if you want me back, he informed herself, in the unlikely event she was listening, *you'd better come up with something good really quick. Like ten minutes ago.*

Despite the silence of the marchers, he tried to keep the Fourth Secretary in conversation. "Tell me more about this fellow Narth who everyone at the fort was talking about. Where is his 'empire'?"

The Fourth Secretary chuckled. "I'm afraid;

Poet O'Neill, that you have been taking our folk stories literally. A long time ago a member of the Committee, a brilliant man—perhaps the most brilliant we ever had—became mentally disturbed from overwork. He asked permission to go out of the City and live in the countryside until he regained his health. Poor man, what could the Committee do? Obviously he would not survive in the outer reaches of our planet. He would hear no argument, so we let him go. No one has seen him since; it is presumed that he died long ago. Most Zylongi have a very superstitious fear of the countryside; legends grow fast in such circumstances. Occasional attacks from hordi bands on caravans like yours don't help."

It sounded like an official party line. O'Neill persisted. "I also heard tales of 'the Hooded Ones' and 'the Young Ones.' Who are they? More legends?"

The Secretary dismissed them with a wave of his fat hairy hand. "Complete fables. I regret that the garrison at Hyperion has filled the mind of an important guest of Zylong with such nonsense. Even in as well-organized and efficient a society as ours, there are occasional accidents—a construction collapse, a crash of small vehicles, a fight between people who have had too much of the wrong kind of la-ir, a less than satisfactory harvest. . . ."

"A monorail accident?" He watched out of the corner of his eye for a reaction.

The Fourth Secretary's thick lips tightened. His answer was a fraction of a second too late.

"Yes, those do happen, too, though very rarely. The computer program . . . In any case, it suits the superstitious needs of some of our less educated people to create explanations for these chance events. So they imagine completely fictional bands of terrorists. Every older generation is dismayed by their young and their 'radical' ideas. Our young people are exemplary citizens—like our good and brave Captain Marjetta, who earned the favor of the people as well as her promotion by her brave actions at a time of great personal loss."

"Thank you, Honored Secretary," Marjetta said, politely staring straight ahead into the desert.

"My dear." He nodded at her, then continued. "The Guardians eliminated supernatural demons from our culture at the time of the Reorganization. There are some residual needs that are served by these natural if fictional demons. While we are dismayed by their persistence and confidently expect that we will eliminate them by proper genetic controls in the future, the fact remains that they do persist. They are socially of no importance."

"I suppose that the stories about the Festivals are also largely fictional?" He was pressing his luck a bit. The Secretary might get suspicious. But this time he didn't hesitate a moment.

"My dear man, surely a widely traveled person like yourself is familiar with the carnival week syndrome that exists in almost every society? You know how people love to exaggerate their misbehavior at a time when the social norms collapse. If you could remain with us, you would find that our carnival time is a time of quite innocent relaxation, despite the wildly exaggerated tales which have grown up around it. It is a very mild period of rest and refreshment after the hard work of harvesting. Our Guardians quite rightly insisted that all honored citizens of our democratic society would participate in the harvest work. I hope you will discount any exaggerations you have heard about the Festivals. Ours is a small and very provincial planet. Stories have a way of getting beyond all proper bounds. They do no great harm, but they certainly would disturb a visitor with less sophistication than yourself."

The so-and-so is plausible enough, O'Neill thought. *If I didn't know better, I might well have swallowed the whole line.*

The attack at the first campsite and the sight of Narth, Imperial Guard surrounding him, were not imaginary, and neither were those killers in the monorail station. The prickling at the back of his neck that meant danger was not imaginary, either—although, oddly enough, the danger seemed to come from outside the marching column. Something was drawing closer every minute.

What's going on in Margie's pretty head? She has not looked your way once during the ride. But surely she trusts in you. Completely. Has to, poor woman. Is she scared?

Of course she is. So are you, Seamus O'Neill, admit it.

Well, there's a lot to be scared about.

Once he had thought her solid rock. Now he

knew there was fire under the rock, disconcerting animal passion and patriotic fervor. And beneath the fire, he was beginning to discover gentleness and fragility. And wit, too, even if she laughed at him.

When she was in his arms, he lusted for her. At other times he feared her but couldn't quite understand why. Would she be reliable in combat, now that some of the fire had erupted? The back of his neck warned him not to be too certain, good soldier or not.

Well, he's still not going to get his greasy paws on her.

They rode on for several more hours. The danger feeling did not abate. But it seemed farther away, as though it weren't in the Fourth Secretary's troop at all, but somewhere else. They were approaching the mountains. He had misjudged where the Zylongi parked the transport, so that they were much farther away from the pass that would lead them out of the desert. Fortunately, two moons had set; the desert was darker. At the leader's guttural command the column wheeled left and began to descend a sloping ravine in the rocky, uneven desert floor.

O'Neill's sense of danger shot up. *They're going to do something now. I don't know what it is, but now's the time. We are going to redeploy instantly. Which means run like hell.*

As they entered the ravine he began the "Whistling Gypsy" tune an instant before shoving the Fourth Secretary from his horse. The sound of screams and shots exploded behind him as he galloped up the slope. He didn't see or hear Marjetta. It was a trap—not for O'Neill and Marjetta, but for their Zylongi escorts.

Out of rifle range, O'Neill stopped to look for Margie. She was there, bless her, right behind him. "What is going on?" she exclaimed breathlessly. "Just as you rode away the head of the column came under fire. The ravine was filled with Narth's cavalry. O'Neill, how did you know?"

"I didn't. I just knew there was something wrong with that ravine. It's a little trick we Tarans have. I'll tell you about it someday."

The two rested their horses while they surveyed the scene spread out below them. Their breakaway had saved the column from complete and immediate destruction. Narth's pony soldiers had started shooting as soon as they saw the commotion caused by O'Neill's and Marjetta's escape. This gave the rear of the column time to dig in behind the rocks at the mouth of the ravine. Narth's cavalry were caught inside, and despite the sharpshooters stationed along the rim, it looked like there would be quite a long battle.

"Our friends on both sides will be busy. Let's put as much distance between them and us as we can before they decide they have one aim in common and we're it." He spurred his horse forward and they raced across the sands toward the towering mountains gleaming in the ghostly moonlight.

An hour and a half of hard riding later, they came up against a sheer cliff face.

"Is not the pass that way?" asked Margie, pointing north.

"It is, but I'm trying to figure out what to do. Narth is that way too. We might try to head back to the fort. But I think the Committee will want us even more after tonight; it might not be all that safe there."

"Poor Retha. She will lead her troop through that." She pointed to the now quiet and sinister desert.

"There's nothing we can do about Retha," O'Neill said, shrugging his shoulders. "Quars is a good soldier. He will know what's happened out here. He may take matters into his own hands and lead an expeditionary force."

They picked their way slowly along the edge of the mountain wall. The horses were tired now. There seemed little danger of pursuit but much danger of stumbling into someone they did not want to meet.

Suddenly the night air was rent by a tremendous explosion. A ball of light shot up from the desert floor, sending a giant mushroom cloud into the darkened sky.

So they have those kinds of things here too, Seamus thought, remembering the worn-out video tapes on the *Iona. Nuclear weapons. And they're not afraid to use them.*

O'Neill and Marjetta struggled to calm their frightened mounts.

"What was that?" Marjetta exclaimed, terror choking her words.

"What do you want to bet that it was some sort of self-destruct charge on the large transport? Narth must have launched an attack on it too. It would be a nice toy for him to have. The Committee probably had it rigged so that it could be destroyed on command of the Central Building. This has not been a good night for the Fourth Secretary and his staff. I don't think you'll have to worry about him again."

She shivered with disgust but bravely replied, "With you protecting me, I did not fear him."

"I may not deserve that praise, woman." He sighed loudly. "But from yourself. 'tis good to hear it."

"It's only the truth."

Well, she's not laughing at me now. I'd better change the subject. "Do you think he was really the boss behind the Committee?"

"That gives him too much credit, Geemie." She patted her horse reassuringly. "He was the one who accomplished things, the only one who was not an ineffectual old man. But he did not have complete power."

"So there'll be a vacuum—into which you and your friends can rush?"

"That seems a long way from here, doesn't it? And highly improbable?"

"I don't know. I'm only a wandering poet. Come to think of it, however, it's not been an especially good night for Narth. He must have lost his best troops in that explosion. Come on, let's see if we can find this pass."

They found it at first light. It didn't look low. The natural trail wound up through the mountains steeply, losing itself in mists and snow near the top.

"Are you game?" Seamus looked over at Marjetta. She was tired already, too early for a dependable officer.

"I have always wondered what the mountains were like. I have never felt snow." She grinned at him, her brown eyes sparkling like a sky of stars. He lost a heartbeat or two in the light of her grin.

So they began to climb. It was arduous at first. Sometime after sunrise the path up the mountain widened to a broad avenue of rock, becoming less steep. It was an ascending canyon with tall walls on either side. Seamus was relaxed, so occupied with looking at Marjetta and spinning dreams that his psychic sense completely failed him this time. They rounded a bend and were astonished to see, waiting not twenty yards away, Narth and a half dozen of his guard. They were trapped.

"So," boomed the crimson-clad, black-bearded "Emperor" of Zylong. "The lovely young leader of the foolish radicals and the inestimable Major O'Neill from the *Iona*. You two have caused me a good deal of trouble. I think you will shortly learn about real revolution instead of café-table talking. Dismount from your horses. Do not try to move your weapons. Try nothing foolish. O'Neill, you are a dead man, but the woman might make an interesting mate, with the proper training and experience. She will need the kind of discipline in

241

which I am expert. She will perhaps even come to enjoy it. Don't risk her life with stupid heroics."

"Ah, now, why would I do anything foolish?" Seamus temporized as he and Margie slowly dismounted. He managed to loosen what he wanted to as he got off the horse. "But since you know about the *Iona*, can't we be after making a wee deal, just you and me? I don't care about the woman. You can have her if you want. She's not much in bed anyway. Your beautiful military types tend to be frigid, as I'm sure yourself knows."

"That's a very interesting suggestion." Narth's thick white teeth flashed in a crooked grin. "Send me the woman and we'll talk."

"You heard what the man said." O'Neill shoved her in the direction of the Emperor and his Guard— a badly battered little crowd. All that was left from the explosion. *Not very alert. Well, we'll see.* He slipped a few inches closer to the canyon wall, drawing his horse with him.

Poor Marjetta stumbled toward Narth. Out of the frying pan into the fire. *You're going to have to be mighty quick, woman, if I'm going to get away with this.*

She stood in front of Narth, obedient and abject. He fondled her for a few moments. She did not resist or respond. Seamus stepped a couple of feet closer to the wall. One of the guards raised his weapon a few inches, but no one else seemed to notice.

"Like I said, your military women really don't have much to offer."

"I will enjoying educating her," Narth slobbered over his captive. "As with so much else in life, it is the process that brings the satisfaction, not the end result. Don't you agree, O'Neill?"

"Sure, the process with that one will not be any picnic." He was almost in position, an angle where the slope of the canyon was behind Narth and his troops. "Now about the *Iona* . . ."

They should have rushed him and tied him up at the first moment. But it was a surprise encounter, as much a shock to them as to Margie and himself. And they were still battered from the explosion. And for all his tough talk, Narth, like everyone else on Zylong, was a bit in awe of the red-bearded giant from outer space. Who knew what might happen if they got too close to him? Better to keep him at a distance with their guns aimed at him.

"Indeed." Narth smiled genially. "I doubt that you can deliver the *Iona* to me, but it might be useful to explore ways of cooperation in any case. Moreover I wish to know more about her. There are ways of finding out, as you may imagine. Need I say that they are in themselves amusing, although neither you nor the lovely Captain would find them such."

"Ask away." Just a few more seconds.

"First of all, what is the complement of the ship? And again, Major O'Neill—" he must have seen the light of battle in O'Neill's eyes "—let me warn you against doing anything foolish. There are easy and there are painful, terribly painful ways to die."

"Ah, sure what is there foolish I can do?"

O'Neill then did something very foolish. Snatching his smoke grenade from its fastening on the saddle, he lobbed it up the canyon wall. Like a ball thrown on a slanted roof, it rolled up the wall, hesitated, and then began to slide down again.

Surprised and startled, Narth and his guards turned to watch the round object accelerating toward them. Seamus grabbed his carbine. Marjetta broke away from Narth and began to run toward him. Seamus raised the weapon, ready to fire as soon as she was clear. She jumped behind a rock.

Just as he opened fire, the Imperial Guard did something equally foolish. Apparently they had never seen a grenade before, so they shot at it as it lumbered toward them. One of them was a pretty good shot. O'Neill, blazing away now with his own weapon, just had time to shout "Hit the ground!" before he was assisted off his feet by the detonation.

A long, long time later he fought his way back to consciousness. The sun was now high in the sky and shining brightly. The canyon was dead quiet—indeed, it was filled with death.

Was he the only one alive? Ahead of him on the canyon floor were the remains of the Emperor Narth's Guard. The imperial robe was now rust-colored with dried blood. Sure enough, the robe itself hadn't burned. So these robes were not flammable. Like a man on a binge, Seamus considered his own robe. *Nope, it hadn't burned either.*

Now what was I supposed to be thinking about?

Oh yes, there's no body in Narth's robe. Now, isn't that interesting. Has Narth escaped? Maybe carried off on a frightened horse?

Sure, if he had, he wouldn't fall for that trick the next time.

So I'll think up a better trick.

Anyhow, if the blast blew him out of his robe, he's probably dead.

There's something else I should be thinking about. No, someone else. Someone real important. Now let's see, who is it?

O'Neill checked his own limbs; everything seemed to be in working order. Well, now he and Marjetta could resume their travels.

Marjetta! Where is she? He stumbled to his feet. Their horses had disappeared, racing back in terror, no doubt, to the lowlands where they belonged. Near the bodies of Narth's guards sprawled grotesquely on a rock slide against the canyon wall, Marjetta lay, apparently as lifeless as the rest of them.

His ears ringing, his legs unsteady, he stumbled to her and turned her over. She appeared to be sleeping, except there was a thin line of blood tracing down her face from a wound above the hairline. Running to the supply pack, which his horse had shed in the rush to escape this place of strange noises, he found a syringe of life serum. With shaking hands he managed to inject it into her arm.

At first there was no reaction. He felt for a

pulse. Still there, but very weak. If some life serum is good, would more be better? Sammy had never told him. Her pulse was slowing down. He dashed back and removed the two remaining vials of life serum and injected them clumsily into her arm.

Slowly color returned to Margie's pale face. A few moments later when she opened her eyes he was holding her in his arms. He busied himself fixing the scratch on her head. She clung to him, fighting for self-control; then grinned again. "Quick thinking, Major," she said with a wink. "But how do you know what I'm like in bed?"

14

Margie recovered quickly. Indeed, she was ready to begin the march more quickly than he, and started going through their packs, choosing what to carry and what to leave behind. "I'm younger and better," she explained. "And wasn't I wonderful? I had Narth convinced that I'd given up on you and become his abject slave."

"Well, you were pretty good," he conceded grudgingly, "though I should be saying it instead of yourself. You could have distracted him a wee bit more."

"Then he wouldn't have believed your slander," she argued genially, "that I was a frigid virgin who would require sexual initiation, would he?"

"Aren't you?"

"I don't think I'm frigid, anyway." She hefted a pack, finding it not too heavy. She jammed some more food into it. "We'll have to wait and see, won't we?"

Well, that's clear enough.

"Ay, we will indeed." He began to shuffle through his supplies, wishing he had ignored her last comment altogether—though he was betting that, like any proper virgin, she might be inexperienced, but hardly frigid. Not by several light-years. "To change the subject to safer matters—" his hands were still trembling "—you were very brave and very quick. I counted on you to be both. Otherwise we would be as dead as they are."

She straightened up and turned toward him, a tall slender woman in a long brown cloak that matched her hair and her glowing eyes, a pack on her back and a weapon in her hand. "Thank you, Geemie. I'm glad you counted on me and I'm glad you were right in doing so."

You're getting deeper and deeper into trouble, Seamus Finnbar O'Neill.

Both of them wanted to leave the horror of the canyon. Narth might be dead, but his troops could still be around; a second in command might try to prove his claim to empire by capturing and displaying as trophies Narth's killers.

They trudged silently up the mountain, both again preoccupied with their own thoughts. As they approached the snow line, Marjetta spoke.

"What is the *Iona*?" she snapped at him, the good feeling of a couple of hours ago suddenly broken by suspicion and distrust. "Narth said you were Major O'Neill from the *Iona*. That is not what you call your spacecraft."

"Did he say that?" Now the lies had to start

again. "That was the name of my command on Tara. Each regiment had its own name. How did he know you were going to take command of the Young Ones when you got back?" He had to get her back on the defensive. There was a lot of rock still in the girl.

"I do not know. I told no one . . . no one but you, that is."

"I certainly wouldn't have tossed that grenade at Narth if I were on his side," he said reasonably.

"I do not think you were on his side." She sighed. "I do not know what to think."

"Was Narth supposed to have any kind of . . . well . . . sort of special powers that were different from what ordinary people could do?"

"Yes. He was said to be able to read people's minds. How did you know that? No one ever mentions it on Zylong except in whispers. It is too frightening." She shivered. "Do you have that power, Geemie? Can you read my mind?" Her brown eyes widened with terror.

"If I could, I'd be afraid to try," he said honestly enough. Then, scratching his head he turned to moderate honesty to placate her. "Most of us Tarans have traces of that sort of thing—kind of an evolutionary throwback, they tell us. All I'm really good at is sensing danger. It only works when I concentrate on it—like back at the ravine. Later I was tired and let other things preoccupy me. I didn't pick up on this last surprise."

"I am glad you can sense danger and I am also glad you cannot read my mind. It would be embarrassing." Her voice trailed off and her lips tightened.

Now what does she mean by that?

As if you don't know, boyo. She wants you even worse than you want her. And is less afraid of it than you are too.

You keep out of this. We have a mountain to climb.

His estimates of the height of this "low pass" were completely wrong. He had figured that maybe there would be a thin layer of snow on the ground, but it was ankle-deep at first and then knee-deep. The top layer melted in the daytime, then froze at night, so that the surface of the snow was crusted and slippery but not firm enough to hold their weight. During the day, the temperature was above freezing—still cold by desert and Zylong City standards. Their desert robes were little protection against the cold, but the boots they wore were high and strong enough to protect their feet.

Marjetta had never known cold like this. She was having a difficult time negotiating the deep snow. O'Neill was sure they wouldn't get through the snowbelt that day. It meant a frigid night at the top of the pass with no fire and only body heat to survive.

He was troubled by Narth's knowledge of *Iona*. How much had he known? Who told him? The Zylongi were not completely unsophisticated about psychic mechanisms even though they didn't use the word. If Narth had known about the monastery, what were the chances that someone else might too?

The questions were soon forgotten in the simple struggle to survive. As the sun slipped slowly toward the horizon, they reached the top of the pass. They saw the dark green jungle far below them and the inviting purple of the ocean beyond that. They had made it halfway. Poor Margie was nearly finished. She was exhausted, frightened, and shivering in the cold. Her teeth were clenched to hold back cries of pain.

"Seamus, it is impossible," she moaned. "I cannot go on. You must leave me here. I will decide to die. It will come quickly."

"No one is deciding anything. Let's find a cave and figure out a way to keep warm." He grabbed her arm roughly and dragged her along.

He wasn't sure he could make it down the other side himself. Better that the two of them freeze to death up here together. With his arm around the faltering Marjetta, he pushed through the snow toward the side of the pass, looking for a cave, a cleft in the rock—even an indentation where they would be protected from the wind, which had steadily increased since sunset.

They found a tiny cave, little more than a depression in the rock face. The two of them huddled together with their packs, carbines, and spears piled up in front of them for more protection from the howling wind.

The bare rock angled away from the wind and was free from snow, but it was very cold. Marjetta shivered wretchedly. He drew her close to himself to share his warmth, and gradually her trembling stopped. They would never last the night.

She knew it. Tears of despair and pain flowed down her cheeks.

"Sure the next time I go mountain climbing I'll be after choosing a woman who doesn't get cold," he joked, his own teeth chattering, and pulled her still closer.

It was now completely dark. There seemed no reason not to light one of the tiny lanterns they carried in their packs. To die in the light seemed easier than to face death in the dark.

Light! That gave him an idea. "Margie, these illumination grenades . . . is there any way we can set them to go off slowly? Can we rig it so that they last an hour or so? There's enough power in them to keep this cave warm for a while."

"There is a slow timer on it," she answered hopelessly, "but even if you push the dial all the way, it will only last fifteen minutes. If you get too close to a grenade, even at that intensity it will burn you to death."

He managed to pry the cover off one grenade and find the mechanism. The timer was a service-able device that inhibited the flow of acid from the supply compartment to the ignition spark.

"What if I tear off a little bit of cloth from my robe and wrap that around the flow valve? The cloth is supposed to be unburnable, and it should slow the acid flow."

"I don't know." She was shaking so hard that

he feared she might hurt herself against the walls of their tiny shelter. In a few moments, her spasms might break out of control.

Well, this thing could explode on us and we'd have more heat than we wanted. Enough to fry us. On the other hand, I'm not going to sit here and watch my woman freeze to death.

He rigged his homemade heating unit, put it on a ledge outside the cave, and pulled the pin. The light slowly began to shine, heat flowed back into the cave—not much, but enough to keep them alive. Margie's sigh as the warmth hit her face was that of one who had been pulled back from the brink.

"See, little one, stick with old Uncle Seamus. He can fix anything." He hugged her.

They ate concentrated supper bars and sipped vitamin-enriched water from their canteens. The cave was uncomfortable; the glare from the light was hard on their eyes until they had the sense to put on the smoked glasses used in desert travel. Then the cave took on a bizarre shade of green that made Margie laugh.

The heat from the homemade furnace lasted close to an hour. They had six grenades in all, so if he used them at hour-and-a-half intervals, they could make it all through the night.

"Young woman," Seamus briskly announced, "on another occasion I may have obscene reasons for suggesting this, but I trust you see the sense of sleeping in my arms tonight."

"I cannot think of a place where my virtue as

a Zylongi maiden would be better assured." She sighed in contentment and then stiffened. . . . "But you will have to change the grenades. You will not sleep?"

"Who is the commander of this expedition, woman?" O'Neill demanded.

"You are." Again the crinkly grin and the starry brown eyes, quickly lowered.

"What did I say?" He put his hand under her chin and forced the eyes back into view.

"That I needed sleep." Now her grin was embarrassed, sheepish.

"Then do as you are told," he said gruffly, drawing her close.

"Yes, sir." She leaned obediently against his chest.

In ten minutes she was sound asleep, snuggled up against him, giving and receiving body warmth.

O'Neill's head was jumbled with confused and complex emotions. He had to think of the challenges of the next day. But this girl disconcerted him, kept him off balance, attracted him, and scared the hell out of him. *Why does she look at me that way?*

I can have her anytime I want. She's offered me her virginity, her self, her life. But it would be a mortal sin to make love to her, wouldn't it now?

If you start, Seamus O'Neill, you'll never stop. She's the proper woman, you'll never give up. You know that. Where are you going to find a better one, I ask you?

Nowhere.

Didn't Carmody tell you that sex was meant to draw people together despite their fears?

He did.

You don't intend just to take her and enjoy her and then leave her, do you?

I should clobber you for even suggesting that.

And will herself ever stop loving you?

Well, I'm not good enough for her, but the poor thing will probably always think I am.

What are you waiting for then?

It would be a great, terrible sin. The Cardinal would never forgive. Making love to a defenseless local.

She's not all that defenseless.

Yes, she is.

Seamus pondered. The Lady Abbess. He shivered, and not from the cold. Then he remembered something she had once said about canon law: If two people wanted to marry and could not find a proper clergyperson for a long period of time, they could exchange commitments and it would be a valid and permanent marriage.

Ah, would it now?

Didn't the Cardinal herself say so?

She did.

Well, that kills another of your excuses. If she's your proper woman and there's no one around to bless the two of you, then she's your wife and that's that.

Well, I'll think about it. We have lots of time yet.

Coward.

There were a lot of other things to think about the next morning. That day's struggle was not easier. By noontime they were out of the snow and on the steep downward trail, which gave them a psychological lift. Margie didn't have much reserve strength; she stumbled occasionally, sometimes reaching out to Seamus to keep from falling. But her spirits were high.

"Let me know the next time you select a low pass," she laughed.

That struck them both as terribly funny. Her irony was beginning to sound like his. The Zylongi were an imitative people, their culture made strong demands for social homogeneity. If she associated with him long enough, she might pick up a good deal of his behavior—maybe even some of his temperament.

That would not be a good thing at all.

Late in the afternoon they stumbled, exhausted and worn, into the warm, gentle foothills where the jungle began. Margie wanted to stop. O'Neill insisted that they try to get across the River while it was still light.

They struggled on. Seamus could think of nothing but soft grass and warm water. Women could wait for another day, another lifetime. Finally, when darkness had fallen, they stumbled down the side of the last foothill and into a meadow bordering a tributary of the River with its own little waterfall and pool. *Paradise*, he thought. *We've made it.*

They could go no further. Both threw off their desert cloaks and sank into the pool with grateful relief. They should never have made it. After a good soak, Seamus and Marjetta lay together on the grass beside the pool, the moonlight turning Marjetta into an alabaster statue.

Her naked body was flawlessly designed, perfection in its rich, supple detail. Yet he still was afraid of her. How could anything that beautiful be dangerous? Why did she seem a trap? It was not just the weariness of their journey which blotted out his lust. Margie's haunting beauty in the moonlight warned him away, a dangerous garden with deadly flowers. *No different than the cold, slimy cave at the end of the long passage that frightened you at Hyperion.*

How many times, you lout, have you fantasized about being alone in a forest with a naked woman? Now look at you. You're in paradise with Eve and you don't want her.

"Geemie—" her sad brown eyes turned plaintively to him "—are you sure you cannot read my mind?"

"Woman, you are the worst unbeliever of them all. No, I can't read your mind, worse luck for me, I suppose. Your privacy is safe from my snooping curiosity." Now he was really having trouble controlling himself, so his tone sounded very angry. Fear or not, there were hungers stirring within him.

"I wish you could." Her voice was small and very soft.

"You're like all Taran women, all right," he laughed gruffly, "always changing your mind." He debated jumping back into the pool. The woman was certainly trying to seduce him now, and himself worn out from the long day's trip. *Why doesn't she wait for a decent time?*

"I am serious, Seamus O'Neill. I do not have much life left, and I want to belong to you. I have wanted to belong to you, Taran, since I pulled you out of the sewer. I have broken all the other rules of my culture, so it is time to break the last one with you. I am just a speck of dust, Geemie, with a bit of life in it. I am precious to myself still, and I am the only gift I have to give. Please take me."

"I am afraid I will hurt you, Marjetta." It was lame but true. She looked so fragile in the moonlight, her limp body a picture of passive vulnerability. *Damn her, she knows how to surrender.*

"I do not care whether you hurt me or not, Geemie. I just want to be yours. I ask nothing from you. Just enjoy me for a little while and then forget me. You are the only good thing that has ever happened to me. I do not want to lose the chance to be with you even if it is only for a few days."

He placed his hands on her slender waist, fingers drawing her to him. "Sure, Margie, I've loved you since the first moment I set eyes on you." He was passing the point of no return. Hunger was now stronger than fear. Her skin felt like the fine Taran linen on the Cardinal's table. "I'll not be forgetting you and it won't be just for a few days that I will love you."

"Do not speak of love, Seamus. I think I feel it,

but too much has happened for me to know what it is. I just know I cannot go on living unless I belong to you." Her lips opened, her eyes grew round and vacant, her heart beat furiously under the touch of his fingers.

Voices screamed in his throbbing head, warning him of the dangers. He ignored them. His hands moved slowly up and down her body, exploring her womanly splendors, and she tensed in response, her face wincing with fear. "I'll speak of love if I want to, woman. I know what it is." *I'm being seduced by a frightened virgin who expects me to take over the seducing.* His lips began explorations of their own, testing the sweetness of her flesh.

There was softness and surrender in her now. "Whatever it is, I accept it." His hands were still moving over her; she had relaxed under their touch.

"Well, it's this. When this night is over, I'm considering you my mate for the rest of my life. If you ever try to get out of it, idjit, I'll spank you within an inch of your life, do you hear?" He patted her glorious rear end in feigned warning and his voice was soft and husky.

She began to cry. "Forever, Geemie. And even after that."

Seamus covered her face with kisses, his passion finally wild. *Easy, me boy, this one will break if you're not careful.* He reined in his ardor and began to slowly and lovingly prepare her for their union.

15

The great ugly lake glared at Seamus O'Neill; its twisting vegetation seemed to grasp eagerly for his soul. The Black Mood was upon him, the worst of all the Taran emotional afflictions. "Self-pity and infidelity," the Captain Abbess would snap when informed that one of her subjects "has taken the Black Mood, Y'r Reverence."

But the Black Mood was not cured by the Cardinal's wrath nor by the ministrations of the medical team, nor by the prayers of the monks. It eventually went away, however. If the Lady Deirdre were to be believed, it went away when the victim decided to act "like an adult and a sworn pilgrim again."

There was no record of a Black Mood being fatal. Nor indeed of it ever being permanent. But that datum brought no surcease to those who were in the grip of the Black Mood. They were convinced that their case would be the exception that proved the rule.

Seamus had been the victim of it only once in his life before. He couldn't even remember the reason, though he always thought that some of his best poetry had been written when the Mood was upon him.

Now he wasn't writing poetry or singing songs. He had repaired his harp, without the slightest hesitation. He had used it to sing love songs to his bride, love songs he had not yet written down and now claimed to himself that he had forgotten.

The Mood had hung on for days. In some twisted way he was beginning to like it. He kicked a rock into the dark waters of the Great Lake. Damn it and damn Zylong; damn *Iona* and, above all, damn Marjetta.

Damn him, too. The mess was his fault. Had his brain become so numbed by sex that he couldn't think anymore? Now he had them lost on this vast water trap. Since coming down from the mountain he had made nothing but mistakes. He was responsible for Marjetta's deterioration. The *Iona* had written him off completely: if it hadn't left orbit before, it was sure to now, leaving him to rot in this moldy jungle by himself for the rest of his natural life, which wouldn't be very long.

Maybe the reason he had been so harsh with Margie was that he was taking some of his self-hatred out on her—though heaven knows the woman would have driven a monk to drink. He had shouted at her that if she felt that way she ought to go out into the jungle and die. Without a word she had picked up and was gone, never turning back. "Don't be in any hurry to come crawling back," he had shouted after her.

She didn't come crawling back, either, as he assumed she would. *God in heaven, the woman would try the patience of a saint.*

He hadn't meant it. Did she have sense enough to know that he merely had been venting his anger? Well, he'd tell her a thing or two when she finally returned.

"The back of me hand to you, woman," he'd shout, though that wouldn't mean anything either. A proper Taran wife ought to know when her man was only talking.

She's not a Taran, you dummy.

Shut up. When I want your opinion, I'll ask for it.

She had left in early morning; now it was almost night. Appalled by the enormity of what he had said and done, he had plunged recklessly through the jungle calling her name. Her behavior was unpredictable. He should have held his temper and fought the thing out some other way. The Zylongi had this crazy "deciding-to-die" thing in which you turn off your vital processes. In the state the poor girl was in, she might have done just that.

This is our honeymoon, he told himself. *We shouldn't be fighting this soon.*

You never should have done it, you idjit. You got carried away by your passions. The Abbess always warned you about that. God knows, she had experience enough of it herself when she was younger. Why weren't you after listening to her?

The woman is nothing more than a child, not much older than Retha. Would you practically rape that little tyke?

And she's never been in love before. And you're an experienced man of the galaxy and a great traveler besides. You were a badly matched couple to begin with. If you'd had any sense at all, you would have never laid a hand on her.

He kicked another rock. It bounced against a floating log and shot back at him. Even the lake was fighting him.

Well, now, it really wasn't rape. She wanted it as much as you did.

You should have said no.

Easy enough for you to talk.

Their first coupling had not been a complete success, to put the matter mildly. They were tired, nervous, frightened, unskilled—himself almost as bad as she.

No, to tell the truth, maybe worse.

It had not been all that bad, either. They both laughed at their own awkwardness and turned what might have been a disaster into a happy comedy. They played with each other's bodies and laughed themselves to sleep.

They improved as lovers with practice. The woman was a quick study, God knows. They didn't provide much in the way of sex education on Zylong, even less than the Tarans received, which wasn't much at all. But Margie was naturally good at everything, even lovemaking.

Especially lovemaking, come to think of it.

"Practice makes perfect," he said to her the first morning, as he munched on some tasty jungle fruit that she assured him was safe, even a delicacy.

"Good. Let's practice more. I want to be perfect." She literally jumped on him.

Well, they had lots of practice during those idyllic days. The woman was insatiable. Not that he minded the fun and games at all. At all. His instinctive decision that she was the proper woman had been correct. Whatever else happened between them in the decades together that he cheerfully anticipated, she would never be dull in bed. Fight they might, but as Carmody had candidly told him, there are some kinds of women you can't stay away from. His Margie was one of those.

And she had only begun to learn the arts of love. What would she be like when she was "perfect," as she wanted to be?

"Practically perfect will be enough for me," he had chuckled, removing his lips temporarily from a compliant breast.

"You deserve perfection, my beloved," she replied, tears of adoration in her eyes.

Adoration one moment, fury the next. Worse than the worst of the Tarans. And that was bad.

Of course, they had begun their life together in difficult circumstances. A walk through the jungles of Zylong was not exactly a leisurely wedding trip.

Maybe, he told himself, leaning a little bit against his Black Mood, *we would have done all right if we weren't caught out here.*

What's the point in thinking that? We are *caught out here. Then again, we can't stay in the jungle for the rest of our lives.*

After they left the pool to continue the long walk back toward the City, the jungle was not actively hostile. It looked like pictures he had seen of Precambrian forests of Earth. The reptilelike creatures who dwelt in it were small and fled quickly at their approach. There was an abundance of fruit and plenty of water. Though they'd lost most of their equipment when the raft he'd built overturned in the tributary he had foolishly insisted on fording at nightfall, staying alive was not difficult.

And the crazy woman had to dive into the River to save my harp.

As though being a bard made any difference anymore, the idjit.

The jungle took its toll nevertheless. Underbrush, swamp, rain, mist, damp, heat—a dark, dismal heat that was almost palpable under the sunscreen of giant trees—drained their strength. With only one spear blade (the precious tranquillity pills hidden in its handle) and a carbine barrel, they fought for every inch of movement through the underbrush. A humid, thick perfume hung in the jungle air like overpowering incense.

They were both sick. The inoculations Samaritha had given him back at the Body Institute protected him from the worst of the jungle diseases, but they were both listless, enervated, depressed.

He was too besotted with fulfilled passion to recognize the beginning of the trouble with Marjetta. They had stayed at their "mating pool" four days, recovering from the mountains and exploring the delights of each other's body. Practicing, as she called it. The days at the pool became unbearably delicious. His tenderness began to unlock her passions. Not only was her curiosity and her hunger a match for his, she was the more passionate.

It was his tenderness that ruined everything. Mating for the Zylongi was not something joyous; it couldn't be in a culture that so strongly repressed individuality. If he had been any kind of an anthropologist, he would have realized that sex for the Zylongi was a brief, brutal act. If people like Sammy and Ernie had discovered there was something else to love, many more saw mating as a brief respite from the loneliness and isolation that a communitarian culture fostered in sensitive people. Tenderness and concern for the other were virtually unknown.

So if a young woman goes through a series of disasters that wipes out all of her contacts with her own culture, and then discovers an unsuspected and overwhelming animal passion within herself, the result will be personality disorientation, even if she loves it and even if she insists on "practice" at every possible opportunity.

And there are plenty of opportunities, if there's

nothing else to do but nibble on delicious fruit and if your man is an oversexed and undersatisfied pig.

His judgment. Not hers.

What happened was that Margie encountered another culture and lost her own. How ironic that it was an ideal of the Taran culture—tenderness to one's lover—that did her in. If O'Neill had quickly and forcefully ravaged her, it would have been what she expected; nothing much would have been lost. After his first bumbling and clumsy failures, he had to become reasonably skilled at tenderness, play the great lover, and mess up everything. He could hear Deirdre now: "It's all your fault, you idjit. You never could control your libido, could you?"

The fighting began as soon as they left the pool area. Within a day she disintegrated. She complained, disagreed, fought, argued, and nagged. He could hardly believe that it was his lovely Marjetta, the cheerful romping mate of a day or two ago. She knew what kind of complaint would irk him the most, what kind of barb would most quickly penetrate the chinks in his self-assurance. He should have fought it out at the beginning. He dodged, ducked, and avoided, typical Taran male reaction to conflict with a woman—and made matters worse. The more she saw she could get away with, the more she pushed him. When he lost his temper finally, it was a blowup of monumental proportions that tore their relationship apart.

The second night out in the jungle she pushed

him away with the icy comment, "I will not couple with a man I do not respect." His mistake was in letting her get away with it. He was so hurt that it hadn't occurred to him till too late that he was being tested by an emotionally overwrought child. He should have laughed at her, joshed her, caressed her, and won her back.

No, she had to go into her funk and I into my Black Mood. The Lord made us and the divil matched us.

Their struggle through the jungle was mostly silent, punctuated by an occasional outburst of recrimination and complaint from Marjetta.

According to the map, the journey should have been less arduous after they reached the Great Lake. The River was too swift in its course toward the lake for them to consider a raft, but after the Great Waterfall it flowed toward the City in what appeared to be a broad band of navigable water all the way down to the Zylong Plain. Again he had misjudged.

When they had hacked their way to its shores, the lake was more sinister and more depressing than the jungle. It was still and smooth, shrouded in thick mists, filled with vegetation and rubble.

"We are going to cross *that?*" Margie had snarled.

"We certainly are," he had replied tartly—though he had decided not to try a crossing. But when she nagged him, he reacted by doing whatever she didn't want to do. So, against his better judgment, he ordered her to start working on a raft. That was a major mistake.

They worked for a solid day, hacking away at trees with a stone ax he had devised and fashioning a crude raft out of logs and vines. Then they spent most of a night trying to construct flat paddles from the soft woody substance of the fernlike trees.

In the morning the mist was even thicker. He insisted on setting off, despite her vigorous complaints.

To give her credit, she did what she was told despite her complaints.

The lake was liquid hell. They repeatedly fouled the raft in vegetation, collided with logs, and swirled dizzily in sudden and unpredictable currents. The heat and humidity were intolerable, the perfume of the forest replaced by the foul stench of rotting seaweed.

The lake creatures were not nearly so timid as the jungle ones. A huge head thrust itself out of the mists of the lake and snapped a paddle in two. It might just as well have been an arm or a leg.

"See," Margie crowed triumphantly, "I told you the lake was dangerous."

They gave up and drifted into shore—though it might have been an island. The Black Mood rose up out of the fetid waters and claimed him. The mists were so thick they couldn't see more than a few feet in any direction. O'Neill was disoriented. He did not know where they were or how they could find their way to the massive waterfall that began the main course of the River. He wanted to explore in one direction, Marjetta wanted to go another. They had gone his way—and discovered nothing but an impassable swamp. They were lost somewhere on the shore of a great dismal lake in the heart of a jungle.

She berated him for all his failures and mistakes. "You are a bad poet, a worse soldier, and the worst possible explorer. How many more mistakes can you make before you will kill us both? I would have been happier in Narth's harem."

She couldn't have meant it, of course. It was the last desperate cry of a frightened and disoriented child. He should have taken her into his arms and soothed and caressed her until she calmed down. Any man with an ounce of sense would have done just that.

But Seamus O'Neill in the Black Mood, by his own admission, didn't have even half an ounce of sense.

"Shut up," he bellowed. "Like all the people on this godforsaken planet, you're a stupid fool, a coward, and a crybaby. You're an intolerable bitch, too, and a lousy lover."

"How can one be a good lover with a clumsy rapist?"

He couldn't take it any longer, he told himself in later attempts at self-justification. He ordered her out into the jungle. God knows, he had provocation enough. How was he to know that, dumb, literal-minded Zylongi bitch that she was, she'd take him literally?

It was the end of everything. The end of the mission, the end of Marjetta, and soon the end of Seamus O'Neill. "Poor fella," they'd say back on the *Iona*. "It was a shame he had to die so young. Not a bad one, you know. A great poet, even if we never did give him enough credit or praise. And of course a first-class soldier. He just didn't have what was needed in a tight situation. Made a fine soldier but not much as a spy and a lover. 'Twas a shame, 'twas indeed, but we didn't have anyone else to send, worse luck." They would all sigh, then sigh again.

A poor spy and a worse lover, such would be the epitaph of Seamus Finnbar Diarmuid Brendan Tomas O'Neill.

After a while they would forget him altogether.

He buried his head in his hands. Now would be the appropriate time to sob for his lost life and his lost love. But his Mood was so black that he couldn't work up the energy for tears, which kind of ruined the effect.

"Geemie," a tiny voice from a great distance. *I'm imagining it.*

"Geemie, my love." *Ah no, it 'tis real enough.*

He decided he didn't want to look up.

'Tis yourself. He did look up. There was Marjetta, standing silently, several yards down the shore of the steaming lake, tears rolling down her cheeks. His heart did a flipflop. Lord, she was beautiful, even after a week in the jungle. Despite the Black Mood he felt a surge of desire.

"So, you decided to come back, did you,

woman? It took you long enough," he muttered glumly.

She had regained some of her self-possession. "May I sit here on this log?" A tiny still voice.

"It's a free planet." He sunk his head lower in his hands, trying not to look at her. "You can sit where you damn please." He wasn't giving an inch.

"May I talk with you?" A polite enough risk, modestly presented.

"The good Lord Himself couldn't stop that if you'd made up your mind." He burrowed his head further into his hands. She was being reasonable, why couldn't he respond?

She threw herself at his feet and embraced his legs. "Dear master, forgive me. I am unworthy of you. I don't deserve you. I'm a worthless . . . bitch. A fool. An idjit. I could never again be your proper woman. Let me at least be a humble slave to serve your slightest whim. Please, please, wondrous master, forgive me. I'll never offend you again. I promise."

Well, now that's a bit much. Seamus removed his hands from his face and considered the trembling shoulders and heaving rib cage. *Ah, she can't mean it, can she? It's nothing but stupid Zylongi exaggeration.*

Seamus O'Neill, you're the idjit. One thing these poor heathens don't do is exaggerate. The poor wee tyke thinks she can make it back only as a slave. That won't do at all, at all.

He stood up, feeling a jab of pain in his back. Ah, his spine would never be the same again. He pulled the would-be slave unceremoniously to her feet.

"You'd make a rotten slave, woman."

"I could try." She would not look at him. "Beat me if you wish, please beat me. I deserve to be terribly beaten. I'll try to be a good slave. I really will."

"That won't do. The only thing you'd be any good at is a wife. You're much too bossy to be a slave. If there's one thing I can't stand it's a bossy slave woman. I've had my share of them, let me tell you. Now there was that time on Galway when a bossy slave woman, two Wild Geese, and myself were having a quiet jar of the creature and . . ."

Her tears stopped. "Geemie, you're joking."

"Not at all, at all. But I'll tell you one thing, woman. There'll be none of this slave and master stuff between us, and that's settled. You're my wife and that makes us equals, which gives me an advantage because if you weren't my wife, you'd clearly be superior."

"Geemie," her eyes were shining.

"As a matter of fact," he was not going to quit when he was on a roll, "I'll even stipulate that, wife or not, you are still a little bit superior to me, but not much. Is that clear?"

She nodded, so choked with emotion that she could not speak.

"Now as for this beating stuff, we Tarans are not into it, if you take my meaning. Sure, occasionally we lose our tempers, but we hate ourselves afterward. A wife like you deserves a good spanking now and then. . . ."

"Spank me if you wish. I deserve it. I . . ."

"Might even like it, huh? Well, you'll never get any of that from me, woman, no matter how much you deserve it. God knows what you might do to me when I'm in the wrong. Anyway, I can think of a lot better things to do with you, some of which I intend to try in a very few moments."

Not bad altogether. If I do say so myself. He kissed her cheek, a promise of reconciling love to come. *God knows, I'll have to tell Carmody he was right.*

"I am forgiven, then?" She was radiant again, hardly able to believe her good fortune.

What else did you expect, woman?

"If I'm forgiven too."

She threw her arms around him. "I love you so. You are such a wonderful man. I am the most fortunate woman in the galaxy."

"At least."

She took a deep breath. The words bubbled out like a tumbling brook. "Seamus, what was wrong with me? I fell apart. I was not me anymore. I am a soldier; I believe in bravery, but I acted the coward. I believe in loyalty to my leader, but I tried to destroy your effectiveness. I believe that one should support one's mate, but I let you down over and over. I love you, but I hurt you terribly. I wanted to die because I had failed you. I was about to die. This voice inside of me said, 'Go back to him, you little idjit, he needs you.' So I came back. But you don't really need me, do you? Of course you do. You love me. What is happening?" She broke down. "Oh, Geemie, please help me. . . ."

How do you explain culture shock to a woman under such emotional stress? He would make more of a mess of things to try. The sheer physical effort to attempt an explanation was beyond him. Better to let things go.

"Margie, I can't help you," he said with heavy resignation, but his heart was beating rapidly and his body was already aching for her.

Marjetta continued breathlessly, her eyes begging, tearing at his heart, "I don't want to hurt you, Geemie. I decided to die out there in the jungle. Then that voice inside me said that I would hurt you even more by dying. So I came back to try again."

"And glad I am you did." His lips began to roam, her eyes, lips, ears, throat, chest. *Love after fights is the best of all, Carmody said. Well, I'll soon find out.*

"Tell me what is happening. Am I becoming insane?" she pleaded.

"I'll tell you, but please, I am tired and worn-out and so are you. Listen to what I'm saying and promise me you won't get angry?"

"I promise." She wiped her tears. "But how can I listen if you play with my breasts that way?"

"That's part of listening."

Only it made talking a little difficult. So he turned to her head and stroked her short, curly hair tenderly. He took a deep breath, crossed his fingers, partly to make up for any wee fibs he might have to tell and partly for luck, and began very carefully.

"Well, it's like this. . . ." He grinned. "You see, you were attracted to me partly because I am irresistible and partly because I am the opposite of the Zylongi, whose whole culture you were beginning to doubt. Remember you said you didn't want to live before you pulled me out of the drain?"

"And after I met you I became a revolutionary?"

Ah, she catches on quick.

"You find out that your government has been systematically lying to you, that they are even trying to kill you. Sure most people would have caved in worse than you did."

She looked at him very seriously, drawing back slightly from his embrace, waiting for him to go on.

"I come along like an amadon, I upset you with a line of come-on blarney that you'd never heard from any eligible Zylongi bachelor, we go through all that stuff in the desert and on the mountain; then I turn gentle. Emotions come out you never knew you had, surrender, trust, passion, sexual playfulness." *I sound like the monk who gives our annual retreat.* "It must have scared the hell out of you, so you try to protect yourself by becoming a child again."

Those last words were a mistake. She pulled back from him, furious.

"How dare you say I'm a child. I'm just as adult as you are. More so."

He gritted his teeth and grabbed her arms very hard. "Woman, you are more so. I already said that. But show you're adult by listening to me."

She clenched her fists and struggled to free herself. Then she began to laugh. "Seamus, you wonderful, lovable idjit. It's splendidly funny." She leaned her head against his chest. "You're just going to have to treat me like a confused child." And then she laughed like it was the greatest joke in the world.

A dark nasty suspicion raised its deformed head in the back of his imagination. "It was a voice inside you that told you to come back? What exactly would that voice have been saying?"

Her fingers stroked his face. "Oh, I don't remember. . . . Is it all that important?" She felt his jaw tighten. "All right, darling, it is important. Let me see . . . the voice said, 'Get back there, you idjit, the poor man needs you.' Yes, those were the words."

"Poor man." *That wasn't Zylongi talk at all, it was pure Taran. Deirdre, I owe you one. So you are still listening and watching. The least you can do, woman, is give a man a little privacy. . . .* She jarred him out of his thoughts by taking his hand and guiding it back to her breasts. *You get out of here, Your Eminence, and leave me and my proper woman in some decent privacy. You hear now?*

277

"Aren't you ever going to couple with me again?" his woman asked plaintively.

"Indeed I am, woman," he sighed. If the Abbess wanted to play voyeur, he'd give her quite a show. "Like you've never been coupled before."

"Wonderful," she sighed happily. "You're such a good man."

"And after that?"

"Yes, master?" she grinned wickedly.

"After that—" *Sure she wasn't the only one whose passions had changed* "—after that, we're going down to Zylong City and clean out that mess so decent people like you and me can live there in peace and freedom."

16

The saber-toothed tiger bounded toward Seamus like a demon sent from hell.

It was, he noted as he fumbled for his spear, the biggest critter he had ever seen. God had made a mistake in upgrading the harmless kitten into such a fearsome beast.

As long as the *Dev*, he estimated as the tiger leaped, its long and fearsome teeth aimed at his neck.

He realized he would not raise his spear in time. *It's been an interesting life.*

"Marjetta!" he screamed, knowing that it would be his last word.

Somehow she slipped between him and the soaring beast, jammed her spear into its chest, and twisted the fearsome animal out of its line of flight.

It rolled over next to Seamus in an angry spasm, growling and pawing the air with its huge claws as blood erupted from its gaping wound.

Marjetta hurled Seamus savagely back from the dying animal. "Are you waiting for it to kill you, you bloody idjit? It's not dead yet."

Trembling and silent, Seamus let her pull him to the side of the tiny clearing in which they were camped. She continued to rage at him.

"What was the matter with you? Why did you stand there and stare at that awful thing? Why didn't you pick up your spear and kill it? You're a bloody amadon."

"Why an amadon?" he began to breathe again.

"Because you're the worst kind of idjit. Why didn't you kill it?"

"Well, partly because I was too scared to move. . . ."

"I don't believe that," she snapped at him.

"And partly because I didn't know how to."

"Oh, of course." Small contrite voice. "I assumed that they had these ugly creatures on all planets and that you had practiced killing them, like soldiers do here."

"You practice on real ones?"

"Of course not." Now she was gasping for breath, terror finally catching up with her. "Mechanical ones."

" 'Tis yourself that has the quick reactions."

"The holy saints be praised," she threw her arms around him. "Oh, Geemie, I almost lost you!"

"I owe you about a half dozen now." He crushed her in his own arms. "Sure that thing had its eye on my throat. Come on, woman, let's sit down before we both collapse."

They huddled together on the floor of the forest, avoiding the sight of the dead tiger and trying to calm their shattered nerves.

"I have a confession to make," she said calmly. "I knew I'd have to tell you eventually. Now I must tell you . . . before something else happens."

Seamus stirred uneasily. She was a complex mixture of woman, comic mimic, grateful child, passionate lover, and fiercely quick soldier. The last had been quiet lately as she docilely followed her husband through the jungle. *Don't kid yourself, Seamus Finnbar O'Neill, she's still a handful.*

"Confess away, darling girl."

"No Zylongi maiden strips for a stranger the way I did that first night. I was shameful."

"Sure now, I didn't mind getting a first view—" he held her close "—of the merchandise, if you take my meaning. They're not bad breasts, you know. I mean I've seen better. Good breasts, not great ones, you know. Now on the planet Cork . . ."

"Be quiet," she insisted primly. "I'll not be distracted by your foolishness. I wanted to seduce you. I was terribly attracted to you the first moment I saw you . . . that's why I was so rude, understand?"

"I think so."

"I thought I would die soon; I wanted to be ravished once before I died; a red-bearded god would be better than most lovers; so . . . well, you know what I did."

"I do. . . ."

"Then I learned what love was. . . ."

"Ah. What is it now?"

"The way you treated me, kind and gentle and good man that you were. I thought it was all violence and pleasure. I fell completely in love with you then. It was hard during the mission because I didn't know who you were. But I've wanted you since that night."

"And you finally got me?"

She nodded, her head against his chest.

"Now what is it that you're sorry for in this whole disgraceful story of seducing the innocent space bum?"

She considered carefully. "Nothing, I guess."

"Herself says that when we know what it is really like to love and be loved, we know what God is like."

"How beautiful. Your god—Jesus, is it?—feels about me like I do about you? He loves me the way you love me?"

"Well, now, Jesus is involved in it all, if you take my meaning, but I guess the answer is yes."

"That's what Deirdre says?"

"Ah . . . the woman's name keeps coming up." He thought for a few seconds. "Were you following me that night?"

"Of course," she seemed surprised that he asked. "I knew the Fourth Secretary feared you and that you needed someone to take care of you."

"From saber-toothed tigers and Fourth Secretaries, deliver us, O Lord." Seamus rather liked the turn of phrase.

"What does that mean?"

"It's a prayer to my guardian angel . . . they're spirits God sends to take care of us."

"Your god is so wonderful. Just like you." She snuggled close to him. "I think I'm ready now to make love, Seamus."

"I was afraid that would happen."

Afterward, when she slept complacently in his arms, Seamus wondered why the great need to confess what should have been obvious to any man who was smart enough to realize that he was the pursued and not the pursuer.

"Someone as smart as me, in other words," he muttered ruefully.

Late the next day they encountered a band of well-armed hordi. Again it was Marjetta who was alert to the danger first.

She sniffed the air. "Someone coming, Geemie, take cover."

It was an order, not a request. O'Neill did what he was told and followed her into a cluster of crimson bushes that reminded his guilty conscience of the Cardinal herself.

Sure enough, a band of about forty hordi males, with females and young trailing behind, padded down the side of the lake, armed to the teeth with knives, spears, and clubs almost as big as they were. On the lake itself several large canoes, jammed with more weapons and supplies and steered by a massive rudder, were drifting at the same speed the aborigines were walking.

O'Neill and his woman waited motionless till the band had disappeared.

"We wouldn't have provided much more than an appetizer for that crowd," he said when she rose from the bushes.

"It's a war party, not a hunting party," she said thoughtfully. "Marching toward the City."

"They're going to storm the City with spears and clubs?"

"As part of Narth's army. He'll send them across the River first to see if the laser weapons are operational. If they die, then Narth knows not to attack."

"He's dead."

"Is he?" she asked skeptically. "I hope so."

"So the Outsiders don't think the hordi are human either?"

"Of course not. They'll use them and kill them too. Why should they be any different from us?"

"But you think they're human?"

"Sometimes I think they're more human than we are. And, however they may have come here, they were here first."

"So even if ... I mean after we win in the City, we will have to do something about them, won't we?"

She stooped to pick up her pack. "What would you do, Seamus O'Neill, to reverse a thousand years of mistakes?"

Well, now that was a very intelligent question. "I'd sign up Quars to begin negotiations with them. He's got his head screwed on right."

She smiled proudly. "That's my Seamus. No one in this whole world would have thought of that."

Seamus was not sure that he agreed or that her proud smile was justified. *What do I know about politics?*

"Freedom for everyone, darling—" she squeezed his arm "—including those poor little creatures."

"For everyone," he agreed with a certain lack of enthusiasm.

"Come, we must hurry to the City before it is too late. Freedom for everyone!"

17

Many days later, having spent a restless night worrying about freedom, Seamus O'Neill opened one eye as the morning sun forced its way into the control cabin of the *Eamon De Valera*. There was a naked woman standing at the entrance hatch, her strong young body bathed golden in the rays of the sunrise. She was gazing at him with tolerant adoration. Quickly he closed the eye.

Ah, the woman will be the death of me. Wasn't it bad enough, her laughing at me every inch of the way from the Great Lake? She wants to make love at this heathenish hour of the morning, and myself trying to decide whether to go into that damn City today.

He sighed quietly for fear of stirring up her pagan passions even more if she knew he was awake. The last thing he'd expected was that the woman would turn into a comic. She had barely smiled till they got to Hyperion. Now she was laughing and dancing all the day long, even with the two of them exhausted.

She must have always been a comic, just hiding it from me so I wouldn't know what I was getting caught in.

He was afraid again, but it passed quickly. Her unexpected humor had kept him going when he was ready to give up, down the long, twisting animal-infested paths from the Great Falls.

Drat the woman. She says the same things she said before our fight, but now they're a joke. What am I going to do with her? He knew what she wanted him to do . . . it'd wear a man out. . . . It all started the day after they had seen the hordi by the lake. . . .

That morning he awoke to find Marjetta gone. The carbine was gone with her. A weather change dissolved the lake mists, the wind was brisk, the sun shone warm. She had probably gone off to do some exploring—he hoped.

She was back, eyes dancing. "We've found our waterfall, Seamus O'Neill. Sure, if you had ears like a Zylongi you would have woken up this morning to hear its roar. Hurry, darling, it's the most amazing thing you'll ever see."

Seamus had seen a lot of marvels in various parts of the galaxy, but the Great Waterfall of Zylong took the prize. Almost without warning the whole lake spilled over into a valley half a mile below. They could not see the other end of it, lost as it was in the rainbow mists. The fall was dazzling in the sunlight; the spray blew in their faces, soaking them. O'Neill and Marjetta hugged and danced.

"Geemie . . ." Her face turned glum, her fingers dug into his arm. "If we get through all this, will they let you back on Tara?"

Why, of all times, would she pick now to ask me that?

"Oh, I think my friends will have enough political power to get things set up for me," he said airily. *Where's the woman going now?*

"Will Deirdre help?" And then, seeing the surprise on his face, she quickly added, "You remember. You told me about the ugly old religious leader who was your friend. How old did you say she was?"

"Oh, eighty or ninety of our years at least, and ugly as sin." He put his arm around Marjetta.

"In the middle of the morning with the most beautiful scenery in Zylong to gaze at . . ." she said reprovingly. "Geemie, you have no self-control at all."

"Sure, the breasts of a beautiful woman will beat a waterfall for scenery any morning."

"Zylongi men are not much interested in breasts. Do you have a fixation? Do all Tarans?" she asked maliciously.

"I'll tell you what, woman. If you don't like my fixations, you can go and find yourself one of those cold-blooded Zylongi creatures. Don't forget you're mated to a Taran, peculiarities and all."

He was ready to climb down the side of the mountain to the base of the falls. But the woman was in her playful mood. She wrestled him to the ground, overcoming his not completely make-believe resistance, pinned him on his back, and peeled off his clothes.

"Taran or not, my darling Geemie, you have a wonderful male body and I want it right now. You can play with my breasts if you want to, but hold still. I want to play with you."

"That seems fair enough," he sighed, willingly yielding himself to her demands. *Sure, I knew all along, she was the proper woman.* "Only stop tickling me, woman. That's too much altogether."

"No, I won't. I'll never stop. How do you like that?"

Ah, the practice has paid off after all.

So they played all morning, swimming in a pool at the edge of the falls, admiring the rainbows in the foam, wrestling and making love again and again and again. It was the beginning of a true honeymoon, an orgy of love that went on no matter what the hardships of their long march were.

And she can never have enough of me. That's a little more than I bargained for.

Ah, but the Black Mood never did come back. There's that, isn't there?

So on the *Dev* that morning while she laughed and danced and sang her heathenish songs, troubled thoughts gnawed at his mind and heart. Margie he'd never give up, no matter what. And he meant it about bringing freedom to Zylong. But true Taran that he was, on later reflection he threw in a qualification that gave him an escape hatch from his spontaneous outburst.

They'd bring freedom to Zylong if it were possible to do that. Only he was not at all sure that it was possible. *No one is held to the impossible, are they? What was the phrase the Lady Abbess used?*

Ad impossibile nemo tenetur.

Right. Tomorrow was "go" or "no go" for the *Iona.* If they wanted to end the mission, this was the day to do it. He had made that very clear to them. He knew now they were listening, probably had been all along. If herself was meddling, unasked mind you, in his private life, she was certainly tuned in to his public comings and goings.

Ah, if we pull this off, they'll be singing songs about me and my woman for a thousand years. Who was this Finn MacCool anyway?

But they had to make up their minds. *Sure, I'm delivering you an ultimatum. Either pull me and me woman out of this heathen place now, or I'm going along with the conspiracy and we'll invite you down, once we take over.*

I don't think we have much of a chance of winning, but it's the only alternative. And I'll be expecting your help, are you hearing me now?

None of this "poor Seamus" stuff while I'm providing early-evening entertainment for you. I'm not breaking any Rules exactly. Haven't they been after asking me to join them? But either you pull me out now—you hear me, My Lady Countess, Abbess, Captain, Cardinal?—or you're going to have to take full responsibility for what happens.

I'll not let you slip away with any of your clever evasions, either.

That makes it pretty clear, doesn't it? All right, you think that because Seamus O'Neill has proved himself a moderately adequate lover—no I'll redo that, a superlative lover—success has gone to his head and he's talking big with nothing behind.

Well, let me tell all of you something. I love the woman. I'll do anything for her. I don't want to have to choose between you and her, but if you force me to, you know whose side I'm going to be on.

Note, he added with a touch of placating reflection, a little bit of mental blarney, *that all I'm doing is following the Bible about cleaving to my woman because we're two in one flesh. You'd expect me to say what I'm saying.*

And if good sex makes me a more obnoxious bastard than I was before, well, guys, you're just going to have to live with that. Understand?

The radio banks of the *Dev* were open; they must know that. He would be alert for a signal. If none came, he could assume that they wanted him to proceed into the City with Marjetta to finish what she planned to start. He was afraid to think of just what kind of finish it would be. *Iona* didn't need any more information. Zylong was in extremis; Podraig's estimate of a fifty–fifty chance of a blowup seemed conservative—especially with the introduction of Marjetta's revolutionary scheme.

He had moved from information gatherer to active participant, which was counter to direct orders from Deirdre. How did she and the Grand Council feel about that? Did they know the two crucial things he had discovered about the Zylongi in this romp through the jungle? The Zylongi, even the strong ones, were prone to intense culture-shock regression, and there seemed to be strong undercurrents of wit that sustained the intelligent and sensitive ones despite the pressures of their rigid society. Ernie's often savage irony was a manifestation of this; Margie was supported by her sense of how ludicrous their hopeless situation was.

She stopped her cavorting, came to him, and put a cool, tender hand on his forehead. *I can't help myself, I've fallen in love with the woman.*

"Do you really want to go back?" she asked gently, as she had last night, "because if you want to take our chances in space, I'll come with you."

"Do you want that?"

"No. I have an obligation to my people. But now I have an obligation to you too. I will do what you want."

Hear her? Two in one flesh. Just like me.

"Well," he had told her last night, "let's think about it tonight and make up our minds tomorrow." Now it was tomorrow, and she wanted to make love again. Which, for all his complaints about exhaustion, was what he wanted too. She was so deliciously, wonderfully, irresistibly beautiful, especially when her clothes were off.

"What I want now is you, woman." He grabbed her arm and wrestled her to the control couch. She giggled and pretended to struggle and then pulled him down on top of her. He held her immobile and drank in her loveliness.

"You are so beautiful, my love."

"Thank you," she twisted in mock resistance.

"And your beauty only reveals who and what you are. Marjetta's body is not as beautiful as she is."

"Are you going to make me cry or are you going to make me love you?"

"How about both?"

"That sounds nice. . . . I like that. Do it again."

"Glutton."

"It's your mouth, not mine."

All right, if it wasn't for the joy and pleasure of this woman, I wouldn't be nearly so fierce.

"I'm happy," he whispered to her, "for the first time since my parents were killed."

"Yours too?"

"Mine too."

"Do you want children, Geemie?"

"If you're their mother."

"Who else? . . . Oh, Geemie, that's wonderful, don't stop."

"You're not trying to tell me something . . ."

If she were pregnant, that would complicate things terrible.

"Just asking. . . . Oh . . . please don't stop."

Then he was too busy to think.

Later, while she was out in the jungle collecting fruit for breakfast, he returned to his reflections. If a signal came from *Iona*, they would certainly leave. Since it hadn't come yet, probably it wouldn't. Give them another half day, just in case there was a debate up there that herself wanted to sort out. He could decide to end the mission himself. A single alert message from his transmitter and protection from the monastery against the Zylongian phasers would be at his service—he hoped. Were he to seek refuge on *Iona* now, what would his reception be? Would a board of inquiry decide he was within his rights to end the mission, that in fact he had performed it at all? Or did continued silence mean the decision had already been taken—to write off O'Neill as an agent whose mission had failed?

Or were the Council and Her Ladyship, the Captain Abbess, waiting for developments? Perhaps the message to him was simply to go on.

He had made friends on Zylong—people he cared about, like Ernie, Sammy, Horor, Carina, poor little Retha, who was probably dead on the desert with whatever was left of that sad, brave troop of soldiers. And Marjetta—she whose strength and humor pulled them through the jungles, she who touched his life like no one ever had, she whose commitment to her people was placing her in extreme danger. How could he possibly leave her? How could he be the instrument of wrenching her away from her people now that they were on the edge of catastrophe?

She shook his shoulders . . . the same firm hands that had pulled him out of the sewer.

"Good morning, lovely lady," he said brightly, putting his arm around her waist.

She kissed him tenderly. "Good morning, Honored Major. Fallen asleep again? Did I wear you out? Here is breakfast. Did you sleep well?"

Laughing at me again.

"I've had worse naps," he admitted with feigned reluctance, pulling her down on top of himself. "Do I see by the light in your eyes that your passions are raging again? So soon?"

Her hands lovingly caressed his face. *Ah, it is the tenderness . . . the terrible tenderness that wrenches your heart, scaring the living daylights out of you.*

"It's what the sight of you does to me, Geemie. . . ." *Now the damn woman is crying.*

Afterward, she sat next to him on the couch. "Are we going to the City?"

"Did you ever doubt it?"

"No."

"Well, then, let's wake them up with the news of our miraculous survival. Hide your pills in my medical kit. We'll leave them out here for the time being. No point in risking their being confiscated in the City."

Several hours later they were on a hovercraft with four soldiers and their commander, Captain Yens—who really did look like he was ten Taran years old—heading back to the City. All of his troops were members of the Young Ones. The conversation about the past several weeks was unhindered by the need to repeat official truth.

"Comrade Captain," Yens formally addressed Marjetta, "we rejoice that you and the Hero Poet are alive."

Marjetta returned, "Comrade Captain, we rejoice that you are here to meet us. Poet O'Neill, may I present you to Honored Captain Yens?"

O'Neill figured that he'd better get to what was on both their minds. "I trust your respected future mate is well, Captain?" he asked with all his formal dignity, his throat constricting at the thought that she might not be.

Yens broke into a broad grin. "She has never been better, Honored Poet Hero Guest. I do not exaggerate. Marvelous things happened to her on her desert ventures."

"Tell me, Captain, do you like the changes?"

"Indeed, Noble Hero. She has gained strength and . . . determination. I would not have it otherwise." His eyes danced with the light of a man who was thoroughly captivated.

"Glad to hear it, Yens. You seem to be a man after my own heart." O'Neill smiled.

"Thank you, Honored Sir. Could you provide the answer to one trivial question for me? What is an 'idjit'?"

"Ah, well now, he's a kind of high-powered amadon," Seamus replied wisely.

"I see, sir. Fascinating." He looked a little puzzled.

Much had happened in their absence. The death of the Fourth Secretary had been announced as simply a "tragic accident." The Sixth Secretary, it was rumored, had assumed power. "The old fool," snapped Marjetta. "During Festival he pursues maidens."

The Committee, already inept and stodgy, was now even less able to cope with its problems. The campaign to dispose of Marjetta was dropped,

Retha and her troops were allowed to return unmolested. Narth's death removed the threat of the Outsiders and other denizens of his "empire." In the City, the Hooded Ones were becoming still bolder. With the confusion and drift at the top, the chances of the Young Ones increased. The Committee would move against no one before harvest.

"Are you with us, Marjetta?" asked Yens eagerly.

"Until death, Yens."

"Until freedom," he amended.

All their faces shone with the fervor of commitment. *Brigid, Patrick, and Columcile, they have imaginative slogans.*

Yens asked Marjetta urgently, "You have the pills?"

"I have. They are safely hidden." Her eyes glowed with a martyr's enthusiasm. A Roman maiden—no, a Roman matron, ready for the lions.

"Major O'Neill is with us?"

"Of course," she responded decisively.

Hey, wait a minute, fellows, I didn't volunteer for anything.

They all turned to him. "Freedom, Seamus O'Neill!"

"Freedom, indeed," he said, without any particular enthusiasm.

They didn't notice.

18

Though his face was burning with embarrassment, Seamus was laughing as loudly as the rest. *All right, the witch is a superb mimic; but she doesn't have to ape my voice and my gestures so perfectly. Nor is there any reason to tell them the story of my tipping over the raft or bungling the attack of the saber-tooth. A man receives no proper respect at all anymore. Well, I'll fix her later in the night.*

"So then the heroic Major said, 'No, we will do it my way,' and the whole craft spun over into the water. He falls very gracefully . . . have you ever seen him fall? I was able to drag him out of the water again. It seems like I must do this all the time . . . it is not completely unpleasant . . . but he is so large that it grows tiresome . . . would any of you like to assume responsibility for keeping our Honored Guest from drowning himself?" She managed to keep a straight face when she asked the question, though the stars in her brown eyes were dancing with mischief.

Hers was the only straight face in the room, though. Samaritha, Ornigon, Horor, and Carina were convulsed with most un-Zylongian merriment. Margie's highly fictional and very selective description of their "voyage" through the jungle had amused them for most of the "small entertainment" at the Music Director's house—and she'd only made it halfway through the trip. O'Neill was cast in the role of the fumbling hero saved by a brave and resourceful woman ... a role which was uncomfortably close to reality.

Sure you'd love it, wouldn't you, Your Eminence? This one is too much like you altogether.

In his own mind, he had made up a bawdy ballad which would describe in the same fictional style the bedding of Marjetta. But he couldn't sing it. First of all, it would shock the Zylongi into horrified silence. Secondly, it was not clear to him that any of the locals realized that Marjetta had become his proper woman. It was a subject that was discreetly avoided.

"Oh, Geemie, you must have had such a wonderful time in the jungle," gasped his hostess, her dark features rosy red with efforts to control her laughter. *Now what did she mean by that? Was it obvious to everyone that Margie's glowing vitality meant she'd found a man to sleep with? Maybe in this society folks didn't dare notice such signs that the rules were being broken.*

"Well, I'm glad I'm providing my hosts with amusement. Sure it's the least I can do." He tried

299

to sound rueful but shifted uncomfortably on his soft couch.

"Ah, now, Honored Guest," protested Ornigon, "you must permit us some amusement . . . there are difficult times ahead. . . ." A quick frown crossed the man's face. He regretted he had said it. There was an anxious pause, suddenly all the faces serious; then Margie hastily plunged on to the days they were lost in the mists. Some of the gusto went out of her wit.

His friends were more relaxed with him than when he first arrived, more ready to laugh and joke. With their openness came a revelation of the deep foreboding with which they faced the coming Festival. They seemed to sense that their society and their lives teetered on the edge of a deep pit. The young people knew that their revolution was just ahead. Even if they whistled in the dark when they were with each other, they must still privately be terrified. *How could Margie laugh? . . . Maybe there were some Celtic genes somewhere from her past . . . just my luck, it would be.*

Later that night they attended a meeting of the revolutionaries. Firmly taking his hand, Margie led him underground. They descended three levels beneath the City, under the basement level of the great buildings, lower than the vast underground transportation and communication network, to the level of the old granaries, now abandoned and musty. In the floor of one of these ancient storerooms there was a rusty hatch that pulled up with surprising ease. Stone steps led down to another, much smaller room, which appeared to be of even more ancient vintage. Out of this room ran a network of tunnels to still more chambers. The City was built, like ancient Rome on Earth, over catacombs.

Margie told him that these underground chambers were more extensive than anyone could accurately describe, because official teaching denied their existence. The Reorganizers were afraid of the underground network—they themselves had used it for planning their own revolution. Tonight's meeting was to be held in what was supposed to have been the Reorganizers' headquarters. "Here," she said with the excitement of the very young revolutionary, "came into being oppression, and here also will come into being freedom."

There wasn't much in the group of forty young people who had piled into the meeting room that would give hope for their success. The idea of their overthrowing an ancient social structure and establishing a new one would have been a joke were they not so serious. Their leader was an old-young man named Chronos, a marginal instructor in philosophy at the university. Though his gray hair marked him as a man in his forties, he maintained the language and enthusiasm of youth.

Chronos was not a military or political leader. He was a mystical visionary with dreamy eyes and a beatific smile. He talked about freedom as if its simple attainment would solve all the problems of Zylongian society. They would seize the Military Center, break into its arsenal for more carbines and ammunition (they had only ten guns, a few hundred pounds of ammunition, and a couple score small explosive charges in their underground hideaway), and then quickly occupy the Central Building and the Energy Center, thus gaining control of three-fourths of the Central Plaza, which should ensure a successful takeover of the government.

It would be a "purifying fire of freedom!" Chronos finished his ringing appeal to action. What would catch fire, how it would be put out, and what would rise from the ashes didn't seem worth his consideration.

The young people loved it. Enthusiasm might enable them to carry out the quick, simple thrust of their bold strategy—although a thousand things could go wrong with it. *After the Committee, what? No one seemed to know or care. These Young Ones were not much different from the Hooded Ones; they both saw no farther than the destruction of existing institutions.*

Marjetta whispered into his ear. "You see why it took so long for me to join them; the man is appalling. He is far worse than an amadon."

Well, at least his woman wasn't being taken in.

"Is this the best there is? No other revolutionary group at all?"

"All the others are even worse; these have some strategy and plan. The rest are mystics, dreamers, and mad anarchists."

Seamus had nothing against mystics, dreamers, or anarchists. Many Tarans were all three. But Chronos would never have been permitted on the

Iona. "Emotionally unstable," Podraig would have announced, with an appropriate volley of foul words. "Six out of ten chances of a breakdown." That would have been that.

After his speech and the singing of the freedom song, Chronos took his leave, greeting the two new members of the group—Marjetta and O'Neill—with polite disinterest. Yens, Horor, Margie, and O'Neill, the de facto high command, remained behind. O'Neill promptly demanded to know about what they expected to happen after power was seized. The idea didn't seem to be important to the young people.

They were not hypocrites, planning to set themselves up as a new Committee to oppress the people in the name of the people. Out of the chaos that was bound to result there could be something much worse than the present dictatorship. The forces tearing Zylong apart would do their work regardless of the Young Ones. The question was, who would pick up the pieces?

After the others left, Margie stood on tiptoe and kissed the back of his neck. "Come with me, Geemie." And she led him to one of the small rooms that branched off a corridor exiting from the larger meeting room. She had somehow managed to furnish it with a number of soft Zylongi cloaks, much like their desertwear but more finely woven.

He was still disturbed, and too upset by the evening's events to appreciate the promise these accommodations offered.

"You don't like it, dear Geemie?" she asked sorrowfully.

"Would you expect me to be jumping up and down in celebration, woman? A pack of amadons and onchoks, presided over by a psycho, and they're organizing a revolution and then a free society. Freedom indeed! You and I will be the targets. Sure they all ought to be put permanently on your tranquillity pills."

"What's an onchok?"

"A female amadon!" he replied tartly.

"Glory be, I learn more about your language every day." She was now tenderly stroking his hair. "Seamus, I have some news. First, the hordi army did not disintegrate when Narth died. There is a new leader, a man named Popilo, our former Army Commander who was sent into exile last year."

"You mean they've got a full-fledged General out there? And I bet he's just the opposite of the poor old fella that's sitting in his chair now." He put his arms around her. *An idjit she might be, but she certainly filled your arms nicely.* He kissed her forehead, though clumsily because he was still trying to think about the revolution.

"He is smart, tough, and very ambitious, which is why the Committee got rid of him. They said he was guilty of the crime of Bonapartism—which he was." She pulled his robe off, running her hands quickly down his back.

"What kind of man was he?" He slipped off

her garment. Sure he wasn't going to be the only naked person at the party.

"Cruel, Geemie, very cruel. I think he is sick emotionally—even worse than Narth. I had him as a teacher when I was a Cadet. He ... he is a very bad man."

"And what's the other bit of bad news? Out with it, woman." He began to kiss her; his lips quickly found their way to her wonderful, swelling young breasts. *Ah, you're a lucky man, O'Neill, despite all your complaints.*

"If you keep that up, I won't be able to tell you. ... I didn't mean stop, Geemie, just a little slower. Uhm, that's *very* nice. Well, the second news is about you. The Committee is so disorganized that they plan to do nothing about you. They feel that you won't do anything unless you are attacked. They now think they can deal with you after the Festival."

His fingers gripped her waist. *Time now to sweep her to the crude couch—no—one last question.* ... "And who's going to lead this thing when Chronos falls apart? ... Some of you must have thought about what comes afterward. ..."

In the dim light of the portable lantern her eyes were now dreamy with longing, her nipples rigid against his chest. She hesitated before answering. "That is not important." The longing eyes darted away from him.

So that's the way the story goes. He pushed her unceremoniously onto the makeshift bed, grabbed for his clothes, and began to dress. "You're a bitch,

Margie!" he exploded. "I wouldn't make love to you tonight for all the coin on this damn planet!" Truth to tell, all desire had left him, replaced by cold fury.

She sat on the cloak-strewn floor, dispirited and guilty. "What have I done, Seamus?" she asked weakly. "Please forgive me. Whatever it is, I did not intend it."

"We weren't even back in the City and you were volunteering my services for this harebrained revolution of yours...." he said, sulking. "Now you've got me pegged to be the leader. Well, let me tell you one thing, woman ... you're not going—"

"—I am truly sorry, Good Mate," she interrupted. "I didn't mean ... I hardly ... but ... oh, I am so sorry. Please forgive my ignorance and stupidity. I will never learn, I fear.... Don't ... I should have told you. I didn't know how to put it." She was weeping now. "Everyone takes it for granted that you will lead us. You act like a leader ... we didn't think you would be just a follower...."

Gracefully she stood up. *Damn naked woman, don't try to charm me.*

She touched his arm soothingly. "Don't be angry with me for too long ... we have so little time together."

His heart turned from butter to cream. He patted her backside affectionately and drew her close. "Ah, sure, woman, you're right. I'd be no damn good as a follower. But I'm no king or ruler either, do you hear me? Just a temporary military chief, that's all. Do you understand that?" He tightened his grip. *Well, maybe I'll not throw her out tonight after all.*

"Yes, darling," she said, nodding submissively.

"All right, then." But he still didn't believe her completely.

Later, after they had slept, she whispered in his ear, "Were you angry because I made fun of you at the entertainment tonight?"

He swatted her backside harder, though not enough to hurt. "It was terrible disrespectful."

"It was not. You loved every second of it. Tarans don't care what you say about them as long as you make them the center of attention."

"You'll be getting yourself raped again, if you say things like that." He kissed her delicately, waiting for his physiology to catch up with his affection.

"It's true," she sighed. "Don't deny it."

"What you haven't figured out, woman, is that we are disappointed if our friends don't ridicule us just a little. Sure a proper wife ought to make fun of her husband now and again so everyone knows that she loves him."

"You didn't fight back." She stroked his chest. "That wasn't fair."

So he sang a few stanzas of the bawdy ballad he'd written about her loss of virginity, the refrain of which was "Seamus, roll the woman over again."

She began her dirty sniggering after the first stanza and exhausted herself laughing as he went on.

"That would have been terrible," she managed to say between spasms of laughing. "It would

have shocked everyone. I would have been delighted
... but it is well that you didn't do it. The poor
Research Director would never recover."

The image of a shocked Sammy seemed to
delight her especially. So O'Neill, ever eager to
keep his proper woman amused, made up some
new stanzas.

"Does it ever stop?" she demanded. "Does the
poor woman ever get loved?"

"A proper Taran ballad never stops, but the
woman does get loved. Let me show you."

So he did.

Later, as they slipped out of their temporary
trysting place into the dim unfriendly light of a
Zylongian dawn, O'Neill, complacent and well satisfied with himself, realized that he would do almost anything she wanted. Lust was spent after a
passionate, almost despairing night together. Love
was stronger than ever. In the clarity of dawn he
saw a truth he had been dodging: he could not live
without her.

*Now look at the trouble Your Fine Eminence
has got me into.*

PART THREE

THE FESTIVAL

19

O'Neill reached for his knife. There was someone coming up from the beach. He tensed for the attack. He knew enough about how the Zylongi behaved during harvest to be ready for anything. He moved to the side of the tent opening and stood quietly.

It was Sammy who lifted up the flap of the tent, her body sleek and wet from the River. "Geemie," she announced breathlessly, "we thought you would be lonely, so we have come to visit you." Her eyes were wide with delight.

Energy Supervisor Niora and State Painter Reena, the two guests at his first nourishment on Zylong, followed her in—equally breathless and equally clad only in their undergarments. There was much laughter, shaking of hair, removing of clothes to dry, and toweling of ripe womanly bodies. Like the women's locker room next to the hockey fields on *Iona*. Not that he'd ever had a peek inside that sanctum save in his fantasy. Mod-

esty apparently wasn't a problem during harvesttime.

He was not to worry, they assured him, nobody
would bother them. They had brought cakes in a
waterproof bag and merely wanted to drink la-ir
with him and sing songs.

The harvest ritual had begun with pep rallies,
citizens singing and swinging their harvesting tools
in all the plazas of the City, three days before the
actual harvest began. On the third day, Sammy
and Ernie had bundled him off to the Island with
a tent, food, a large quantity of poteen, and a pile
of books. The word had come down from the Committee that he couldn't stay in the City and couldn't
visit the fields during the sacred ritual of the
harvest.

He was worried about Marjetta, despite the
careful plans that had been made to rescue her
and the rest of their friends before the Festival
winds began to blow, and to provide them with
the pills to control their emotions and the weapons with which to defend themselves.

It was a harebrained scheme if he'd ever heard
of one, but he couldn't think of anything better.

On the first day of the harvest, the Zylongi
assembled in small bands at their preassigned
places and marched out of the City, singing lustily.
Many came right down the plain to the River,
where O'Neill could see them easily from his vantage point on the Island. Women worked below
the River and men above it. Every action was
ritualized and supported by chants—the swinging

of the tool, the packing of the bundles, the loading of the hand-drawn carts, the rest periods, even swimming in the River before the evening meal.

The rituals, the songs, the stylized movements were hypnotic; the workers were in deep trance during their working hours. Their evening swim was designed to shake them out of it so that they could get some natural sleep before the wake-up signal for the next day's activities.

The horn sounding on the last day of harvest would be the signal for O'Neill to steal a hover-craft and head back to the *Dev* for the tranquillity pills that his young allies would need when the sun set. Then their crazy revolt would begin.

He had enough on his mind: he missed Margie desperately, he was worried about the crazy revolution. He didn't need the stimulation of these hyped-up and uncharacteristically excited women.

Well, never let it be said that a Taran is not hospitable and prepared to entertain.

The circumstances called for soft, sad, and erotic songs. So he began by teaching his lovely visitors a neo-Celtic love song.

If you come at all
come only at night
and walk quietly
——don't frighten me.
You'll find the key
under the doorstep
and me by myself
——don't frighten me

There's no pot in the way
no stool or can
or rope of straw
——nothing at all.
The dog is quiet
and won't say a word
—it's no shame to him:
—I've trained him well

My mammy's asleep
and my daddy is coaxing her
kissing her mouth
—and kissing her mouth
Isn't she lucky!
Have pity on me
lying here by myself
—in the feather bed.

Then he asked them to teach him their songs. There were some embarrassed giggles, but as the la-ir was consumed, they became bolder. Their songs were much more explicit than his. And these were the same women who would have been shocked a few days earlier by his mildly bawdy ballad about the winning of Marjetta.

Whoever conceived the system of carnival orgies followed by long months of repression had given considerable thought to the conditioning techniques necessary for the change from a sexless existence to madcap Festivals.

There was a certain logic to the system, once you admitted the basic premise that sex interfered with responsible human living. Concentrate it all in two bashes every year, enough for reproduction (more than enough, considering the antichildren bias of the planet) and for sexual release, and sedate citizens mentally and physically to repress it the rest of the time. Logical system, but mad premise—not completely unknown in the rest of the galaxy, or even in the history of Christianity, for that matter.

The temperature in the tent rose; his guests were crowding him, their faces and bodies close to his. Sammy rested her head on his chest. He hurriedly started to sing something comic. She put her hand over his mouth and laughed softly. The other two women were watching avidly. Sammy began to stroke his face with the tips of her fingers. Her eyes were round and large, her figure passive, available, inviting. With the three lovely bodies gleaming with sweat and pressing against him, O'Neill felt himself drifting slowly back toward a primal unity with all things fertile and creative. He was being absorbed by the strong, overpowering power of the loving Earth Mother. He had wanted her from the first moment he had seen her, and now this superb creature was forcing herself on him. He didn't want to break his Rules or hers. He summoned every bit of self-discipline he'd learned during the pilgrimage and pulled back, with a playful slap on her rump. It broke the spell. She eased away from him, disappointed and hurt. Her friends sighed subaudibly. They had come to watch the show.

After more singing and storytelling, most of it dispirited, Sammy and her companions excused themselves to swim back across the River to prepare for another day's work.

They returned twice more; each time he entertained them with ballads, though he avoided the more erotic ones. Their behavior was more restrained. Sammy seemed hurt but still friendly. He was relieved when on the night before the end of the harvest the women did not come. *Well, I survived that, the Lord be praised.*

His gratitude to the Deity was premature.

Just before dawn he was suddenly awakened by a powerful incense odor. As he struggled awake, he saw Sammy standing above him, naked, available, vulnerable. Coquetry had been replaced by frank and anxious invitation: Please love me before we both die.

She had banked the tent in flowers, lighted an incense capsule, and tied a ring of blossoms around her waist. She knelt and placed a wreath of similar flowers on his head.

"I am yours, Geemie, for whatever you want to do with me. You have always wanted me and I have always wanted you. Since the first day. Let us exchange the gift now while we still have time."

Seamus gulped. This was no blushing, energetic but untried youthful virgin. This was an experienced, mature, extremely desirable woman. He'd never made love to such a one, despite all his fantasies.

Why not?

Well, there are a thousand reasons, the first two of which are Margie and Ernie.

Neither one of them would ever have to know.

"You hesitate?" she seemed ready to weep. "But it is not wrong. In two more days I am soon to be the play object of every heavy-handed smelly man who wants me. Why not give myself first to a man who loves me? My Good Mate would not mind. He prefers that I be loved by those who respect me."

"He doesn't think I would do it, does he, Sammy?" O'Neill groaned and clenched his fists.

"He did not say that he would disapprove. Surely just once . . . we will soon die, all of us, you know that. Then there will be nothing."

"Of that I'm not so sure, but even then . . ." He turned away from her flesh, all the more appealing because of the gentle marks of age on it.

"Marjetta is no longer a maiden. We all know that. She too will be taken by others. It is our way. She will not blame you."

She might and she might not blame me. But she isn't going to be taken by others, not if I can help it.

"I'd blame myself." He stood up, walked to the other side of the tent, and put on his robe. "I don't think your culture would approve. Maybe it would, I'm too confused to understand anything anymore. But, Sammy, I know mine wouldn't." *Damn, why do I have to sound so priggish?* "But the point is that if we do it now and we survive this Festival, we'll never be able to be friends again. You know it and I know it. I'd rather have you as a friend in years to come than a lover for a few minutes."

"You don't love me, Geemie." Sad, quiet tears were streaming down her cheeks. "You have never loved me."

"I do love you," he said miserably, trying vainly to sort out the demands of both cultures and of his own heart.

"It was the day you kissed me in the Body Institute that I rushed home to tell my mate that I was ready now to ignore the rules. He was so happy." She covered herself with her hands, now shy and awkward. Hastily Seamus found a thin blanket to drape around her shoulders. "You made me love him, but you won't love me."

"It's because I do love you that I am saying no."

And because you're a damn fool, you moralistic idjit. You'll never have a chance like this again.

She collapsed into his arms, now a chaste and exhausted child. Seamus crooned a lullaby so that she might sleep for a little while.

She's the blackberry flower,
the fine raspberry flower,
she's the plant of best breeding
—your eyes could behold:
she's my darling and dear,

my fresh apple-tree flower
she is Summer in the cold
—between Christmas and Easter.

He was about to waken her and send her back
to the harvest work when the police arrived.

20

"Seamus Finnbar O'Neill, you are the prize idjit of all human history!"

'Tis herself! Glory be to God, why do women always have to wake me up? Where am I? It's cold and hard here—not at all comfortable. He turned over to go back to sleep.

"In addition to that," the voice was relentless, "you are a blatherskite, a flannel-mouth, a scapegrace, a coward, a gombeen man, a disgrace to your regiment and to *Iona*, and one of the biggest fools God ever permitted to exist!"

" 'Tis yourself," Seamus said weakly, opening one eye and then closing it. " 'Tis your mirror-self. Faith, woman, this must be the distance record for such spookiness." He pulled himself up to lean on one elbow. He looked around for the source of her voice.

"You'll be silent until I'm finished," she ordered imperiously. "You have failed in everything you were assigned to do. When the disciplinary board in the monastery gets through with you, there will be not one regiment in the whole galaxy that will take you in as a potato peeler."

I'm in trouble, all right. Still, it was best, when dealing with herself, to permit her to vent her anger. Then she became much more reasonable. "Sure now, what did I do wrong?" he pleaded in the direction of something that glowed eerily in the corner of the room.

"What did you do wrong?" The voice became shrill. "Are you such a fool that you don't know? You should ask what you did right; that question I can answer quickly: Seamus O'Neill, you did nothing right, absolutely nothing."

The glow at the corner of the room coalesced for an instant into an astral body that flickered in the gloom of the place. Strong emotion interfered with astral projection. Her Ladyship would have to contain her temper or she would be back on *Iona. That would be nice.* Seamus closed his eyes again and sighed, "Faith, I couldn't have been all that bad."

She recited: "You interjected yourself into their political affairs; you fought in their domestic wars; you killed their Fourth Secretary, who for all his faults was the one person still capable of governing; you got rid of the bungler Narth and replaced him with Popilo, who is a military genius, his army is set to attack in three days; you supported a crackpot revolutionary movement made up of a bunch of children; you stole goods from one of their forts; you seduced their women, some of them little more than schoolgirls. Do you want more? Zylong was in trouble; Zylong is in much worse trouble now, thanks to you."

Seamus braved saying something in his own defense. "They seduced me."

"I trust you will concede me some expertise in the subject of what affects women." Her lips were thin and menacing, her eyes shooting ice-cold sparks. "Seamus, you are not merely an incorrigible womanizer, you are an inept one—which is worse. You began to flirt with that poor thing from the first minute you set eyes on her. What did you expect to happen in a repressed culture like this when a great, red-bearded godlike idjit appears? You are such an incurable seducer that you didn't even know you were doing it." She finished as though she were a prosecutor before a jury, folding her arms in satisfaction at the damning case she had presented.

"I didn't realize what was happening." *Why am I whining like a little boy?*

"You're too dumb to know what you're doing. Those women should never have got past the door of your tent. You knew the strain they were under; still, you not only let them in, you encouraged them with songs and drink."

"Sure, I was tired and lonely. And anyway, I didn't take her."

"No, you merely tease her and then break her heart."

"Don't tell me that morality never is better than morality late," he began to argue his case. It called for a crafty approach. *Use the woman's own words against her.*

"Tell that to the court-martial board. Or tell it to the poor woman down in the bottom of this infernal prison, hysterical with self-loathing. Poor heathen. 'Tis not Samaritha's fault, 'tis yours. They're going to execute her the day after tomorrow. Why didn't you have sense enough to send her promptly on her way? They've got some indecent pagan notions about how to kill adulteresses. Because of your stupidity she will be cruelly tortured for a crime she didn't commit. You should have known they'd be watching your tent. You might tell her before she goes up there to be cut apart that you were tired and lonely."

O'Neill looked wildly around him and realized he was in a small metal cell. He leaped up and shouted, "Deirdre, you've got to get me out of here!"

"You will be pleased to know that Marjetta and your young rebel friends are also here in this prison. The police put a psychic probe on you."

"Margie?"

"Of course they have her too. I believe they have some special plans for her."

"Deirdre, I wish I were dead," he moaned.

"You won't get off that easily," she said triumphantly, brandishing a delicate accusing finger. "The wise men on the Committee are going to ship you off the planet tomorrow morning before the Festival begins. They want no part of you. So, whether we like it or not, we get you back."

"Good God, Deirdre, is there nothing to be done?"

"You are beyond redemption, Seamus O'Neill. You destroy people's lives. You intervene in a dying culture and aggravate the situation; then all you can do is ask if there is nothing to be done." Again the pose of the successful prosecutor.

"What can we do?" he begged. *If herself is putting on such a show to make me feel guilty, then there's still a chance.*

"The holy saints Brigid, Patrick, Brendan, and Columcile give me control of my temper. What is to be done? Why, what else but get those people out of here and go ahead with your mad plot to take over this planet. If it works, then they can invite us to land. If it doesn't, well, we'll have a nice Requiem Mass for you, idjit."

Maybe he was not in as much trouble as he might have been. "What did you think of herself?" he ventured quietly.

"What? Oh, you mean your . . . er . . . proper woman. Well, she's a pretty wee lass, I suppose. In fact, she's much too good for the likes of you. We'd just as soon take her and leave you here."

"She seduced me, you know." *I'll see how far that defense can be played.* "Sure wasn't herself after admitting it."

"That's what the man always says."

Ah, but you don't deny that the woman is a handful altogether. I'm betting there. He ventured, "You should give me credit for good taste."

"More than I'd give her, God knows."

"And we are properly married. Canon Law says—"

"The divil quotes scripture—" she dismissed his argument with a disgusted wave of her elegant hand "—and Seamus O'Neill, gombeen man extraordinaire, quotes canon law."

As the Captain Abbess calmed down, her image became more defined. Seamus had the sense of talking with a real person instead of a ghostly image.

"Podraig has revised his estimates. He says now that there is only one chance in ten thousand that the Zylongian society can survive the Festival in its present structure. He will give you one-in-two odds that it doesn't survive the first day. We do not yet know what combination of biological, physical, and cultural forces are at work in this frenzy—we told you that before. It is of such intensity that its force in the early days will be more than enough to tear the society apart. The Hooded Ones have grown in number. The psychopathic spirit that animates them is infecting the broader society. I do not like being here even in out-of-body mode; it is a pagan, indecent, heathen place. The population will run amok tomorrow morning when the wind blows. The day after, the mountain army will sweep across the River and destroy what's left. Podraig says it is likely to capture the City unless something intervenes." She shrugged. "If you establish even temporary control, you may find allies."

"Do you have any ideas?"

"None, Seamus. I'll cut a corner or two if I have to, but we cannot intervene directly in the end of this culture. We have no right to play God to these people. If we can help afterward, we will. If worse comes to worst, I'll try to get you and your Marjetta off the planet. I'll not endanger the ship or the pilgrimage to do it."

"You do like my woman, then?" He was like a child eager for approval.

"You idjit! Why must you make me angry? The holy saints know I have done my best to keep my temper under control. Yes, I do like the wee leprechaun child. Everyone on *Iona* who has had contact with her adores her. Now get her out of this prison! The guards here are lax. The lass is on the floor below, two cells closer to the stairs than yours. Jesus and Mary be with you. Now move, you idjit!"

Her Eminence faded out, then in once again. "You'll marry the poor thing, do you hear me, you scoundrel?"

"Woman, I will. In fact, I have. I have no intention of doing anything else."

She paid him no heed. "We'll stand for nothing else from you."

"I told you, I've made up my mind to do it. I don't need to be told by you what to do." He was getting angry, his pride and confidence returning.

"Don't try changing your mind, either." She was gone, with the last word as always.

Then she reappeared. "And herself expecting a child too."

"So soon!"

"You wouldn't leave the poor thing alone." This time she vanished for good, having delivered at the very end the essence of her message.

O'Neill grinned. *A wee one is it? Well, now there is something more for which to fight.*

The cell was small, square—a cube actually, nearly as high as it was wide. In one wall was a small alloy door or panel that slid into the wall to open. Through the small window, he could see two guards sitting and talking to each other at a small table just in front of his cell. His captors had allowed him to dress before taking him to jail. He removed his robe and cloak, arranged the latter in the far corner of the cell to resemble a form, after which he stood by the side of the panel uttering a low moaning that he gradually intensified until it reached banshee proportions. The panel slid back and one startled guard rushed into the room. O'Neill tripped him and simultaneously flung his robe over the second guard. Before either guard recovered, he had them both bound and gagged in the corner of his cell.

He paused at the head of the staircase to consider the situation. The Festival frenzy was about to begin; he didn't have the pills yet. He couldn't possibly handle his Zylongi comrades and get the pills too. They were much safer in jail. Quickly he mounted the stairs, disposing efficiently of two more guards who met him at the corner of a stair landing.

At street level, the narrow back streets that

led into the plazas were practically deserted. There was a small hovercraft at the place Margie had designated. As he sped through the City toward the wall, he caught glimpses of crowds of people in the plazas milling around. There were fights between small groups and individuals in the side streets. Zylong was deteriorating, though its Festival did not begin until the morning.

He sped over the wall (no obstacle to the hovercraft—it just soared over it) and out toward the River and the now harvested fields. Full speed to the *Dev* and those blessed pills. The predecessors of this crowd must have been real hopheads, with all the drugs they used in this culture. He was worried and preoccupied. The jungle path when he found it was shadowed by tall overhanging trees. He never saw the huge reptile ambling across the path until he hit it.

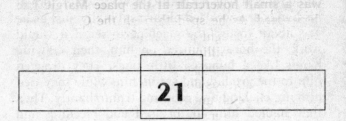

21

"So—" Narth leered like villains are supposed to leer "—we meet again, Commandant O'Neill."

Trussed up like a sack of praties with a dozen hordi spears pointed at his gut, Seamus O'Neill was not inclined to wit.

"The next time I'll make sure you're dead."

Narth's enormous stomach rolled as he laughed. "You amuse me, Taran. I might just keep you alive long enough to watch the destruction of the City. It would be pleasant to watch you as my warriors dispatch—slowly and lovingly, of course—your friends, particularly that delightful woman you seem to have taken for your own."

Standard bad-guy threats. But how does the hero—me, that is—escape?

The dinosaur had fled terrified into the jungle. Seamus unfortunately had banged his head at the end of his spectacular flight from the hovercraft to the ground.

When he regained consciousness, he set to work

straightening the metal sheets on which the machine rode. It was hot, difficult work which tore at his hands and wearied his arms. Finally, just as he was about to test the machine to see if it would work, the hordi pounced on him, their clawing hands like a hundred little bugs. They dragged him to the ground and sat on him while they tied him up, clicking and grunting triumphantly. Then they hauled him off, bruised and bleeding and deprived of all his dignity, to Narth's encampment in a jungleside meadow that was dangerously close to the *Dev*'s landing site.

Had they found his ship and destroyed it and the precious medicine?

As he considered the camp and the thousands of well-disciplined troops in crimson uniforms with vast crimson banners, O'Neill realized that the question might be pointless. This army might not be stopped by dubious and ancient laser cannons. Certainly there was nothing he had seen in the City that could match the organization and efficiency of Narth's forces.

"Impressed, O'Neill?"

"No combat experience," he said hopefully. "They'd break and run at the first sign of competent opposition."

"Which we don't have here. I know. I organized the defense plans. They are folly, but it is all those senile fools would permit. As for the guns, they might just as well explode and destroy the City as harm my troops."

"You'd better hope they do. Otherwise this

crowd will scramble back to the hills as fast as they can run."

"Care to wager?" he sneered.

Ah, he is not all that confident. But neither am I. The man is a genius to have pulled all of this together. If he weren't mostly round the bend altogether, he might be unbeatable.

But that doesn't get the hero out of the hands of the villain, does it?

Much more dangerous than Narth was his second-in-command, Popilo, Narth's rumored successor. A tall, thin, mystical-eyed fellow with a lean fanatic's face, Popilo was the ascetic Merlin to Narth's frothing King Arthur. He might not be a genius at organizing this weird assembly of mutants, savages, and exiles, but he would be ruthless in using it to destroy everyone he hated, which seemed to be just about everyone.

"Kill him now," he said coldly. "His talk is dangerous."

If it were up to Popilo, Seamus O'Neill would have been fed to the eager hordi on arrival.

"Let us first see about the *Iona*. We can listen to it, but we cannot speak to it. Moreover, I do not understand this strange Spacegael you talk, with its strong mixture of Proto-English. It may be that we can make some arrangement with your masters, Major O'Neill."

"Might it now?"

"Bring him to the tent," Narth barked at the two one-eyed, three-armed giants who were in charge of fending off the hungry hordi.

O'Neill was dragged to the tent. Inside was a very ancient transceiver system, powered by a liquid-fuel generator. A tank of fuel rested against the generator. Twenty-second-century communication equipment in a world where solar batteries had not been invented.

"An old bugger." O'Neill saw, very dimly through a dark cave, the way out.

"Can you make it send as well as receive? Or do not Majors in the Wild Geese have such skills?"

"Of course we do," Seamus lied. "But 'tis a real old machine. I'll have to tinker with it."

"You think we will release you and then you can fight your way out of here?" Narth's big belly rolled merrily.

"What chance would I have? You want this fixed, or don't you?"

Narth produced an old machine pistol, an Uzi Mark XXI, Seamus guessed, from underneath his cloak. "Untie him. A single false move and I'll empty this into your gut. Fair warning?"

"Fair warning."

You'll have to release the safety before you do that, but I don't think I'll point that out just now.

They poured some of the liquid into the generator and cranked it up. Seamus, rubbing his hands to restore a bit of circulation, listened to the sound croaking out of the speaker—mostly static and an occasional word or two of Spacegael. *Why hadn't the idjits up there picked up this unit? Too weak to be noticed?*

" 'Tis a powerful old machine," he murmured.

"I think you will make it work." Narth raised his weapon warningly.

"Give me a bit of time," he pleaded, running his numb fingers over the machine. " 'Tis terrible old altogether."

Now, let's see, if you bring this red lead and this black lead together and hold them long enough there'll be a spark, maybe a big one. Then if you throw the sparking wires into that open tank of fuel, you'll create a frigging explosion that they'll remember for a long time around here. The hordi may have to eat you toasted.

"I think we have it here, let me see, if you tie these two lines together." He braced himself for the current of electricity. *Roast Wild Goose.*

Nothing happened.

He wound the wires together. "What's the matter with you idjits?" he demanded. "Why don't you have the current in these wires?"

"What current?" Popilo demanded. "Kill him, Lord Narth, he is a trickster."

The man's eyes shone brightly, his face glowed like he'd just enjoyed sex. *He's even more off the wall than his boss. Great pair. The Lord made them and the divil matched them.*

Carefully Seamus laid down the twisted wires only a few inches from the open fuel tank. *I was lucky the switch wasn't on. Now if I can find it and then jump . . .*

"Ah, here's the frigging switch; you have a lot to learn about such things, Lord Narth."

He took a deep breath, flicked the switch and

jumped out of the way, ducking under Narth's gun and ramming his head toward Narth's belly. He was assisted in the last foot of this charge by the explosion behind him.

The tent blossomed like a Yule fire at Christmas. The hordi clicked wildly, the Zylongi screamed, the mutants rumbled. Seamus O'Neill roared like a squad of Wild Geese, removed his head from Narth's great, soft belly, picked up the machine pistol, and ducked out of a flaming hole in the tent.

He banged an Imperial Guard on the head with the butt of his gun, yanked off the man's crimson cloak, swirled it around his shoulders, jumped on a horse, and galloped through the camp.

A squad of Narthian guards tried to stop him. Seamus raised his pistol and pulled the trigger. It would not fire.

Like Narth he had forgot the safety. His horse tumbled into the crowd of soldiers. They jabbed at him with their lances, missing by a hair's breadth. Finally he managed to free the safety and blasted away. The guards fled in all directions, and Seamus thundered out of the camp, screaming like an infuriated banshee.

Beat them this time.

What will we do when they show up at the gates of the City and we try to fight them off with sticks?

22

The sound of a big explosion rattled the walls of the City and temporarily deprived Seamus O'Neill of his hearing. They were blowing the frigging place up! Cursing the frigging dinosaur, he had parked the battered hovercraft in the lee of the City wall in one of the less populous sections of the North Quarter of the City. It had taken an hour to bend the front end of his hovercraft into place. Now his arms and back were sore, his hands were bleeding, and he was several hours behind schedule. Zylong was already beginning its Götterdämmerung.

Every light in the City was turned on. Shouts, laughter, cries, and wild music echoed even in the North Quarter, which he had selected to reconnoiter. He heard the sounds of small explosions and the screams of women raped and raping—if anyone knew the difference anymore. Throngs of people, most of them completely naked, were milling about, containers of la-ir in their hands. They were pushing, shoving, bellowing, fighting. So this was what a full-blown orgy was like. As the Abbess had said, it was a heathenish place.

He was worried about the Young Ones. If it weren't for the damn dinosaur, he could have made it back by sunrise with their pills. Now he didn't know how to get through to them. The wind was blowing fiercely. Perhaps his friends were protected from its effect in their cells.

He concealed himself behind a wall of a storehouse. He could not slip through the streets of the City in the hovercraft. His machine was too battered to jump over the City wall. To try it on foot would be suicide. His only hope was to use the underground highway system, which would be relatively free of people—he hoped. It seemed like everyone was outdoors enjoying the Festival breeze. Ugh.

The prison, like the Energy Building, the Central Building, the Military Center, and the Worship Plaza, was part of the "Old City" or Central Quarter. Here many of the buildings were of masonry with wood trim, and most were only four or five stories high, bordering the irrationally narrow and crooked streets of the earliest city.

The prison and police buildings stood like a solid block at the end of a small side street that wound into the Worship Plaza. Horor had led him to a door of what appeared to be an abandoned shop on that street on the night he first met the entire group of conspirators. In the floor of the shop was a trapdoor down to the unused granary that was the conspiracy headquarters. He could maneuver through the underground maze to the granary; his problem was to get from there to the prison. He would worry later about how to get through any guards that might be around.

He heard another loud explosion. Someone was using powerful charges like those stored in the headquarters of the Young Ones. So there were more rebels in the streets. Or were they still another group that had got at the powder supply within the Military Center?

The transport system would run to the storehouse, which at the moment was protecting him from sight. He discovered what appeared to be a manhole cover. A thin alloy ladder led down through a tunnel filled with cables, pipes, and various sizes of conduits. Another hatchway opened at the bottom onto the well-lighted roadways he was seeking. It was deserted. Hovercrafts were parked along the side of the tunnel in alcoves. He selected a new one with its key in the ignition. Like all such cars, it was reluctant to start. Seamus coaxed it into action with several choice words of Spacegaelic obscenity to which the machines in this dreadful heathen place seemed remarkably responsive. (The words were borrowed, as the Abbess was fond of observing, from Anglo-Saxon, since ur-Gaelic was a gentle language free of such vulgarities.) Clutching the *Dev*'s medical kit, within which were the magical pills, his trivial-looking Holy Grail, he turned on the lights—since the underground was now totally dark—and eased the

car down the road and under a monorail structure. Now he had to find the direction to the elevator that led up to the Old City.

At one intersection he slowed for an instant,
uncertain which way to turn. Three hooded characters emerged from behind a panel in the tunnel
wall and threw a flat package at him. Jamming
the hovercraft into fast forward, he narrowly escaped the blast. The Hooded Ones had explosive
charges. That was a complication Seamus and his
friends didn't need. He pushed aside the fear that
the Young Ones' headquarters had been discovered and the charges stolen from them.

After losing his way three times, he found the
old elevator. Should he go down into the granary
or up into the street? He decided to check the
granary first. He heard a woman's screams. Jumping out of the car, portable light in one hand,
tranquillity pills jammed into his belt, carbine in
the other hand, he ran in the direction of the sound,
turning a corner to see two men savagely brutalizing a young girl. Seamus sent them scurrying down
the passage with a shot from his carbine ringing
over their heads.

Less in the grip of the Festival frenzy than her
attackers, she was sobbing with pain and fear. She
clung to Seamus in terror, her teeth chattering. As
her fear receded, the spirit of the frenzy returned.
Her body arched toward him lasciviously. He
shoved one of the precious tranquillity pills into
her mouth.

The reaction was immediate. She went limp

against him for a moment and then drew back, humiliated and grateful. "Truly you are a generous god, Taran Poet."

What was he going to do with her? He had other pressing matters to attend to. She was small and frail, with pretty little breasts and a nice ass. *Too many unclad women on this planet.*

"I'm not a god," he insisted. *I can't leave her here and I can't take her with me.*

"Could you be so generous as to give me one more of those pills?" she begged. "I would take it to my mate, perhaps we could survive this Festival. I love him very much." She put out her hand timidly. The plea in her eyes tore Seamus's heart in two. He wanted no godlike power of life and death over this pretty child and her mate. He gave her a second pill. "Who are you?" he asked gently.

"I am Meena, Lord O'Neill." She bowed her head respectfully. "I am responsible for the small shop just above. I came to make sure the shop was locked before the Festival started. My mate is not yet back from the fields."

"Meena," O'Neill exclaimed, "you are a godsend! Do you know the underground area around here? Is there a way I can get into the prison without the guards seeing me?"

She was confused at the urgency of this great Taran's question. "I have lived here all my life; when I was a child I used to play in the old granary below." She hesitated fearfully, then looked at O'Neill with adoration. "I know a way. Come with me. We used to go into the basement of the prison when we felt very brave and were looking for adventure."

His brain filed a new bit of information. Zylongi children actually sought adventure. A good sign for the future of the survivors of a shattered culture—if there were any survivors.

Meena led him to a narrow opening in the passage wall—an old ventilation outlet, perhaps. Moving the beam of his light in front of them, Seamus followed her down a narrow, dank corridor that was not made for tall Tarans. Despite his light, they both had to feel their way along the walls. "That ladder," Meena whispered to him when they came to the end of the passage, "leads into the prison. You must shove hard against the hatch, but it will not be difficult for one of your strength."

O'Neill nodded. "Thank you, Meena." He bent and kissed her forehead. "Now go home to wait for your mate and stay indoors with him until this is over. I hope he is a good man to deserve someone as brave as you."

She grabbed his hand and kissed it. "Thank you for giving us life, Lord O'Neill. He *is* a good man. Save our people." She scurried back down the corridor. Seamus watched the dust-covered brown body disappear in shadows illuminated only slightly by the low-power light at his belt. Again the terrible sweet wrenching of tenderness.

She had called him "Lord O'Neill." *There'd be no more of that.*

The grimy old corridor rocked with a tremendous explosion. Someone had blasted the jail.

Seamus was shoved against the old stone wall, his
head bounced into the metal pole of the ladder.
For a few precious minutes, he wasn't sure who he
was or what was happening.

Then, with terrible slowness it seemed, his
senses returned. He climbed awkwardly up the
ladder and shoved at the hatch on the top. It did
not budge.

He took a deep breath and shoved again. Still
no movement.

Then there was another ear-shattering, mind-
twisting explosion, very near. The ladder rocked
and swayed. Seamus hung on for dear life. As soon
as the reverberation ceased, he pushed at the hatch.
It opened. There was a cacophony of screams,
shouts, shots. He was in a smoke-filled hallway
filled with running hordi. Had Popilo attacked?
No, they were domesticated hordi. Seamus slipped
unnoticed into a smaller passageway as a throng
of screaming Zylongi, filled with the spirit of the
frenzy, surged by. They wore the red robes that,
Sammy had told him, marked those who were to
be sacrificed at the climax of the Festival, to be
helped along on their journey to the god. Either
intentionally or not, the Hooded Ones' explosion
had freed them to join the mad mobs in the streets.

There were no guards in sight. They must have
been swept along by the escaping prisoners or run
off, maddened themselves, into the wildness of the
Festival's destruction spreading through the City.
Frantically searching up and down the corridors
of the various levels of the old prison, he feared he

would never find his Young Ones. *Dear God in heaven, help me to find my woman. And my child.*

Finally, when he was about to leave the prison to look for her somewhere else—where he did not know—he heard a muffled roar at the end of one corridor, the sound coming from behind a great door with a huge bar holding it shut. *Maybe it's themselves.*

He threw up the bar and looked in on a scene of pure horror.

The Young Ones were far gone. They were like a pack of caged dogs, their faces contorted with rage, their mouths pulled back in snarls, their teeth bared, their mouths dripping saliva, their limbs twisted into grotesque shapes, their hands clenched for battle. Some were fighting one another, others were pounding their heads against the wall, others were lying on the floor groaning.

The dead body of Chronos sprawled against the inside of the door, his skull cracked open like an egg. When they saw O'Neill, the Young Ones came slinking toward him, panting and growling, reaching out for him in a kind of mindless appeal. He thrust his carbine at them, they dropped back.

Marjetta stumbled toward him, agony on her contorted face. "Quickly, O'Neill, quickly," she entreated him.

He shoved a pill into her mouth, then brutally pushed her aside to poke the carbine at a young revolutionary who was coming at him with violence in his eye.

"Nice way to treat your woman after a long

separation," she mumbled, a shadow of the old crinkly grin reappearing. "Give me some of your precious Holy Grail."

You save the woman's life, and she turns around and starts giving orders. It could be a long, long life, Seamus Finnbar O'Neill.

Together they began to administer the medication to their friends, O'Neill pushing them one by one into a corner with a gun, and Margie shoving the pills into their mouths. The effect continued to be almost instantaneous. That should mean something, only he didn't know what.

"How come you were not as bad as the others?" he asked as they backed a screaming Retha into the corner.

"More release of sexual energies," she whispered back. Laughing aloud, she said, "Come now, Retha, it is all right now. You are not disgraced. Help us with the others."

The tiny officer shook her head, trying to clear from it the last traces of the frenzy. "Chronos killed himself, Lord O'Neill," she mumbled. "He hit his head against the wall."

He wanted to kiss her. Instead, he did the next best thing. "You call me 'Lord' once more, woman, and I'll take you back in the desert and leave you there."

Tranquillizing the Young Ones went slowly at first, but soon the team was "defrenzied." Many of the young revolutionaries were ashamed. They had lost face with the Taran. "We have never been this bad before. The wind is much worse than it has ever been—even inside these walls it transforms us."

The prison itself was silent now. There was a continuing roar of explosions outside. They were hopelessly behind schedule. They had to get back down into the bowels of the City, collect their carbines, and begin the attack on the Military Center. Somewhere in the building, Sammy might still be alive; he would search as they went down back into the corridor leading to the granary. If he could not find her, she would have to wait until the MC was seized. Guilt swirled through him as he saw her son and future daughter-in-law among his band of rebels. Did they know what had happened? No time to ask. All the decisions were tough ones now; the prime objective had to be the Military Center.

More time was consumed in the slow descent from the jail to the revolutionary command post. O'Neill sent Marjetta and Yens ahead with instructions on the route. He brought up the rear himself, searching in vain for Sammy.

When they got to the arms cache, he found the Young Ones had captured two Zylongi—Meena and the tallest Zylongi he had ever seen. "These two people say they want to join us," said Yens.

O'Neill gripped the young man's hand. "We take our allies wherever we can find them. Meena's mate is as brave as she."

"We will follow you to the death, Lord O'Neill," he said simply.

O'Neill winced. More of that "Lord" stuff.

"You'll do no such thing. You'll stay alive to take care of your wife and the children she's going to give you. Do you hear me? I want no martyrs."

"Yes, Lord O'Neill."

"I want to give him many children."

"Good enough for him. Now promise that you'll both be careful."

They nodded solemnly. God knows what meaning they read into that gesture.

Armed with carbines, spears, and explosive charges, the Young Ones and their Taran leader climbed back to the surface of the City, but the City was already in a shambles. O'Neill left the main force on the landing just below the surface and went up to scout the situation before launching the long overdue attack. Leaving Margie in command, he and Retha went ahead into the crooked side street. Their first step took them into an inferno. Fires danced all around, some of them great leaping conflagrations soaring high up into the night sky, others tiny spurts of flame seeping out of door panels. Though the street onto which they had emerged was deserted, they could hear cries from the plaza at the end of it.

"You trust a mission to a coward, Lord O'Neill?" asked Retha with a touch of sarcasm as they rushed down the street.

"Damn it, woman, you pick a fine time to remind me of my mistakes! And you call me Jimmy, do you hear?"

They reached the end of the street. The Hooded Ones and remnants of police units were fighting a desperate battle for control of the plaza, the police armed with carbines, the Hooded Ones with their small explosives. The police must have been immunized. They were shooting accurately and taking a deadly toll on their attackers. The frenzy of the Hooded Ones disregarded death. They drove the police back to the far edge of the worship platform. While the battle raged, Retha and O'Neill heard the noise of a huge crowd beyond the Central Building in the Great Plaza. The Festival orgy was continuing without any attention to the deadly battle. It was like a scene from a mad artist's painting of hell.

The sound of carbine fire and explosions, the shouts and screams of smaller battles raging throughout the streets of the Old City, the continued hum of demented cries of pleasure and pain—this was the end of the Zylong that was.

Would there be a new Zylong?

The answer to that lay with Seamus O'Neill and a handful of brave but inexperienced kids.

If I were a betting man, which I am, come to think of it, I wouldn't bet on us.

23

The final conflict would be fought where the City had begun, where the first colonists, pilgrims like the Tarans but with a very different faith, had built their tiny, fragile little village and set about the task of creating a free and just society. So much for human hopes and efforts.

While O'Neill and Retha watched with horrified fascination the scene before them on the worship platform, a new stream of Hooded Ones emerged from a street that emptied into the plaza only a few yards from where they stood. O'Neill pulled the tiny Lieutenant back into the shelter of their own flaming street. The Hooded Ones darted around the platform where the Great Globe of Zylong gleamed in the reflected light of the fires and ran in the direction of the Military Center itself. *Uh-oh*, thought O'Neill, *they're stealing our strategy*. The refulgent globe dissolved in a powerful explosion, toppling into the pit in front of it. Then an even more powerful explosion split the night air. The whole center of the platform collapsed into the ground.

Retha gasped. "When the Globe falls, Zylong falls!"

"What?" he shouted over the roar of secondary explosions. He bent his head close to hers.

"It is an old axiom: 'The Globe is the City and the People.' If the Globe falls, so does the City. We are destroyed." Her voice choked with terror.

"Not yet." O'Neill shouted, conscious for the first time that the ancient Celtic battle lust was upon him.

> The great Gaels of Ireland
> Are the men that God made mad
> For all their wars are merry
> And all their songs are sad.

His branch of the Gaels had come, long ago, not from any of the thirty-two counties of Little Ireland, but from a county in Great Ireland, which was an island far to the west. County Cook, as best as he could remember it, was the name of the place, though historians often confused it with the older County Cork.

Wherever his ancestors had come from, Seamus Finnbar O'Neill was now spoiling for a fight. And determined to win it.

The police had fallen back to the rear of the Central Building itself. The battle shifted across the Worship Plaza to the streets that led into the Central Plaza. Explosions were beginning inside the Military Center. There were intense danger signals in his brain.

"Run, Retha, run! Don't argue! Back to the rest of them—top speed!"

Flames were beginning to lick the wood trim around the door panels of the Military Center. The first big explosion knocked him off his feet. O'Neill scrambled after Retha. He snatched her up and ducked into the doorway of one of the tiny shuttered shops. He was just in time. A great ball of flame exploded upward, the shock waves shook the building and flattened them against it. The deafening roar of the Arsenal of Zylong blowing up in spectacular destruction echoed in their heads for minutes after the sound itself was gone. Great chunks of rubble, metal, and rock fell all around them, and then it was silent except for the crackle of flames.

"All right, wee lass?" asked O'Neill softly, holding her tight.

"Yes, Geemie," she muttered, her eyes wide and dull with shock and fear.

"Get back to Yens and Margie. Tell them to withdraw back into the underground and set up a defense perimeter at the corner beneath where they are now. I'm going to take another look around." O'Neill watched her stumble back, his heart filled with compassion for her and all her compatriots.

Don't worry, kids. Uncle Seamus is going to pull this one out.

He picked his way through the rubble to where the street opened onto the Central Plaza. He had to brace himself against a half-standing wall to recover from the shock of what he saw.

There was nothing left. The Military Center and the Central Plaza were one vast crater. There was no trace of the crowd that a few moments before had been "celebrating" on the plaza. The Central Building was a devastated ruin. Smoke and dust hung over the scene, flames were beginning to leap up among the ruins. Only the damaged Energy Building still stood. The center of Zylong no longer existed.

He hurried back to his followers. They were a discouraged and frightened-looking lot, his young soldiers, students, artists, technicians, writers, administrators. Not the kind to go to war with. He told them briefly what had happened, adding, "The Hooded Ones have done our work for us. The Committee doesn't exist anymore. Unfortunately, we don't have yet the kind of weapons we need to restore order in the City ourselves." He stopped. They looked at him expectantly, but he could think of nothing more to say. He needed time to think.

Come on, Uncle Seamus, let's go.

He had kept putting off making a plan. Now it was time to come up with one. He was tired, bleeding from cuts caused by small pieces of rubble; his head hurt from the explosion. He could not think what to do.

And his wife and child depending on him too.

The lights in the tunnel flickered. Horor, standing next to O'Neill, asked, "What of the Energy Building, Lord O'Neill?"

"Part of it is down. The rest of it can't last long with the fires. There may be a few Hooded Ones left too. I'm sure they'll hit it next."

"It may not matter anymore ... there is a nuclear reactor."

Holy Saints, you're an idjit! The computer was buried underneath the rubble of the Central Building, but the fission pile was beneath the Energy Building.

"If the City is to end, perhaps an atomic explosion is the best way for it to go," went on Horor dispassionately. "Yet, if there is anything left afterward, it would prove unfortunate to have lost our principal energy source. There is a control room near the reactor with a mechanism for banking it down. I ... I think I know how it works, and Ranon—the mate of Meena—is a mechanic. He can come with me should I need his aid with the device."

"How do we get there? We can't go down the streets."

"One of the underground rivers which flow beneath the City provides the cooling for the reactor. We can follow it to the control room." The lad's voice was utterly detached. Though his civilization was falling apart, he spoke like he was in a seminar room.

The Young Ones left in Margie's charge, Horor and Ranon, O'Neill in tow, prepared to depart for the underground river. The lights were flickering and dimming frequently. The Energy Center might

be in its last agonies. Margie had been warned
that the lights might go out anytime.

"Take care of yourself and the brat." Seamus
touched her face.

"You *know?*"

"The Lady Deirdre told me."

Which was the honest-to-God truth.

The tall sturdy Ranon and the slight bookish
Horor crowded into the hovercraft with O'Neill.
They moved slowly down the street, avoiding the
chunks of rock that had been dislodged by the
great explosion. He longed for Margie's presence.

Horor touched his arm. "We stop here, I think,
Lord O'Neill. We should test our handlights because if we are successful, we will return in total
blackness."

They descended through a hatch in the rock
floor of the street, down several sets of ladders, the
last of which was in a shaft lined with black dripping rock. O'Neill heard the sound of rushing water.

"How deep is this river of yours, Horor?" he
asked skeptically.

"Not very deep, but at this time of the year it
will be very slippery." The ladder went right down
into the river, whose waters were icy cold.

They slipped and stumbled along the river-
bed, supporting themselves on the tunnel wall.
Horor led the way, occasionally flashing his light
at the top of the tunnel to see where they were.
Finally he stopped, announcing, "We are below
the control room now, I think. Yes, there is the

ladder. Exercise care, Lord O'Neill, it will be very slippery. We must climb up a long distance."

"I'll be careful, never fear!" he yelled.

Thirty feet on a ladder, you bet your life I'll exercise care.

O'Neill's care wasn't enough. Fortunately, Ranon grabbed him as he began to fall. *Probably the only Zylongi around who is strong enough to prevent a Taran from breaking his neck in a shallow river by falling twenty feet off a ladder*, he thought.

"Favor returned," he murmured to Ranon.

The big Zylongi laughed. "No, Lord O'Neill, much more will be required to repay. It is a good beginning, perhaps."

When they reached the top of the ladder, Horor couldn't budge the hatch to the control room. O'Neill pulled himself up on the same rung; with the two of them clinging precariously to the slippery ladder, they managed to shove the hatch open.

Explosions had shaken the Energy Building to its foundations. The safety center of the nuclear reactor was a tumbled mess of tables, chairs, charts, and pieces of machinery. Horor shook his head in dismay at the wreckage of the control panel. "I don't know, Lord O'Neill. It is all badly damaged. We will have to try to repair the mechanism. What do you think, Ranon?"

"There is no machine made that cannot be fixed if you have the time."

"You don't have much of that," said Seamus. "Do what you can. I'm going to have a look around.

Where's the fission pile? There?" he pointed uneasily at a sinister black wall.

"Yes—behind several feet of lead. We are in no danger from radioactivity now. Of course, if it were to be detonated, the lead would not be of much help, I'm afraid."

Seamus O'Neill prayed hard as he prowled the corridors underneath the Energy Building, especially for his daughter, as he had decided the brat would be. *It might be necessary to name herself Deirdre . . .*

He smelt the thick, rancid smoke in the corridors; there were fires brewing someplace in the bowels of the building. It wouldn't be very long before it went up in flames too. But the fission pile represented the future.

Uncle Seamus's future.

And if the Hooded Ones, or a fire, moved it to critical mass, there would be no future for any of them anyway.

He opened a door into another corridor, and narrowly escaped running into a severed electrical cord that danced about, shooting sparks. The staff of the Energy Center must have abandoned the building—if any of its immunized custodians had survived.

Rounding a corner, he met a small group of Hooded Ones. The insurrectionists knew what they were doing. They had outflanked the police in the Worship Plaza battle and were now heading for the energy vitals of the City. O'Neill fired his carbine into them at point-blank range before they could throw an explosive his way. He ducked back around the corner and down a stairway. At the foot of the stairs he turned and raised his carbine just as three more of the black-clad hooded figures emerged at the top. He fired quickly, but one of them pulled the pin on a grenade.

He fought back into consciousness. His head ached even worse than it had from the concussion at the Central Plaza explosion; one of his arms wasn't acting the way it should. Above him the stairwell was demolished—no sign of the Hooded Ones. Flames were eating the paint off the alloy walls. Staggering to his feet, he groped his way back to the control room. His poor battered head was clogged and musty; he couldn't think, he couldn't find his way, he wasn't hearing or seeing too clearly. He stumbled into the control room.

"Lord O'Neill! What happened to you? We were afraid that you had been killed. Are you badly injured? You are covered with blood."

"I'm surviving. Have you got this damn thing working yet?"

"Judging by the fire up there, we have about five minutes—ten at the most."

Horor turned to Ranon. "What do you think?"

Ranon shook his head.

"We will acquaint you with the situation, Lord O'Neill," said Horor calmly. "We may have found a way to shut down the reactor, but it is possible that an explosion will occur that could allow the nuclear reaction to ... er ... run out of control. The outcome would not be pleasant. If we had time—fifteen minutes—we could better guarantee a safe shutdown. What shall we do?"

There was no point in wasting time agonizing. "Shut the damn thing off."

24

Horor flicked three switches. With a quick glance at Ranon, he shoved a rod on the wall over the control panel. Nothing happened for a few seconds. An indicator needle on a great dial swung from right to left. The lights in the room went out.

"Did it work?"

Horor answered, "I think, My Lord, that it is safe to say that it did. Let us light our handlights and rejoin our colleagues."

O'Neill had to be supported on the way back. His injuries were not serious, nothing more than cuts, bruises, and a rather painful and disabling pulled muscle in his arm. But, for some strange reason, he could hardly walk.

Concussion, he supposed. *One bang on the head too many. Like a hurley player who has been hit by the stick too often.*

The chilly waters of the underground stream did nothing to dissipate his daze from the explosion. When they reached the hovercraft, he was in a state of incipient shock. The City was now completely black, the battered vehicle's single headlight shone dimly through the streets. As they approached the street-corner defense perimeter that the Young Ones had set up, Horor flicked the light on and off several times to signal their arrival.

Yens was at the door of the hovercraft to greet them. "We were attacked by many Hooded Ones," he began excitedly. "They came down the tunnel from the jail."

"What happened?" O'Neill managed as they were helping him out.

"We defeated them and destroyed them—though the tunnel to the jail is now blocked by the rubble from their explosion." He sounded exultant, as only the young warrior successful in his first battle can.

O'Neill thought, *Poor Sammy. No way to get to her now.* Aloud, he said, "What casualties?"

"Only three, Lord O'Neill, two of them not serious."

"Who is serious?"

The young officer's voice faltered. "I fear that Captain Marjetta has a broken leg. . . . All our medical equipment was destroyed in the blast. We cannot move her."

Seamus elbowed his way through the dark to where his mate lay on the hard tunnel floor, her leg twisted and her face drawn with pain.

"How does it feel, my love?" he asked awkwardly, wishing he could drive the pain from her face.

"It hurts, you amadon," she snapped. "How do you think it feels? It took you long enough to get back." She reached out to touch his battered face. "Oh, darling, what happened to you? Are you all right?"

He was about to shout for someone—anyone— to come and help her when he remembered that he had taken the Taran medical kit along with the tranquillity pills when he left the *Dev*. As soon as the pain medication was in Margie's bloodstream, he set her leg in the line the indicator on the portable template said it should be set and applied the thick plastic and metal strips. Then he injected rapid bone-mending serum. With any luck at all, she would be able to walk on it shortly— though it would be a painful effort for many days.

"The holy saints protect me," he murmured ruefully, "if it has to be reset. . . . How's the brat doing?"

"He's not in my leg, you idjit," she said through clenched teeth.

"She."

"Really?"

"She'll look like her mother, but she'll have her father's personality."

"Poor child," she sighed, a perfect imitation of his own sigh.

"Damn lucky thing for you, woman, that her mother has such a brilliant wonder-worker around." He was busying himself putting supplies back into the medical kit.

"I keep asking myself, Seamus, where I would

be now if it weren't for you. I know I would not be here like this." She nodded in the direction of her bound-up and useless leg. She grasped at the kit Seamus was filling. "Give me that medicine kit. I'm going to give you a dose of your own medicine."

Seamus enjoyed the affectionate attention. As he was relaxing under her tender ministrations, Retha joined them. "I have just returned from a patrol at the City level, Lord O'Neill ... er ... Geemie. There is nothing left of the center of the City except fires."

"Could you hear explosions from other parts of the City?"

"None. I think the Hooded Ones are gone."

"All right. Tell Captain Yens to maintain the defense perimeter for the present. We will move on to the next phase shortly."

"Yes, Lord O'Neill." She hastened away.

Sure, we will move on to the next phase—as soon as I can figure out what it is.

His mate echoed his thoughts. "You'll have to figure out what the next phase will be, won't you, Geemie?"

"I will, woman. If you would stop disturbing me with your blather, I'll do that very thing."

25

It was hard to think. In fact, his thinking through the whole mission had not been too impressive, as the Cardinal would doubtless remind him for the rest of his life, should there be any of that.

Zylong was no more. Its driving life energy and political structure had been wiped out. Its population was in chaos, thousands dead. The Hooded Ones were not all killed; some must have survived and returned to their underground lairs. Perhaps some more escaped the City itself. They could expect the wild hordi under General Popilo to attack. Soon? Did the wind blow so strongly outside the City? Did the wild hordi avoid the frenzy?

Perhaps they wouldn't be able to attack before the end of the Festival time. Even if they could not enter the City, the food supplies for next year were stored in dumps at the edge of the City. They could be destroyed easily, meaning famine for those who managed to last through the Festival.

The food supply . . . maybe that was where his band of rebels belonged. They would be close enough to open ground for the *Iona* to evacuate them. Deirdre had said nothing about more survivors than he and Marjetta. . . . Still, for all her bluster, she had great affection for young people. His troops would go to pieces if he kept them here in the dark, damp tunnel much longer.

His thoughts were interrupted.

"Seamus."

"What now, woman?"

"I have another problem for you. I think the tranquillity pills are losing their effect. I can feel the frenzy returning. You are going to have to give us more pills."

"The first twenty-four hours are not over yet. There'll be no pills left after another dose."

"The wind may die in the morning. It usually does. So we should last through the day. After that . . . it may not matter by then." Her teeth were clenched; the words were forced and a little harsh.

"One problem at a time, please." Seamus thought desperately. He began to dispense the precious drug to his embarrassed followers. They were ashamed of their strange lunacy before the eyes of their Honored Leader.

"Chronos never said anything about freedom from the frenzy," muttered Yens when he took his pill from Seamus.

"Poor man," replied O'Neill. "He probably understood it even less than everyone else."

The decision to evacuate was clinched when Carina stumbled through the darkness, announcing, "Lord O'Neill, there is water coming down the tunnel! Either one of the reservoirs has collapsed or an underground stream has been diverted by the explosions. There are only a few inches so far, but it is coming rapidly!" Already O'Neill felt the water trickling around his feet.

He called his band together. "This command," he announced with more official confidence than he possessed, "is the only organized group left in the City. Therefore we must assume responsibility for protecting resources that will be absolutely indispensable when rebuilding begins. Horor and Ranon have ingeniously preserved the energy source; now we must redeploy to the City's edge to guard the food dump just outside the main gate. We will not go hungry, though I do not think unrefined jarndt will be particularly tasty."

They obligingly laughed at his very thin joke.

Seamus ordered them to stay close together during their march through the City. They would defend themselves against the "populace" only when attacked. With spears and carbines at ready, they would discourage civilian attack. There were not many Hooded Ones left, so he did not mention that if there were any, such a compact marching phalanx would be an easy target for an explosive charge.

They climbed back to the surface of the City with their handlights and marched across the ruins of the Central Quarter, through streets where neither darkness nor disaster had quieted the wild revelry, and finally to the main gate.

Their progress was impeded by repeated scuffles with bands of celebrants; the spears and determined faces of the Young Ones frightened the revelers. Most of the fires were contained within the Central Quarter, but the streets were littered with mutilated bodies, and screams rent the dark night air. Singing, shouting, drinking, and "love-making" were going on all around. The grimly determined Young Ones did not falter despite the exhortations of the fellow Zylongi to join them.

Limping painfully beside him, leaning on his arm for support, Marjetta told him, "It has never been this bad, Seamus. It is really the end of everything."

"And the beginning. Chaos, then cosmos again."

He wasn't altogether sure what that meant, but he had heard it in the monastery school, in a class most of which he had slept through, and it sounded nice.

They arrived at the gate after first light and quickly moved out into the sloping meadows that lay in front of the vast pile of jarndt on the riverbank. Only Seamus was detached enough to look back at the City—now completely dark except for the towering fires still blazing in the Central Quarter and silhouetted against the brightening sky.

As they passed the hospital, he saw it was

undamaged. Was there a supply of tranquillity pills in the hospital? Maybe later in the day he could lead a patrol back there to explore. Now it was important to set up a defensible position near the jarndt dump and snatch a little sleep. He was so tired. . . .

Margie woke him. The sun was shining brightly in his face. "Seamus, we have visitors coming," she said calmly.

A mob was pouring out of the main gate of the City, flaming torches in hand, running toward them. Their screams polluted the clear, cool morning air.

Seamus O'Neill shook the sleep from his eyes. "Why the torches, Margie? It's daytime."

"I don't think they're coming for us, Seamus. They want the food."

The advancing mob was many thousand strong. His young people had wanted to save Zylong; it was appropriate enough that they die defending the jarndt, which had been the basis of their civilization. He turned to look at his ragtag band. A sudden movement on the opposite bank caught his eye.

"Narth's advance guard, no doubt. Well, good luck to you, fella; you're welcome to whatever is left."

He ordered his troops into a skirmish line in front of the grain, instructing them not to shoot until he gave the order. A sudden collapse of the leading wave of the mob might panic the others. He noted irrelevantly that it was the beginning of what would be a marvelously beautiful day. The sky was a deep purple, the sun a lovely rose; great white clouds were already marching by in stately ranks, the pile of still-brown jarndt smelled of good rich land. His skirmish line stirred nervously but did not break under the strain of the howling mob's approach. They would hold, he knew, to the end.

"Look," said Carina, who was standing with Horor next to Margie. "See who is leading them?"

"Who is he?"

"Farge, the Police Commissioner."

Farge was a sturdy, handsome, silver-haired man, clad in the robe of the Hooded Ones but with his head bared. The leader of the police was also the leader of the Hooded Ones. A corrupt Zylongi to the end.

The frenzied Zylongi were now quite close. "Ready to fire!" he ordered. *Ready to die.*

"First shots over their head."

"I love you, Seamus."

"Fire!"

The guns of his ragtag crowd sounded like a packet of cheap firecrackers. But they seemed to do the trick. The frenzied Zylongi turned tail and ran screaming back into the City.

"We won!" He hugged Margie fiercely. "I'll take an anticlimax any day. So long as it's a victory."

"I don't think we've won yet," she pointed toward the River. "Look!"

Narth's army.

26

The rebel army stretched along the bank of the River in either direction as far as the eye could see, lances and spears glinting in the sunlight, crimson banners straining in the stiff wind. Across the water came the sound of rhythmically clicking hordi and pounding horses' hoofs.

As Seamus watched in stunned silence, swarms of aborigines rushed to the riverbank with giant rafts on their heads. They cast the rafts into the River like paper boats. Other hordi, monsters, and red-clad exile cavalry swarmed on them. The current carried the rafts downriver as solid massed ranks of poles on either side of the rafts steered them across. A cluster of hovercraft put out from the bank, carrying several dozen troopers and their horses.

The Imperial Guard, with a number of grudges to settle.

"What do we do now?" Marjetta asked, still ice-calm.

"We engage them in combat, that's what we do."

As soon as I get an idea of what that means.

"Reform the battle line. Hold your fire until I give the order."

That's not a very original idea.

Then he had another idea that was also not original, but seemed at least to be useful. He didn't think through the possible outcomes, because there was neither the time nor the need.

The Guard disembarked on the bank. Narth, on a mammoth black stallion, led them off and remained a safe distance away from Seamus. *Learned his lesson, did he? Well, we'll see about that.*

"I thought I'd toasted you for the hordi, frigging lardass," Seamus bellowed. "What happened? Don't they like grease?"

"I'll cut you up in little pieces, Taran worm."

Not a very creative response, at all, at all.

"You're a loudmouthed coward, you fat disgusting slob," Seamus continued.

"Seamus . . ." Margie whispered.

"Shush, woman, I'm engaged in strategy." And again at the top of his voice, "Maybe if I carve you thin, the hordi would find you more palatable."

"You and your whore will die for days." His face was now as red as his cloak.

"You notice, fellas, how he's always big talk when he has the weapons, but he won't fight fair man to man."

Popilo, guiding his mount daintily off a hovercraft, rode up behind his leader. "Kill him now," he screamed.

Sure the man is wound up tight enough to go into orbit. He's completed his pilgrimage round the bend.

"Ah, he can't do that, Poppy old fella; you'd have to charge us first and some of you might get killed before you killed us. Maybe most of you. My crowd are crack shots." A shameless lie. "And he won't be in the first rank either."

"Prepare to charge!" Narth moved his horse back from the front of the troopers.

"Tell you what, I'll fight you myself, man to man."

Narth stopped his horse. "Your whore will tell you that I'm the greatest ax fighter in all Zylong."

"He is." Marjetta was as cool as ever.

"Regardless," Seamus whispered. "I'll make you a deal," he yelled, his voice hoarse from shouting. "You come on foot with your ax and shield and I'll fight you with one of these little spears." He grabbed Marjetta's weapon. "Winner take all. If you kill me, we won't kill your troops when they charge. If I kill you, your Guard lets us leave before they destroy the City."

As Seamus had hoped, the troopers stirred restlessly. They expected their fearless leader to respond to the challenge. Narth had been trapped.

"Kill him," Popilo screamed again.

"I'll do just that." The fat rebel climbed ponderously off his horse, discarded his cloak, took a shield from one of his lancers, hefted the biggest ax Seamus had ever seen, and strode manfully toward O'Neill.

"Tell me about him quickly," he said to his woman.

"He's most vulnerable when he raises his ax for the kill. He's fat and out of condition. I'm sure he hasn't fought in years. But he's dangerous and you are wounded and exhausted."

Did the woman have no nerves at all, at all?

"Well, then I guess I have him outnumbered."

"Seamus . . ."

"Yes?" He hefted the spear and waited for words of love.

"What do we do if you die?"

"Run like hell."

"Will they honor his word if you win?"

"Probably not."

No argument, no disagreement.

"Form up behind me," she ordered their band. "Be prepared to respond to my orders instantly." Then in a whisper, "Be careful, Seamus."

Sure she was a lot like herself.

"Ah, fat man," he began the ritual insults, "how can someone as gross as you even lift that frigging ax?"

"I will show you." He lifted the ax over his head and swung it violently—and skillfully.

Seamus ducked quickly, almost not quickly enough. The man was indeed good with the frigging thing.

"Careful, now, big belly, you'll hurt yourself

swinging that thing around like a drunken grandmother with her pisspot."

Seamus's strategy, if you could call it that, was to continue to duck until his opponent's mighty heaves began to exhaust him. Then, taunted perhaps into an unguarded assault, Narth might leave himself open for a quick thrust, like Marjetta's assault on the saber-toothed tiger.

Roaring like an angry elephant, Narth charged again. The great ax whistled so close to Seamus's ear that he feared he had lost it.

"Ah, grandma is finding the pisspot heavy, isn't she?"

Some of the Imperial Guard snickered. Insane with rage, Narth hefted the ax again and charged at Seamus much as the tiger had. This time the Taran was quicker; he dodged the swinging ax and tripped the rushing rebel.

"Earthquake, earthquake," he shouted as Narth tumbled onto the ground. Quickly he darted in and jabbed his spear into his opponent's body.

And missed. Completely. His spear stuck in the soft ground and would not come out when Seamus tugged it.

Too tired from the sleepless night and too weak because of my wounds. The man had been an easy target.

For the first time Seamus was afraid.

Narth rolled up and swung the ax at Seamus's leg. The Taran had a choice, pull his spear out of the ground or save his leg. He elected to save his leg.

But now he had no weapon and Narth was advancing on him with the light of victory shining in his black eyes. Exhausted and breathless, Seamus wondered what came next. Out of the side of his eye, he saw his woman waiting, calm and implacable.

Holy saints, she thinks I can't lose!

He retreated toward the riverbank, leading on his slow and panting opponent and wondering what he would do when they arrived at the edge.

Finally Seamus was cornered with the water behind him and the great ax in front of him. He feinted in either direction, as though he were trying to run back to his spear. Narth, supremely confident now, blocked his escape with a negligent wave of the ax.

"Now I've got you, lardass," Seamus taunted him. "Come on now, don't let your men think you're a gutless coward."

With a furious howl, Narth charged him; the ax poised over Seamus's skull, and then swept downward.

As if he was blocking a defensive charge in hurley, Seamus banged into the rebel's knees. *Personal foul, fifteen yards for unnecessary roughness*, he thought as Narth sailed over him and into the waters of the River.

Now all the Imperial Guard laughed. Standing in two feet of water and out of his mind with rage, Narth reached for his ax.

He could not find it, because it was on the bank of the River. The fat man rushed to grab it, quickly for someone his size, but not quickly enough.

"I don't want to kill you," Seamus said, struggling to lift the incredibly heavy weapon. "Do you want to talk peace?"

Narth grabbed for the weapon. Seamus shoved it at him, cutting into his foe's leg. The rebel collapsed on one knee, his hands still gripping the handle of the ax. His blood was spurting out on the soft sand of the bank, but with a mighty heave he pulled the weapon out of O'Neill's grasp. Seamus scampered for his spear and then danced toward the riverbank.

"I don't want to kill you," he repeated, raising the spear.

"I want to kill you," Narth bellowed. Despite the blood escaping from his artery, he rose and lunged toward Seamus, his ax raised for one final mighty swing.

He charged limping and screaming into Seamus's spear, dropped the ax, curled up on the ground like the dying tiger, and expired. Quietly.

The falling ax hit Seamus a glancing blow on the head. He fell to the ground, momentarily stunned. He'd won fairly. Would that mean anything to Popilo? Of course not. Why hadn't he thought of that?

"Kill him *now!*" screamed the madman.

The Guard hesitated.

"I said *kill him!*"

The cavalry lowered their lances and began to trot forward. This was the end. Seamus had a fleeting wish to embrace Marjetta, but it was too late now. He made a quick sign of the cross. A long way from Jerusalem.

The lead lancer was only a few yards away, his deadly weapon pointed at the Taran's chest. Seamus Finnbar O'Neill heard a mighty roar from across the River, inundating them all with a terrible, shattering shock wave of sound. The noise was the loveliest sound Seamus had ever heard—retrorockets.

The lancers' animals bolted, leaving only Popilo, a stone's throw away from Seamus.

A final explosive burst shook the ground, and a cloud of smoke enveloped Popilo and Seamus. Then there appeared, standing between them, a slender woman with long black hair blowing like a great frigging banner in the Festival wind. She was clad in dazzling cardinal-red robes and shining ermine and held in her right hand a thin gold crozier with Saint Brigid's cross on the top.

"Who are you?" screamed the demented Popilo. He raised his gun to fire at herself. She extended the Brigid crozier and lightning jumped out of it, knocking the gun from the madman's hands.

It was only psychic lightning, but sure it served the purpose. The hordi rafts, paralyzed in midstream, began to swing around. Some of the Imperial Guard had already plunged back on their hovercrafts.

"I am," announced the vision, "Lady Deirdre Fitzgerald, Countess of Cook, Archbishop of Chicago Nova, Fleet Commodore of Tara, Captain Abbess of the Pilgrim Ship *Iona*, and Cardinal Priest of the Holy Roman Church of Saint Clement. Who, may I ask, kind sir, are you?"

That was enough for poor Popilo. He turned his horse and raced for the landing area. The frightened animal stopped at the edge of the bank and tossed its rider over its head into the River—right in the path of a fleeing hovercraft. The madman went under without a sound in a burst of bubbles that turned from white to red. He did not come up.

The Cardinal raised her staff higher, the Brigid cross on the end of it glowing momentarily with the brightness of the sun. Lightning, still make-believe and still effective, jumped in all directions—along the City walls, across the River, into the ranks of Narth's army, up the side of the Island, down the newly harvested plain, and to the tops of the snow-capped mountains in the distance.

Ah, it was quite a show.

Panic-stricken, the rebel army broke and ran in wild chaos, the insanely clicking hordi, poor things, leading the way. Hovercrafts nosed over, rafts capsized, canoes loaded with weapons floundered, horses galloped off in terror. The River filled with bobbing hordi heads. Fortunately the poor things seemed able to swim.

For good measure, herself raised the cross higher still. It glowed with space darkness for a fraction of a second. The sky turned black and the whole world shook with thunder. And more thunder. And yet more thunder in an ear-splitting cadenza of primal sound.

Imaginary thunder of course, but it worked just as well as the real thing. The clouds dissipated quickly and it was once again a lovely harvest morning.

The late Narth's army was finished. It would be at least a generation before anyone would attack the City again.

Conscious that his woman and his friends had gathered around him, awed by what was really, to tell the truth, only a minor trick show, Seamus stood stock-still in the fullness of his relief and pride. *Ah, the bitch is loving every minute of this*, he thought as she lowered her crozier and seemed actually to wink at him.

Just to the right of the awestruck rank of Young Ones, two squads of Wild Geese poured out of the *Michael Collins* and the *Thomas Patrick Doherty*. They carried their blue plow-and-stars flag and were dressed in white electronic-protective armor, their black cloaks flowing behind them, phasers ready to fire. Further down the River, there was another blast as the *Napper Tandy* glided to a soft landing.

"It took you long enough to get here," said Seamus O'Neill.

"O'Neill, will you never learn that you are not the hinge of history?" She was grinning broadly. "When the City was obviously collapsing, we decided more positive action was required before Narth gained control of the food and energy resources and eliminated the only remnants of sanity and order on this heathenish planet. I admit that it's a little strange to think of you representing sanity and order, but the Holy Rule says work with what you have. We trusted you could hang on in the City long enough for us to get to you."

"You might have given us a hint you were coming," he argued.

"Och, Seamus, you didn't think we'd leave you here among all these heathens, did you?" The Lady Deirdre was not only grinning broadly, which was unusual enough, she was laughing. "Sure weren't you after inviting us to come, and aren't you—" the woman actually guffawed, something Seamus had never witnessed before "—Lord O'Neill himself?"

More Wild Geese were pouring out of the *Tandy*, and the *Brian Borou* was settling down in the distance. His own platoon—with a grinning Fergus in command—was marching on the double toward them. The young Zylongi skirmish line remained in astonished silence, not comprehending what had happened or what was being said.

Deirdre continued in Spacegael: "Now, O'Neill, I have something for you to do that just may suit your talents, something you can perform adequately for a change." Then in perfect Zylongian, "Far be it from me, Colonel O'Neill, to give you military advice, but if you wish to supplement your own excellent troops with a few platoons of Wild Geese, you may want to restore some order in the City. You may also wish to leave your talented and charming ... uh ... 'proper woman' with us so that we can treat her injury. She can help us with communications." And the Captain put her arm gently around the astonished Marjetta. "Can't you, my dear?"

"Yes, Deirdre," the little imp replied, inordinately pleased with herself.

The Young Ones, fascinated by their new allies, fanned out with Fergus's platoon of Wild Geese and began to march back into their City. The silence of the morning air of Zylong was rent again, now by the mournful but implacable wail of Celtic warpipes. They had almost reached the gate when the sound of massive retrorockets roared behind them again.

Out on the Island the smoke cleared; there on the highest hill a great, gray spaceship settled slowly to the ground. The *Peregrinatio* of the *Iona* was over.

The chapel bell rang softly across the waters. It was time for Morning Song.

27

The Captain Abbess did not normally entertain in her own quarters, considering that such entertainments were not in keeping with her understanding of holy poverty.

Besides, it was such a nuisance.

However, exceptions were made on special occasions. It was her custom to entertain a very select group after the midnight Mass of Christmas. This Christmas, the first on the planet recently renamed "Tyrone," she shared fruitcake and brandy in her austere study with Diarmuid MacDiarmuid, the ancient and venerable Prior, Sean Murphy, the young and very shrewd Subprior, Brigadier Liam Carmody of the Wild Geese regiment and his wife, Maeve, and General Seamus Finnbar O'Neill, Earl of Tyrone, and his pregnant wife, Lady Margaret— called Pegeen by almost everyone—O'Neill.

The Countess, now charmingly plump, announced to the small company that of all the things she liked on the island of *Iona*, the best was the Lady Deirdre's fruitcake.

Her husband was glum. He was always glum at Christmastime, but to make matters worse, he had had a shouting fight with the Abbess before the Mass. Now, he was angry at himself for having lost his temper. She had not returned his anger, which meant that she had won. He wished Pegeen would stop babbling, damn the woman. *Was that all she was good for anymore? Prattling about fruitcake? She had become a Taran biddy in short order.*

Pegeen. Glory be to God, what can you do about a name like that? Of course she loved it; she loved everything about the *Iona*—the stained glass in the chapel, the library, which she was devouring book by book, the plainsong, the services, the monks, the nuns, and the Wild Geese. It was as though the whole damn pilgrimage had been put together for her entertainment. The "wee leprechaun lass" was an instant hit with the whole monastery. Having to share his wife with monks, nuns, and a regiment of Wild Geese was poor reward for all the risks he'd taken on this planet.

It isn't fair.

His ruminations came full circle—back to his argument with Deirdre. It had begun with his complaining about the close—too close, he thought—relationship between Marjetta and Deirdre. He was tired of having an Abbess for a mother-in-law, he had said—half in fun and half in earnest. "Ah, sure, Seamus, what's a poor old woman to do when she sees a queen coming into her territory?

She had better be after making her peace with the new woman."

He answered irritably, "You're daft, woman. What do you mean a 'queen'? She's just a Captain in an army that doesn't exist anymore."

" 'Tis not so, Seamus O'Neill," she replied calmly, fingering her pectoral cross. "You may not be much of an Earl—that will take time to tell; sure it was nothing on your part that deserved it—but you have found for yourself a real queen in that wee lass."

That's when all hell broke loose. After the big blowup and after she had floored him with the whole story of his mission, Deirdre must have felt sorry for his obvious deflation because she had asked with more concern than she usually displayed, "You are not really dissatisfied with Pegeen, are you?"

"Ah, musha, I've not taken leave of all my senses. I suppose I've got nothing to complain about along those lines. She'll do until someone better comes along."

Even now, blathering away and munching on the fruitcake, Marjetta was enough to make O'Neill's throat tighten and his eyes fill with tears. A touch from her hand and he melted into slush. There was hardly a minute of the day when she wasn't in the back of his mind. There she was, accepting another "wee sip" of the abbatial brandy. He sighed. The creature had a very bad effect on the woman's sexual appetites; it increased them enormously, pregnant or not. It looked like another long night for Seamus O'Neill—and on the Holy Feast of Christmas. He sighed again. He thought of Ernie and Sammy. It had been a long time.

The thought of Sammy took him back to that first day after *Iona* had landed. His orders were to restore some discipline in the City. He sent the main body of his force of pacifiers into the Central Quarter to secure what was left of the Energy Center. O'Neill took a squad in the direction of the jail to rescue Sammy. Along with them was Cathy Houlihan as medical "adviser," a superb doctor who never lost her nerve in a fight or a crisis. The wind was dying; it was time to begin bringing in the wounded and injured to the hospital.

He led his team rapidly through the now quiet streets of the City, past the dead bodies and over the rubble to the ruins of the jail.

"Seamus, you idjit, what are we after doing here?" Cathy exclaimed.

"Somewhere in this mess we may be able to find the Director of their hospital. Sure she'll be useful before the day is out."

It took only a few minutes to find the staircase that led down to the tiny dungeon where Sammy was. "Glory be to God!" burst out of Cathy when the heavy metal door was opened and she saw what was inside.

Sammy was still alive, bleeding badly from wounds opened by her furious struggle with her chains. She was still in the full fury of the frenzy, howling, snarling, screaming. He crammed a tranquillity pill into her foaming mouth. It had its usual effect. Sammy went limp against the chains, collapsing in a heap when Seamus freed her. She would not look up. Seamus gently put the back of his hand against her face.

"Dr. Houlihan, I would like to present Dr. Samaritha, who has just become the Director of the Body Institute here—hospital, to you. You will excuse her unprepossessing appearance. Through no fault of her own she has had a rather rough time of it." O'Neill spoke in a formal and dignified tone. Sammy began to pull herself together. She would not look at him, however.

"I am sure that the Doctor will want to go to the hospital immediately to begin the arduous task of ministering to the wounded and dying. Houlihan, you and the rest of the squad go along with her; offer every assistance possible. I will ask the Captain Abbess to instruct the *Pat Moynihan* to land in front of the hospital to provide you with auxiliary power. We will send the rest of our medical team in as soon as Dr. Samaritha has determined what needs to be done. Carry on, gentlepersons." He left quickly to rejoin the main force of the Wild Geese.

Cathleen told O'Neill later what had happened after he left. A tiny immunized skeleton staff had survived the night of horror hidden behind the walls of the hospital compound, fearing attack by the Hooded Ones. When the popular Samaritha arrived, they sorted themselves out and began to work. Within an hour the Tarans and Sammy's staff were laboring efficiently together to aid those

Zylongi who had dragged themselves to the hospital for treatment. The *Moynihan* landed a medical team from the *Iona* shortly thereafter. By the end of the day, the cross-cultural medical team had saved hundreds of lives.

As Cathy had put it later, with the characteristic ethnocentrism of the Tarans, "She's a quare heathen person, she is, but a daycent woman just the same; and I'll speak up for her to anyone, I will. Seamus, she's a hell of a fine doctor."

When O'Neill left the jail, he hastened to the command post that the Wild Geese had established just off the ruins of the Central Plaza. The noise of the shuttlecraft landings, then the troop carriers, and finally the huge monastery, the terrifying appearance of the Geese and the fierce banshee wail of their pipes sent most of the celebrating Zylongi scurrying back to their living spaces in terror. The wind died down in the morning, easing the force of the frenzy. Those Zylongi who still seemed of a mind to continue the killing and raping were quickly dissuaded by the "stun" charge of the phasers carried by the Geese. By noon, what was left of the City was quiet.

O'Neill was beginning to get things under control when he remembered the tranquillity pills. He got on the communication link to Deirdre. "What have you in the way of defrenzy pills, woman? My people are going to need them by nightfall—not to mention the entire population of Zylong."

"Someone as wise as myself could be trusted to have thought of that, O'Neill. Your, er, lass was good enough to help us with a sample of her blood for us to analyze so that we could produce some kind of medication. A secondary investigation into the nature of the wind has produced the theory that the frenzy is in part an allergic reaction to what the wind picks up blowing across the harvested jarndt fields. Just as your man down in Hyperion thought. If you stop the wind, you stop the frenzy."

"Sure, 'tis analyses like that that got you those pretty red robes. Now all you have to do is stop the wind."

"If we can divert a meteor with our psychic powers, we can stop a wind."

Sure enough, the wind stopped just as abruptly as it had begun. A great peace descended on Zylong, a peace so profound and reassuring that Seamus could see Retha and Yens relax as though a vast burden had lifted from their shoulders. They looked at each other with tears in their eyes.

"In years to come, we must celebrate this day in a new way. This Day of Peace shall be a new Festival by which all our descendants will remember the final ceasing of the wind," said Yens, holding his wife's hand.

"Geemie O'Neill Day," the delightful little tyke giggled.

"There will be none of that," Seamus insisted, without—to tell the truth—too much conviction.

So the work of reconstruction began. Horor and engineers from the monastery busied themselves repairing the energy station; the computer technicians arranged lines into Podraig—whose language had been considerably cleaned up in deference to Zylongi sensibilities. Yens, as the Chairman of Public Order, in consultation with Fergus Hennessey, posted the daily assignments of Wild Geese patrols. Order slowly emerged.

He worried about Sammy. One day as he was crossing the hospital plaza, Cathy stopped him to sing the praises of Dr. Samaritha again. She had done a brilliant job of restoring the hospital to its former efficiency. "Ah, sure she's worked hard, she has," said the golden-haired Cathleen, and pounded the side of the *Moynihan*, which was still parked there. "The poor thing."

"She is that." He tried to break away from the conversation. He didn't want to have to think about re-establishing that relationship.

"It was strange what happened the second day after the hospital reopened—it almost broke my heart, 'twas so sad," persisted Cathy. "A new group of badly injured Zylongi had been brought in by a squad of Geese from a quarter of the City that was just being pacified. One of them was a man with a badly shattered skull. Dr. Samaritha hesitated for just a moment, then plunged ahead with dramatic and skillful surgery. Sure she saved that man's life on the spot. Then," Cathy paused dramatically for effect and went on, "she turned to me and said, 'Honored Adviser, perhaps you would not mind if I rest for just a few moments?'

" 'Heaven help us, woman,' I said, 'you've

earned more than a bit of rest. That was as brilliant a piece of work as I have ever seen. You saved that fellow when I would have given him up for sure. He's a very distinguished-looking fellow. Must be someone important around here.'

" 'He directs an orchestra, Honored Adviser,' she said. 'I'm glad you find him pleasant. He . . . he is my mate.'

"Praise be to Brigid, Patrick, Columcile, and the Holy Mother of God, Seamus, what was there for the two of us to do but break down and weep in each other's arms. I tell you, man, she's a fine lady—heathen or not!"

He told himself that he had to see Sammy and Ernie, had to exchange forgiveness and understanding, had to renew their friendship. Could he do it? He'd asked the Cardinal what she thought, the old witch.

"Why have you been after waiting so long? And herself expecting a child, like almost every other female on this heathenish planet. The poor things still love you, you idjit. More than ever. Which you don't deserve at all, at all."

The reconstruction of the City passed from physical rebuilding to the reformation of the political structure. The first political act of the Council, as the Young Ones had constituted themselves, was to unanimously elect Seamus King. He stormed out of the meeting, saying he would be damned if he would be king of anything, whereupon they revised their agenda, tabled the "King" vote, and respectfully requested that he rejoin them to advise them in their deliberations. They voted themselves into office for a year (providing for their replacement by citizen vote after that time—a detail that was strongly urged on them by O'Neill and of which they had somehow not thought).

The meeting was adjourned until the next day, when a public ceremony was planned to present the Tarans formally to the citizenry of the City and to exchange pledges of mutual help and support for the future peace and prosperity of the planet.

It had been a grand sight. In one of the smaller and still intact plazas near the wall, the Council, with their Taran "Advisers," gathered for its first meeting under the deep purple Zylongian sky. The Young Ones were still clad in their torn and dirty robes ("Turrible pagan clothes," muttered old Diarmuid); the Wild Geese stood tall and proud in their black and white armor; the monks and nuns waiting for the ceremony to begin made a solid block of Celtic blue in their long dress habits. The Zylongi crowd that had gathered to watch the show were awed at the spectacle. Then the pipers struck up "Deirdre's March," and the Abbess approached slowly, clad in her full crimson robes of office with golden Brigid crozier aloft, ascending to her throne in a most regal fashion. The ceremony began officially with speeches, exchanging of scrolls of peace and friendship, and other appropriate gestures of protocol.

Subprior Murphy had risen to say that he

strongly agreed with General O'Neill's decision to reject the kingship. Sure no good had ever come to any planet from having a King. All they did was want to fight. So, as an alternative, he recommended that the City be governed by someone who should be entitled "Earl," someone who would preside over the Council and its Taran Advisers and administer the government on a daily basis for no longer than a year's term—subject, of course, to reelection. He felt that General O'Neill could hardly refuse to accept office under those conditions.

Fergus promptly seconded the nomination, adding that General O'Neill was the only one, with the possible exception of his lovely lady, who knew enough about the two cultures to maintain the delicate links that would combine them in their glorious efforts to make this planet a happy and free place for all who lived on it.

Horor then rose to speak for the Council of Tyrone. He assured the Tarans of the warm welcome their citizenry extended to their new friends and allies, saying that as the first Taran friend, the Noble Lord General O'Neill surely should act as the Earl for at least a year. Horor was the only one who kept a straight face throughout the farce.

After that, herself asked if there were any more nominations. There were none. O'Neill was elected Earl by acclamation.

What could he do? When Deirdre solemnly asked him, "Will you accept, General O'Neill?" he responded with the shortest speech he ever gave in his life: "Woman, I will."

There was a huge cheer from the plaza, then much good-natured laughter when his wife caused him acute embarrassment by hugging him in public.

Politics, O'Neill discovered, was much harder than war or reconstruction. In a battle, you either won or lost or ended up in a draw; reconstruction was just a matter of efficiently organizing relief and such. In government, you never really knew whether a decision was a good one or a bad one, and you usually had to be content with a compromise that most people could live with. You could never be sure whether the compromise had been wise or not until much later. Sometimes you never found out.

He and Quars met halfway down the continent within a week of his election to set up permanent communication between Hyperion and the City and to appoint Quars Regent in charge of hordi, mutants, and exiles.

"It will take a long time," the gruff officer admitted, "but it has to be done, and it should have been done long ago. I'll say this for you. That scene on the River when your friends showed up scared the hell out of them. They really do think you are the red-bearded god. That will help us get started in making peace with those poor folks and giving them a chance."

"Will you be after doing it?"

"It'll keep me busy, Seamus, but my wife says she'll leave me if I don't do it. Claims I'm irritable when I'm bored. By the way, I see you finally captured that lovely girl."

"Ah, was that the way it was? Sure I thought she captured me. To listen to her tell it, I was a pushover."

Then there was a hesitant invitation to a "small entertainment" in honor of Quars, who had recruited Samaritha into his team of hordi specialists.

"I won't have time to go," Seamus told his wife. "You represent me."

"We're both going, Seamus." She put on her steely-eyed military face, which terrified him more than the Cardinal's frown.

"Well, why didn't you say so in the first place."

So Seamus turned on all his charm, touching hands in the friendship sign with Sammy and Ernie at the door of their quarters, hugging Carina, and swinging the pregnant hordi servant over his head, to the accompaniment of delighted clicks.

Quars's wife was the only female at the party not expecting. The Zylongi were producing the children they had always wanted, some, like Sammy, presumably in the nick of time.

Seamus sang and told stories about his fictional adventures, the space bum once again. Forgiveness and the renewal of love, mutual, implicit, and fervent, was so easy as to be an anticlimax.

"We will not presume to invite you again, Noble Lord," Sammy said as he and his proper woman were leaving. "We know how hard you must work."

"If I don't see you two once a month, I'll have you locked up in the bowels of the monastery."

"Very nice, Seamus," herself had whispered to him on the way back to the monastery. "Just like the night I knew I loved you."

"Sure I was much better tonight."

"I should hope so, and yourself a married man."

Good enough it was, but there was too much of it altogether. As Christmas approached, Seamus began to think about taking his woman and his child and returning to Tara as soon as they could. His weary brain had been awhirl for weeks with never-ending administrative and political crises.

I'm a poet, aren't I?

Not a frigging politician.

He was in a vile mood on the night before Christmas when he cornered the Cardinal just before First Vespers. Tired and nervous, he ranted that he had been tricked into the job, he hated politics, he was no good at it, couldn't imagine why they had maneuvered him to become "Earl," he wanted out—now, not next year.

"Now, do you hear me, woman? I am sick of all your wee plots and your fey schemes and your spooky tricks. Just give me and my wife the old *Dev* and let us get the hell off this bloody planet!"

She let him rave. When he stopped, she said quietly, "Why would you be thinking we sent you here in the first place?"

"Musha, you sent me here to be a psychic sponge."

"Och, Seamus O'Neill, can you be that much of an idjit still?"

He began to see the pieces falling into place.

"You mean you were after sending me here from the beginning to become a politician?" The ground was quaking beneath his feet.

"Whatever other reason would you be thinking? Surely not because of your self-control?" She smiled complacently.

"You mean you connived from the beginning to make me King of this place?" Anger was surging through him like the waters of a river in flood.

"King for a year."

"Regardless."

"Would I dare to do anything like that without consulting the Council of Tyrone? Or our own Council?" She adjusted her ruby ring, worn especially for Christmas.

"I'm no good as a politician, woman." He was screaming at her now. "You wasted your time. I'm a third-rate poet, a fourth-rate anthropologist, and you yourself said an incorrigible, inept womanizer."

"And a flannel-mouth braggart, I believe I also said?" A quizzical eyebrow raising slightly.

"All right, add that too!" He kicked the wall, something he hadn't done since he was a child.

"It all sounds to me like a perfect job description for a politician, Seamus." She ignored his tantrum. "Be sensible. You have been a decent soldier, you are brave, and you think rapidly in a combat situation, but we will not have many wars on this planet, I hope. You write decent, if not outstanding, poetry. You are good at winning people to like you and to agree with you. You charm these poor heathens every time you smile at them. That is what this planet needs."

"I'm not good at any of it. I'll not do it. I don't believe that the fellas in the regiment want me to be some great damn bloody Earl." His anger ebbed. He was ashamed at himself for acting like a baby.

"Ah, you've noticed how much they complain about all the mistakes you've made since you've been an Earl." She smiled that damn complacent smile and folded her arms in satisfaction.

"They have not complained, Deirdre Fitzgerald! You're lying in your teeth. There hasn't been a single major complaint from a one of them, I'll have you know. After all the work I've done holding this bloody place together, I'll not have you saying that the fellas in the regiment don't like it . . ." His voice trailed off as he realized what he was saying.

"Precisely my point," she said, her triumph complete.

So he had a lot to think about through the vespers and the Mass of Christmas. Now it was late. Time to take their leave of the assembled guests in the Abbess's room. With Pegeen leaning on his arm, he bade the Lady a formal good evening and a happy Christmas.

"You'll do it, Seamus?" she asked, with more anxiety than she usually permitted to creep into her voice.

"Musha, Your Ladyship, the whole bloody mess was a near thing from beginning to end." He sighed his most Taran of sighs.

"It was, Seamus O'Neill," she conceded.

"Well, sure we had some luck coming."

"God knows," her sigh easily outdid his. Always the last word.

He and Pegeen went out silently into the cool, starlit night.

"Are you all right, Geemie?" she asked him, affectionately squeezing his arm.

"And why wouldn't I be?" he protested.

"When my man is quiet through a whole evening, he has something on his mind."

"Can't a man do a bit of thinking without everyone in Tyrone getting in an uproar about it?"

"What were you and Holy Lady Abbess talking about when we left?"

"Ah, 'tis a long story." He sighed again.

"A story that could be told on the night of our Savior's birth?" She sighed back.

Damn it, she's even imitating Deirdre's sighs.

"Saints preserve us, the woman's becoming a damn religious fanatic!" he exclaimed, hugging her. "Well, it could be told, I guess, if a woman doesn't mind finding out that her husband is the worst damn fool in the galaxy."

"What if she knows that already and wouldn't have it any other way?"

The Earl of Tyrone turned to mushy plum pudding. *Sure, it might not be a bad Christmas after all.*

In the monastery the bell chimed out a very old Celtic Christmas song. Before O'Neill began his story, he sang the carol in Gaelic for his proper woman.

God greet You, sacred Child,
—poor in the manger there,
yet happy and rich tonight
—in Your own stronghold in glory

Motherless once in Heaven,
—Fatherless now in our world,
true God at all times You are,
—but tonight You are human first.

Grant room in Your cave, O King,
—(though not of right) to this third brute
among the mountain dogs
——for my nature was ever like theirs.

Mary, Virgin and Mother,
—open the stable door
till I worship the King of Creation.
—Why not I more than the ox?

I will do God's service here,
—watchful early and late.
I will chase the hill-boys' dogs
—away from this helpless Prince.

The ass and the ox, likewise,
—I will not let near my King;
I will take their place beside Him,
—ass and cow of the living God!

In the morning I'll bring Him water.
—I'll sweep God's Son's poor floor.
I'll light a fire in my cold soul
—and curb with zeal my wicked body.

I'll wash His poor garments for Him,
—and, Virgin, if you let me,
I'll shed these rags of mine
—as a covering for your Son.

And I'll be the cook for His food.
—I'll be the doorman for the God of Creation!
On behalf of all three I'll beg,
—since they need my help to speak.

No silver or gold I'll ask
—but a daily kiss for my King
I will give my heart in return
—and He'll take it from all three.

Patrick, who through this Child
—by grace got Jesus' crozier
—O born without body's bile—
—and Brigid be with us always.

Patron of the Isle of Saints,
—obtain God's graces for us.
Receive a poor friar from Dún
—as a worm in God's cave tonight.

A thousand greetings in body tonight
—from my heart to my generous King
In that He assumed two natures
—here's a kiss and a greeting to God!